JONATHAN **MABERRY**
WESTON OCHSE

THE
SLEEPERS
WAR

BOOK ONE

Apha Wave by Jonathan Maberry and Weston Ochse
Copyright ©2023 by Jonathan Maberry and Weston Ochse
Published by arrangement with Aethon Books
Cover art by Tom Edwards
Cover design and typography by Steve Beaulieu

Printed in the United States of America

First edition: 2023
ISBN 979-8-212-32312-3
Fiction / Science Fiction / Military

Version 1

AethonBooks.com

‹ΛLPHΛ WΛVE›

BOOKS BY JONATHAN MABERRY

BOOKS BY WESTON OCHSE

From Jonathan:
This is for Ray Bradbury and Richard Matheson.
Mentors and friends. Key players in my path to being a novelist.
And, as always, for Sara Jo . . .

From Weston:
This is for Robert Heinlein and Ray Bradbury who first taught
me the wonder of science fiction. For all of those who stuck by me
in the dark writing nights of the soul.
And, of course, for Yvonne . . .

ACKNOWLEDGEMENTS

This has been a long, strange trip and some smart, fun, affable folks have helped us along the way. Thanks to our agent, Sara Crowe of Pipping Properties; our audiobook reader, Ray Porter; astronomer Lisa Will; Dr. Ronald Coleman; Merle Rogers; and to the world's best literary assistant, Dana Fredsti.

PART ONE
THE FIRST FLOCK WAR
2265 C.E.

"The true soldier fights not because he hates what is in front of him, but because he loves what is behind him."

—G. K. Chesterton
Illustrated London News, Jan. 14, 1911

"So long as there are sheep Nature will insist on beasts of prey."

—H. G. Wells
The Sleeper Awakes

1

Lance Corporal Alex Chow had never fired his weapon in anger. Not once during the entire war.

He did not ache for that experience either. Even with the deaths of his mother, his cousin Joon, and four friends from high school. Chow was just not that kind of soldier.

Not that he floated the "lover not a fighter" nonsense. Chow *was* romantic—his wife agreed with that—but it no more defined him than did the Sigmund 45pp snugged into his hip-holster. He could fight—he had been eighth out of sixty recruits in his training pod—but all of that was a side effect of wanting to use service as a way of paying for college. OTC was not for him. Chow was a history buff and wanted to land a post-war job chronicling the expansion of the human race across the galaxy. *That* was who he was.

And as for the Flock? He only *kind of* hated them. Mostly

he was afraid of them. Of what they could do. Of what they had done.

Titan? Detmer Station? The Hermippe Star Port?

All of the horrible things he downloaded from the news streams. Raids. Massacres. Minefields hidden in the asteroid belt.

So, yes, the Flock was nasty. Violent and dangerous.

Evil . . .? He wasn't at all sure where he landed on that point. History was filled with conflict, with wars and slaughters, but historians tended to remain objective, to view things as cause and effect rather than good or bad. Only genocide was, in his opinion, actually evil, and even the Flock wasn't trying to exterminate humanity.

At least not as far as what he'd read about them.

The best thing about the Flock, though, was that they were very far from Calliope Station. Since the war began this star system had been quiet. It was strategically unimportant to both sides, which is why the station was used as a nursery, school, and library.

Chow's friends—Private Chowdhury and Sergeant Kofax—were bored out of their goddamned minds, though. They wanted to be *in* this fight. Kofax had joined up after Detmer, and Chowdhury enlisted when her wife's patrol ship was blown out of the skies above Neptune. Yeah, they were at the shooting range three times a week, and anyone could read it on their faces—they ached to take it to the Flock and burn some feathers.

Ached for it.

But not Chow.

He thought about that—the differences in what his two closest friends wanted and what he did not—as he walked another slow lap around the interior walkway for Wheel 377. Calliope was a gigantic ring-city completely encircling the tiny moon dubbed Little Petra, but every half mile of its circumference was a smaller lateral wheel that turned with slow deliberation to provide Earth-G gravity. Micro-gravity was fun at times, but it did nothing for muscle mass or bone density. Even if he wasn't on patrol, Chow would have spent a lot of his time in one of the rings. Who wanted to be a slack flabster?

Chow slowed his pace as he reached the first bank of windows that looked down on the nursery. And as he strolled along, he counted—as he always did—the number of tiny bodies down there. Eighty-four as of Tuesday. Eighty-four little ones. Every color in the human rainbow. Crying and sleeping, kicking little legs or pawing at brightly colored mobiles over their basinets, trying to sort out the first mysteries of being human.

That always made Chow happy.

This was what mattered. This was what made him put the uniform on, strap on his sidearm, keep current with training, and be proud to be a soldier.

One of them, a newborn with a shock of wild black hair, was not even a day old. It made him want to cry. Twenty-two hours into being a person. Alex understood that the baby was really nine months and twenty-two hours, but he couldn't help seeing birth as the real start in life.

He paused and waggled his fingers at the infant. Not that the little one could see him way up on the observation treadmill, behind dura-glass. It didn't matter. What mattered was Chow *saw* the baby. Number eighty-four.

"Hey, kiddo," he said, speaking quietly to himself so that none of the other walkers on the wheel heard him. "What are you gonna be when you grow up? Pssst . . . here's a hint—historian. Historians are cool. Ask anyone."

The baby kicked at the air.

Chow nodded and turned away.

Which was when the first missiles hit.

2

Calliope reeled.

The entire massive wheel had a circumference of 1.8 kilometers—nearly identical to Styx, a moon of the dwarf planet Pluto. Calliope Station was necessarily bigger, with a radius of 2.2 kilometers and a circumference of 13.823 kilometers. It was built of polysteel alloy mined from asteroids and the latest polymers. It was constructed to endure the gravitational pull of Little Petra as well as the greater stresses of the planet Gipley. During pre-construction testing it was able to withstand direct impacts from asteroids of up to a tenth of a kilometer and could even survive most C-class missiles.

It was meant to endure, meant to last.

The missiles fired by the Flock warship were something new. Talon M4s. Weapons rumored to exist but which no one had ever seen before. Warheads like cluster bombs that split apart upon target-lock and released dozens of smaller guided explosives packages. These flew toward key stress points and detonated on contact. The effect was that each missile strike hit like thirty-six. Nothing like that had been factored into the design schematics or materials testing.

The first Talon hit Calliope's graceful curve as the host moon swung through shadows and into the light on the far side of the planet. Sunlight painted the wheel with golden light for exactly three seconds before the weapon deployed its payload and hit.

The blast tore off the entire upper level of the wheel, ripping away shielding and disintegrating four thousand tons of reinforced structural polysteel. The expanding fireball faded quickly in the airless vacuum, but within Calliope, a storm of burning gas punched left and right along the curve, melting through three complete sets of blast doors. One hundred and eleven people died in the first second, vaporized back into stardust. The limited-range electromagnetic pulse slammed into the barriers designed to contain exactly that kind of threat, but overloaded them with such ferocity that half of the gigantic wheel went dark.

Emergency systems struggled to seal the massive hull breach even as oxygen and other gasses shot out into the void. The EMPs fried thirteen satellites, including two of the wheel's four early detection orbiters. Not that these had done much good because the Flock ship had come out of a bore-hole—a kind of wormhole that tore through the fabric of space.

That was the first missile.

The second struck more solidly, hitting Calliope in the heart, blasting through the side of the wheel right in the middle of the main community housing. Nine thousand men, women, and children died. Many within seconds; but many more as hull-integrity systems began to fail. They choked on smoke, they starved for the oxygen that was now venting into space. Or they burned.

Many, many of them burned.

The third missile struck a glancing blow, but by then Calliope was losing orbital integrity. Stabilizing jets fired to try and keep the crippled wheel in place, but it was already twisting and shifting. When the third Talon struck, it hit the Ops center, killing the command team, filling the response craft launch bay with clouds of fire, and the resulting EMP destroyed all interior communication.

Of the sixty-two-man Spinners and fourteen Tiger-Shark short-range fighters parked in the station's big bays, only seven craft managed to launch. Six Spinners and one Tiger-Shark. They tumbled out of the bay as much as flew, the pilots fighting to avoid clouds of debris, flying on willpower, nerve, and faith.

There were two midsize Mantis guard ships in stationary orbit near the local Deck—the transduction corridor used for intragalactic travel—but they dared not join the fight because that Deck was the only link to the rest of the galaxy. However, they went to red alert and spun up their combat systems. They were on the far side of the planet, and the Deck station commander sent urgent warnings down to the planet and across the vastness of space using the Cho Corporation Vox system.

The big Flock raider ship—designated as an Albatross-class stealth cruiser—hung between Calliope and the sun. It was immobile, as if painted onto a backdrop of fire. As the Spinners tumbled through the blackness, targeting systems located missile ports and the gunners began firing. The first three Spinners launched their full array of Lionfish torpedoes, filling the void with enough high explosives to blast the bird cruiser back to hell. But then the front of the lumpy, ugly ship seemed to break apart before the torpedoes could reach their targets. In moments that confusion resolved itself into a hundred Needletails—one-bird fighters known for their incredible speed and maneuverability.

The dogfight was furious. Spinners were one of the most

maneuverable craft in existence—fast, agile, with cutting-edge inertial dampeners that allowed them to make radical sharp-angle turns at top speed. They could outfly anything the birds had, even Needletails.

But the Flock had the numbers.

The aliens had no hesitation, no mercy, no concept of individual self-preservation. They tried to shoot down the incoming Lionfish, and when that did not work, they simply flew into their path. The torpedoes exploded, each one taking out one or more of the Flock fighters. And then there were no more torpedoes to fire and the sky was filled with enemy craft.

As one Spinner ducked and dove around shattered junk and incoming fire, trying to get close enough to the Albatross to use pulse cannons to do as much damage as possible, three of the Needletails rushed it in a converging run that looked like a hawk's talons closing on a leaping fish. The Spinner and the three bird ships vanished into a fireball.

More of the Flock fighters joined the dogfight, deploying from slots along each side of the Albatross.

The Tiger-Shark—stronger but slower than the Spinners—fired all guns and for a moment there was a flicker of hope. The pilot—a decorated veteran with two Silver Nebulas on his chest—owned the sky for nearly a minute. His AI interface allowed him to target multiple bogeys at the same time, secure hot locks, and fire all while allowing the pilot to focus on flying and tactics. One after another of the enemy fighters blew apart, and then the Tiger-Shark punched through a resistance blockade of five Needletails. The pilot hit the burners, cranked the shields to max, and slammed into them.

The remaining Spinner pilots saw the big fighter disappear inside a storm cloud of fire and death, and every one of them held their breath. But the Tiger-Shark hurtled forward, its hull scraped and scorched, one stabilizer fin gone. The pilot shot toward the Albatross and opened up with everything it had—pulse cannons, torpedoes, short-range missiles, EMP bombs. He brought death to the Albatross.

The big ship reeled, its port side erupting as the shields failed and torpedoes savaged its hull.

But even as it canted sideways toward the pull of the moon's gravity, its station-keeping engines failing, the Albatross had one last surprise.

It wasn't alone.

A flight of Talon M4s came out of nowhere and blew the valiant Tiger-Shark into pieces.

The Spinner pilots wheeled around to see a second Albatross emerging from a borehole, cannons firing, missiles punching forward, scores of fresh fighters deploying.

The last recorded message from the Spinner squad leader was, "God have mercy."

There was no mercy at all. The Spinners died in a storm of cannon fire.

The Flock fighters split into two groups—fifty Needletails headed off to attack the Deck and the Vox comms satellites, while the balance of their force swung around and began firing at the Calliope. Ripping at it. Tearing at it.

The Wheel was not dead, but it was dying. Left alone, gravity would conspire with the failing operational systems to send it crashing down on Little Petra. And below, on that tiny moon, thousands of miners and their families stared up at a sky filled with horror.

The sky was falling.

3

Lance Corporal Alex Chow clung to the handrail beside the walkway, his feet braced against the glass of the observation window. He looked down between his feet and saw the babies screaming. He could not actually hear them, but in his mind he could.

They screamed even though they were too young to understand what terror meant.

They screamed even though they were unable to grasp the concepts of human frailty and death.

And Chow screamed too.

For them. For the thousands who lived and worked on Calliope.

For himself.

He had not seen the Talon missiles, but this was wartime and so he *knew*.

He wrapped one arm around the rail and used his free hand to tap the comms unit seated into his left ear.

All he heard were shouts, yells, weeping.

And then static.

The lights in the nursery flickered and faltered. However, they did not fail entirely, because this part of the wheel was farthest away from the three points of impact. The walkway wheel, though, had begun juddering and slowing, shedding much of the artificial gravity effect.

Sirens blared like shrieking banshees. Red warning lights flashed and whirled. The intercom was a jumble of incomprehensible panic.

Although Chow could not see the Flock attack craft, he saw tons of debris hurtle past the big triple-paned windows. Twisted pieces of metal. Chunks of machinery so badly mangled their purpose could not even be guessed. Star fields of tiny glittering shards of plastic and glass.

And people.

He stared with a shock so profound that he forgot to even breathe as bodies tumbled by, their faces wide with a terminal surprise, eyes wide and frozen. They twirled and spun, singly or in groups, as if they were part of some grotesque ballet. Doctors and scientists, gardeners and shopkeepers, adults and children.

People.

Whole or in pieces.

Swirling away from the battered Calliope. Falling through space, pulled by the gravity of the tiny moon, and the greater and hungrier lust of the planet Gipley. They would enter the atmosphere and ignite. They would scrape like matches across the outer envelope of the world and then plummet toward the merciless ground. Small falling stars that would leave nothing but a smear of ash on the winds of the world below.

Chow's chest heaved as he gulped in a breath. And it heaved more painfully as that gasp became a sob. Deep, broken, filling his chest with splinters.

"No . . ." he said, gagging on the futile denial.

No.

This could not be happening. The war was too far away. There had never even been a Flock ship spotted in this star system. The closest battle was eighty-nine light-years away.

The sound of the klaxons was drowned out by a deeper, sharper, more troubled groan of metal twisting away from its intended shape. The delicate balance of the wheel-shaped Calliope was now in a losing battle with gravity. If the main station-keeping engines remained offline for more than an hour, the whole ring would break apart and those pieces would rain down on Gipley. There was enough mass to do terrible harm below. If the whole station fell, then the impact would create a shock wave and firestorm to rival that of the asteroid that wiped out the dinosaurs on ancient Earth. And he—along with those screaming infants—would be part of that apocalyptic rain of debris.

"Please," he begged, though Chow had no personal religion. No faith. No god to pray to. And yet he cried out that word, begging the smoke-filled air for mercy.

He pulled himself along the handrail to where his grav shoes were hung. Putting them on was something he did every day, often multiple times each day, and the actions were so ingrained that normally there was no conscious thought. Today, though, he fumbled with them, dropping them, fishing them out of the air as they tried to float away, connected the binding straps wrong three times, and then finally got them on. He swiped the sensor on the inner arch to activate the mechanism inside the soles and only then could he stand and walk.

Badly.

He staggered along toward the crippled gravity wheel until he reached a wall-mounted communicator, but it was as useless as his personal comms. He stayed there, swaying, uncertain what to do next when he heard a new sound.

Gunfire.

Several kinds. Projectile weapons and pulse pistols. And something heavier whose shots made the walls shudder. A portable cannon, maybe. Or . . . a Flock weapon of some kind.

Forty meters along the corridor was an arms locker, and Chow began hurrying in that direction. Grav shoes were excellent for walking but dangerous when running. They required a certain amount of body weight inside the shoe and equal pressure from deliberate footfalls to work, and a runner often had both feet off the ground. And so, he lumbered as fast as he could. By the time he reached the locker the sound of small-arms fire was much louder. Close.

"Shit, shit, shit," he breathed as he pressed first his palm and then his right eye against scanners. The system paused so long he was afraid its internal systems were damaged, but then the locker door hissed open to reveal six handguns and three rifles all snugged into their foam slots. He grabbed two pistols, slapping them against his belt to engage the catch-magnets that held them secure. Then he took a pulse rifle and slid a hundred-round battery pack into place. The display flashed on, offering the first splinter of comfort he had since the attack started. Although some of the troops used projectile weapons, those were nonlethal, with either stun beads or hard-rubber bullets. Great for riots, useful for taking down a runaway hog from the kitchen pens. Nearly worthless against Flock armor. Those rounds could hurt the birds, but that was about it. Bruises didn't stop them.

The pulse rifles and pistols, on the other hand, were very lethal. A shot to any part of the head and torso was a kill shot. Hits to legs, arms, and even their vestigial wings were crippling.

He also snatched up a pair of XO-120 fragmentation grenades. Too powerful and dangerous to use this close to the nursery, but just having them hanging from his belt made him at least *feel* better.

Chow turned and looked around. The bay windows that overlooked the nursery seemed impossibly fragile. He had to make sure that if those avian bastards came through the hatches on either side of that section of the wheel, he would be ready for them. There was a big air conditioner unit extruding from a wall nearly at the midpoint and so he hurried that way and crouched down, moving the rifle from one door to the other and back again. Trying to do those sweeps at a slow speed, at a controlled pace, but he was totally wired. Adrenaline was pumping through him too hard and too fast, and his hands were making the barrel twitch and dance.

"Please," he said again, and this time it was both a plea for the Flock to go hunting elsewhere but also for them to come in so he could send them to hell.

He waited. Sweat ran in cold lines down his face and his heart hammered with dangerous intensity.

He waited and waited. Ready for anything.

But not for what happened.

4

Chow swept right and left, right and left, and just as he moved the barrel from his left to swing it once more to the opposite end of the corridor, *both* hatches blew inward.

They bulged and then imploded with a massive *ba-roooom* that shook the whole station. Each two-ton polysteel door leapt inward. The left-hand door fell onto its face and slid ten meters before the micro-grav won the battle with the impetus of the blast, and the steel began to lift.

The right-hand door landed on one corner and spun in a weirdly slow pirouette.

Through the smoke swirling around both doorways came the figures. Dark, bizarre, unnatural by any sane definition.

Most of the Flock were about the same size as humans, ranging between five and six feet. They were thin, though their slender appearance was deceptive because their muscle tissue was unusually dense. They were far stronger than they looked and could move very fast. Physically they looked birdlike, with feathers on small and somewhat stunted wings. They had arms and legs apart from the wings, and their skin was tough and reptilian. A running theory was that their race evolved from animals similar to Earth's dinosaurs, but since there was no catastrophe like the asteroid that wiped out the saurian giants, they continued to evolve. Their heads were an even split between avian and reptilian, with crests of feathers running like Mohawks along their skulls, and long beaks not unlike those of Shoebill storks.

Their body armor was structured for elongated necks and beaked heads. They had grav-boots on strange feet that allowed for their heel hooks to remain free. These hooks were poisoned and could put down a human in less than five seconds if given the chance. It wouldn't kill, but it would incapacitate until the human system flushed free of the poison. They also wore mech gloves on long-fingered hands. Each of them had a small device strapped to one forearm, and the birds held rifles of strange design.

They moved with a jerky stride that called to mind ostriches from old Earth nature films. Or the terror-birds that the History Zoo on Luna had brought back from extinction with reclamation genetics.

Terror was the right word, because these were not the foot soldiers seen in thousands of newsfeeds. These killers wore the sleek silver-blue armor of the combat elite—the Raptors. Bigger, tougher, faster, and utterly ruthless. This group was even bigger than the normal Raptors, which spoke to radical genetic enhancement. These Raptors were brutes with increased muscle mass and bleeding-edge tech.

And they were *here*.

As they stalked through the smoke, Chow felt his heart begin to freeze over. He forgot the weapon in his hands. His mouth went dry, but his eyes filled with tears. There were so many of them, and just one of him.

Raptors.

"God help us all," breathed Chow, unaware that he had now started to pray.

Behind the glass, the babies shrieked their silent shrieks. Did they somehow understand that their lives were meant to be this short? Were their spirits—if spirits even existed—doomed to be born and then to die like this, with no life lived except what was measured in hours?

That thought—and the pitiful horror of it—did something to Lance Corporal Alex Chow. It lit a fire in the cold hollow of his chest. He knew—absolutely knew—that he was going to die here. Just as he knew he was the only human standing between those babies and the Flock raiders. They would probably die too, but he could think of no greater crime, no more damning sin, than to allow that slaughter without some kind of response. A statement about the value of human life.

"Damn you all to hell," he roared and opened fire.

If his yell came out broken and full of tears, it mattered to no one. The pulse rounds smashed into the first of the Raptors. He fired and fired, hitting center mass every single time.

And it did absolutely no good at all.

5

The plasma bursts exploded in showers of sparks and burning gas, but it seemed to stop short, hitting what Chow thought was empty air. But as he fired, he saw that the bursts seemed to somehow detonate too soon—inches from the Flock soldiers' bodies—and then slough off in a strange curve. It was as if the aliens were covered in some kind of circular shield.

Then he saw that the air around them was shimmering; there was a faint radiance that spread outward from their chest armor and around them, expending the force of each shot harmlessly. It took Chow a moment to understand, to grasp something seen in real time with descriptions he'd read in newsfeeds. He suddenly understood the nature of the devices strapped to their forearms. Every single Raptor was protected by a grease-shield—nicknamed so because it made bullets and even most force blasts slide off like sausages in an over-greased frying pan.

Knowing this made Chow's mind connect that newsfeed report with something else. According to government reports, only one kind of Raptor team had them, and they had wiped out everyone on Ganymede Stations Five and Eight. That team had been the dreaded *egg hunters*. And with terrible clarity, Chow understood that these Raptors were the top tier of the Flock Special Forces and they weren't here to take Calliope Station . . . *this assault was to take the children themselves.*

This was a new and terrible Flock tactic—to capture the children and thereby demoralize human defenders here and across the galaxy. Rumors were that these children would be raised in slave pens and forced to serve the will of the Flock.

The thought of that—the knowledge—that he was seeing it firsthand—nearly destroyed Chow. It tried to shatter his mind and take all of the strength from his muscles. Even as he kept firing, he could feel defeat rise like a black tsunami in his mind.

The Raptor egg-hunters who massacred the two stations on Ganymede suffered no casualties. Not a single one. They'd slaughtered all of the adults and kidnapped every child below the age of two. And here they were, with only a single armed person in their way.

Another soldier might have been frozen in the face of such overwhelming odds. Even some seasoned veterans might have been overwhelmed by the horror and certainty of it all. There were stories of mass suicides by soldiers who faced defeat and enslavement by ordinary Flock soldiers. After Ganymede the number of suicides by grieving families was appalling.

Some people, soldiers or staff, might simply have fled. Maybe selling themselves the lie that the dura-glass wall was unbreakable and that the children would survive. Others would flee because there was no possible win.

Few people would have stayed and tried to fight. Very damned few.

Alex Chow was only a lance corporal. He had never been in combat, had earned no medals, no Purple Hearts, no battle scars. He was a simple young man wearing the uniform as part of a plan to go to university, get his degree in history, and spend his life in the stacks of a great library on one of the university moons.

He was not a hero.

And yet . . .

Chow held his ground and fired that magazine dry.

Then he thew the rifle away and drew both pistols, rose up, aimed a gun in each direction, and fired. He screamed as he pulled the triggers.

The bullets did nothing. The grease-shields knocked them away, stealing much of their foot-pounds of impact so that the rounds merely bounced around until they were spent. After that the bullets merely floated.

The Flock advanced slowly, not firing at him. Chow wondered if they were afraid of damaging the windows over the babies. Or was this some kind of field test, seeing how their grease-shield worked in the close confines of a space station?

Chow released the pistols and let them float, too.

He looked at the little ones. So beautiful. So helpless. The thought of them becoming slaves to these monsters was unbearable.

"I'm sorry," he said as he plucked the grenades from his belt. "It's better this way."

He raised the grenades, ready to detonate them both, knowing that the combined blast would shatter the nursery window and the exterior window both.

"Better this way," he repeated as tears streamed down his face.

He placed his thumbs on the arming switches. The Flock troopers rushed toward him, their hideous eyes visible through the visors of their armored suits. They reached for him with taloned hands.

"If there's a god," he said to the children, "may He take you and—"

The head of the closest Raptor *exploded*.

6

The head and shoulders of the creature simply blew apart, splashing Chow, the rest of the Flock, and the walls with gore. Blood and bits of brain, bone, and gristle swirled madly through the air, turning with bizarre gentleness in the micro gravity.

For a moment everything seemed to *stop*.

Maybe it was a few full seconds or maybe it was all one warped microsecond. The rest of the Flock on both sides of the corridor froze. Chow froze too. They all watched as the decapitated Raptor swayed there, its feet anchored to the deck by grav-boots, its weapon floating free.

And then time caught up to perception. Reality became a fist and it struck hard.

Chow whirled to see the Raptors at the far end of the corridor turning, raising their weapons, firing.

And . . . dying.

The knot of them seemed to break apart as a figure burst through them. It was a human, wearing a kind of armor Chow had never seen before. Close-fitting, appearing to be some kind of metallic cloth rather than hard-shell protection. It allowed the man to move with incredible speed and agility. Small packs placed at key locations on the suit spat bursts of gas that let the man move like he was in standard gravity. He had a strange-looking pistol in one hand and an even stranger knife in the other.

The man was huge—heavily muscled and fast as hell.

"*Heads down!*" came a command over Chow's commlink.

Chow was not much of a fighter, but his training kicked in and he dove for the floor, wrapping his arms around support struts on the walkway to keep from floating back up. The grenades, unarmed, went drifting as he curled into the tightest, smallest ball he could.

The big man fired his gun into the Raptors around him, killing them even as they wheeled around to fight. The grease-shields did not stop his rounds; they didn't even slow them. Chow saw the birds freeze in surprise.

"Overconfidence is a bitch," he said, and it turned into a laugh. Shaky, humorless, and nearly hysterical. But no one was listening to him.

The birds who were a half second too slow recovering from their shock just died where they stood. The rest—the majority of the two groups—shook it off and drew their weapons.

Those egg-hunters were fast. Very fast. The big man was faster still.

He twisted away from a pulse blast, ducked, spun, rose and whipped his knife across a Raptor's groin. Alien bird-creature or not, armored codpiece or not, the blade did hellish work. The creature threw back its head and uttered a scream that was so shrill, so piercing that Chow flinched, fearing the dura-glass would shatter.

It held, and the man with the knife kept moving. He jumped into the air, twisted, and struck a savage downward blow at a second egg-hunter. Miniature in-suit gas jets were synced with his movements, giving him the same essential range of motion and gravity effect as if he were on Earth. *Les Danseurs Étoil*— the micro-grav circus performers—used that kind of tech to allow them to do all manner of acrobatics and choreographed stage combat.

And the weapon the man used had similar micro-jets. Chow saw that it was a gas-knife such as salvage teams used on asteroids, but the level of sophistication was far superior. These jets seemed to work at the speed of actual nerve conduction. And coupled with the man's incredible speed and power, it became a true extension of his will. Everything he wanted to cut was cut; everything he wanted to kill died.

It was unlike anything Chow had seen in real life. It was more dynamic and terrifying than the special effects in holo-films.

It was itself a ballet of slaughter.

One of the Raptors jogged right and chopped at the man with a long, curved blade. Chow began to yell a warning, but the big fighter seemed to sense the blow and turned toward the bird, slipping the cut with a fast backward lean that any professional boxer would have been proud of. He twisted as he came out of the evasion and snapped out with his gas-knife in a series of fast taps. Each short blow opened a slit in the Flock body armor; from each slit dark red avian blood erupted. The short cuts—picks, Chow remembered from a training video during basic—attacked a nerve cluster, key muscle, or vein. Even in standard gravity that kind of precision would be nearly impossible given that both players were in motion. But the Raptor's arm seemed to die, the talons spasming open, the arm muscles going slack, and the curved blade floating free. The big man did not pause to admire his work but was clearly thinking two or three moves ahead. He hip-checked the Raptor into two others, then ducked under a pulse blast to slash tendons on the shooter's leg. As he rose up, he drove the point of his knife under a third bird's chin.

One, two, three, and a trio of the attackers at the far end of the corridor were wounded or dying. They squawked in agony and surprise—and fear, no doubt—as they stumbled away from the onslaught. Chow had never seen anything like this. Not in real life.

The other members of the Flock crowded forward to attack, but their human target was moving too fast, invading their space, using their numbers against them, cutting with the knife, taking short-range shots with the pistol. The level of shocking violence was astounding to behold. The Raptors always had the bigger, stronger, faster fighters in any conflict. Any one of them could handle two or even three soldiers unarmed, and a score when in full kit. And yet in seconds Chow had lost count of the number of the creatures that had been crippled or killed.

There was a screech of noise—all cries and clicks and whistles—as the Flock leader bellowed orders to its team. The group of them closest to Chow began to rush forward, raising their weapons to deliver a fusillade that would have killed the man as well as their own fellow Raptors.

Would have.

But before they could open fire, two of them plunged forward with sudden force, their helmets erupting with fire and blood. Chow stared as a second figure—another human soldier—slammed into the second group.

It was a woman.

She was smaller than the man, but she moved with the same oiled grace, the same blinding speed. The same lethal efficiency.

She had a pulse gun mounted on her left shoulder, allowing her to use both hands to wield a pair of military *kukri* knives.

Old style—no gas jets, but that did not hinder her in terms of speed or effect. Wherever she looked, the gun fired. Where her hands went, death happened.

Chow clung to the strut and watched as two people, two human beings, tore apart the Raptor squads. Chow had watched videos of Marine Star Recon, Army Special Forces, and even Omega Teams in pitched battle with the Flock, but they were not on this level. Those other groups were the best of the best.

But these two people were better.

An order of magnitude better.

He saw that they relied on their knives to do most of their wet work, firing their exotic blasters only when there was a clear shot along the corridor. If a Raptor was between them and either the nursery window or exterior ports, the killers did not fire. Even at the incredible speed of the battle they made no such mistakes.

The woman was closer to where Chow crouched, and he watched in dreadful fascination as she moved. Her reflexes were unnaturally quick, and time and again she dodged pulse blasts and evaded grabs as if she had foreknowledge of each specific threat. It was like watching a movie at double-speed. He caught sight of her face as she turned. She was a pale-skinned, pale-haired woman with one half of a beautiful face, the other half a melted horror from some terrible burn.

And she was smiling.

Laughing . . . as she slaughtered enemy soldiers that everyone else in the galaxy feared as virtually unkillable.

She proved that wrong. Laughably wrong.

Her knives were silver blurs and they seemed to lunge for each target. Joints and suit seals, throats and arteries. Blood swirled in the air around her as if she wore a whirlwind of red as her armor.

One of the Flock darted away from her, letting its fellows

face the blades while it launched itself upward to make a grab for the floating grenades. If it could grab and arm even one bomb, then this fight would end with everyone dead—the Flock, the human fighters, and all the babies. One of the reasons Raptor teams were so feared was their willingness to die in order to win a battle. Suicide runs and mission collapse fail-safes. Any version of a standard defeat—especially if capture was likely—was anathema to them. They would rather perish, and in doing so, take as many humans as possible. This was why so many politicians and military strategists called *victory* against the Flock an unattainable goal. The cost in human lives to defeat so committed an enemy was horrific.

Chow did not give a damn about his own life, having made that decision earlier, and so he shoved himself violently away from the strut, kicking off the floor, rising, reaching, trying to beat the inhuman monster to that device.

The Raptor's clawed hand closed around the grenade, but Chow clamped both of his around that hand, squeezing with strength born of total panic. They tumbled through the air together and slammed against the nursery windows. Chow kicked out, hitting the Raptor in the thighs and stomach.

The Raptor used its free hand to tear a knife from its belt, but Chow kept his hands clamped around the grenade.

"*Please*," he prayed once more, seeing that blade sweep toward him. Even then he kicked and fought.

Then the big man was there.

The face behind the visor was grim, with high cheekbones and a strong jaw. There was some kind of tribal tattooing on his face. Like the woman, he was grinning, and that grin did not flicker one bit as he caught the Raptor's wrist in one gloved hand and wrenched it sideways. Even through the bird's suit and the sounds of battle, Chow heard bones break. White ends of bone tore through the suit, seeding the air with fat drops of red.

The gas-knife swept around and down and suddenly Chow was floating free, still clutching the severed Raptor hand and the grenade.

The Raptor died screaming. Those screams were short, shrill, and wet.

Alex Chow bumped up against the window, clutching the grenade to his body. His heart pounded with hysterical fists against the walls of his chest. He stared with unblinking eyes at the floating bodies that swirled now in gentle clouds of blood

The big man sheathed his knife and held out his hand.

"You can let go now," he said. "This is over."

It took Chow a few long moments to realize that the fight was over. That these two fighters had accomplished the impossible.

"I . . . I . . . I . . ." was all Chow could manage.

The man checked that the grenade switch was off. His face was grim, even brutal, but when he smiled it was oddly gentle.

"You're a brave son of a bitch, Corporal," he said.

Outside, seen through the big windows, squadrons of Tiger-Sharks came blasting out of the deck, and behind them a New Zealand-class destroyer.

"God Almighty," whispered Alexander Chow. And then he put his face in his hands and began to weep.

7

The big man took Chow's arm and used his gas jets to lower them both to the deck. The woman waited there, her chest barely heaving from the exertion. She caught one of the floating corpses and wiped her blades clean on the fabric, then pushed it away as if the Raptor was nothing. Nothing at all.

Chow gasped and pointed. "One of them is still alive."

"Where?" demanded the woman, drawing the knives she'd just sheathed. "On your four o'clock, Horse. You missed one."

The big man—Horse—shook his head as he engaged his grav-boots and walked over to the injured bird. Chow expected the man to shoot the alien or cut its throat, but Horse did neither. He hauled it upright, stripped the thing of all weapons and comms, took a slap-plaster out of a pocket and put it over the deep puncture in its side. The medicated bandage immediately fitted itself around the wound in an airtight seal. Chow had no idea if the antibiotics and painkillers in the plaster would work on a bird, but the thing became more stable. Horse then produced a self-tightening cuff ring and fitted it over the alien's hands. It cinched tight, and he used a link chain to secure the cuffed alien to a steel guardrail.

"Stay," ordered Horse as if the bird were a dog. The Raptor cringed back, throwing horrified looks at the two fighters, then at his dead comrades, and back again. People always said that Flock would make dangerous poker players because it was impossible to read the expression in those bird eyes, but Chow no longer believed that. He looked into the egg-hunter's eyes and saw naked, unfiltered fear.

"You getting soft in your old age, Horse?" the woman asked, coming to stand between Chow and her partner.

"Oh, absolutely, Pryss," he said, "I'm considering retiring and dedicating my life to good works and piety."

"Any church you walked into would immediately catch fire," said Pryss.

"Fair point," said Horse. He nudged the captive with the toe of one boot. "We're keeping this asshole because command wants one with a pulse."

"What the hell for?" demanded Pryss. "They going to build a cage and keep it as a pet?"

He grinned at her. "Fun as that would be . . . no. The plan is to patch it up and then let it go."

"You shitting me?"

"Serious as a heart attack," said Horse.

"Let it *go*?" demanded Chow. "Why? I mean . . . *why*?"

Horse turned to him. His mouth smiled but there was no trace of humor in his dark eyes. They were hard as iron.

"Because we want one of their fucking *elite* egg-hunters to take a message back home to their nest," he said coldly. "Command wants them to spread the news that *they* are now the prey, and the war is coming to them."

Chow gaped at the two of them.

"Who *are* you people?"

It was Pryss who answered. "These assholes have been

winning because they're on the leading edge of combat technology. Until now. They never met battle-trained HEs before. Until now, and that's tough shit for them. You want to know why, Corporal? It's because *we're* in the fight now. We're the fucking *future*."

"But . . . but . . . the things you did . . . the way you fought. How could anyone human do that?"

"Human?" snorted Pryss. "That's not even us anymore, is it?"

She snatched the Raptor from Horse's grip and punched it in the face so hard it split the helmet and knocked all sense and light from the creature's eyes.

"Was that necessary?" asked Horse.

Pryss shrugged. "Nah. But it was fun."

Chow found his voice—which took one hell of a lot of effort—and again begged, "Who *are* you people? What are HEs?"

Horse gave him a stone-faced stare that was unreadable and uninformative. But Pryss offered a small, wicked smile.

"Oh, we're just like you, honey," she said in a sugar-sweet voice. She picked up a Raptor pulse rifle and with no apparent effort, bent the weapon in half. The polymers snapped and the steel shrieked. She handed the mangled weapon to him. "Just bigger, better, faster, sexy as fuck, and super badass."

"I . . ." began Chow, but he had nowhere at all to go with that.

8

They came out of nowhere.

Invisible to scanners, too small to be seen against the vastness of the eternal midnight sky, quick and deadly. Breaching pods by the dozen, fired from special launch tubes in an unmarked stealth ship. Each pod had small thrusters burning highly compressed fuel that moved at dangerous speeds that no ordinary human could endure. The drivers inside steered them with the aid of thrusters controlled by AI that interfaced with chips wired into their motor cortex.

The breaching pods looked like oversized and cumbersome space suits of the kind used for mining in the most inhospitable places in the galaxy. Except these suits were totally flat in front and the border ringed with dura-steel. Inside, the drivers wore light-duration suits. They fired forward thrusters that slowed them with shocking abruptness and then guidance thrusters settled the breachers against the hull of the overrun station.

At the instant of contact, small quick-weld packets mounted all around the flat borders suddenly detonated, hard-welding the entire forward suit to the skin of Calliope Station. A screen of self-sealing gel filled with carbon nanotubes that were extremely light and tiny and yet one hundred times stronger than steel. They protected the drivers from blowback and flying debris while cryo-tech kept the occupants cool. The burns flashed intensely bright and hot . . . and then stopped completely.

And for one moment there was stillness.

Then the drivers ignited their suits' primary breaching tool. Ultra-high-intensity cutting lasers fired in perfect sync. The beams were tightly focused to cut a silhouette just inside the bread of the welded seal. Cut-time was four seconds to burn through twenty-two inches of polysteel

As soon as the cuts were done, the soldiers in the suits struck outward with the heels of their palms, and the human-sized panels of metal collapsed into the station. The drivers paused only long enough to make sure the welds were intact and that there was no atmosphere breach that could trigger decompression and—worse—activate more interior alarms.

And then the special operators were inside Calliope Station. Searching for more birds to hunt. They knew that the nursery was already secure, but there were Flock everywhere.

For the moment.

That was about to change in a big, red, terrible way.

9

The battle was over all through Calliope Station.

The big Flock cruiser was now a cloud of debris two miles wide. All but six of their fighters were slag, and of those, five were sent through the Deck with guidance rockets attached magnetically to their hulls and a pair of Tiger-Sharks as escorts. These were headed toward a military R & D site where they would be stripped down to the last screw in order to reverse engineer the latest Flock tech. That was a big win, because these ships were a new design—faster and more maneuverable even than Spinners. Luckily, their autodestruct software was the same as had been used in previous generations, and military techs were able to shut those down. The sixth ship—the one in the best shape—was ferried to a space dock on the far side of Gipley where the U.S.S. *Waratah*—the New Zealand-class destroyer— waited in geostationary orbit.

Alex Chow wandered the steel corridors of Calliope Station.

With the rescue and support teams swarming everywhere, his services were not needed, and his CO had given him a few days to rest and restore. He spent much of that time interviewing people about their experiences during the attack. Chow had a StarCast channel about history but decided to repurpose it to cover the human stories unfolding around him. War stories. Survival stories. Stories of courage and fear, of loss and survival, of grief and hope. He downplayed his own heroism during the attack, though inevitably his interview subjects tried to get him to tell his own story. Over and over and over again. He found new ways to deflect and decline. His aim was to be the historian, not the history.

He was walking through a series of corridors in an undamaged part of the Calliope wheel when he heard voices around a corner. Chow recognized the distinctive deep-chested voice of Horse and he flatted out against the wall to listen. There were layers of polysteel support struts, and Chow pressed his eye to one little gap that allowed him to see Horse, Pryss, and some others whose names—or combat callsigns, he supposed—that he did not know. He quieted his own breathing so he could hear what they were saying.

". . . boys upstairs are pretty happy with us," said Horse, smiling. "Zero causalities except for Short Dog."

"Hey," said another of the group. "It's just a splinter from a ricochet."

Like Horse, this man was very powerfully built, but unlike Horse whose stature gave his muscularity a very even symmetry, the stranger was much shorter and nearly as wide as he was tall. He wore a tight black T-shirt stretched over the broadest shoulders Chow had ever seen. His overdeveloped arms were covered all the way to the wrist with complex Japanese tattoos. His skin was darker too, suggesting mixed race heritage.

"Yeah," said Pryss, grinning. "But it was a splinter from a ricochet from your own damn gun, you dope."

"Heat of battle," protested Short Dog. "Could've happened to anyone."

"Anyone dumb enough to carry a frigging antique pistol into combat in deep space," countered Pryss. "I mean . . . why do you even *carry* that thing?"

"It's a family heirloom," said Short Dog defensively.

"My ass," said another man. He was shorter and had a thin, scholarly face. "I was *with* you when you bought it at the vendor fair on Mill's Rock."

"Okay, okay, Trig," conceded Short Dog, "so maybe it's not the actual family heirloom. Big whoop. Sue me. But it's the same make and model as the one my grandfather gave me. Everyone in my family who went into SpecOps carried one of these going all the way the hell back to Colonel Charlie Beckwith. And, sure, this is a perfect replica of Beckwith's Colt Mark IV Series 80 Commanding Officer's Model .45 ACP."

"Yeah," said Trig, "but it's not a true heirloom."

"Hell, you wouldn't expect me to bring the original out here, would you?" protested Short Dog. "It's worth a fucking fortune."

"Let me get this straight," said Pryss slowly. "You bought a *replica* of an old-fashioned handgun to a firefight with aliens who carry pulse rifles. No . . . no, don't interrupt me . . . because your great-great-great-great-whatever grandfather carried one. So, tell me, Short Dog, did Beckwith also shoot himself in the ass with *his* gun? Is that the family tradition? Bringing outdated guns and shooting themselves in the ass?"

"I did not shoot myself in the ass," snapped Short Dog, clearly aware that he was losing this argument. "I shot at a bird because I thought his grease-shield was down, but the round bounced off, pinged off a few walls, hit a support strut, knocked out a splinter and *that* kind of . . . well . . . you know . . ."

"Debris from a ricochet from your own shot counts as you shooting yourself in the ass," said Pryss. "Am I right, Horse?"

The big man with the indigenous features looked serious. "That's what I'll put into my report."

Short Dog looked around. "You guys are a bunch of total frog-fucking assholes, you know that, right?"

There was a beat, and then they all started laughing.

"Kiss my ass," grumped Short Dog, and that made them laugh harder.

Chow smiled and relaxed a little. This was just a bunch of those SpecOps guys chilling. He was about to push off the wall and join them. He hadn't really had a moment to thank them. But before he could move, the conversation changed into something entirely different as a new voice entered the conversation.

"Hey, there you guys are," said a newcomer hustling down the hall toward them. He had a Japanese face and thick scars on his upper lip. "Been looking all over for you."

"Sup, Sushi," said Short Dog, some relief in his voice that maybe the conversation would take a new direction.

"Horse," said Sushi as he joined them. "Just ran into Colonel Seldon. He wants us to meet him in the east shuttle bay at oh-four-hundred. The techs cracked the nav system on the Needletail and they're programming it for the return flight."

"Outstanding," said Horse.

Sushi lowered his voice to a more confidential level. "Off the record, boss . . .?" he asked.

"Sure," said Horse and the others clustered around. "What's up?"

"I saw a little of a vidcall the colonel was having with some brass higher up the food chain. I think it might have been Admiral Sims."

"Shit," murmured Trig.

"Go on," encouraged Horse.

"Well, they were kind of arguing, you see? About payback for what happened here. Seemed to me that Colonel Seldon was pushing back on some eye-for-an-eye shit." He paused and licked his lips nervously. "I think the brass want to hit the Flock hatcheries."

Hatcheries? Dear God, Chow thought.

The thought of human soldiers doing to Flock children what the Raptors had planned for the babies on Calliope made Chow feel sick. Alien hatchlings or not, those were children.

It became apparent that Pryss had reservations as well. "Don't tell me we're going to go all egg-hunter on the birds. I mean, I'll kill as many Raptors as you want to send my way, but come *on*, Horse."

"Nah," replied Horse, shaking his head. "That's not the actual plan. The intel I got—and this is just between us, feel me?—is that we want to show that we *could* hit their egg barns. We send some stealth craft to drop dummy bombs near those hatcheries. Duds. And inside each one is a message translated into the bird language."

"What kind of messages?" asked Short Dog.

"I don't know the exact wording," said Horse, "but from what the colonel told me, it would amount to something like, 'look what we can do if you force us to.' Something like that."

Chow watched as many of the faces as he could see. There was doubt and skepticism and a little anger.

"I thought that was what *we're* for," said Pryss coldly. "We're the message."

"That's pretty much what I heard the colonel telling the admiral," said Sushi. "But I got the impression that the brass were having second thoughts about that. And, hey, I could be way off here, but it seemed to me that the boys upstairs actually want to take some of those hatcheries out."

"Jesus H. Somersaulting Christ," snarled Trig. "Glad this is off the record, Horse, because I have a whole bunch of six, ten, and twelve letter words I'd like to say to the brass."

"Cool your jets, boy," said Horse. "I'll talk to the colonel. Maybe you didn't hear enough of that conversation."

"Maybe," said Sushi, but it was clear that he did not believe it. Chow felt really sick.

"Look, guys, you have to understand how the brass thinks," said Horse, trying to keep everything in a low gear. "Right now, we're losing the war. We're a response to that, something to up the game, but what if we'd failed here? What if the other teams failed? What if we aren't scaring the birds enough? What then? The command strategists don't want to be seen standing around with their dicks in their hands. They have to answer to those pencil-necks in the government. Maybe by putting together a last-ditch plan that includes hitting the hatcheries as well as a bunch of other critical targets. Maybe dropping some duds with messages in them is a smart move. It shows that we can hurt them the same way they hurt us. I mean . . . the birds are hardly a sentimental race, let's face it . . . but they love their kids."

"Is 'love' the right word for them, though?" asked Pryss.

"Love, need, whatever," said Horse. "They don't want us to steal their future. So, that strategy would show that we're willing to go there if they push this war. That threat, coupled with what our teams are doing."

"And . . . what?" asked Short Dog. "They'll get scared and just back off?"

"Something like that," said Horse.

"But we won't actually kill their kids, though, right?" Pryss demanded.

"According to what Colonel Seldon told me."

"Off the record, Horse," she said, "but that's a bridge too far for me. I won't do that."

"Off and *on* the record, Pryss," said Horse, "neither will I. But I have no compunctions about making those birds believe we will."

"And if they call our bluff?" asked a second woman who'd been silent the whole time. "What then?"

Horse was silent for a few seconds. "Well, Girlie, then things are going to go from bad to the bottom of the shitter."

"Meaning what?" demanded Pryss and Trig at the same time.

"Meaning that command will send all of our teams in to kill everything with feathers. That's what we XEs do. You said it yourself, Pryss—we were *made* for this. If the birds push back, if they want to keep this war going, then we'll go in and teach them the truth about how the universe is wired. Not how it was, but how it *is* . . . and how it will be. We'll scorch the ground and sow it with salt if that's what it takes to end the war and save the human goddamned race."

Girlie snorted. "Human race," she echoed sourly. "That's not even *us* anymore, is it?"

No one answered that question.

After a very heavy pause, Horse said, "Let me go talk to the colonel."

The group of soldiers moved away, leaving Chow to try and process the implications of what he'd just heard.

10

The officer in charge of the small military unit stationed on Calliope, Major Melissa Farnham, found Chow among the teams sifting through wreckage to find and identify the dead. She took him away to the duty office. Inside, there was a silver-haired man in a black uniform with no rank or unit insignia. That he was very senior was evident in both the personal power he conveyed and the extreme deference the major showed him.

"Lance Corporal Chow," said the man, extending a small but very hard hand for a shake. He released the grip and waved Chow to a chair. "I'm Colonel Seldon, and it is my genuine pleasure to meet you."

Seldon. That was the name Sushi mentioned. The officer in charge of the team of—what had Pryss called them—HEs?

"Me, sir?" asked Chow, surprised.

"Oh yes," said Seldon warmly. "Your actions in the nursery saved the lives of those children."

"No sir," Chow said quickly. "I wasn't able to do anything. Not with those grease-shields. I couldn't even scratch those Raptors."

The major quietly cleared her throat and glanced at the colonel. "You held off two squads of egg-hunter Raptors."

"I lost that fight, sir," insisted Chow. "I was about to use a couple of grenades to . . . to . . . I mean . . ." He swallowed. "If it wasn't for those two soldiers—Horse and Pryss—all those kids would be dead."

"If you hadn't held the birds off as long as you did," said Seldon, "the egg-hunters would have breached the nursery walls. You gave my team time to get there."

"Sir, I—" began Chow, but Seldon cut him off with a firm shake of his head.

The colonel had eyes of a stark crystal blue and he rarely seemed to blink. Chow found it hard to look into those eyes and had to fight the impulse to look away.

"But, sir, *they* saved the kids."

"Listen to me, son," said Seldom. "*You* saved those children. No one else was there. You were not rescued."

"But sir, I—"

"Chow," said the major quietly. When he looked at her, she gave a small shake of her head.

Colonel Seldon's voice lost some of its warmth. "You never met anyone named Horse or Pryss, Lance Corporal. No one came to your aid. You successfully defended those children. Those kids will live to grow up and have full lives because of you."

Chow opened his mouth to reply several times, but each time shut it again. He was a student of history, even if he had not gone to college yet. He understood politics.

When he finally found his voice again, he said, "I wasn't supposed to see what happened." He did not make that a question.

"Tell me, Corporal," said Seldon, "what *did* you see?

Chow did not look at his commanding officer. Instead, he stared right back into those crystal blue eyes.

"I saw two squads of Flock egg-hunters enter the nursery, sir."

"And . . .?"

"I secured weapons from the locker and engaged the enemy."

"You did. And because of your training and the weapons provided for use in such situations you prevailed."

"Yes sir." It hurt to say it, but Chow understood.

"What did Mister Horse say?"

"Mister who, sir?"

Seldon leaned back and smiled. He glanced at the major. "You said he was sharp and you did not exaggerate."

The major smiled too.

To Chow, Seldon said, "You could have a solid future in the service, son, but I understand that you have other plans. History, is it?"

"Yes sir. I have an application under review at Harvard."

"Harvard?" mused Seldon. His mouth smiled but his eyes were cold. "I don't think you have to worry about whether your application will be approved."

Chow stiffened. "Permission to speak freely, sir?"

"In this room? Certainly, son," said the colonel. "Speak your mind."

"I don't need to be bribed to keep my mouth shut."

The major's face lost three shades of color. Seldon merely looked amused.

"Son," said the colonel genially, "if I was afraid of you talking about classified matters, I'd have you transferred to one of the ice moons on the ass-end of the galaxy. I could do that with a single call."

"I . . ."

"I don't make a habit of bribing noncoms."

"Then . . .?"

"But I will always reward heroism. And before you say

anything, hear me on this," continued Seldon. "I saw the footage from the vid-feeds in that corridor. I saw the entire fight. The truth is that if you'd had weapons of sufficient potency, you might have won that fight in the exact way our news stories will describe. You were outgunned and outnumbered, but you did not desert your post. You stood your ground and fought that fight. You were going to detonate those grenades to keep those babies from being taken. Yes, that meant you were willing to die and take them all with you. That's heroism. There's that old saying, 'A hero is no braver than an ordinary man, but he is braver five minutes longer.' You were willing to fight *and* die to protect those children from lives of slavery, torture, humiliation, and horror."

"I'm no hero, sir," protested Chow.

"Son, maybe you can lecture me on history, but don't tell an old war dog about what makes a hero."

Chow sat there, barely able to process what was happening.

"The official story is that you saved those kids," said the officer. "We could have had better weapons available to you on this station. That we did not is on us. Sure, we could blame the rapid expansion of the war, the cost of materials, the logistics of distributing newer weapons and materials, and so on, but the truth is *we* failed you and failed everyone on this station. If that became known, then the resulting in-fighting and political game-playing bullshit would do us a lot of harm. Morale, which is shaky at best lately, would crumble. Right now, we need public support because we are about to go on the offensive. That will get expensive but maybe—*maybe*—we'll actually triumph over the enemies who want to exterminate or enslave the human goddamn race. Do you understand?"

Chow stood at rigid attention. "Yes, sir."

"At ease, Lance Corporal."

Chow assumed parade rest, which was as close to relaxation as his nerves could manage.

"If," continued Seldon, "the press has a story about a hero— and there are other people on this station who went above and beyond—then that becomes something to rally around. It stokes the fire of courage. It *unites* rather than divides people. Are you following me on this?"

"I understand, sir."

Seldon sighed. "Is it the truth? Hell, son, you're a student of history. You know how history is largely interpretation filtered through personal or national bias. History is written by more than the victors. Is it propaganda? Yes. Of course, it is. But it's at worst benign propaganda. It serves the common good when the truth might erode that good will." He paused and spread his hands. "As for the Harvard thing . . . it's not a bribe. It's a reward. Your major has shared your psych and performance evals. You have a lot going for you, and if I can help a very promising young man—someone who has clearly proven his courage, vision, and compassion—to explore his full potential, I'd have to be a damn fool not to do what I can."

Chow sat with his fingers knotting together in his lap. "I don't know what to say, sir."

"Nothing is required, Lance Corporal Chow," said the offi- cer as he stood. He once more offered Chow his hand. "It is an honor to meet you. That is *not* propaganda. Prosper, flourish, do well, write the history of this war, tell the truth, maybe get married and have kids and raise them to tell the same truth. In either case, I hope you live long and live well."

With that Seldon turned, nodded to the major, and left the room.

11

Everything about Horse and his team was designated above top secret. No one was supposed to know. Chow, true to his word, said nothing. Nor would he even if he had not met Colonel Seldon. It was a chapter of history he knew would never be written.

But secrets, however closely guarded, tended to find their way into the public conversation.

The story of a team of some kind of super soldiers got out. Luckily none of what made the intragalactic news feeds covered his particular action. He was the hero of the nursery battle, and that bit of fiction seemed to stick.

Somehow other sections of the vid-feeds leaked. Chow watched the screens as Sushi and Trig, Short Dog and Girlie, and other HEs tore through swarms of heavily armed Raptors. They were not named, but that didn't seem to work. What mattered to the hundreds of billions of people scattered throughout the galaxy was the fact that the Raptors were no longer invincible. There were newer, tougher kids on the playground.

Soon vidcaps of other HE teams began leaking into news feeds and social media channels.

"Am I dreaming this?" asked Chow's friend Margo as they sat at a table in the mess hall.

"Maybe we all are," said Chow.

He never saw Horse or his team again. He never saw or heard from Colonel Seldon. But Pryss's words echoed constantly in his head.

Human? That's not even us anymore, is it?

And as for the other thing Pryss said, calling herself and by implication the rest of her team HEs . . . all of the conspiracy theorists cracked that within hours of the story breaking.

There had been back-channel rumors for years about something called the Chimera Project run by a government molecular biologist named Dr. Ingrid Teller. Details were scant and exaggerated speculation rampant, but the bottom line was that leaked documents hinted at a program to create *Homo eximius*. Enhanced humans for military use. Hearing Horse use that acronym was a telling remark. It called to mind things Chow had read and heard about from other Special Forces players who had volunteered for physical upgrades. Yes, it made them more efficient fighters, but they found the adjustment back to civilian life filled with all kinds of challenges. Not merely being physically different from friends and family, but not knowing how to be normal again. To be truly human again.

What would it mean to be as radically enhanced as Horse and Pryss seemed to be?

We're the future.

How far from recognizable humanity had they been taken?

Chow chewed on that day and night. He was deep into speculation one morning as he shaved in front of his bathroom mirror. Wondering if the time might ever come when he could tell his story. When he could tell the truth. If he could never do that, if he had to smile and wave and be some kind of false hero, then what kind of historian could he ever hope to make of himself?

These thoughts were tumbling through his brain when massive alert buzzers shattered the air and scattered his thoughts.

"God, no," he cried, bracing for the thunder-strike of more Flock missiles.

Then he heard the shouting. The screams. The yells that filled the corridor outside of his small cabin. Without pausing to wipe the shaving cream from his jaws, Chow pulled free his sidearm and plunged out into the corridor.

He stepped into madness.

Everyone was pouring out of their cabins. People were laughing, crying, and hugging each other and hugging with wild abandon. People disengaged their grav-boots and soared into the air, shouting at the top of their lungs, their faces glowing as if huge fires were igniting within.

Sergeant Rilke, one of his best friends, saw Chow and grabbed him. She *kissed* him with towering, spiraling, boundless joy.

"What's happening?" he demanded, pushing her back.

"What's happening?" she laughed. "Didn't you hear? It's over!"

"What's over?"

"The war," she cried. "It's over."

"Over? What are you talking about?"

Then he saw the big holo-screens lit up, the president of the Confederation of Planets stood there, his face bright with joy as if this was Christmas morning for the whole galaxy. Chow stood in stunned silence, listening to the president say impossible things. Reading the text crawls and pop-ups; staring at cutaway vidclips. Everyone around him cheered and wept.

It.

Was.

Over.

The Flock had surrendered. Unconditionally, completely, and immediately.

Chow felt as if he were falling. As if the structure of reality had been torn asunder by this new reality.

And then he, too, was yelling.

He, too, was hugging everyone in sight.

He, too, wept.

The war was over.

12

He had no official rank.

Once upon a time Jason Horse had been a first sergeant, but then he died.

Officially.

The casket they buried in Hawaii had just enough ballast in it to make the pallbearers think there was a body in there. The flag was folded and given to his sister—the only living relative he'd had. Taps was blown, rifles fired, salutes given, tears shed. Then the box of stones went into the ground.

Jason Horse watched it all via a live feed from a pigeon drone.

He wept too. For his sister. For his life.

No one said shit to him about those tears. Not his commanding officer or any of the technicians and doctors at the Chimera Project.

Jason Horse died and was buried. At least they had the good taste to sell the fiction that he had died in combat with the Flock. Some Tier One shooters died in "training accidents" or "atmosphere failures on ships or exo-bases." He—as far as the official story went—died fighting. Hoo-fucking-rah.

"Now I'm a ghost," he said at the time. No one laughed.

That was then.

This was now.

He stood by his *second* coffin. This one was gleaming metal and crystal polyglass. There were meters and dials and display screens all over it; there were tangles of wires and cables hanging from it and leading to ranks of supercomputers.

"So much for the war being over," Horse said, trying not to sound as bitter as he felt.

"It's over," said Colonel Seldon.

"Why? Because the birds said they were sorry?"

It was the same argument they'd had since the war ended. Once the Flock surrendered there was the big reveal that communication—actual meaningful communication—was now possible. Teams of cultural translation specialists had been able to sync more than ninety Terran languages with the Flock's language via radical new software. While not exactly the universal translator linguistic specialists had been promising for decades, it was close. Close enough, at least.

What became clear was that the war had been the result of a miscommunication of a spectacular and unprecedented level between two species. That was how the president phrased it. Without the need for propaganda, the story emerged that early human exploratory missions intruded into Flock space, and by accident destroyed several of their incubator facilities, killing thousands of unborn birds. The Flock, naturally, took this as an act of war and retaliated with understandable outrage and aggression.

Those faults in communication had now been corrected, and the Flock—realizing that it was all a terrible accident compounded by an extreme overreaction—sued for peace. They realized now that human intentions were not at all intended to do harm, and their overreactions had been greatly out of proportion.

Colonel Seldon shook his head. "Look, Horse, we have to try and make the peace work. Especially now that both sides realize the errors we've all made. This surrender was unconditional. They asked for no concessions. Not one. They have offered to make any and all reparations we demand. Allowing them to do that is a serious win for us, and the government unanimously sees it as the best pathway to a lasting peace."

"And you actually believe it?" demanded Horse. "After all that slaughter? After all the devious shit they pulled? The politicians on both sides just blow each other and smile?"

"What should we do?" asked Seldon, wearying of the ongoing argument. "Tell them to shove their surrender up their asses and go back to killing each other?"

"Permission to speak freely, sir," said Horse.

Seldon looked both pained and annoyed. "Don't give me that chain of command shit, Horse. Speak your mind."

"You're putting us on ice," said Horse, his tone heated. "That means you think we aren't needed."

"That's not the right way to read this," growled Seldon. "Alpha Wave and the other teams are going into cryosleep for a limited time. You're each being sent to a strategic location in case this peace isn't what we all hope it is. Dr. Teller feels that this is the only way we can guarantee that there is no loss of physical potential or operational readiness. This allows all teams to be thawed out and therefore 100 percent ready for combat."

"And if this bullshit peace actually works, then what? How long do we stay frozen?"

Seldon shook his head. "You read the analysis papers. Ten months to a year. Tops. Then you all get thawed and by then we'll have a bunch of options mapped out. Discharge and some surgical de-enhancements . . . at least for the biometrics. You get to keep the other bonuses. You'll always be stronger and faster than anyone you meet. That's got to be fun. There will be any of a hundred military assignments that will be yours for the asking. And if you go civilian, the list of companies—everyone from the entertainment industry to exoplanet exploration corporations—will trip over each other to hire you. You can get rich, grow old, and die happy."

"Colonel . . . Bill . . . I wish I felt a bit more trust," said Horse wearily.

"Come on, Jason, you know me. We've been through the valley of the shadow more times than most people have had hot meals. You *know* you can trust me. I will always have your best interests—and those of your people—at heart. I give you my word."

"I trust you, Bill," said Horse. "You're a soldier, not a politician. But you work for politicians, and I don't trust them worth a damn."

"I do," said Seldon. "On this? I really do."

Horse sighed, nodded, and tried to give Seldon a salute. But the officer slapped his hand down and gathered the big soldier into a fierce hug.

"When we thaw you out, brother," said the colonel, "your first hot dinner is on me."

"Can you at least tell me where we're going?"

"Sorry, boy, that's above even my pay grade. A team is coming to oversee transport. All I know is that each team will be on a different moon, the nature and location of which are above top secret. You understand why, don't you? If word gets out and the peace *does* fail, the last thing we want to do is paint bullseyes on you lot while you're sleeping. But don't worry. My guess is this will all be over sooner than later."

And that brought them right up to the brink of it. Horse knew that he had no real option. Bill Seldon was his commanding officer, and he was a friend. If there was anyone who would speak up for him and the rest of Alpha Wave—hell, for all of the XEs—it was Seldon. That was the one thing Horse was certain about. It was what he told Pryss, Short Dog, Girlie, and the rest of the team before they went cold.

There were twenty-one sleep capsules. The full Alpha Wave platoon. No officers. Jason Horse—nominally still first sergeant—two staff sergeants, and eighteen specialists that could be deployed in squads and fire teams of various sizes. Elastic in structure, adaptive in ways even the most experienced normal human soldiers could not be. And all of them slumbering in the arms of Morpheus.

Jason Horse was the last one. Always the first up and the last down.

He climbed into the cryo-chamber and worked on his breathing and blood pressure while Dr. Teller's technicians hooked him up. Ten months to a year was a long nap in the ice. The longest he'd done so far done.

The only good thing was that it wouldn't feel that long. Cryosleepers did not dream. Waking up always felt like only a minute after lying down. He was acutely aware of Colonel Seldon watching him. He saw his friend's face. Saw the sadness in it, maybe a flicker of guilt because he had been the one to deliver the news and carry out the order.

Horse figured, *fuck it,* and forced a smile onto tight lips. He gave Seldon a thumbs up as the polyglass hissed down and sealed him in.

Then he waited, using his enhanced senses to smell the first whiff of the gasses that would lull him to the edge of sleep before the cryonics flash froze him. Oddly, those gasses always smelled of roses. It had amused him before, but now it called to mind the roses his sister had thrown onto his first coffin as it was being lowered into the ground.

Then Horse took a deep breath, allowing those fumes to flood into his lungs. The first sensation was always a faint tingling around his eyes. Then a sense of peace.

He glanced once more at Seldon and saw that he was speaking. Not to any of the techs. Seldon was looking directly at Horse and he seemed to be saying something to him. Horse couldn't hear the officer's voice through the glass, but he could read lips well enough.

"I'm so sorry, my brother," the colonel seemed to say. "I only pray to God that you'll find some way to forgive us."

Horse jerked against the tubes and cables and tried to find the emergency release.

Forgive you? Forgive you for what?

But the gasses owned him now and in the blink of an eye, Horse's mind went dark.

And he slept.

For a very long time . . .

PART TWO

SUCH STUFF AS DREAMS
ARE MADE OF
2479 C.E.

"A dreamer is one who can only find his way by moonlight, and his punishment is that he sees the dawn before the rest of the world."

—Oscar Wilde

Intentions

"It is a serious thing to live in a society of possible gods and goddesses, to remember that the dullest most uninteresting person you can talk to may one day be a creature which, if you saw it now, you would be strongly tempted to worship, or else a horror and a corruption such as you now meet, if at all, only in a nightmare."

—C. S. Lewis

The Weight of Glory

13

Two hundred and fourteen years later . . .

14

Millions of years ago, when humans looked up and noticed the stars for the first time, they couldn't possibly have contemplated how the very idea that there was something greater than themselves would change the trajectory of their existence. Although the moment was lost in time, many of the greatest human minds attempted to capture the instant humanity shifted—our most dramatic moment of evolution. For without that moment, we would have been a much different species indeed.

Arthur C. Clarke, one of the most famous authors of the twentieth century, partnered with then acclaimed two-dimensional film director, Stanley Kubrick, and attempted to capture the potential of that moment in cinema. In the movie *2001: A Space Odyssey*, the idea of their partnership was to try and bring two of the most forward-thinking minds together and postulate the possibilities of the human race influenced—not necessarily by an outside force—but by the idea that the human race was not alone.

Although much was lost to popular culture and the appropriation of the pseudo sentient computer known as HAL and his conversation with the astronaut representing humankind during the period the movie was portrayed, the ultimate statement of Clarke and Kubrick could be dissembled in the opening scenes.

Picture this: Earth, primates are the only creatures capable of anything approaching a consciousness and the ability to deconstruct and create. Had they been given the mirror test, they would have passed. The number of cortical neurons has reached a critical mass where they are no longer reactive but proactive. A troop of primates in search of food stumble upon a watering hole where other animals are drinking. While obtaining sustenance, another troop of primates comes and they argue, but no violence ensues.

Later, they all sleep.

When they awake to a brilliant red sunrise, their landscape has been marred by the presence of a monolith, which is synecdoche for the unexpected, or the first acknowledgement of the stars. The monolith is impossibly tall and smooth and rectangular, clearly something that could not have been created by any troop of primates known by the group who discovered it.

The primates approach and immediately begin to worship the object, even though they do not know what worship is. They cannot help themselves as they touch and fondle the impossibility of the advancement among them. In an effort to identify the unidentifiable, their cortical neurons blast and sizzle, creating the need to acknowledge something greater than themselves and in that moment, they realize that they are not alone.

They were incapable of understanding it like humankind because they lacked the appropriate number of cortical neurons. They understand the monolith means something, though, but they lack the heritable traits of successive organisms as they replaced each other over generative spans allowing for discoveries such as: Aristarchus of Samos (310-230 BC) was a Greek astronomer and mathematician who presented the first known heliocentric model that placed the Sun at the center of the known universe, with the Earth revolving around the Sun once a year and rotating about its axis once a day; Hipparchus of Nicea (190-120 BCE) who created accurate models for the motion of the planets, the first star chart, and developed mathematical principles for calculating astronomical events; Ptolemy of Egypt (100 CE-170 CE), known for the geocentric theory of the universe, which would form the basis of human understanding of the motions of stars and planets for over than a thousand years; or Galilei, Kepler, Hershel, Laplace, Eddington, Hubble, Kuiper, and Sagan.

In fact, it is Clarke as mentioned previously, who makes two statements to describe the ideas flaring through the primates' minds.

"I suspect that religion is a necessary evil in the childhood of our particular species. And that's one of the interesting things about contact with other intelligences: we could see what role, if any, religion plays in their development. I think that religion may be some random by-product of mammalian reproduction. If that's true, would non-mammalian aliens have a religion?"

And more succinctly: "Any sufficiently advanced technology is indistinguishable from magic."

For the primates in the movie, the monolith was magic and it was also something to be worshipped. But what occurs next in the film is where my thesis really shines.

(*The speaker takes a moment and drinks from a container, centers herself, and then once again addresses the congregation of scientists.*)

In the next moments of the movie, the primates seem to

discover for the first time that around their watering hole are a number of bones. Whether they have used them as tools before has not been indicated by the filmmaker and his advisor, but the belief is that, although they may have been used as tools, it was as tools to dig for more sustenance.

This is where the thesis of the film director and mine merge.

Instead of approaching the other troop with wonder and sharing the discovery, perhaps even attempting to use the combined neurons of all the members of the troops together to jumpstart an idea, they discover violence. Note that they have been violent before, but the violence has been evolutionarily selected to be wrought in such a way as to benefit the group as a whole, such as attempting to capture and slaughter other species for food.

Let us return to the imagination.

Imagine, if you will, millions of years ago when the first primate grasps a piece of broken bone from the ground and appraises it as a weapon of war for the very first time. One troop has argued with others. They may have even chased each other and rained down fists in an effort to manage food and water sources, but war and violence for the sake of violence is as unknown as the monolith.

You are the primate. The bone feels solid in your grasp. Behind you is the wonder of wonders. In front of you is a troop of primates who wish to have an equal share of this wonder. Instead of allowing it, your cortical neurons fire and you lift the bone, then bring it down on top of the lead primate's head. Members of your troop see you and do the same. Soon, the land around you has become an abattoir. You have discovered that you can obtain that which you want through violence.

Boom.

More evolution.

With the primates dead, the trajectory of your species changes. In a million years, Aristarcus places the Sun in the middle of the solar system, Hipparchus creates the first star chart and Ptolemy changes our understanding of the universe as a whole.

Carl Sagan explained, "It's an ancient human theme. You can find it in virtually every culture in some guise or other, in religion, folklore, superstition, and now in science. The search for life elsewhere is remarkable in our age because this is the first time that we can actually do something besides speculation. We can send spacecraft to nearby planets; we can use large radio telescopes to see if there is any message being sent to us lately. It touches to the deepest of human concerns. Are we alone? How common is this thing called life, this thing called intelligence? Where did we come from? What are the possible fates of intelligent beings? Need we necessarily destroy ourselves? Might there be a bright and very long future for the human species? We tend to have such a narrow view of our place in space and in time, and the prospect of making contact with extraterrestrial intelligence works to de-provincialize our world view. I think for that reason, the search itself, even without a success, has great merit."

We would never have left our planet had we not discovered that violence is more powerful than the fundamental principles of lift and gravity.

The primates represent us before knowledge of the universe.

Violence is our way to seek knowledge of the universe.

The Flock is the result of our seeking knowledge.

Had we not sent out millions of invitations, they never would have come, and having come, they demonstrated that their knowledge of the universe was created in the same fashion as ours.

By seeking knowledge through violence.

Sagan was more optimistic than reality provided. He was right in the idea that "making contact with extraterrestrial intelligence worked to de-provincialize our universal view." But how many of you wish the return of provincial ideas? The ideas that we are alone? That we never sent out invitations? Had we never done so, we wouldn't be the subservient race. For now, we are not the troop who are closest to the monolith, we are the ones doomed to try and forever touch it but are beaten down before we can ever get close.

(The speaker finishes and waits for a few moments for applause. There is none. She turns and walks off the stage, aware that six observers from the Flock have watched it all from the shadows of the upper balcony.)

15
IN DREAMS . . .

Lexie Chow ran along the burning street, keeping to the shadows, using the toppled buildings and burned vehicles as cover. Running, pausing, waiting, running.

All around her the world burned.

The mighty towers built by man in his creative majesty and his unended hubris were ablaze. Many had already collapsed, and the smoking debris formed impassable mountain ranges that clogged the side streets. Lexie knew where they were blocked, though, and she knew where the passages were. She was practiced at this. She had done this a thousand times.

She paused near a hover-hauler that had fallen from the sky. It was crammed with people. Refugees trying to hide among the crates of supplies. Fifty or more.

They were all dead, their bodies torn to cinders. Lexie had seen this before. Raptors must have knocked the hauler down, blown open the bay doors, and simply hosed everyone inside.

Men.

Women.

Children.

Pulse weapons don't incinerate. They burn, they sear, they char, but the blasts leave enough of the victims so that they look like what they are. People. Savagely killed, their blackened faces contorted into everlasting masks of screaming fear. They were all unarmed. The dead clung to one another. Friends holding friends. Lovers entwined. Parents huddled over their children in a vain attempt to save them.

All dead.

Lexie turned, feeling that old fire. Not the heat of pulse weapons, but the deeper, hotter fire inside her body. It started in the pit of her stomach and burned its way into her chest and tried to escape as shouts, as screams.

But she bit down on that. Swallowing the heat and the pain, feeding on the horror and the hate.

A sound warned her. A pebble tumbling softly down from a mound of rubble. Lexie hurled herself to one side, tucked, rolled, and came up into a shooting position, one knee down, the other raised and braced, her hands bringing twin *pistols up, the grips heavy with fully loaded magazines. On some level she was aware that these were old-fashioned models, but at the same time a part of her recognized them as new, as cutting edge.*

Her barrels locked on a shadow and with blinding speed Lexie tracked upward from shadow to shadow *caster. To the thing that squatted atop the mound.*

A Raptor. One of the big ones. Dressed in exotic biomech armor, the grotesque helmet around its head and beak, multi-spectrum goggles taking in data, seeing more than human eyes could ever see. It held a heavy pulse rifle in its taloned hands. The vestigial wings beneath its arms twitch in a mockery of agitated flight.

The Flock fighter swung the rifle toward her, but Lexie was moving, rising from her kneeling posture, firing fast.

The damned bird did not even try to evade. It had such faith in its armor that Lexie could actually hear its dry, staccato laugh as it prepared to shoot.

But the rounds in Lexie's gun were not standard issue 9mm caseless armor-piercing rounds. That was for the regular army. That was why the regular soldiers had been dying by the thousands, taking down one Raptor for every dozen humans.

Lexie smiled as she fired. The big guns bucked in her hand despite the shock-absorbing polymers in the frame. The CS rounds began spinning in the magazine, activated by syncing with Lexie's biosignature, and each round struck like a diamond drill, corkscrewing as they hit the Flock armor. Drilling through their gear in a microsecond before the micro-charges in each bullet detonated.

The Raptor staggered, its body dancing and jerking as each CS blew apart a nerve cluster or muscle group. It dropped the rifle and actually raised its hand as if somehow that could ward off the shots.

As the people in that hauler had done.

Lexie offered the bird the same mercy it had shown them.

The bird spun away, seeding the air with dark red blood.

A second Raptor raced up the far side of the mound, shoving its dying companion away with the indifference to suffering that marked their species. It raised a flame unit, but before it could spew the self-igniting chemicals, Lexie shot the thing in the face. The corkscrew rounds tore the helmet and head to crimson junk.

Then Lexie was moving again, running around the base of the mound, firing at anything that moved, catching two more Raptors as they tried to move a heavier gun on its tripod mount. She killed them and then three more.

She burned through three magazines for each pistol, then holstered the empty guns and took a pair of firesticks from their thigh scabbards, ignited the laser blades and went running to find more of the birds.

They saw her coming.

They tried to defend themselves.

They tried to flee.

But she caught them and killed them all.

Without pause. Without mercy. Without caring that they screamed and tried to surrender.

She found one more, a young Flock foot soldier, wounded, bleeding, huddled in the doorway of a burned-out store. It had a pistol, but it wasn't trying to fire. Instead, it kicked backward, trying to fold itself against the door, trying not to be seen, or at least not to be seen as a threat. Its helmet visor was shattered and those bird eyes stared wildly at her.

That's what they said.

They were wrong.

Lexie saw the fear in those alien eyes. She smiled as she drew a knife. The smile was so cold it actually hurt her face. As she approached, Lexie caught sight of herself in the cracked remains of the store's plate glass.

And she froze.

The whole world froze.

The reflected image moved when she moved. It held the same knife. It looked back with exactly the same expression of complete surprise and shocked bewilderment.

Lexie stared at herself.

But it was not Lexie looking back.

It was a man's face. Hard, scarred, with dark eyes and some kind of tribal tattoos climbing up the neck and over his square jaw and high cheekbones.

The body was a man's body. Huge. Muscular.

Lexie said, "What the hell . . .?"

The words came out in the deep timbre of a man's voice.

And then Lexie Chow woke up . . .

16

Lexie screamed herself awake.

She kicked out furiously at sheets now tangled around her like some tentacular sea beast. Cursing and slapping at them until she was free, Lexi huddled against the headboard, gasping and staring around as if expecting to see burning debris and dead bodies. She looked at her hands, surprised there was no knife.

"What . . .?" she asked the empty room, totally confused by her unmarked, unbloodied skin. There was not even the residual faint sunburn effect from prolonged use of a pulse weapon. Nothing.

Only skin, beads of cold sweat, and endless rows of goosebumps.

"God . . . damn . . ." she said, breathing heavily, forcing those words out through a tight throat. "*God*damn."

Something small and desperate struggled out from under those sheets and stood trembling on the edge of the bed.

"It's . . . it's okay, Ahab," she stammered, her voice lacking all conviction.

Ahab, sixteen pounds of simulated Jack Russell nervous

energy, looked at her with wild eyes. Wanting understanding, needing reassurance, but also game to bite anything he could see. Except there was nothing to see. Even robot dogs with sophisticated AI couldn't see dreams. It had no idea what a dream even was. To Ahab, dreams were nothing more than static amid the commands that had been worked into its operating parameters.

"It's okay," Lexie said again, though she didn't believe that. She inhaled deeply then exhaled. "Goddamn . . ."

Her bedroom was small and draped in gray-brown shadows. Outside there was the *whoosh-whoosh* of traffic cruising on electromagnetic lines of energy. It sounded like waves exhaling onto a shallow beach, and that usually offered a measure of distracting calm. Not today. Now it grated on her, abrading her frazzled nerves. Lexie's heart hammered inside her chest as if it was trying to crack apart, and every inch of her was bathed in icy sweat.

It took a long time for her breathing to slow. She huddled back against the headboard; her whole body clutched as tight as a fist.

The dream was still with her, playing and replaying on the inside of her mind with all of the sounds and smells. She could smell the acrid stink of burning plastic, the coppery odor of blood, the rawness of her own sweat.

No . . . not her sweat. *His.*

Whoever he was.

After nine dreams like this, she still wasn't sure who was invading her dreams. At first, she'd felt violated, as if the brawny soldier in those dreams was stealing her mind from her. But that wasn't really it. He wasn't taking anything from her. Instead, it was like he was inviting her into his mind. Perhaps into his dreams.

Was that what was happening?

How, though? It couldn't be some kind of psychic transference. There was no one alive who'd ever fought the Flock in a battle. Hell, there hadn't been a fight *with* the Flock in more than two hundred years. So, this couldn't be some kind of mind-swapping bullshit.

Who was it, then?

Was it one of *them*?

Could it be that?

That frightened Lexie on a profound level. It terrified her. If the man in her dreams was a Sleeper, then why were her dreams so different from everyone else's?

Even though she dreamed of brutal combat, she did not wake up ready to kill. She had not gone from dream-state to a murderous rampage. She had not built a bomb and taken it to a rookery. She hadn't bought a rifle from a black marketer and gone sniping for birds. Nor had she bought a set of kitchen knives and crept through the night cutting throats of unsuspecting Flock.

And, there were the *other* dreams. The ones in which she and that strange man, that exceptional soldier, were not sharing one skin, but exploring each other's flesh. There had been dreams like that. Steaming hot. Scalding. Yet tender. Not merely sex, but lovemaking.

What the hell was *that* all about?

Ahab crept toward her and pushed his muzzle into Lexie's side. Its emotional response and interaction software compelled it to want and need comfort in that moment. Lexie—like most people with a RealLife pet—reacted to it as if the dog were truly alive.

"It's okay," she said, the words thick and rough.

Ahab whined softly, and Lexie's trembling fingers running jerkily down its fur did nothing to sell the idea that anything was okay.

The dream. Those *dreams.*

Those damn dreams.

Lexie knew that she was dreaming of the Sleepers so why was she still sane? If "sane" was a good word to use. Her therapist and all three ex-boyfriends might choose other adjectives.

Even so, if this wasn't her slipping into a dream of the Sleepers, then what the fuck was it?

Too many questions. No whiff of an answer. And she did not want them to escalate. She did not want to become a full-blown Dreamer. No fucking way.

"They'll go away," she told Ahab, and the croaking old-woman voice that came out of her throat was jarring. She coughed, cleared her throat, and repeated those words. Her voice sounded more normal than not. There was too much fear there. Too little control. Ahab's little tail whipped back and forth with whatever encouragement he could muster.

Last night's dream *would* fade, ebbing like a slow tide from the shores of her awareness. The memory of it would not diminish, though. Not completely. It would linger, like the foam left on the bank by the outgoing tide.

As had all the others.

As had the dreams of making love with him . . .

Given what she was planning, Lexi wasn't sure she wanted any of it to vanish completely. Not if the dream was some kind of message. Or omen. Or whatever the hell it was.

"Goddamn bastard," she said through gritted teeth. Directing that arrow to wherever it would stab hardest. The Flock, the Sleepers, that *particular* Sleeper—if he was real—or whatever misfiring neuron was creating those dreams.

The echoes of gunfire still seemed to haunt the room. Ahab flinched as if he heard it, though she knew he was just reacting to her wild energy. Her fear.

"Walk it off, you stupid cow," she told herself.

Lexie swung her legs over the edge of the bed and stood up. The room took an immediate and nauseating spin and then she was falling. She cried out, reached out, tried to check her fall, tried to regain her balance, tried to keep last night's dinner from exploding up from her gut. In all of these things she failed utterly.

Lexie landed hard on her palms and kneecaps, and then crouched on all fours like a sick dog, vomiting up her food, the alcohol, her fear, her pain, and her horror.

The bedside alarm went off. It did not ring—those kinds of alarms were only allowed on days off. The workday alarm squawked at her in a Flock voice. Sharp, grating, and yet patronizing.

"Rise and celebrate a new day in which you can joyfully fulfill your purpose by serving the Flock."

Lexie wiped her mouth with the back of her hand.

"Fuck you," she snarled. But at that moment her vitriol was directed inward every bit as much as outward.

Ahab, ever the opportunist, darted forward and tried to eat the mess, but Lexie growled him back. It did not matter than Ahab's materials processor could have cleaned it all up and excreted it in sanitized little lumps. The Jack moved six inches away, sat, and stared with a hunger that made her stomach churn even more.

It took about two thousand years, but Lexie got to her feet. She braced her feet against the swaying floor, hands outstretched for balance, ignoring the critical eye of the small dog.

"I love you," she said hoarsely, "but you can kiss my ass."

Ahab smiled a doggy smile.

Moving with great care, Lexie stepped over the stinking puddle of her own puke, placing each step as gingerly as if she were picking her way through a minefield. When she was clear of it, she punched a wall pad with the side of her fist.

"Songbird," she gasped, speaking to the household AI system, "spill on aisle seven." A small panel hissed open on the wall and MATT—a little triangular cleaner-bot—rolled out, its small whiplike antennae twitching. It immediately glided over to the mess on the floor and began spraying an enzyme blend that would break everything down to a grayish powder that could be vacuumed up. Ahab growled at MATT, disliking it on principle.

"Stop it, Ahab," snapped Lexie. "Go . . . charge, or something."

The dog contrived to look sulky as it walked over to a small wireless pad next to her dresser. It lay down with every appearance of disappointment and annoyance, then closed its eyes as the charging pad interfaced with its batteries.

Lexie staggered into the bathroom and leaned heavily on the sink. That was the best she could manage, despite the clock in her head telling her to hurry up or risk being late for work.

For a moment she resisted looking into the mirror, afraid of seeing the same reverse image she'd seen in her dream. It took courage to raise her face and look.

The face in the mirror was what was *left* of her own. The same black hair—uncombed and with particles of last night's chili clinging to the strands. The same gray-green eyes, though they looked shifty and guilty. Her mouth was slack, caught between sadness and self-loathing. Her body—once curvy and lush during her college years—was now wiry and nearly sexless. She had hard muscles and good tone, but at the moment she felt rubbery and useless. She felt weak and vulnerable, and that made twenty-eight look like sixty-eight—and a sixty-eight that was the end result of hard use and bad decisions.

"Fuck you," she said again, directing it solely at herself and really leaning on it.

The apartment was very quiet except for the whisper-soft

humming of MATT's motor.

"Songbird," Lexie called, "sing something old. *Rocking the Universe* playlist nineteen. Shuffle."

The interactive AI system loaded thousands of rock and roll songs going back five hundred years. A desperate and plaintive male voice began singing.

"*We gotta get out of this place*," it said, "*if it's the last thing we ever do . . .*"

Lexie listened for a minute, unmoving.

Then, despite every single reason not to, she burst out laughing.

17

His name was Hell.

That was not his birth name, but it defined him.

He was born Ren'Mgo, with no third part, no battle-earned name. Not like Ngo'Pgo-Callisto or Ugi'Sgo-Mars. Only families from one of the Privileges could have a battle name. Centuries ago, there had been members of his rookery with such names, but no longer. After the debacle on Calliope Station, his ancestor had been sent back as the sole survivor, beaten, humiliated, and forced to carry the human ultimatum that ended the great war with the Flock's surrender, humiliation, defeat, and shame. So many of his ancestors had been executed for being traitors to their own rook. All blame was heaped onto his family. The government would never admit their own strategic missteps.

That blame was forever the stain that tarnished the feathers of his rookery. They were not allowed to fight in battles, not even after the Flock rose up and conquered humanity. Glory was for the heroes of the Flock. With no battles, there was no war name. Instead, the brothers and sisters from his clutch used convenience third names. Places in which they lived rather than sites of fierce conflicts or heroic victories.

Only when circumstances demanded a full name did Hell give the one he felt he had earned.

His name was meant to give pause.

Ren'Mgo-Hell.

That said so much.

When the call was sent out for him to visit Earth, Hell came.

Now he stood at the top of the short ramp, clawed fingers resting lightly on the open hatch of his Pterosaur ship—a modified bomber with ordnance bay swapped out for bigger engines. It looked old and slow but looks were often deceiving.

There were no markings anywhere on the ship, nor on his armor. The craft, like its owner, did not officially exist.

Two Flock officers stood waiting at the bottom of the ramp. They were not warrior class and stood only a few inches above five feet in height. They were thin and lightly muscled, with severely trimmed feather crests running from brow over the skull to the napes of their necks. The feathers on their vestigial wings were painted to match their clans and status within the Flock military hierarchy. Their armored skin was unmarked, more proof they had not earned their rank through combat. Hell despised them on principle. Not that he had any love or patriotic affection for the Raptors who stood in two precise lines to form a kind of corridor between his ship and the exit hatch at the back of the landing bay.

All of them—the slender nobles and their towering Raptor soldiers—wore red. The guards were likely second, third, or even fourth-born from their egg clutches, but while that might matter within other rooks, all of the soldiers who wore red were from one of the Eight Privileges. Even the heel spikes that curved outward and down from their otherwise booted feet were stained red. Hell disliked that most of all, because it was a decoration that tried to sell the fiction that those spikes were dripping human blood.

He wondered how many of them had actually seen combat. Certainly not the effete officers waiting for him at the bottom of the ramp. Hell wished he could show them what combat felt like. He wondered how long they would last. Three seconds? Less?

Each Raptor wore a cuirass and kilt in some shade of medium red. The color marked them as sons and daughters of the noblest families. The darker the shade, the more important the lineage. The nobles wore crimson that was nearly the color of fresh blood.

Hell wore white.

The color of weakness. The color of shame. The color his family had been forced to wear since the debacle on Calliope Station. The cuirass and kilt he wore were spotless white. However, his cloak was stained with red. Not clan red, but the color of dried human blood. Here and there were splashes of a watery reddish-yellow—Flock blood. That cloak was his statement, and as he descended the ramp, the senior Raptors waiting for him stiffened. In other places, on other worlds, members of the Flock had scoffed and jeered at him as a white-feather. None of those Flock were willing to do so now, and it was clear to him that these Raptors knew this.

Every Raptor in that docking bay had the legal right to insult him, disregard him, even strike him. He was a white-feather from a clan of broken wings. A spoiled egg. Hell was a Raptor by heritage and genetics, but not by status. He had no rank, no title, no credentials. The cloak, however, was enough. He could see in their eyes that they knew his reputation. Not one of them spoke a word of disrespect. Not one. Instead, they all stood to rigid attention and none of them dared meet his eyes.

Hell was not amused by this. Delight in such games of castes and rookeries had mattered to him as a hatchling and a youngster, but that was a long time ago. So much had happened since. He had stopped caring about it. Nothing could change his family colors. He found it useful, though. Very useful indeed.

The two Flock officers did not bow, but he could tell they felt compelled to do so. Not in mere deference. No. Out of fear. And that was right and proper.

The senior of them spoke. "I am Kgo'Ngo-Thames," he said, announcing his family name, the order in which he had been hatched, and a battle name earned in the service of the Flock. The Kgo clan had crushed the London uprising several years past. They were indeed a Rook of Privilege.

Hell did not reply in kind. Instead, he merely lifted his chin toward the door at the far end of the docking bay. One Flock officer nodded—an action that *almost* became a bow, but which the officer caught in time. Almost in time. He and his fellow officer turned and led the way down the corridor of clan champions.

They led him from the bay and along several corridors in The Grand Nest, a towering building composed of thousands of hues of every color in the spectrum. Except white, of course. They reached an elevator that was guarded by another pair of red-swathed Raptors. When the door whisked open, the officers lingered at the entrance.

"You will go up alone," said Kgo'Ngo-Thames. "The lift is programmed."

He stood back as Hell stepped in. As the door closed, Hell caught a flicker of contempt in the London hero's eyes. He took note of it and filed it away. Perhaps one day he would meet that one again. Somewhere that offered the chance for a private discussion. As he considered that, he absently touched his bloodstained cloak.

The lift rose very high and Hell closed his eyes for a moment, enjoying the soaring feeling. When the door opened, his eyes were open and his attitude composed.

More Raptor officers were there to greet him, and they ushered him in total silence to a conference room. Hell saw that there were three older Flock seated at a curved table. Theirs were the only chairs in the room. A statement, Hell knew; a tacit comment about their status within the Greater Flock, and his as a white-feather. He took no offense. If they truly felt superior, then they would not have bothered with such theatrics.

Without haste he went and stood before the table. The three elder Flock were not Raptors. They were smaller, ordinary. And old. Their garments, however, were so dark a red as to be nearly black.

The eldest of them wore a starfield of medals and ribbons on the sash of rank. Hell took in their historical and political importance, filing that into their proper places in his vast and orderly mind.

The elders did not give their names, birth rank, or conquest names. Nor did he.

By way of preamble, the Eldest said, "You have done great work for the Flock."

Hell said nothing. For any other operative such a statement would be followed by an obligatory remark about how his family would be proud, or a platitude like "I see a red kilt in your future." But everyone in the room knew this was impossible. White-feathers were the lowest branch in the tree of castes that made up the Flock. White-feathers did not gain color, and certainly not red.

And so, he merely waited.

The Eldest nodded, as if he followed the flow of Hell's thoughts. He glanced briefly at his colleagues. Each of them gave a small, silent nod.

"There is work for you."

"I serve at the pleasure of the Flock," Hell replied.

"No," said the Eldest. "You do not."

Hell waited.

"You serve your hate," said the Eldest. "You serve what you hate most in all the galaxy. Not us, not the elite, not the many clans who celebrate their colors, not the other Raptors who are heroes of the Greater Flock. Not the Eight Privileges. You serve your hatred of the human race."

Hell said nothing.

"When the human military slaughtered the egg-hunter team at Calliope Station all those generations ago, that hate was born. Not with the death of any ancestor," continued the Eldest. "No, it was born when your ancestor was *not* killed. He was not one of the Flock heroes who died for the glory of our race. He suffered the humiliation of being captured, beaten, chained, and sent back to our homeworld with the ultimatum that brought about our defeat."

The older Flock at the table hissed and clicked and rustled their stunted wings. Their heel claws tapped agitatedly on the floor.

"Hate," mused the Eldest, "is a useful tool. It can be a dangerous one, though." He nodded toward the bloodstained cloak. "There is a vanity in hate for some."

Hell regarded the smaller Flock. "Am I here to be lectured on emotions?"

"Watch your mouth, hatchling," snarled one of the others. Hell turned his head slowly and glared at him. He said nothing, but the look in his eyes was eloquent enough. The Elder found something interesting to do with the papers on the table.

The Eldest said, "It is your hate that we want."

Hell raised his head, finding this very interesting. "And how is that?"

"It was not humanity as a species who brought about the ruin of your family. We both know this. Tell me who it was."

It was difficult for Hell to say the words aloud. He had not done so in many years. They were forbidden words within his family and throughout the Greater Flock. Saying it now, in the presence of these elders required much of him. Very much.

"*Homo eximius*," said Hell.

"Yessss," said the Eldest, that word stretching like a hiss.

18

Dr. Alexandra Byeol Chow had three jobs. She curated the historical documents collection at the Museum of Shame—the last place humanity could be curated for how great it truly had been. She also worked as a level six adjuster for the Flock Office of Cultural Presentation, which meant that she wrote about the history of the Human-Flock Fellowship. It was a nicer title than deputy propaganda minister, which both the museum and writing jobs were.

Mostly, though, she was a historian. This was not a paid job. It was not an official job, and she would never admit to such a profession in front of the Flock, the humans who worked for the Flock, any humans she did not personally know, or . . . well . . . most people. Only she knew, and her contacts within the Resistance. What she wrote—articles and papers on the history of the Flock War, the Great Harmony—as the birds called it—the Uprising, and the galaxy under the spiked heel of the avian invaders.

Chow and her human colleagues were not allowed to present any evidence of the Great Submission because the Flock wanted to excise it from their records. That burned Lexie. Such an idea was anathema for a historian like her. Real scholars of the truth. History was sacrosanct. To destroy it was to destroy all the efforts of those who had come before, regardless of the outcome. How could one learn from history if the very nature of it was fiction?

The Flock were not brilliant by any stretch—perhaps with a few exceptions—but they were the most detail-oriented of creatures. Over the last two hundred years they had found ways to massage history to decrease their own appalling war crimes and aggression in favor of a more genial and open-hearted race whose passion was to serve humanity.

Even now, fourteen years after the Uprising.

People like Lexie were overpaid, praised, and promoted, to ensure that current events were edited to reflect that fiction of harmony.

If it had not been for a Resistance member contacting her two years ago, Lexie was pretty sure she'd have found a way to kill herself.

Now she had a reason to live, but her optimism was on shaky ground. Always.

Lexie was a descendant from a line of historians stretching back two hundred years. Her parents, in a burst of optimism and—she secretly believed—a bit of discreet rebelliousness directed at the Flock, had named her after the most famous member of the family. Professor Emeritus Alexander Chow, author of forty-six volumes of history, department chair at Harvard.

Lexie liked that about her parents. She liked being named after someone so brave, so important. Alexander Chow had been on Calliope Station and had singlehandedly defeated a team of Raptor egg-hunters. How cool was that? Truly legendary. He had gone from military service to university, and to the interplanetary bestseller list with what, in another era, might have been dry academic throwaways. But Alexander had written with passion and insight, and his very first book sold eighteen million copies.

That was the story passed down through generations of the Chow family. Hell, some of it was even true.

Some. Not all.

Lexie knew the difference between the propaganda and the actual history. That information was worth more than a mountain of diamonds, and it was as dangerous as a supernova. Lexie had never even told her parents, siblings, or relatives about what really happened on Calliope Station. They would not know how to cope with that knowledge. The truth would definitely not set them free.

Not from life under the Flock. No way.

The truth was *hers*. Her burden, her fuel, her knife.

Lexie knew that she was not brave, and she was certainly no hero. None of her eleven books had sold more than a handful of copies outside of academic circles.

Even so, she thought that Alexander—were he still alive— would be proud of her.

After all, she was going to try and start a war.

19

"Peaceful sleep, honey," said his wife. "Hope you don't dream."

Hiram VanOwen gave Linda a brief, warm kiss and then turned onto his side, pulling the blanket up to cover himself.

"You know me," he said. "I never dream. Besides, I took a couple *Nulls*."

The drapes were closed to keep out the morning sunlight. The household AI lowered the lights to the precise level conducive to sleep and selected a gentle ambient noise. They both liked the sound of rain on forest leaves, with a hint of animal sounds.

Linda stayed up late. She stroked the right spot on her left forearm to active *Mon Tout*. The microchips imbedded beneath her skin offered her the choice of flat or 3D screen. She chose flat, but when the hologram appeared just above her skin, she nudged it to stand upward above her chest. Once she called up the novel she'd been reading, it self-adjusted to her posture and the angle of her eyes. Linda sank back into the story. It was all about love in the art world, the text moving in sync with her gaze

Hiram was asleep in seconds.

He felt himself fall into that velvety darkness and was always semi-conscious as his body dropped down, down, down. Being aware of falling asleep was not uncommon, according to his therapist. Linda hated those sleeping pills, insisting it felt like she was being pushed down and smothered. Hiram liked them. To him, it was more like being gently pulled down onto a bed of soft foam.

Null was the latest sleeping pill, and it was very popular. The BIRDS encouraged everyone to use them. Which made Linda all the more obstinate.

Besides, he really did not dream. He swore to it. Hiram never remembered dreaming. Not a fragment, not even a fading image. That used to bother him, but ever since those rumors started going around about people having weird and violent dreams, he was glad of it. He was a peaceful man. A natural pacifist and a pragmatist. Last thing he wanted to do was dream about doing what some of the Dreamers did. Blowing up buildings, killing Flock, putting on suicide vests and running into government offices.

If dreams were driving people to violence, then no thanks. He was quite happy for his mind to shut off as the Null hit his nervous system and then wake up refreshed with no thoughts about being a menace to goddamn society. He was a builder, night supervisor for one of the big 24-hour-cycle construction projects. His love was to create, not destroy.

And so, he slept and did not dream.

For nearly an hour.

And then . . .

The dream returned.

It did not matter that Hiram VanOwen never remembered these dreams when he woke. What mattered was that when the dreams drew him close and pulled him under, the dreaming version of his self—his subconscious? His immortal soul?—remembered all of the previous dreams. What mattered is that they happened. It mattered that he was a Dreamer.

It mattered that God spoke to him in his dreams.

God called his name. His actual name. The dreaming Hiram often broke down into tears of gratitude amid humility, of wonder and joy.

Some of his dreams were so strange that he could not make sense of them even as they unfolded. Other times the message God wanted him to understand was crystal clear.

That day, as the sun burned above the European Metropol, as his body slept next to his wife, Hiram entered a completely different kind of dream. Like nothing he had ever experienced before.

He woke *into the dream, coming to gradual awareness. His body was in motion, walking, as if he had been doing that all along and was only just realizing it.*

The place was very dark, lit only by light spilling down from holes in the ceiling, and yet when Hiram tried to look up into those holes, the light was too intense. There was no way to determine if it was sunlight or artificial. In either case it provided no warmth, and he was bitterly cold. A steady breeze nipped at him, making him shiver. Goosebumps stippled along his arms. He rubbed his skin to coax warming blood to the surface, but it did not help. He pressed on regardless.

Hiram had no idea how far he walked, or how far he had come before he woke. It was enough to understand that this was a very long journey. And a very important one. That part was crystal clear. This was what God required of him.

That mattered.

That was all that mattered. And so he walked.

An hour later—or was it a thousand years?—he realized that the ice corridor was beginning to slant downward. It curved too. This way and that, as if he walked inside a gigantic frozen snake.

That unnerved him because he knew all about the serpent. The serpent. The one who tempted Eve and corrupted Adam and gave birth to original sin.

"Goddam snake," he said aloud, and the words echoed off the frozen walls, distorting as they bounced away and ricocheted back to him in ways that sounded different from his own voice. He paused, listening to that warped sound.

"Goddam snake," he muttered again, this time much more quietly.

Hiram walked on.

For an hour, for an age.

Then he heard a new sound. Not an echo of his footfalls or his labored breathing. This was more real than that. He paused again; head tilted in an attitude of listening.

Was it something scraping or scratching the ice?

No, he decided.

Was it the serpent slithering through the darkness?

No. Not that either.

It was more like a soft, muffled crackling sound. Like leaves brushing against each other, or the folds of clothing, or . . .

He stiffened.

Or like the rustling of feathers.

Terror exploded like fireworks in his heart.

"Birds," he whispered. "It's the goddamn birds."

Fear wrapped its coils around him, and Hiram nearly turned and fled.

Nearly.

But through the icy darkness another sound reached him. A voice. A man's voice. Faint, filled with pain, desperate. Hiram hesitated, unsure of what to do. If there were birds down there, then he was outmatched. He was only a man and the Flock was the Flock. Those alien bastards were vicious. The huge Raptors were the worst, but even the smaller ones who ran the government were dangerous. They had weapons and Hiram had nothing except the clothes he stood in. Hiram was no kind of fighter. He was strong, sure, but that was because of his job as a construction worker. Maybe if he had his tools with him—a hammer, a welding pistol, even a length of rebar—then he might have a chance, but he had nothing at all. He had never been inside a boxing gym or a martial arts dojo. The only fight he'd ever been in had been a schoolyard scuffle in fifth grade, and Hiram had lost that fight.

He wanted to do something, but he knew that fighting the birds was a death sentence. Everyone knew that.

Hiram stood stock still, caught in the vise of indecision.

Then he heard the voice. Clearer this time. Deeper and stronger.

"My son," cried the voice, "help me. If you love God, then help me."

And with sudden, shocking clarity, Hiram knew who was speaking. It made no sense and yet it did. A twisted kind of logic that stabbed him through the heart. The understanding coalesced, but his body had already launched itself into movement. He ran, fists clenched, anger flaring hot enough to melt the cold around him.

"I'm coming," he yelled. "I'm coming!"

He ran down into the shadows, skidding as he rounded sharp curves, his body banging against the walls. None of that stopped or even slowed him. He was ablaze with purpose now.

"I'm coming!"

Then the corridor suddenly gaped around him, the walls and ceiling rearing back to form the shell of a massive cavern. There, in the center of the chamber, he saw a tableau that tore an anguished cry from him.

A great slab of ice rising from the ground. A dozen birds were clustered around it, each of them big and dark and impossibly powerful. On the slab, like a lamb on an altar, lay a man. He was held down by the birds, and his body was crisscrossed with scratches and bites that leaked dark lines of crimson. That color seemed to be the only real color in that grim place. There was so much of it.

One of the birds—larger and more terrifying that its comrades—held a large dagger, the blade curved like the talon. The blade was wide and ugly, and it tapered to the sharpest possible tip.

For a few fractured moments Hiram was unable to make sense of what he saw. The birds were evil and numerous, but they did not conduct sacrifices; human or otherwise.

Then Hiram began to understand what he was seeing. The Flock did not engage in human sacrifices. But the man on the altar was not human.

Not really.

His physical form and aspect were not what Hiram saw. No. What he beheld was a construction of his own mind because, after all, no one could endure seeing the true face of God.

God.

As if they heard his thought, the birds raised their heads and turned toward him. Seeing him. Knowing that he saw them and saw what they were doing.

The figure on the altar turned his face toward Hiram and spoke in a voice that shook the entire cavern.

"My child," said God, "the Flock is killing me."

Even in that moment of shock and revelation, Hiram was aware that he was dreaming. What he saw was some kind of metaphor, or, perhaps, a prophecy structured in a way that he could understand.

But he couldn't help but cry out, "No!"

The birds chittered with anger and agitation. Their large, dark eyes seemed to bore into him. To freeze him.

"Only you can save me, my child," said God. "Only you have the strength to save me and all that I have created. Only you."

"No, no, no," begged Hiram.

"Save me, my child, my son, my beloved one," said God.

The bird priest uttered a piercing cry that struck Hiram like a physical blow, staggering him.

"Leave him alone, you goddamn birds!" roared Hiram, forcing his feet to move. The air seemed suddenly too dense, and each step felt as if he were pushing against a solid wall of ice.

"Save me, my son."

And the raised knife plunged down, the steel flashing as the point bit deep . . .

Hiram VanOwen woke up.

His body convulsed and he was suddenly standing in the middle of the floor in the darkness of the room. The dream, those screams, the chittering of the Flock, the blurring silver fall of the knife, and the pleading eyes of God . . . they were all still with him. They filled his mind and ignited his heart. He stood there, chest heaving, fists clenched, his eyes bright with the fires of terrible purpose.

20

Lexie stepped out of the shower and stood on the bath-pad while air jets dried her off. Her black hair was short enough to finger comb into an approximation of disheveled chic mess that was in fashion right now. She found fresh clothes, dressed, and got herself to work on time. Somehow, no matter how bad her mornings were, she always managed to get everything done.

Her officemates called her a worker bee. She hated that, but never said so. She was a Chow, and being this she had a need to be better, to represent the first Chow. She'd never dared want to be someone else. Her destiny had been written before she'd even been born. Still, sometimes she felt the weight of it, and it held her in place, almost pushed her to the floor.

Like now.

Before leaving her apartment, she had stood in front of her mirror and studied herself. Discreet business clothes, minimal makeup applied to hide the dark smudges under her eyes. Sensible shoes because she preferred to walk to work whenever possible. She used the mirror's record and playback which reversed the image so she saw what everyone else would see.

Nothing weird or awkward or alarming. An uninteresting mid-level office drone who was a threat to no one.

The smile she wore was one she'd practiced every day since taking the job. Upbeat but not starry-eyed; competent but not in any way that would alert a Flock inspector or human informer. What she hoped was a look of someone who enjoyed her job despite the circumstances. It was a crock of moose shit, a deliberate performance, but she sold it well enough. She knew she couldn't coast along on how people perceived her the previous day, or the previous few thousand days. It was like that old saying, that an officer was only as good as his or her last battle. So was survival in a galaxy under the heel of the Flock.

Lexie Chow lived the life of a collaborator and she hated herself for it. While the vast majority of humanity fought for every opportunity to scrape together a meager existence from the castoffs of their conquerors, she wanted for nothing, reaping the rewards of her cooperation and pretense of ignorance of the fate of most of her species.

As she walked, Lexie stared out across the European Metropol, a singular, flat thousand-kilometer plain with rookeries scraping the sky every thousand feet, based on Flock family territories.

She'd seen photos of what Paris had looked like hundreds of years ago. The beauty and elegance were all past tense. Gone were the arrondissements and the Eiffel Tower and anything remotely historic, swept aside by the Flock and their own avian cultural needs. Most people did not mourn those losses because they did not remember them or even know of them. They were ignorant of history; allowed to know only what the Flock approved. Historical context and insight had dwindled and—far too often—faded complexly.

Because Lexie was a historian, she was tolerated without

enthusiasm by the masters. She was useful when the Flock needed an item of human history to serve some propagandized end, or when they needed a version to sell the fiction that the birds had always been there to guide humanity. Her job was to provide the food for thought so that the Flock could ram it down humanity's throat—the concept that all the greatest human accomplishments had only been possible because of the superior technology and benign guidance of the Flock. No talk of war, rebellion, resistance, freedom, or human superiority was ever allowed, and Lexie spent much of her working life making those revisions.

She fought down her bitterness with tricks learned and refined over a lifetime. She was their creature in all outward ways.

The Flock owned the Earth.

The Flock, in all practical ways, owned the galaxy.

What she saw epitomized that domination. They lived as if Earth had always been theirs. Earth, and the hundreds of other worlds humanity had settled since the first transduction decks were built. No corner of the human realm had been spared. All of it had been subsumed. All of it was beneath the poisoned heel of the Flock.

For now, she thought as she hurried along the moving sidewalk toward her office building.

Each of the giant rookeries she passed held an extended family unit. A hundred-meter-tall building topped by another hundred feet of dense construction created to resemble nests the Flock had once called home millions of years before they took to the stars. Now, they demarked territories, each rookery a thousand meters from the other, creating a geometrically identical landscape of vertical responsibility on the flatness that once was rolling hills and the mountains of Aquitaine. Between them were a special breed of cattle, born without legs, moving through the sludge like two-ton slugs, husbanded and harvested for their meat by the occupants of each rookery.

Lexie's apartment was in a building less than half the height of a rookery. Despite being considered a premium location for certain humans, it was squat and ugly, and sat in a row of similarly drab buildings. On the outside, they lacked the shine and fine lines of the Flock's quarters, but anything was better than living below. To even see the sun and its indifferent warmth was an exquisite gift afforded to less than 1 percent of 1 percent of the remaining population of humanity. She knew she should be thankful, but she wasn't. She was, however, appreciative of the place she had in the Flock Hegemony.

Without it, she wouldn't be in a position to change everything.

Every.

Single.

Thing.

That kept her going, kindling a fire inside her chest. It fed scraps of fuel to the meager flames of hope.

Hope.

Such a strange word. Its real meaning lost beneath the weight of the Flock occupation. People said things like, "I hope you have a good day," or "I hope you get over those sniffles." Using the word as a conversational courtesy instead of exploring the range of what "hope" used to mean. Should mean. Maybe *will* mean again.

If she had anything to do with it.

If . . .

Another word as dangerous as hope.

If what she had in mind only worked. If she was right. If, if, if . . .

But she had to play the game very carefully. To get what

she wanted she had to give the Flock what it required. Without the access afforded by her work for the Flock, Lexie knew there would be no way for her to awaken that which the Flock most feared.

"Please," she murmured silently.

The metroplex was always buzzing with activity, some of it quite contradictory. As fast as new rookeries were being built, key Flock families were also moving out and building new rookeries in the mountains, by the ocean, in the middle of vast farming communities. It meant that some of the most important members of Flock government and military were no longer inside the metroplex. That made Lexie's job tougher because documents often had to be sent out by special couriers, with nail-biting delays before approval was granted for what she'd written.

It was a maddening inconsistency for a species that prized efficiency above all else. And it had only started happening over the last eighteen months. It was as if the Flock, after all these years, suddenly discovered the joys of living in isolation, even with the added expense, lost time, and reduction in overall efficiency. The one time that Lexie asked her supervisor about it, the bird's response was a cold rebuke for her impertinence, uttered in a way that conveyed a veiled threat.

It bothered her. Then and now.

As she approached the office, Lexie saw a street beggar leaning against the wall. The homeless were everywhere, above and below ground. Oddly, the Flock did not seem to care about their presence. It almost seemed as though the birds did not see them—or chose not to react. Lexie wondered if their allowing the homeless to wander everywhere was to make some kind of statement to humanity. Maybe it was intended to show that even nonproductive members of society were allowed to exist within the overall peace of the Flock. Or perhaps it was a veiled threat suggesting that anyone's safety and comfort could be taken away for the slightest infraction of the law. Lexie rather thought it was a bit of both.

The man—so ragged and filthy that he was a homogenized gray, his age impossible to guess—held his hand out to each person and bird who passed by. The birds kept walking. One in maybe two dozen humans fished something out of their pockets and placed it in his upturned palm. Each time, the man said, "Blessings to you."

Lexie had no physical currency and so she paused at a food cart and bought the man a vegetable sandwich and a bottle of water. She brought these over to him.

The homeless man took the proffered food and hugged it to his chest.

"You're a good person," he said in a voice far less ragged than his clothes. "I bet everyone likes and respects you."

Lexie stiffened in surprise. Before she could respond, the man turned and walked away. After a dozen steps he paused and looked over his shoulder.

"Thrive in the peace of the Flock," he said.

Lexie swallowed. "Thrive in the peace of the Flock," she replied.

Then she hurried into her building. She kept her face totally blank, even though her heart was suddenly racing, and her mouth wanted to smile.

The homeless man's words rang in her head. Even though she had never seen him before, she now knew who and what he was.

He was part of the Resistance. The things he said were codes.

You're a good person.

That was the right day code.

I bet everyone likes and respects you.

That meant that members of the Resistance would be coming for a visit.

It's starting, she thought, and nearly stumbled as the truth of that struck home. *God . . . I'm really going to do this.*

She hoped and prayed that her face was not as flushed as it felt.

Lexie took a few calming, centering breaths, and went into her office. She remembered to smile at the Flock guards as she passed through security and headed to the elevators.

It's starting.

She wanted to shout it. She wanted to cry. She wanted to run.

Instead, she merely went to work.

The weight of the invisible armor she wore felt like a world and she tried not to stumble. All depended on the next twenty-four hours.

21

Hiram VanOwen stood at the foot of the bed, trembling with tension and nervous energy. His hands opened and closed, opened and closed as if rehearsing how they might close around something that would scream.

Hiram's face, though, was utterly slack. His conscious mind recorded nothing that his eyes saw. His lips hung open, his skin oddly pale—though his cheek still bore the impressions of small folds from the pillowcase. His body quivered with raw energy, but his heart beat very slowly.

His wife slept, reading tablet by her hip where it had fallen. Her lips were parted and her soft, buzzing snore was the only sound in the room.

Hiram watched her for nearly an hour, unmoving. Then he abruptly turned and walked out of the bedroom. Yesterday's soiled work clothes were in a hamper in the laundry nook, and he put them on. He stepped into his shoes by the door, hung his ID lanyard around his neck, and then paused. For a moment his eyes flickered as if he were trying to focus. His lips formed words but there was no force, no sound behind them.

Goddamn birds.
Goddamn birds.
Goddamn birds.
Over and over.

Leaving his house, Hiram walked out into the midday sunshine. He turned east and walked along narrow streets between the humped domes of the Hills—the vast underground human habitats. A trendy name for ghettos. Everyone who worked for him at the site lived there. All the men and women on his team were asleep.

He gave none of them a moment's thought.

Goddamn birds.
Goddamn birds.

His feet moved with metronomic precision, arms swinging, eyes forward. It took him nearly an hour to reach the site. Had he taken the airbus he would have been there in four minutes, but it never occurred to him.

Goddamn birds.

Crews were busy working on a series of support struts that would reinforce the rookery they were building to give it more stability in case another of the big supercell storms smashed through the region. Three years ago, a rookery had been very badly damaged by hurricane winds, and a whole section of it had collapsed. Fifty-seven Flock were killed, and a hatchery was seriously damaged. Now, crews like Hiram's were working on a massive project to make all the rookeries stronger and safer,

Goddamn birds.

Hiram swiped his badge and walked through into D-building. It was dark because the types of things stored in there were not used in this phase of construction. Hiram did not even bother to turn on the lights. The dim security bulbs offered all the illumination he needed. He went straight down the main aisle, turned at the end of the fifth row of shelves, turned again at the end of that, and then stopped. Everything he needed was laid out neatly on shelves. The freezer in which the tubes of Coban-42 were safely stored. A tray of slender silver detonators. Boxed remote triggers with their bright red buttons. All of it.

Goddamn birds.

Goddamn birds.

Goddamn birds.

He mouthed those words as he assembled the bombs.

He repeated them as he fitted each one into a pocket of a canvas tool vest.

He kept saying it as he shuffled out of the building, crossed the busy construction site, went back through the security gate, and walked the one thousand meters to the fully occupied rookery. The words were on his lips as he walked into the lobby and straight up to the tall, muscular bird who stood guard by the lifts.

The bird watched him approach, then held up a hand to stop him. "Identify yourself," he said, clearly bored. "In pattern."

The request should have been answered in precise order: last name, first name, Human ID and number.

It was only then that Hiram VanOwen spoke aloud.

"Goddamn birds," he said.

It was the very last time Hiram spoke. As he said those two words, he raised his hands to show the small devices in his palms. Both thumbs depressed the little red buttons.

Six full tubes of Coban-42 concentrated explosives detonated at once. The combined force of those explosives—normally used to disintegrate the dense rock of a massive hill on which the new rookery was being built—vaporized Hiram and the bird. They blew through the entire first floor like a tsunami of fire, sweeping away everything in their path. The fireball roared upward,

obliterating three entire floors and all the polysteel and structural polymers as if they were tissue paper. The upper floors
shuddered and seemed to hang for a moment atop a swelling
mushroom cloud of superheated gasses, and then they fell, pan-
caking down floor by floor, crushing everything in between.
Thousands of birds. Tens of thousands of eggs. One hundred
and sixty-six human servants. All of it.

The shock wave rippled outward, tearing the roofs off nine
underground human habitats, killing scores of people, injuring
hundreds. The glass windows of the rookeries positioned around
it in their precise geometric patterns exploded inward, showering thousands of other birds with storms of glittering splinters.

The other rookeries reeled, the foundations cracking on
two of them.

But they did not fall.

Instead, they stood as battered witnesses to the death of one
of their own. There was a long moment of ghastly silence, and
then the sirens began to scream.

22

"The HEs are lost to time," said Hell to the elders of the Flock. "Am I here for a history lesson? Or is this some kind of retraining in humility? Do you make me say it to put me in my place?"

He did not raise his voice, did not let anger seep into his tone, but there was something—some quality beyond his immediate control—that made the two other Flock lean back as if sinking into their seat cushions could increase more than the subjective distance between them and the white-feather.

The Eldest did not share that reaction. He remained very calm, his palms flat on the tabletop.

"What if I told you that the HEs are not dead?" he asked.

"The Flock has looked," said Hell. "For generations we've looked."

"The galaxy is vast and even if ten billion Flock searched, they could not search everywhere," said the Eldest. "And the humans are clever. It is why we wanted to assimilate them. It is why we allow them a measure of freedom still, because freedom—however conditional—is the secret of their creativity. Do you agree?"

"I do, but what of it? Are you saying that the HEs still live? That they have survived these centuries somewhere the Flock has not looked?"

"Not exactly," said the Eldest. "I will ask you another question. What do you know of the Sleepers?"

"They are a myth," sneered Hell. "They are a cover story to hide their own resistance efforts. They claim that dreams have inspired their acts of sabotage and destruction."

"All of that is true except one thing."

"And what is that, Eldest?"

"It is not a myth."

The room was plunged into immediate and total silence. Hell stared at him, unable to speak for the first time in his life. The elders waited him out.

When Hell finally found his voice, he said, "I . . . I am at a loss here, Eldest. What does that have to do with the HEs?"

The old Flock leader studied him; his taloned fingers laced quietly on the tabletop. When he spoke, his words were even more of a punch to the gut than his last pronouncement.

"The HEs *are* the Sleepers," said the Eldest.

It took Hell a moment to process that information. He stood still, aware he was being scrutinized though he was looking inward. He pulled on bits of data, rumors, things from Flock spy networks classified as misinformation or disinformation.

The HEs are the Sleepers.

If that was true, then it would be the glue that would bind a lot of other things into a picture that made sense. His two hearts raced as he thought it through. Then—slowly, maintaining his outward calm—he looked across the table at the three elders.

"You would not have called me here," he said quietly, "just to tell me this."

"No, Ren'Mgo-Hell," agreed the Eldest.

"Then what do you need of me?" asked Hell. "Is this about the *Juggernaut*?"

That question plunged the room into tense silence.

"How do you even know that name?" demanded one of the other elders. "You could be executed for speaking it aloud."

"Are we afraid of words now?" asked Hell. "Or are you afraid this room is bugged?"

"We will not talk about that at this time," said the Eldest, his tone icy with reproof.

Hell paused for a moment, then bowed in acknowledgement. It had been a gamble to mention *Juggernaut*, and the reactions were telling. For years it had been a rumor circulating through back channels among the Flock, and even in some parts of the human world. Until that moment, Hell had not been sure it even existed. Now he knew for certain, and he tucked that coin of knowledge away for later.

"You are strictly to deal with the HEs," said the Eldest. "We have been gathering considerable information for some time. Our human spies are seeded throughout the Resistance. Things are beginning to move in certain directions. It is possible, even likely, that one of our spies will be able to lead you to where one or more of the HEs may be stored in cryosleep. We want you, Hell, to find those Sleepers."

It took great effort for Hell to keep his wings from trembling. "To what end?" he asked. "To butcher the lot?"

The Eldest leaned slightly forward, his eyes intense. "Separate yourself from your hate for a moment, Hell," he suggested. "Consider what would be best for the Flock. Here on Earth and throughout the galaxy. The evaluations we have on you suggest high intelligence, an understanding of propaganda, and innovative thinking. Let those guide you as you tell *us* what the best course of action would be."

This was a trap and Hell knew it. But it was also an offer. Everything depending on how he answered it.

"Killing the HEs outright would be a missed opportunity," he said. "If they can be discovered—if the intelligence your spies have gathered is accurate and actionable—then these Sleepers need to be found and brought to Earth. They need to be brought out of cryosleep, isolated, and interrogated. Once we have extracted the locations of any other Sleeper cells, and once those HEs have been collected, then any members of the human Resistance should be rounded up, along with their families and close friends. At this point it would serve the Flock to have the Resistance and the HEs tried publicly, with the live feed going out across the galaxy."

"And then?" asked the Eldest.

"We execute them all."

The other elders nodded, but the Eldest did not. "All of them?" he asked.

Hell shook his head. "Oh . . . no. Not all. We determine which of the Sleepers have been able to intrude into human dreams. We can fake their executions, but the HEs should go to the Black House."

The Black House was a sprawling research facility hidden where no human eyes could ever find it. It did not officially exist, but even among the Flock there were rumors—almost certainly deliberately leaked. To the citizens of the Flock, it was spoken of only in whispers. It was a place of horror, of dread. It was the stuff of nightmares to them. Hell had been there, and he knew it was all of that. And more. Much, much more.

Like him, the Black House was a kind of hell.

The Eldest nodded.

"For the greater glory of the eternal Flock," he said, "we charge you with this mission."

Hell took a moment before replying. He did not want excitement to play any part in what he said, or what he did. That was a hatchling's error. Instead, he nodded thoughtfully and studied the air between him and the Eldest, letting his gaze become unfocused so as to leach any insight into his thoughts from his eyes.

Then he said, "To do what you ask would require access to resources and freedom of movement I do not currently possess."

"Would you dicker over trifles when we are offering you so much?" asked one of the other elders.

Hell turned very slowly toward him and just stared for five long seconds, then he looked once more at the Eldest.

"Every resource you require will be made available," said the Flock elder.

And that, Hell knew, told him everything he needed to know about how serious this was. He bowed and spread both his arms and his wings in an old-fashioned salute. One that had not been used since the surrender.

The Eldest rose to his feet, eyes bright with unreadable lights.

Then he returned the same salute, and after a shocked moment, so did the others.

23

Micah Fontenot lived the first forty-two years of his life in freedom.

Sort of.

He thought he was free. A lot of people did. Most did. Freedom seemed to be a given. Not even a right, just a thing. Everyone had it, it was free, and there was never a worry because it had always been there and always would.

Until it wasn't.

On Thursday, Micah Fontenot was a travel consultant for a company that ran adventure tours. Scale Olympus Mons, the tallest volcano in the Solar System, and one of the most dangerous climbing sites on Mars. Go hunting for crystal crabs in the emerald caves of Theselan Beta. Spend a honeymoon on a floating dome in the upper atmosphere of Harriet—a gas giant in the constellation of Cancer, formerly designated 55 Cancri-f. Fun stuff.

For Micah, the challenges of that job were many because it wasn't easy to wrangle the right ships at the right price, scout talented pilots and experts in the various otherworldly events, and get the tourists there and back. It meant that Micah had to wear a lot of hats—diplomat, salesman, con man, black marketeer, moneyman, problem solver, and overall fixer. He was good at that and made a lot of money, and he felt free.

Free.

Then the Uprising. That absolutely surreal day when the Flock—the nice, quiet, agreeable, useful, background noise of a race—decided to take the hell over. All at once. Everywhere. Boom. Done.

The transduction decks were shut down to everything except Flock use. The Vox communications system blanked out. Tourism was ground to a halt, and Micah Fontenot stopped making money. He stopped having fun.

He stopped being free.

At first he was shocked. Of course he was. Everyone was. After all . . . the Flock? The fucking *Flock* . . .? The docile, bland birds? The ones who loved to serve man. They were the ones taking over?

Correction, they were the ones who *took* over.

It made no sense.

To most people.

Micah, after he recovered from the shock of it all, got it. He had always been practical and adaptable. If this was the new truth, then it was the new truth. Accept it and find a way forward or stand still in denial and get run over.

Fixers don't give up. If things are broken, they fix it.

Most of the best people Micah knew were some kind of fixer. For banks, for salvage companies, for the entertainment biz, for drug cartels—legal and illegal—for colonists willing to take some risks in terms of what they were allowed to do and where they could. Lots of fixers. Some guys who ran numbers, sexbots specialty shops, and even murder for hire. Micah was a realist. The universe is, was, and always would be corrupt. No reason not to make some money off the inevitable.

But the Flock uprising had stopped virtually all kinds of trade, including his. They closed hundreds of thousands of businesses and redirected those workers to other tasks. Building rookeries; building the underground cities. They took skilled dice-men, sex workers, and extreme gamers; pro athletes, relic hunters, and pyramid scheme players; outer-rim burn-runners, body-mod cage fighters, and all the rest of the cool kids and put them to work turning Earth and all of the other human worlds into glittering cities for the Flock.

Micah Fontenot hated all of that. A lot.

So did his friends. All of those wheelers and dealers, procurers and con men, thieves and hijackers, smugglers and computer hackers. Not one of them liked having the world taken away from them, the various Inter and Intra Nets limited, and having patrols of vicious Raptor security teams out knocking heads.

Micah saw this as a problem. But his personality was more hammer than nail. Observing and complaining burned up the wrong kind of calories. What he saw, as everything went to shit, was an opportunity.

To give the people what they wanted, sure. Commerce was a river that should never be dammed. But more importantly—and with an honest-to-god flare of patriotism in his cold little heart—Micah decided to turn opportunity into a war.

Devious. Quiet. Subtle. Lethal as fuck when the moment called for it.

He started slow, moving key diplomats, scientists, scholars, and military to places of safety. That was risky, but the risk was fun. So was smuggling goods. There were a lot of Flock, but they were not everywhere. Micah's people were.

Then, as most of his old colleagues—and business adversaries—joined in, Micah thought it would be fun to level up.

Smuggling people and contraband was the pathway to

financing something bigger, infinitely more dangerous, but equally important. For the human race and for business.

He decided to build himself an army of specialists—fixers and those with particularly useful but underutilized skill sets. It took years. It took money, but they were making plenty of that. It took commitment, and that had to be encouraged and sustained. It took faith, and that had to be inspired.

Mostly, it took balls.

Micah Fontenot had balls.

He also thought it was fun. In a weirdly dangerous, likely suicidal way. But he didn't care. Someone needed to do it. He decided it would be him.

So . . .

He launched the Resistance.

24

"Where are you going?"

Lexie stopped with her finger an inch from the elevator button. She composed her face before she turned.

"I'm going home."

A figure stood behind her. It had come up on her blind side without making a sound. Not even the rustle of a feather; not the click of a beak. It loomed over her, its shadow completely covering her. It was not a Raptor, so there was that small slice of cold comfort. But it was one of the deputy administrators. The complex color codes on its sash gave its rookery, rank, and name. Although it was not a deputy in her department, all Flock had the right to question any human at any time.

"The sirens are not a call to end the workday," said the bird.

"I know," she said. "I heard that something awful happened a few districts over. God, I hope none of the Flock were hurt."

The creature stared at her for a long, silent time. When it spoke, it did not acknowledge her comments or remark on the sirens. "You are scheduled to work for another two and a quarter hours."

"I came in early yesterday so I could leave early today," she said. "I can show you my timesheet. My supervisor signed it."

The unreadable alien eyes studied her. They blinked rarely and very slowly. Even after a lifetime of interacting with them on a daily basis, it was still unnerving. The eyes gave nothing away. The face was not constructed for even a minor range of expressions. Nuance, for them, was in clicks and chirps and other sounds, some of which were either above or below the perception of the human ear.

The moment seemed to stretch as the Flock continued to stare.

"You may go," said the officious bird.

"Thank you," she said, bobbing her head. "Thrive in the peace of the Flock."

The creature said nothing.

Lexie fumbled for the button, found and pressed it, and tried to shrink into the carpet pattern while she waited for the lift. When it arrived, she gave another obsequious bob and stepped into the car. The bird kept watching until the doors closed.

But Lexie did not relax. Every elevator was wired for audio and video pickup, and someone was always watching. Always. Mostly the watchers were more of the Flock. Sometimes they were humans in service to the birds. But even then, there were watchers watching the watchers.

She tried to look casual. Leaning back against the wall, she raised her wrist, tapped the screen of her *Mon Tout* and activated a holo-screen so she could check her email while the car descended. The watchers could read the screen although it would be reversed in the camera view. Lexie opened a video message from her mom and let it play. Dinner on Saturday was going to be fish and could Lexi bring a bottle of wine to go with it?

"The kind your father likes," said Mom. "You know the one. Blue label with the sailfish on it. I forget the name."

"I will, mom," Lexie said, allowing the message to auto-record. "I might make some brownies too. I got fresh walnuts the other day. They cost a bomb, but they're going to taste soooo good with the chocolate."

She sent the message, closed the vid with another tap on her *Mon Tout*, and smoothed her clothes, all the time hoping that she looked as bland and boring as she needed the Flock to think she was.

A scar-faced security Raptor in the lobby watched her and she gave it a cheery wave.

"See ya!" she called.

Hope you get sick and die, you jumped-up chicken, she thought as she headed out onto the street. That made her smile a little brighter.

25

Hell sat in the cockpit of his ship, with news and data feeds on multiple screens.

The ship was not the one on which he'd come to Earth.

No. This was a different model. It was a Shadow-class stealth cruiser. Not one of the many Flock ships based on human technology—and they were inventive bastards—but on a hull design scavenged from a world his own people had never named.

The humans called it UDF 2457. It was 18 kiloparsecs—59,000 light-years—from that troublesome planet. The civilization that had once thrived there had died out seventy thousand years before the Flock discovered it. Even by transduction the journey was extremely long.

And yet the ship was waiting for him when he left the meeting with the elders. Ready, fully outfitted with tech from thirty non-human cultures. Hell wondered if some of this same science was being used for the secret *Juggernaut* project.

This ship was an extraordinary gift. The Eldest must have ordered it made ready long before the latest terrorist attacks. Months before, perhaps years.

That was curious. This issue with the Sleepers and the Dreamers was new. Or was it? Had the elders known before the greater Flock became aware? Certainly, he decided.

Had *he* been their choice since then? That was a harder question. That his career had been guided was clear. That it had been overseen with this much attention to detail showed a degree of foresight he seldom credited to politicians. This was strategic thinking, not the fluttering of wings so common with civil servants.

And there were too many damned civil servants in the Flock. Too few strategic thinkers, for that matter.

He found himself admiring the Eldest.

Not that he trusted the creature. Never that. Trust was hard to come by for someone whose family had lived with shame and been the butt of jokes for two hundred years.

He leaned back in his chair, feeling the gel-pack backrest conform to his body. He disliked most common comforts, but an accommodating fighting chair was acceptable. One less thing to think about in a battle.

For Flock administration purposes, the ship had been given a name. Not one pulled from the Flock's complex mythology—a mishmash of beliefs, legends, and junk borrowed from ten thousand civilizations across the galaxy—but from Earth. From where his ship currently squatted. The Eldest had named it, and in doing so showed that he—if not the others—understood the fires that burned in Hell's heart and soul. The ship was *Tartarus*. Named for an abyss in Earth's ancient Greek heritage; a dark and horrific abyss used as a place of torment and suffering for the wicked. But also a prison for a race of godlike giants known as the Titans. They had ruled before the more commonly known gods of Greece, but they had fallen from grace and were imprisoned for all eternity. In Tartarus, souls were judged and the wicked received divine punishment. Hell understood the message within that name and knew that the Eldest intended him to do so.

His family had been champions and honored soldiers before the surrender; now they were fallen. He represented his family, and every action he took, every decision he made would be judged. Hell realized with some horror that there was also a punishment implied—should he be found unworthy through word or action, then his family would likely be cast down farther than they were. There were only two levels of Flock society beneath that of being colorless.

There were the labor camps on worlds so inhospitable that death was truly a mercy.

And there were the labs. Genetics, radical experimental surgeries, drug trials, and worse. No one who went to the labs—to the Black House and places like it—ever returned except as freaks in a museum, or as tales told to frighten hatchlings.

The Eldest was not showing him mercy. All the resources and freedom of action were a lash, and brutal one at that.

Hell pushed the horror away and focused on the data screens.

Catching up on the Sleepers and the Dreamers. Learning about the Resistance.

Drawing his plans with cold, cruel clarity.

There was a copilot seat as yet unfilled. His mandate allowed him to requisition staff, but Hell had few friends and no relatives whose backbones he trusted. For the moment, his only companion aboard the *Tartarus* was a sleek and slender multifunction robot. He named it Worm.

"Worm," said Hell, "status of the ship?"

"We are fully fueled, provisioned, and ready for takeoff, my lord."

It amused him that the robot had a human-sounding voice. Appropriate for a slave.

"Did you complete the task I set for you?"

"Yes, lord," said Worm. "Would you like me to schedule a treatment?"

"No. Give me one now."

"Yes, lord," said Worm, and a piece of its curved chest opened to reveal a shallow compartment in which were a dozen hypos. Hell sat back, pushed up his sleeve, made a tight fist, and watched as Worm removed one of the hypos and prepared to inject the glowing blue-white fluid. "This may hurt."

"You say that every time," mused Hell.

"It is true every time, lord."

Hell laughed. "Get on with it."

The robot pulled the trigger on the hypo and the liquid shot into Hell's bloodstream. Hell gritted against it even before the pain hit. And when it hit, the level of agony was immense. Towering. Searing.

Yet he endured it without making a sound. Not a groan or a cry.

The pain soared higher and higher, and for ninety long—very long—seconds there was no part of him that did not feel as if it was on fire. He wanted to scream. No one but the robot would hear him if he did.

Except that he would hear his own scream, and Hell would not, could not, allow that. And so he took the pain and fed on it, ate it, swallowed it whole, even when his eyes seemed to fill with blood and his brain boiled in his skull.

When the worst of it passed, Hell sagged forward, releasing the tension he held as a shield against his own reactions. He sat there, gasping, nearly weeping.

"Is there any way in which I could provide comfort for you, lord?" asked the robot. And if Hell thought there was a hint of real compassion in Worm's voice, he ignored it. As he had every other time.

"No," wheezed Hell. "It's passing."

He waited until the swirling lights vanished and his eyesight was restored. Already he could feel the strange chemicals flooding through every blood vessel, every nerve ending. He raised his hand and made a slow fist, squeezing it tightly until his tendons creaked and his knuckles cracked. The pain had been terrible, but in its wake . . . the *power*. By the stars, that made everything worth it.

"Worm," he said after several minutes, "lay in a course for the Paris Metroplex."

"At once," said Worm.

Tartarus lifted from the pad, the VTOL thrusters pushing away from the ground in a ghastly silence.

26

Lexie made her way back to her apartment, strolling past empty rookeries and rookeries half built. She thought about humanity's fall from grace, from common sense, and from dominion. Historian though she was, there was a spark of poetry inside her, and she longed for things to have happened with at least a flicker of grandeur, with a slice of dignity.

We lost because we were stupid, she mused. *Lazy, shortsighted, naïve, and just plain dumb.*

A Flock patrol cruised by on a hoverdeck. Two of them. A big one who was probably a Raptor, though wearing a local patrol sash. The other was smaller, frailer, but Lexie feared that one. The big ones were the muscle. The little ones were the brains and the eyes. They were the sharp-eyed ones who were always watching.

Lexie was reminded of her own history lessons of Nazi-occupied France so long ago when humans thought their own worst enemies were themselves. The Nazis had a special unit known as the SS—an abbreviation for the German Schutz-staffel—or protective guard. Many were not even soldiers but were given command because of their guile and nastiness. The large ones even back then were muscle, but it was the smaller of stature a person had to worry about. Many of these were masters of manipulation and torture.

In another time she might have written a historical treatise on size relative to guile in human historical conflicts, but that was a luxury Lexie could not afford. So, she forced a smile onto her mouth and sketched a wave.

The smaller bird looked down at something—probably a citizen ID table—then raised its head and regarded her with those flat, unreadable eyes as it matched the data it had with the reality of her appearance on the street. It acknowledged her with the smallest nod. Marking her. Perhaps recording her affable expression and gesture.

Good thing they could not read thoughts—Lexie imagined the bird baked and breaded and surrounded by cooked vegetables.

The hoverdeck moved on and she continued on her way, hyper-aware that out of sight was never out of mind with the Flock. Their patience was legendary, and humanity had already been fooled by it.

It was how they conquered everyone everywhere.

After the war, after the Flock's total surrender and offers for any and all reparations, humanity had welcomed them in. Sure, not at first—there were too many bodies in graves or floating in airless space. There were too many ghost cities that had once teemed with life.

But as the years passed, the Flock offered to help. Without any remuneration, without even a promise of forgiveness for their massacres. They accepted blame, they endured anger and resentment and even outbreaks of violence with a humility that was astonishing. When groups ganged up on unarmed birds, there was no protest, no formal demand for apology. No cries for the crime to be addressed in any legal way.

There was a famous vidcap of six grown men beating a Flock family to death, smashing the hollow bones with clubs, hurling unhatched eggs against a wall. A year before something like this would have been celebrated by the more hawkish humans—and at that time nearly everyone was some species of hawk. But the audio track that accompanied the video was crystal clear. As the Flock died, their translators broadcast what they said.

"We are sorry," cried the birds as they died. "We deserve this. We are sorry."

That was when the change started.

Not among the Flock but throughout the populations of five hundred worlds. The cruelty was inarguable, the supplication of the birds evident. The tragedy and immorality of it eloquent. If it had been a single incident, then it might have had the usual social media lifespan. But it was merely one incident of many. Of very many.

Even so, that one lingered. It lit its own kind of flame.

Within days there were calls for official condemnations of the men who had committed the atrocity. But then the Flock played its next card, and it was such a clever one. The ambassador to Earth went before the Grand Council of the Galactic Union and made an impassioned plea on *behalf* of the killers.

"What they did was no crime," he said. "What they did was just because we deserve punishment. I will offer myself up to any group or family who need to express their hurt and outrage for what we have done. This I offer without reservation. If my death and the deaths of everyone in my family unit will ease your pain and give you peace, then we will lie down and let you do what you will."

It was a shocking video. Those words could not be unheard, could never be ignored.

There were some who posted replies via the messaging

utilities, and of course there was more hate, more taunts . . . but those voices were immediately overwhelmed by the public outcry *in support* of the Flock.

In the months following that incident, the Flock played its next card. As violence against the birds decreased, the aliens reinforced their desire to make reparations. They presented a plan to the Grand Council outlining how they would use their technology and their vast numbers to rebuild what they had damaged, and to go further—to help build mankind's galactic presence to a greater degree. The workforces they sent took jobs like trash collection and recycling, handling toxic and nuclear waste, farming the fields even in the most brutal climates, and any kind of manual labor that might be unpleasant for humans. They asked nothing in return. They never complained. They lived up to the promise.

Month after month.

Year after year.

Decade after decade. Freeing humans from drudgery, increasing the yield and variety of produce, building bigger and safer cities, and volunteering for the most dangerous jobs in off-world exploration and terraforming.

No one ever called them a slave race—except in underground conspiracy newsfeeds. After all they "volunteered" for it. They seemed genuinely happy to be of service. If any violence against them sparked up, the birds apologized for it. Apologized for whatever they did, knowingly or not, to upset humans.

Over time they became invaluable. People came to accept them, tolerate them, depend upon them. Apologists for how mankind allowed this unequal relationship to endure trotted out talking heads in behavioral psychology, philosophy, exobiology, and social engineering to claim that servitude was the natural state of the Flock, that it was where their true happiness flourished.

"A hardworking bird is a happy bird," was a common line.

"They love to serve," was another, often coupled with, "If you give them too much freedom, they hate it."

A few historians railed against that, arguing that the lessons offered by our own history could and should not be ignored. One, Dr. Alexander Chow—Lexie's great-great-great grandfather—was one of the first to warn against such a distorted assessment. But as the years passed and the violence diminished, his cautions fell on increasingly deaf ears.

By the end of the first fifty years after the end of the war, the Flock was in service on every settled world, and completely on Earth. At the close of that century, there was no part of the more mundane aspects of human infrastructure on Earth that was not managed by the Flock. Humanity, freed of such labors, evolved a new leisure class. The arts flourished as a new renaissance was born. Literature, medicine, science, and travel exploded in countless new forms and directions.

And the Flock was happy to help. So very happy. Helpful, agreeable, uncomplaining, diligent, tireless, efficient, and so willing to please.

Until they weren't.

Two hundred years to the day—to the actual minute—that the surrender was signed, all of that changed.

Lexie had to admire the subtlety and patience of the Flock's long game.

They waited until all resentment was gone and humanity became completely dependent upon the birds. When they rose up, it was coordinated with an ease and sophistication only possible when the enemy controlled the infrastructure.

There was no real Second Flock War. Not a *war* at all.

It was merely a conquest in place.

27

Although the Flock was an evolved species, Hell knew that evolution was not a static thing. It was evident in younger species like humans who had been grunting apelike hominids less than a million years ago. However, for some reason the Flock's development had slowed over that same span, and more so in the last fifty or so millennia. Hell ascribed it to a standardization of health care, the discarded need to hunt for food that was now processed, and more intellectual than physical problem-solving.

Yes, the Raptors were more physically powerful, but that was the result of careful genetic manipulation of female Flock, and treatments of selected eggs. Not true evolution. Nor had it elevated the mind of those thuggish Raptors. They were hammers, fists. Their size and strength were enviable, but little else.

That had always felt like a missing opportunity on the part of Flock scientists. A failure of vision, or perhaps timidity.

Hell had amassed considerable funds and resources by skimming from the various off-book projects the Elders had assigned to him. Nor had they paid much attention to see *if* he skimmed. They were bottom-line minded. And that, too, was a limitation.

The HEs were different. The human scientists, through courage or callousness, had gone farther, pushed against boundaries, broken through walls. *Homo eximius* was not *Homo sapiens sapiens*. Not in any meaningful way. They were a next step in evolution, or perhaps even the next leap, skipping lesser intermediate steps.

That was what Hell wanted. He wanted that for himself and, if the process worked as he hoped, for Flock he handpicked and whose loyalty to him was unquestioned.

His laboratory—hidden on a moon that was not registered on any record by either Flock or human—had made great strides.

Hell knew that the area of the avian brain for executive function was called—in human language—the *nidopallium caudolaterale*. That area was heavily dependent on dopamine signaling. Part of the chemical cocktail Worm injected into him was a radical blend of dopamine precursors—levodopa and carbidopa—mixed in with a mélange of nanites that cross the blood brain barrier and embed themselves in the *nidopallium caudolaterale*. These could then generate small $100\mu s$ pulses of 1.5 to 4 volts at 185 hertz. From the very first shots he could feel his cognitive abilities quicken, his executive functions sharpening to an incredible degree.

But what was a powerful mind without an appropriately powerful body? Hormone therapy, with testosterone as its core. There was also a soup of growth hormone-boosting peptides that were nicely accelerating muscle-specific genes. His body scans showed marked increases in skeletal muscle development.

And the nanites were rewriting the functions of his neuromuscular electrical stimulation to slowly build the strength of the muscle. The scientists had promised as much as a 10–15 percent increase, but the last scans said he was at 19 percent and the course of treatments was nowhere near complete.

28

Douglas Wheaton was the hardest working electrician in his work group. While others would take a lunch break and gab about what they might do that evening in their Flock-supplied quarters while eating their Flock-supplied food and watching their Flock-supplied entertainment, Doug worked. He was the first in and the last out. When asked why he worked so hard, all he said was "A hard worker is a happy worker," mimicking words from his dreams that had once been spoken by the very Flock he now served.

At first, the other workers made fun of him for working too hard. But the longer he ignored their comments, the less effect they felt their words had and the less they regarded him until eventually he was invisible. Never part of their group, he wasn't missed so they gabbed on without him.

It was as if they weren't the subservient race.

It was as if the lives humans lived were what was best for them.

But his dreams told him otherwise.

Like last night . . .

It came like it always did . . . like a call in the darkness.

Everything was black. His dream-self held up his hands and could not see them an inch from his eyes. Yet, he knew he wasn't blind.

Then the call came again, *Wheaton, you have been chosen.*

Eventually, a single light would appear traveling from a great distance. A pinprick in the utter black quickly became a blinding burst of sustained energy that made him wince from the pain of it.

And when it spoke it pulsed.

"Save me, Wheaton."

"From what?" He could see nothing nor any threat.

Then the light solidified, and it showed a giant of a naked man hung upside down by his feet. Tears of blood poured from his eyes, falling into the abyss of darkness.

He was easily twice the size of a normal human. His hair had been shorn, his bald head reflecting light from everywhere and nowhere. His teeth were cracked and broken. His arms hung down as gravity tugged at them, the nails ripped clean, leaving nail beds that also dripped blood.

His manhood was gone—plain gone—leaving nothing but a gaping bloodless hole where insects curled and cavorted.

"Hurry, Wheaton. Help me. They are coming."

"Who is coming?"

That's when he turned to see a dozen pricks of light on the horizon firing toward him at an impossible speed. Like bullets fired from an old-fashioned vid pistol, they were aimed right at the man.

"Wheaton. I can't take anymore. You have to make them stop."

And suddenly the pinpricks of light were fully formed.

They were Flock.

Doug should have known.

Each of them had leers on their faces as if they were part human, the joy they felt worn like medals of honor on their visage. Their beaks snapped as if they were speaking to each other in code. Snap-snap . . . snap-snap-snap . . . snap-snap.

And their talons. *Oh my God of Dead Humanity*, their talons were five times the length they should be.

They grinned at Doug as if they could see him, acknowledging him as their sole witness, then plunged all their talons into the body of the man. Two times twelve sets of talons spearing the man, whose entire body stiffened.

And then he screamed.

And the scream shattered the darkness.

The black exploded into a billion shards, and as they struck each other tinkled like predatory laughter. And as they fell away, they revealed an abyss revealing a solitary rookery covered by electrical codes.

He stared at them for a long moment until they coalesced into something he recognized. Then he read them and understood what they demanded.

"Help me, Wheaton. You must stop them."

Then one of the Flock turned to him, put a talon to its beak and said, "A hard worker is a happy worker. Work hard, human. Be happy."

Then it skewered the God again.

And in that moment Wheaton realized that it was indeed a god. This was no mere mortal man. This was something special. Something created by the universe to save humanity and yet he was allowing the Flock to eviscerate him.

That was last night's dream.

A dream he'd had dozens of times with the single difference being the electronic symbols on the rookery. They told him all he needed to know. The Flock could change many things, but they could not change science.

They were users, not makers. So things such as Ohm's law and resistance meant nothing to them. Watts Law might as well have been an order of food at an auto-dispenser.

Then there was Joule's law.

Coloumb's law.

Kirchoff's law.

And the laws of Biot Savart, Ampere, Gauss, Lenz, Curie, Vardeman, Hopkinson, and Wiedemann-Franz. The Flock were parasites falling onto other people's discoveries without any thought or idea how they were created or the limits that were put in place for safety. They were children of technology, but children should never play with something they didn't understand.

"Electrical Tech Wheaton, what is it you are doing?" asked his human supervisor and collaborator, Wisnewski.

"A hard worker is a happy worker," Wheaton mouthed, the image of the upside-down god still pulsating in his frontal lobe.

"It looks to me like you are adjusting the resistors."

"The Flock require more energy, so I have been ensuring that they have all the energy they need."

Wisnewski poked his fat head into the space. His eyes widened. "Where are the resistors?"

"Go back to your lunch and remember that a hardworking human is a happy human."

"What is it you are talking about?" Wisnewski took a step back and tapped the comms on his wrist. "Supervisor Electronic Tech Wisnewski requests security at my location."

Doug grabbed the man's hand and shoved it into the cables he had so recently removed from their protected sheathing. His supervisor immediately began to dance as enough electricity to power an entire rookery roared through his system. Then he smoked, and the sizzle of hair and skin filled the room with the stench of human meat.

The others were of two minds.

Half of them rushed him.

The other half backed away.

Doug knew it was time. He held up a remote he'd made and secreted in his waistband.

At that moment, three Flock arrived with submission sticks.

Doug appreciated the irony of them trying to keep him from doing what needed to be done with electricity. As if they understood it. Fucking parasites, every damn one of them.

Sarnoff, one-time friend, said, "You have to stop this, Wheaton. Are you crazy?"

"What's more crazy?" he replied. "Allowing birds to be your masters or fighting for what you believe in?"

"We aren't fighters, Doug," Sarnoff said, using Doug's first name to try and placate him. "We're electricians."

"Electricians who know more about the potential of death than most fighters. There's a reason why they are called *resistors*."

"What's that in your hand?"

"We might be children of a lesser god, Sarnoff, but that doesn't make our god any less powerful. It is time to fight back."

And with that Doug depressed a button.

Electrical circuits blew all over the city as they were overwhelmed by the power coursing through them. And where the power could flow, it did with all the energy of a dying god.

Screams erupted from rookeries as light pulsed off and on as far as the eye could see, like Doug's own personal Christmas.

Doug couldn't help but laugh as he watched the effort of two weeks' worth of work.

He imagined even from so far away he could smell the Flock who were even now cooking in their own feathers.

"Human. Stop what you are doing!" came the command.

"A hard worker is a happy worker. Thrive in peace of the Flock," Doug said, laughing, And then he joined Wisnewski in a forever dance where he was able to ride the lightning until his brain liquified and began to boil.

29

Lexie's dreams had begun last December . . .

She had been walking home exactly as she was now, and suddenly awoke mid-stride. It was snowing heavily as she trudged up the slope. She slipped several times, the slickness of the flakes merging with the rich soil underfoot to create a slippery sheet of ice. Twice she fell forward, forced to use her hands to catch herself. Where she was going she had no idea; she just knew she needed to go up. The sky above was blocked by the flakes, but she swore she saw the hand and sometimes the face of a giant being.

Was she an ant? An insect, perhaps? She glanced at herself, and saw it was merely her dressed in her sleeping shorts and baggy shirt.

She was dreaming.

But what sort of dream?

She reached out and grasped the root of a tree for balance and then the world turned upside down. She felt her universe shake and tightened her grip, lest she fly away into the sky. She hung from the root, her feet dangling into nothing. Then more shaking and her world righted itself once more.

Her legs struck the ground with an audible *thump*. Where

there might have been pain, there was only cold as her bare legs were covered by falling snow.

She climbed once more and then found herself on a flat space. She stared around her, careful to find something to hold onto. She knew this place. She'd seen it every day. Then it hit her. She was in a Buddhist temple. Not just any temple either. She was in the courtyard of Sudeoksa, the head temple of the Jogye Order of Korean Buddhism. She'd just tread up the slope of Deoksungsan in Deoksan-myeon, Yesan County, South Chungcheong Province, Unified Korea.

And the snow.

She grasped a flake out of the air and tasted it.

She immediately spit it out.

Soap flakes.

The giant hand came again.

She held onto the stone rail with two hands as the world flipped and shook once more.

When it righted, she laughed.

She was inside of her snow globe.

Then she spied a figure wearing a saffron-colored robe with a hood that hid his features. She could tell it was a man by the width of his shoulders and his height and the way his muscles rippled beneath the material. He moved toward her, oblivious to the shaking and the flipping of the world. It was as if he were a god and nothing could affect him.

The flakes fell away from him as he strode to her. Just as the world was about to flip once more, he reached out, embraced her, held her close.

As the world spun, she could feel his strength, his warmth, his comfort.

He held her, his feet locked to the ground as if they had been planted there.

The universe shook and then they were once more standing as they should have been.

While one hand held her fast, the other reached for her and touched her in places she hadn't been touched in a long time. She was the book of a blind man and he read her like braille. Then his lips were on hers. If his grasp was warm, his kiss was nuclear and the temperature of it washed over her in waves.

Then he took her inside where a bed awaited them.

Outside the universe flipped, but inside it remained fixed.

He lifted her, then lay her on the bed. He gently removed her clothes, his eyes never leaving hers. She stared back at him as he disrobed, his muscled body more impressive than anything she had ever seen. He was covered in tattoos that seemed to be a blend of Polynesian and Indigenous American, and when she looked again at his face, she could see those cultures in breadth and angle, brow and nose, chin and mouth. He was the most beautiful man she had ever seen. Masculine, powerful, in full command of himself—and yet there was a vulnerability in his eyes that promised gentleness.

Who was he?

What was he?

When he entered her, all questions disappeared in a hurricane of pleasure.

They stayed that way for an immeasurable amount of time, each of them moving slowly in concert with each other's wants and needs, two became one, the universe flipping around them.

As they climaxed, he whispered her name. "I love you, Lexie."

And to her astonishment, she replied with his. "Oh Jason . . . I love you."

That had been the dream.

Now, awake, she expected it to fade, to become nothing but the conjuring of a dreaming and lonely mind. And yet . . .

She could feel the heat of his breath on her skin. The gentle way in which he touched her with those big, callused hands. The breath they had shared as they strove together. The way their hearts beat in a perfect, shared and timeless rhythm.

"What's happening to me?" she murmured aloud.

30

Lexie walked along a sculptural garden whose complex patterns were intended to appeal to Flock aesthetics. To her it looked like the landscapers had tried to make math problems into topiary art. Despite lush green and rampant floral colors, it felt cold to her.

More so that day, because the impending meeting with members of the Resistance sparked connections in her head. The people her friend Pickle was bringing over would be strangers to her—but the Resistance operated with a series of cells that had many layers of security. Pickle was a *fixer*—part project manager, part logistics expert, part con man. His job was to find the right specialists from different cells in the hopes they would be the right fit for Lexie's crew. If they were . . . well, that made her heart flutter wildly.

If they were the right choices—and Pickle was rarely wrong—then she might get the greenlight to put her plan into motion. That might mean that her time as a *faux* collaborator for the Flock would come to a very sudden end.

Everything would change. Her life on Earth would be

over—hell, maybe her life itself would be over. Either way, once she had her crew and received the go order, then there was no going back. Not a chance. She would be an enemy of the Flock, an enemy of the State, and that would paint a target on her forever.

But goddamn it, someone had to throw the first punch. Or fire the first shot. Who would ever guess it would be mousy, docile little Lexie Chow?

Her excitement kept building, but Lexie made herself walk at a casual stroll. There was always someone watching.

That excitement also filled her with anger and frustration for everything that led to the Resistance being necessary. So many mistakes had been made, and humanity had paid for them. It hurt her to accept the truth that there was no actual second war. There were no great battles, no heroes. None of that.

It all happened so fast.

It was on the 200th anniversary of the Flock surrender. On Peace Day, as it was called.

Peace. What a goddamned joke.

On *Peace* Day fourteen years ago, the military found that they were locked out of all their combat systems. All forms of planetary, interplanetary, and intragalactic communication—everything based on the Vox stellarcom systems—went silent. Every single transduction deck that humanity had used in its population explosion throughout the Milky Way powered down. With no communication, no transportation, no military, no governance by the Galactic Union, and no infrastructure, the Flock, in one day, made the galaxy their own.

Just like that. Boom. Done.

They did not need fleets of ships to enforce their conquest. There were more than enough birds in every city, on every space station, on every moon and world. These billions of Flock civil servants rose up at once—not only armed but trained. The how and why and where of this was something no one—not even Lexie—understood.

The Flock rose, humanity fell. That was the math.

Their placement in every useful level of government, industry, medicine, and even the military allowed them to transform human infrastructure to Flock infrastructure without so much as a blip.

Raptor teams emerged from within the legions of hard labor—and that, at least, explained why there were so many fit and tough birds. Their work for humanity had been part of their training. And it also explained why such a disproportionate number of humans were weak and lazy.

Lexie, always a voracious reader, likened it to the radical and humiliating cultural topsy-turvy world the 19th century author H.G. Wells wrote about in his novel, *The Time Machine*. In place of the cannibalistic Morlocks were birds. Humans, though, were alarmingly similar to the Eloi—grown soft and helpless through dependence on a workforce in which they played no useful role. With that ennui came a drastic reduction in ambition, innovation, creativity, and drive. Each generation before the peace had been marked with jumps in technology. War always accelerated innovation and sparked intuitive leaps. Peace did not. It was a weird truth about the human condition, and during those two centuries, nearly all aspects of technological advancement slowed to a crawl.

Lexie knew that future historians would have a hard time writing about man's downfall in any encouraging way. By any metric or angle of discussion the human race was dealing with the consequences of their own bad choices. Humanity would be compared to Rome with the entire race fiddling as their planet burned, only to be taken over by another hegemony.

Of course, life under the Flock was not easy. Granted, easier for her than the bulk of humanity who had been forced to live underground; but living up in the sun had its own challenges. In the fourteen years since the Flock's uprising, everything had changed. The key to survival—especially for someone working with the Resistance—was to adopt a new set of habits that would sell subservience, and yet demonstrate a peaceful acceptance. Every action was monitored. Every word spoken or texted was weighed and evaluated by Flock security specialists as well as their trusted human spies. Lexie knew of many people who had vanished in the middle of night never to be heard from again, and she did not want to be one of those.

Playing the role of domesticated office drone was insanely taxing on the nerves. It also required acting on a level that in another age of the world resulted in awards for superior performance. But the only award these days was another day of freedom, another day of life. And every day it felt like she was aging a month.

Lexie did her best to not let the anger these thoughts provoked change her gait.

Just another happy day in paradise, she thought sourly. *Just out for a fucking stroll in the afternoon sunshine.*

Her bland smile and easy pace sold that fiction.

Luckily mind reading was not among the Flock skill set. Within the shelter of her thoughts Lexie was free to be fully herself. To feel her feelings. To think her thoughts. Even the dangerous ones.

Like the fact that the Flock's victory was only possible because some military geniuses had long ago decided to put humanity's greatest weapons on ice.

Literally on ice.

The weapon that had inarguably frightened the Flock into that total surrender was frozen and hidden away where no one could find it. Supposedly safe and ready in case the new truce didn't last.

Lexie wished she had a time machine so she could go back and find the idiots who thought *that* was a good plan, and kick their balls up into their chest cavities.

Naturally, most people had no idea that weapon had ever existed. Alexander Chow's books—particularly the one he wrote upon his retirement from Harvard—hinted at the nature of that weapon. That post-retirement book told the whole truth, but it was never published. All known copies had been ordered destroyed by the government. It was radical, they said. It was inflammatory, they said. It would only create problems and disturb the peace, they said.

They *said*.

Alexander had turned over his files and physical copies. He let a government investigator do a thorough sweep and scan of his entire home. He allowed that work to be eradicated and the truth silenced.

Kind of.

Among his possessions—handed down with other family relics over the generations—was an old-fashioned snow globe. Not the holographic kind, but an actual glass sphere in which was a tiny and beautifully wrought model of Sudeoksa—an important and ancient temple of the Jogye Order of Korean Buddhism. It was set on a hill intended to represent the southern slopes of Deoksungsan in Deoksan-myeon, in the South Chungcheong Province of Korea. Nothing about that appeared to be in any way significant except as a family treasure and a historical oddity. But that was exactly the point. It was an oddity connected with history. Only someone who really understood Alexander Chow on a deeply personal level would ever pause to consider a subtler meaning.

Lexie knew that Alexander Chow was not a person of faith. In his journals he wrote about how he had only come to it tentatively after the Battle of Calliope Station, and even went to that temple as an experiment to see if he felt anything. And while he respected the traditions of Buddhism, he never became devout. So, why then would he have that snow globe? There were no other souvenirs from his travels on Earth and elsewhere. Just that.

Because the snow globe was handed down from one generation to another, eventually becoming a relic of the family's most famous member, it was always kept in good condition. Alexander guaranteed that by putting in his will that the globe be kept in the family to honor what happened at Calliope. Generations of Chows had followed those wishes because traditions were sewn into the fabric of the Korean heritage.

Lexie, perhaps more cynical that her forebears, did not for a moment believe the object was what everyone else believed it to be. When it came into her possession, she spent an entire weekend figuring out how to dismantle it so that it could be completely reassembled later. Like most puzzles, the solution was worth figuring out before the thing itself was tampered with. Historians, like archaeologists, were very patient and very analytical types.

Patience was more than a virtue. It was a skill. A strength. Hadn't the Flock proved that beyond a doubt?

Inside that tiny temple was a fountain no larger than a grain of rice. And inside that fountain was a fragment of crystal. To any observing eye, it was there to give the fountain a reflective quality and the illusion of movement within the captured water. But Lexie was not fooled. The fountain was *inside* the temple. You couldn't even see it very well, even with a magnifying app.

She extracted it using the most delicate of tools. Then she

put it under an analyzer that was not connected by wire or WIFI to any source the birds could monitor. The analyzer was itself a relic of long ago . . . or at least made to look like an old clunky analog device. The guts were bleeding edge.

That crystal fragment was a storage cell, and within it were encrypted data files.

That was when Lexie first learned the truth about what happened.

About the strange and apparently superhuman soldiers led by the mysterious Jason Horse. A man who, according to military records, was dead and buried long before that fight. An XE—a concept Lexie had heard vague mentions of on the conspiracy theory channels.

Homo eximius.

The most advanced, sophisticated, and dangerous fighters in human history. It was they who had saved Calliope. It was the XEs who were pitted against the toughest of the Raptor groups—the vicious egg-hunters. It was the XEs who turned the tide of that long war and struck at the heart of the Flock empire.

It was the XEs who so thoroughly terrified the birds that they sued for peace and surrendered unconditionally.

Alexander had not known the full extent of who and what the XEs were when he first met them. It took him decades of careful research to put all the pieces together. And that led him to a great and terrible secret that had at first been hidden from the public by a guilty government and later erased from all human databases in the galaxy by the Flock.

The XEs were made to stand down and then all of them were put into cryogenic sleep. They were an inconvenience because they were bred for war, with no chance of being able to re-enter human society. The genetic engineering had changed them too much, pushed them too far, possibly even a rung or two up the evolutionary ladder.

The idea was to have them handy, though. Ready to be thawed and put back into play if the surrender fell apart and the war started up again. A "sheathed sword" was how one general referred to it in Alexander's notes.

But the war was over, and the sleepers slept on.

As the War Generation aged out and died off, and the Flock became more thoroughly spread within the infrastructure, references to the XE program were quietly, covertly edited out of history.

Alexander Chow had done his homework, though. He truly had been a brilliant historian. An investigative historian. He found that the *location* of each team of frozen sleepers was encrypted. He somehow managed to decrypt that data and then erase the original mentions. In his notes he wrote about how diligently the Flock looked for those old codes. Unfortunately, Alexander did not include how he had managed to hide the data. And even the crystal data core did not have that information.

What it had, though, were clues left for some future descendant. For someone with the wit and skills to find the data core and mine its secrets.

Like Lexie. A woman born two centuries later.

Now it was up to Lexie to decide what to do with that knowledge. Any hint of its existence—even a whiff—would without a doubt result in a Raptor team coming for her. They would likely wipe out her and her entire family. If they needed to, they would carpet bomb the city, even if that meant butchering a few million of their own. The Flock had no compassion, no sentimentality.

If thine eye offend thee, pluck it out. A Biblical reference she thought quite apt.

Even though there had not been any kind of official war,

the Flock were not above making statements to quell unrest. Wherever a pocket of the Resistance was discovered or made itself known through violent protest, the Flock's response was immediate and overwhelming. In the last fourteen years they had destroyed more than a dozen deep space bases, three moons, and an entire world to maintain control.

What would a single city be to them?

Not a goddamn thing, that's what.

Sometimes Lexie just wanted to scream. To climb to the top of the tallest rookery, douse it with gasoline, toss a match, and scream as it all burned. Her with it.

The one thing that kept her from either making such a grand—though pointless—gesture, or from sinking into the gray mud of mindless acceptance was knowledge.

It was her understanding of the power she possessed.

Knowledge.

What she had was the ability to awaken those ancient weapons. Awaken the sleepers and aim them like a gun at the heart of the Flock.

She had that.

As she crossed the square near her apartment, she saw a smudge of gray smoke on the horizon, but that wasn't surprising. Whatever had happened was too far away from her to be seen, but there was a rookery in that direction. Maybe someone had blown it up.

Part of her hoped that was true, and that it had been crammed floor to ceiling with birds. But the rest of her hoped it *wasn't* true, because right now the last thing she wanted was increased security.

If that blast was another Dreamer going crazy, then things would be bad. Maybe very bad. After the last bit of sabotage—a suicide bomber walking into a Flock police barracks and triggering enough Semtex-99 to kill twenty birds and four human prisoners—patrols had doubled. Her Resistance contacts had been covertly posting alerts that human spies working for the Flock were out in force.

That was what really scared her. Especially since a Resistance group was coming over to her apartment. What if one of them had been incautious? What if a human spy was watching and following?

Those thoughts—dark and growing darker—filled her mind as she left the park and crossed to her front door.

She thought about the war that she prayed was coming.

She thought about the mission she hoped to lead. Leaving Earth and going hunting in the dark of space. Looking for answers. For proof.

For her war.

31

He stared at the rug and it spoke to him.

Not with words, but with images as the sequences of colors changed and merged and flipped and became something entirely different. He felt the fluttering of young Flock deep in his belly as the excitement of the moment returned. He'd dreamed for weeks and knew that today was going to be a spectacular day.

He really had no name. He'd long since forgotten it. He'd once lived in the Bottoms, but then became homeless when his family had tried for something better. What they'd found instead of being uplifted was a life of invisibility. To the Flock they didn't exist, or if they did, it was as living evidence of what humans did to other humans.

The Flock would never leave their own to suffer. Each member of the Flock belonged to a family unit represented by rookeries and each member had a purpose. No Flock threw away one of its own.

Not like humans.

Not like his own species.

In his dreams he'd been speaking to the fire and the fire

spoke back to him. It talked of belonging and how he could be one with the flame. Pieces of it with different voices, shaped like the bees that no longer existed. Big fat bees made of flame and fire, each one with a different attitude as if they were part of the same family trying to get him to do something he'd never thought of, arguing amongst themselves as much as they directed him.

Like him they had no names, just energies that begged for him to join them. Then they spoke of the sacred one. How a long, long time ago a single man in a saffron-colored robe had sparked the world with his own fire.

Immolation—it was called.

Embrace—the bees renamed it.

And he longed for the embraces of the bee-made fire. He'd lived too long as one of the gray masses that were ignored, his hand forever outstretched, his stomach eternally empty until his insides rang like a hollow bell that only he could hear.

And him wearing the saffron of the chosen, the color of the middle of the fire, the hungry flame that could never be satisfied. Not the blue of gas or the yellow of satisfaction, but the saffron of the need to belong to something greater than he had ever known.

Every day he would like the gray.

Every night he would dream the fire.

Until last night when the bees said it was time. They were ready to finally allow him to wear the saffron. They would embrace him, and if he was lucky enough, he could become one of the nameless bees as well, forever buzzing in the dreams of the unwanted. Gone were the bees of Earth, but the bees of dreams remained, pollinating the spirits of the damned with the fire of inclusion.

They explained to him what to do and where to go, and he

did as they asked once he awoke. The place they'd chosen was crowded. It was a transportation hub where Flock moved from place to place above ground, sometimes soaring to their rookeries and sometimes diving beneath the earth. In the center of the place was a statue of the first Flock to be killed by the then "mad humans."

A male, female, and a child Flock all standing in a family unit forever caught in the fear of being beaten, vestigial wings up to protect their beaks and heads, doomed to die and become a rallying cry for humans to put away their weapons and show mercy.

A mercy that was met with laughter.

A mercy that was met with dominance.

A mercy that was met with merciless rage.

A mercy that would never be repeated.

He had a container of a special accelerant that would burn far longer than was necessary. This would allow him to greet the Flock at the hub, entreat them, and share the wisdom of the flame bees.

He sparked and then flared and laughed with the joy of the feeling of seared skin. The bees had told him that he'd be changed, and that change was necessary. He reveled in the feeling of the fire and spun as the flame ran from his feet to his head.

He was barely aware of the Flock backing away from him, but that wasn't right. He wanted to explain what true mercy was. What true understanding and belonging could be. So he ran at them and where he touched, they too caught fire, encouraged by the accelerant. Soon, they were rioting and running, bumping into each other, catching each other on fire, becoming bees themselves.

Oh, the joy of the moment.

To share in the wisdom of the flame.

He stood for a few last seconds and admired his handiwork as all around him burned with the knowledge given to him in his dreams. Then he fell to the ground, a single mote of who he had been leaving and following the winds created by the firestorm.

Him.

Now a bee.

A flame.

To pollinate the idea of freedom.

32

Lexie sat with Ahab on her lap and tried not to go completely out of her mind.

"Where the fuck are you, Pickle?" she demanded of the empty air.

The clock on the wall stubbornly refused to move as fast as she needed it to.

"Useless piece of shit," she muttered.

Ahab gave her a wounded look.

She mindlessly petted the RealDog. "Not you. The clock. The time. Everything."

What was she even doing? She was a historian, not the leader of a resistance . . . and yet, the resistance looked at her as one because of her family name.

Chow.

As if it were a magic word that would gift the universe with freedom.

When there was a soft *bing-bong,* Lexie actually screamed.

Not a big scream. More of a *yeep,* but it was so sharp and shrill that Ahab leapt from her lap and began barking furiously.

Lexie got up quickly and hurried to the comms panel on the wall. She brought up the front door feed and saw a small knot of people outside, bodies stiff with tension, heads turning this way and that like nervous dogs.

"Oh, very discreet," she muttered. "You don't look at *all* suspicious. Jeez."

Lexie tapped the lock release for the street-level door. The five of them came in fast. One of them, Bert Fickle, known to everyone including his own parents as Pickle, closed the door and peered through the peephole out into the street. His shoulders relaxed only a little, but she saw him nod. Then they turned and headed for the stairs. A few moments later there was a small tap on her door. Lexie pressed a concealed panel on the wall by the door, removed a very illegal *Buzz* neuro stunner, and slipped it into her sweater pocket. She settled back on the couch, shifting into what she hoped looked like a totally casual posture, and then told the door to let her guests in.

Ahab stood four-square, watching the door, tail high, eyes focused, growling faintly as the door opened and Pickle entered her apartment, followed by the four strangers.

Pickle always looked relaxed. Actually, he always looked high, though Lexie knew he seldom was. But he could rock that look no matter what was going on around him. It was one of the talents that made him invaluable to the Resistance. He was one of those people who simply could not look devious or threatening.

"Say hello to our mission team," he said by way of introduction as he plopped down on the opposite end of the couch.

Ahab gave Pickle a couple of perfunctory wags, but then his tailed still as the newcomers shuffled in and formed a ragged line in front of the couch. The dog kept making small growly noises, until Lexie snapped her fingers once, softly, and he grew quiet. He still stood rigid, though, alert and unconvinced. And he kept showing his teeth to anyone who looked his way.

Pickle propped his feet on the coffee table, crossed his ankles, and flapped a hand at each stranger as he introduced them.

"The tall pretty one is Jack Dubbs," he said.

Dubbs was six feet tall and tanned to a golden brown. He had broad shoulders, arms crammed with ropy muscles, and a mop of blonde hair that seemed never to have had any meaningful encounters with a brush. He wore an affable if uncertain grin and said nothing as if unsure of the protocol.

"As you can see," continued Pickle, "he doesn't live in the Bottoms."

"Clearly," said Lexie. "He have any skills beyond sunbathing?"

"Oh yeah, and he's smarter than he looks," laughed Pickle. "Sun god here is a cryospecialist, which we clearly need because I can't defrost a chicken dinner without help. And he also studied the history of cryogenics, so he knows about the old methods. If we're going to wake Sleepers after two hundred frigging years, Dubbs is our guy. He's also studied the effects of the Mahabharat Phage Virus—the PMV virus, including ways in which to sublimate continuing effects."

"Really . . .?" said Lexie, drawing it out, allowing her doubts to seep through. "That's a challenging field all on its own . . . and you're read in that as well as cryonics?"

"Rumor has it," agreed Dubbs, looking straight at Lexie. "Got my first PhD at nineteen."

"Child prodigy?" mused Lexie.

"Nah," said Dubbs. "It just shows what you can accomplish with threats and bribes. Parents wanted to take away my skimmers and my vacays to moon colony. So, I crammed and we both got what we wanted."

Lexie liked the tanned scientist. He seemed grounded and

interesting and not at all hard to look at. But she let none of that show on her face. Much more accessible and real, as opposed to the overmuscled gun freak in dreams.

She caught an amused look in Pickle's eyes, but then he continued his introductions. "Next up are our two new security specialists and general do-anything crew members. Fierro Sanchez and Veronica Davis. Better known as Fire and Fodder."

"Fire and Fodder? Really?" asked Lexie. "Or is that more Pickle humor?"

"Sadly, those *are* their nicknames."

Fire was a pale white woman with Western European features that were both delicate and fierce. Her nose and cheekbones could have come out of the mountains of Romania, but the fire in her eyes and the scarring on the skin of her face promised everyone who saw her that to mess with her was suicidal.

Fodder's demeanor was no better. But where Fire had delicate features, Fodder's looked as if they had been painted on with a house brush. Her mouth was wide enough to bite off a handful of fingers. Because of her wide and busted features, it was difficult to tell where she was originally from. It could be South America, North Africa, or even Spain. Fodder was a head taller than Fire and weighed half again the other woman's weight.

Both of their heads were shaved and wildly tattooed—Fire's with flames that matched her nickname; Fodder with hundreds of highly-detailed insects. They wore similar nondescript jumpsuits with top-worker patches, but Lexie assumed these were their disguises. Both of them had skin paler than was common even in those who lived underground.

Their skin was gray white with some mottling that made them look like two different species of mushrooms. They most likely lived far belowground and obviously lacked vitamin D— or as some called it—Vitamin Sunshine. The complex tattoos told Lexie that they were ghetto rats from the Bottoms, the lowest levels of forced human habitation. Places even the Raptors didn't go. It was all gangbangers, criminals, lowlifes, and societal dropouts. Their heads were shaved to keep away the bugs and lice.

Lexie had never been down to the Bottoms, but Pickle had told her about it, and it was a truly awful place. Lots of drug use, including the latest craze—Loop—which sent users into a mind-altered state where they relived a single memory over and over. The faint yellow staining around the nostrils were telling. Loopers all had that.

"In case you're sweating it," said Pickle, "they're straight. Yes, they have *used* but they've been clean for five weeks. I tested them again before we came here."

"And they're security?" asked Lexie, not hiding her skepticism.

"Yeah," said her friend, grinning. "They spent the last two years as muscle for King Rat."

King Rat was the war chief for *Arratoiak*, a gang of ethnic Basques, and one of the most feared crews in the Bottoms.

"They work for him and still they want to risk money, security, and their lives for us?" asked Lexie.

"For the cause," corrected Pickle.

Fire said, "This is only the fourth time I've seen sunlight in my life."

"Fuck," said Fodder, "it's only my second. Do we want to get out of the devil's asshole down there? Do we want to find a way to put our boots halfway up the ass of every bird we see? I dunno . . . what do *you* think?"

"Noted," said Lexie. "But if either of you uses Looper again—or anything stronger than a breath mint—then you're both out. If that happens while we're in space, the "out" means out the airlock. I'm not joking. This thing is going to be risky enough."

The two Bottom-dwellers just looked at her through heavy-lidded eyes. Her threats probably seemed tame compared to King Rat's. Still, the idea that these two woman were her security was stunning. By their looks, Lexie had little doubt they knew their way around a fight.

"Hey," said Pickle sharply, "the lady wants an actual answer or you two can crawl back down into the sewer."

Fire nodded; Fodder just grunted. It wasn't much, but Lexie knew it was all she'd get.

Pickle indicated the last of the newcomers. "And to round out our merry little band of brigands," he said, "is Ingwae Mugabe. Master mechanic and ship driver, not to mention black hole wrangler. He's been working on our little pleasure boat." Pickle winked. He was not a good winker. He couldn't really manage it, screwing his whole face up. Lexie privately thought it was endearing.

Mugabe was the tallest of the group. He had very dark brown skin, a face that was more majestic than handsome, and rows of tribal scars on his cheeks. His eyes had been replaced and were golden, without irises. Lexie had seen the tech modification before—on him it was striking and, along with his bone structure, made Mugabe look like the mask of some ancient king. Those eyes, though, made her feel uncomfortable because it was virtually impossible to read his expression.

"Why the eye mods?" she asked bluntly. "Decorative or functional?"

"Full spectrum," said Mugabe, his voice deep and sonorous. "Ultraviolet, infrared, thermal scans . . ." He let the rest hang.

"Mugabe's originally from Mars, but spent his formative years in the Cloud," explained Pickle. "Had to work in all kinds of conditions. Used to run the gauntlet between Jupiter and Mars with various—how should I put this—cargo . . .?"

"Cargo is a good name for it," Mugabe said.

"I take it you moved people, then?" Lexie said.

"Those who needed a change of scenery," Mugabe replied.

Lexie noticed that the others stood slightly apart from him. "Is there something else?" she asked. "Now's not the time to be coy."

Pickle cleared his throat. "Well . . . as it happens, Mugabe here is also a Prophet of Morpheus."

Lexie found that very interesting. More and more people were having those bizarre dreams. The Flock's official view was that it was the result of some new street drug, but that was horse shit. Lexie never took drugs and yet she had those dreams. However not all of the dreams were the same. There seemed to be different kinds, ranging from what could best be described as memory dreams, where people dreamed of places and things they could never have personally seen—things from centuries ago—and yet their knowledge of details was astonishing. More precisely, those details were impossible because these folks were born into a different version of Earth, and there were no available records or vid files that would correspond.

Another group of Dreamers were called Travelers, because they dreamed about living on other worlds, some of which had long since been destroyed by the Flock.

The most dangerous group were those people whose dreams drove them to commit appalling acts of violence against the Flock. These people—those who were interviewed before the dreams overtook them entirely—claimed that the dreams were sent to them by beings they called the Sleepers. Beings—possibly human but arguably not—who slept in remote places in the galaxy and projected their thoughts across the gulf of space.

One Dreamer who was arrested before she could detonate her bomb said that she had not built it. She was a landscaper and had no understanding of explosives or detonators. She insisted that her own personality was shoved to one side by another and more powerful one that hijacked her. Even under Flock interrogation—which included a dreadful array of drugs and physical torture—she held to that story.

Lexie was not at all sure where her own dreams came from, because they did not fit those other categories.

This Mugabe, however, belonged to a whole different class of Dreamers. He belonged to an actual religion—one of several—that was built on the belief that ancient warriors of great and mystical power lay sleeping in tombs hidden on small moons. Their belief was that these warriors were chosen by God to liberate humanity from enslavement, and that one day they would rise and lead a holy war against the birds. One of their more interesting tenets was that the galaxy was, in essence, God's brain, and that travel along the transdimensional pathways opened by the transduction decks meant that travelers literally passed through the electrical conduction pathways of the Almighty's mind. They held that certain humans, who ascended as masters, reached a new level of existence once they traveled from deck to deck. The legendary warriors were these ascended masters, raised to demi-godhood. As they slept in their tombs, their minds reached out through dreams—which their faith held were more connected to the transduction pathways than the conscious mind—and chose people to be their instruments on Earth. They referred to these people not as Dreamers or terrorists or suicide bombers, but as saints.

One of the more interesting tenets of this faith was that the Mahabharat Phage Virus had been able to open interdimensional neural pathways that enabled those who were asleep the ability to communicate across vast interstellar distances. That, in essence, their dreaming selves had become one with the transduction network. With the electrical network of God's actual mind, and the god in question was not the one worshipped by Jews, Christians, or Muslims but the ancient Greek god of sleep and dreams.

Morpheus.

The mixture of religions from Old Earth showed how all humans were in it together. Whether it be Jews or Christians or Muslims or even older religions such as Hindu, humanity was in it to win it. The name of the phage virus itself came from an ancient Sanskrit text dating back to over four hundred years before the first Torah was ever transcribed.

Lexie was an atheist, so she did not buy into that, but the fierce dedication to that belief was unnerving. And here was one of that faith's prophets.

"Are you here to preach or to help me find the Sleepers?" she asked.

Mugabe gave her a tight little smile. "I don't see how those two concepts are in opposition."

She nodded once, then studied her new crew and knew she needed more. The problem was that screening took time and she couldn't afford to wait. She'd already received the coded message from the Resistance that it was today or never.

"Okay," she said. "Do you all know why we're here?"

They milled in place a bit, none of them willing to speak.

"The lady asked a question," said Pickle, his lazy smile turning cool.

"We're here to find the Sleepers," said Mugabe.

"We're supposed to steal a ship and somehow slip by Flock patrols," said Fire.

Fodder nodded. "And then go off to start a war. At least that's what I heard."

Everyone glanced at Dubbs.

"And you, surfer boy?" asked Lexie.

"Couple things," said Dubbs. "One, I don't surf. Second, I don't give a lizard's left nut about religion or Dreamers or any of that freaky shit. Far as I see it, all of that is a means to an end. But the bottom line is that, yeah, we're going to steal a ship, get the hell offworld, sneak past the entire Flock satellite network, hopefully find a bunch of frozen super soldiers, and then try and save the whole goddamn human race. If that means starting a war, then booyah. Either way, we can't keep living like this. I was free when I was born. We all were. And I sure as hell don't want to die a slave. So, whatever it takes to change things, you can count me all the way in."

That hung in the air for a long moment.

Fire pointed a finger at Dubbs. "What he said."

Lexie stood up and shook hands with each of them.

"Welcome to the war," she said.

33

Pickle stood. "Okay, okay, let's not break into song."

That broke the tension, and everyone laughed except Mugabe, who measured out a tiny slice of a smile as if he had a daily allotment and needed to conserve.

Lexie stepped back and gestured to the table on which she'd placed bottles of energy water and an assortment of protein-rich snacks. There were also platters of fresh fruit swollen with juice and bursting with color; fresh bread, and plenty of sliced meats and cheeses. "Help yourselves. Might be a while before we get our next meal."

Fire ogled the food. "Is that real fruit? And meat?" She salivated staring at the spread.

Fodder did the same, side-eying anyone who appeared too near her anticipated meal.

After the two Bottoms-dwellers grabbed what they could and found a corner, Mugabe and Dubbs took a more leisurely approach to the food and picked at what tasted good at the moment.

"Pickle, let's you and I chat," Lexie said.

Lexie, cynically, understood that food was sometimes more powerful a recruitment tool than money or ideology. And food was never plentiful underground. There was no such thing as a fat person living belowground. Smugglers got very rich selling scraps cast off by the Flock.

Equal to her cynicism, Lexie was embarrassed because she exercised every day to keep her own weight down.

While the others dug in, Pickle paced the length of Lexie's apartment and stared out the window, where Lexie joined him.

He gave a low whistle. "So, this is how the high and mighty live."

"You could have lived this way too."

"Not really," he said. "Not that I'm judging."

"That's just what you're doing."

He grinned and held his fingers up an inch apart. "Maybe just a little. Not that I would have ever allowed myself to be bought so cheaply."

She snorted. "I have more access to what I need up here. You know that."

"I guess," conceded Pickle. "Somebody has to be on deck, keeping an eye on the birds, paving the way. So . . . sure, I get it."

Ironically, for all of their superiority over humanity, the Flock weren't technologically superior. They were scavengers and opportunists, stealing tech from any race they conquered. In Alexander Chow's notes, he had outlined information from various sources in and out of the military that he felt proved this. Earth explorers in the early days of transduction intragalactic travel discovered the remains of dozens of other civilizations that the birds had destroyed. Evidence of scavenged machinery was everywhere to be found. Lexie's theory was that by volunteering to do the grunt work in manufacturing facilities and office work in all aspects of the human infrastructure, the Flock had learned everything they needed to know in order to conquer. She wondered sometimes if that surrender was planned all along, that it was perhaps a tried-and-true strategy for a race that prized conquest over the lives of their foot soldiers.

In a much quieter voice, pitched so that only Lexie could hear, Pickle murmured, "You sure you're ready to do this?"

Lexie licked her dry lips. "Yes," she said, leaning on the word a little too hard.

He nodded. "You better be, sugar," he said. "Word keeps coming down that we've been infiltrated."

"Wait . . . *what*?" She gaped at him, fear coiling inside her.

"Jesus, keep it off your face, sweetie," he said quickly. Lexie, abashed, composed her features and shifted so that her back was to the others.

"How?" she begged. "Who? How many?"

Pickle's face lost all traces of amusement. "You didn't hear about London?"

"No. Why? What happened?"

"A woman—a mathematician working on a stellar cartography project for the Flock's interworld supply chain—joined the Resistance after she had a whole series of dreams about the Sleepers. I don't know if she actually had dreams or was lying. No real way to find out. They screened her nine ways from Sunday, and she passed every test, so they brought her into a cell that was working on our own star maps group. And before you ask, it's the same group looking for Sleeper sites Four and Seven. They kept an eye on her, but she seemed like one of us. A believer. After seven weeks of excellent work, the head of her cell arranged for her to meet the head of the London network. Ten kinds of security at every stage, but halfway through the meeting the place was hit by Flock teams. They killed at least half of the people there, but not the ones the woman singled out.

Those folks were taken, and—Lexie, this is the bad part—they were Griggs and Patel and a couple others."

Lexie felt she'd been punched in the chest. Leslie Griggs and Jok Patel were the scientists overseeing the entire Sleepers project.

"No . . ." she breathed.

"Yes," Pickle corrected. "That's why the entire timetable is being moved up."

She clutched his arm. "Moved up by how much?"

The genuine strain Pickle felt was beginning to show through his forced composure. "These jokers here . . . they aren't candidates—they're our actual crew. What Dubbs said is pretty much the truth. We have no time to finesse our way out, Lexie. Mugabe has the ship as sound as she'll ever be. Billabong and his team are fueling and onloading stores right now. Once we brief these guys, we're splitting."

"When? *Now?*"

"Tonight, for sure," said Pickle.

Lexie felt her entire body go ice cold. She fought not to shiver. *"Tonight?"*

"Yeah, kiddo," said Pickle. "Wish I had better news, but the match is lit. So . . . please tell me you have it."

It.

He said that word quietly, but it hung in the air between them with the combined weight of the sword of Damocles and the boulder of Sisyphus.

"Y-yes . . . I . . . I . . ."

"Hey," said Pickle, "we have an audience, *capiche?* Be cool."

Lexie forced her body to relax despite the alarms going off in her head. The Flock knew. They were onto the entire endeavor. They might have already found some of the Sleeper sites. Hell, they might even know of her mission.

Lexie nodded.

"Okay," she said. "Okay."

"Another thing," said Pickle, still looking out the window. "Navigation's likely to be a bit tricky."

"No doubt," said Lexie "With all the Flock patrols and—"

"That's for sure," Pickle interrupted, "but there's another factor. We've been hearing rumors that the transduction network has been wonky."

Lexie peered at him. "Define 'wonky.'"

Pickle shrugged. "That's just it. What our astrophysicists have been seeing is something that acts like a gravity well or maybe a planetary mass. Something is warping space in ways that don't make sense based on what we know to actually be there. And it's playing merry hob with navigation. Excess drag in some areas and a kind of push elsewhere."

"That doesn't make sense."

"Hence 'wonky.'"

"Will it prevent us from taking a ship?"

"Prevent? No. But we have to factor it in, and that means some tricky navigation. I can handle that part and Mugabe will drive the boat. He has enough space hours logged. And, in a pinch, I can take the wheel. They set me up with simulators, so I'm moderately sure I can manage."

"Should I be nervous about 'moderately sure?'"

"I am," admitted Pickle. "So . . . yeah."

They shared a smile that was more hopeful than confident.

"Now," said Pickle, lowering his voice even more. "I ask again . . . do you have it?"

Without answering she went to a small table and ran her finger along the carved filigree around the edge. There was the faintest click and a section of the top slid open. Inside was a modular pack. The outside was made from faux leather and looked like a travel case for cosmetics. Pickle picked it up and unzipped it. Inside there were, in fact, a duplicate set of the cosmetics she used.

"Take out the powder brush and the cinnamon lipstick," said Lexie quietly. "Then put them back in the opposite slots."

He did and the panel on which the cosmetics rested came loose. Pickle opened it and there, between sheets of leaded Kevlar, was a small, flat oblong device about a half-inch thick.

"Wait, that's it?" Pickle asked. "It's so small."

"That's it," agreed Lexie, nodding.

It. The word seemed so insignificant considering what the device represented. *Everything* might have been a better word. The salvation of humanity was what the small object represented.

It.

It was everything.

It was hope.

"Okay, sugar, you'd better pack," said Pickle. "We're out of here in an hour. Not a minute more or we'll—"

The buzz of the doorbell cut him off. All heads swiveled toward the sound.

"Are you expecting anyone?" Pickle asked.

Lexie's mouth went completely dry. "No. Just you."

"Shit."

The door buzzed again. A little longer this time. Ahab began to yap, but Lexie shushed him. She dipped a hand into her pocket and closed it around the stunner.

Pickle snapped his fingers and when the team turned, he put a finger to his lips and with the other hand waved them toward the bedroom. They moved quickly and silently, and as Dubbs closed the door, the bell buzzed a third time. Pickle lingered in the doorway long enough to give Lexie a brief nod. Then he, too, was gone. Ahab whined softly.

Lexie's heart was hammering now. If it was who she thought it was, then they wouldn't buzz a fourth time.

She inhaled deeply and approached the door. Up until this moment, she'd been nothing more than a curator, working at a museum that promoted the idea of the Flock's greatness and the shame of humanity. Now, with two criminals from the Bottoms, a prophet of Morpheus, and two top-dwellers who had no legal business to be in her apartment, she was technically a traitor to the Flock. The small stunner in her hand offered no real comfort. The fear in her was so thick she felt as if she were moving in slow motion.

She palmed the panel by the door and the reader embedded in the electronics read the chip embedded in her wrist. The door slid open with a faint whisper.

Three Flock stood in the hall.

34

Lexie nearly fainted.

One was medium-sized and dressed in civil authority attire. Flanking him were two much larger birds who wore black shiny armor over their chests and legs, and carried plasma induction rifles. Raptors without a doubt. The smaller one wore a black suit over his wide torso. His legs were visible beneath a matching kilt that also had a computer pad hanging from a belt. His feet were uncovered, revealing three large talons on each, with a wicked heel hook that curved upward. Like all Flock, this held a mild neurotoxin that would put any opponent to sleep.

"Lexie Chow?" asked the smaller one, and it was obvious he was in charge. His modulator made his speech sound almost human.

"I am—" Her throat had closed, and she forced a cough. "Yes sir . . . I am she."

"You will come with us."

She was reminded of the Nazis again. The SS.

"Come with you? Why?"

"You are under arrest," said the bird, his tone matter-of-fact.

He held up a slender, flat comms-strip on which her likeness was shown full-on and in profile. Various data about her—age, height, weight, eye and hair color, and other details scrolled across.

"N-no . . ." She stammered as backed into her living room. "There must be a mistake."

"There is no mistake, Ms. Chow."

"But . . . *why?*" she begged. "What's my crime?"

"Treason."

"*Treason?* No, that's crazy. You got something terribly wrong, I swear," she cried. "I'm just a historian. I work in the museum and I do propaganda to promote the greatness of the Flock. Treason? God, no way. Please . . . no way!"

The Raptors shifted. They were inscrutable most of the time, but she could tell they weren't prepared for her answer.

The Flock in charge remained staring at her. "There is no mistake. We have our orders."

Lexie glanced back to the couch where her pack was, but it was gone. *Thank god*, she thought. At least, someone thought to take it. They might take her, but her life's work was safe.

"Where is the device?"

They knew about it? Her heart sank. "What device?" She stared into the Flock's unblinking eyes and tried to keep herself from shaking.

"Do not play with us, Ms. Chow. We were informed of the device and its importance. We will leave here with it." He edged forward and his voice became colder. "We need it, do you understand? We do not necessarily need you as well."

And there it was.

Pickle was right. The Resistance had been infiltrated. They knew her plans. They knew about the device. Did that mean they also knew of her family inheritance? Did they know that she had found the crystal memory chip left by her ancestors, passed down from generation to generation?

The neuro stunner was in her pocket. Could she get it in time? She doubted it, just as she doubted that she could stun all three birds and make a getaway. Still, her fingers began creeping toward her pocket.

At that moment, Pickle came out of her bedroom, seemingly naked with a towel around his waist. He used another towel to rub his wet hair.

"Hey, babe, I think we order some takeout from—" He stopped dead and pretended to be surprised. It even fooled her. "Whoa! Sorry. I didn't know you were expecting company." He smiled at the birds, then glanced at Lexie. "Who are they?"

The Flock in formal attire said, "Identify yourself. In pattern."

Pickle straightened and stared straight ahead, not making eye contact with the Flock. "Sure thing. Pickle. Bertrand. Human ID Earth Core 8893873."

"Fickle Bertrand," said the Flock. "Bring us the device."

He grinned and glanced at Lexie. "What device?"

"Ms. Chow's device."

Pickle looked from the bird to Lexie and back again. "You . . . want her vibrator?" He sneered. "Seriously? 'Cause that's kind of weird. Gross, really. I'm not even sure she cleans the thing after . . . well . . ."

The three Flock operatives clacked their talons all the way into the apartment, with Lexie yielding ground. Ahab barked a few times, but she waved it back with a hand at her side and the little robot dog cowered behind her legs.

One of the Raptors raised a rifle.

The leader said, "We only need one of you to show us where the device is hidden. Are you willing to die for it, Bertrand Fickle? Now bring us the device."

Pickle's eyes went wide and his mouth fell open. "Oh, *that* device," he said. "Why sure, it's in the bedroom on the night table. Help yourself." He watched the Flock stare toward the room. "Mind you, we've been busy and it might be a little dirty in there." He grinned mischievously.

Lexie stood there, frozen, her head swirling, sick at heart. After all of her family's efforts over a two-hundred-year period, the Flock were going to get it.

Processing what Pickle said lagged far behind her view into no future at all.

The Flock official gestured toward the bedroom and warbled for the two-armed Raptors to retrieve it. They marched into the other room. The moment they passed the threshold, Pickle dropped the towel at his waist revealing a pair of shorts with an old-fashioned ballistic pistol sticking out of it, accounting for his suspect bulge. He jerked it free and jammed the barrel under the official's beak.

"Shut the Flock up, chicken wing," he said in a fierce whisper, "or you won't live to see the next few seconds."

The Flock's head tilted upward and he warbled something impossible for the human ear to understand.

And everything went to shit. Just like that.

There was an answering high-pitched screech from one or the other Raptor, and suddenly a pulse blast punched through the interior wall. It burned past Lexie's cheek close enough for her to feel the heat. She ducked and flung herself at the official, grabbing his arm as he reached for a small pulse pistol in a shoulder holster beneath his jacket. The bird got the gun halfway free when she hit him with the stunner. His body jerked and spasmed; pain tore an even higher shriek from him. Lexie hit him again and again, driving him backward against the open front door. The official's armored back struck the door hard and his impetus slammed it shut. Lexie hit him over and over again. His shriek became higher and thinner and then faded away as he sagged down. Ahab rushed in and began ineffectually nipping at the unconscious bird's cuffs.

Lexie spun as two figures came crashing through the bedroom doorway. It was Dubbs, locked together with one Raptor. He had the creature by the throat, and it was choking him with one hand while it rained punches with the other. The bird's small wings slashed and tore at the burly scientist.

They collided with the side table, which collapsed under their weight, sending food and snacks everywhere. Lexie darted forward, trying to stun the bird, but the figures were moving and writhing so quickly that she had no clear line of attack.

Then Pickle was there. He had his pistol and fired two shots. The first burned an angry red line across Dubbs's left deltoid and missed the Raptor entirely. Dubbs screamed and recoiled, which allowed the bird to land a solid punch to the young man's floating ribs. Dubbs let forth with a dull, deep, painful *ughh-hhh*, and fell sideways. Pickle's second shot took the Raptor in the mouth as it opened its beak to bite Dubbs's throat. The soft lead bullet punched through soft pallet, through esophagus and windpipe, and launched outward through the brain stem, splashing the wall with dark blood, brain, and chips of bone. There was no battle armor, no grease-shield. Just avian skin, bones, and blood. It was all very immediate and messy.

Lexie whirled and ran to the bedroom, bending to snatch up the official's pulse pistol. Before she could follow, the second Raptor appeared in the doorway, disheveled but unhurt. Had it fired from the hip it would have had her, but instead the bird raised the rifle and spent a splinter of a moment tucking the stock against its shoulder. That was time he did not have. Lexie and Pickle both fired, hitting it in the chest and groin, and then a pulse blast from inside the bedroom caught the alien in the back of the skull, burning an exit hole through its left eye. The Raptor took one step forward; then its leg buckled, and it went down.

Silence dropped like a ton of bricks.

Lexie stared in horror at the blood and bodies. Pickle stood next to her, eyes glassy with shock. Behind them Dubbs got to his feet, hands shaking as they simultaneously probed the burn on his shoulder and the damage to his rib. Fire came into the living room with Fodder and Mugabe behind her. All three of them were bruised, cut, and scorched from pulse blasts, their faces registering the kind of shock from someone who'd realized how close to death they'd been. Ahab ran around the room, yipping and whining.

Abruptly a panel in the wall opened and MATT trundled out. It spun around, letting its sensors assess the mess, then it began sucking up the bits of brain and bone that had landed on the floor.

The silence held for a very short time before Lexie said, "We have to go. *Right fucking now.*"

35

Micah Fontenot sat at one end of a huge polymer conference table, legs stretched out underneath, his seat tilted all the way back. The holo-screen floated around to follow, establishing a geostationary orbit above his head at the best angle for watching without strain.

Micah was using an old smuggler's trick of affecting nonchalance to use posture and deliberate muscle control to lure the unsuspecting into thinking he was relaxed, thus releasing the right soothing hormones. He'd done this for everything from news stories about Resistance cells being raided to police counterpunches for the bombs the Dreamers set off. He was so practiced at it that he was always successful.

Only this time it was not working.

The image on the holo-screen was the Calgary Metropol in Alberta, Canada. There were seventy-seven million people in that region. Five hundred and six rookeries. A thousand apartment metroplexes for key human workers. Countless thousands of humped mounds covering the undergrounds. The Hives.

All of that was true as of yesterday.

Today, when Micah pulled up the news feed about the Calgary Metroplex, the vid image looked like high-def images of one of the inner rings of Hell.

The fires reached like the arms of Satan himself, clawing at the atmosphere with yellow talons of flame. The whole of the sky seemed to rest on twisted columns of gray smoke.

Smoke from burning apartment houses, burning Hives. Burning flesh.

Even from his office in London, Micah could almost smell that stink—wood ash, melting plastic, burning rubber, and charred meat. The perfume of Armageddon.

The news reporter—a human with watery eyes that never quite managed to look directly at the camera, and by extension the people around the world who watched—said it had been a gas main leak. Methane buildup in tunnels illegally blocked by societal washouts from the Bottoms.

That was the story they were trying to sell. When Micah switched channels, the news reports were all the same. Most of the reporters read from the identical script, varied only as was required for translations into dozens of languages. Same story.

Same propaganda.

Same lies.

Although there was no footage of what happened, Micah was sure he knew. He prayed he was wrong, but he knew he was right.

He told his AI to call his aunt.

The call went through over nine thousand bounce-routers before a woman picked up.

"Line?" asked Micah.

"Clear," said the woman.

The very low hum told Micah that the jammer was in place.

A hologram digital readout appeared to his left, counting down the probably safe time of the call.

Micah was brief.

"The news. Calgary," he said. "You saw."

"We did," said the woman who was not his aunt. Lulu Feng ran an administrative cell in Shanghai. She was the third person—the third of his old fixer friends—Micah had contacted after beginning work on the Resistance network. "They're calling it a massive gas explosion."

"And?"

"Well, that's nonsense."

"Of course," agreed Micah.

"This is more your area than mine," said Lulu. "What do you think it is?"

"You *know* what I think."

There was beat. "No one has actually *seen* it," said the woman. "You know that, right? You do get that this is purely hypothetical and that you're almost certainly wrong. You get all that?"

"I'm not wrong," said Micah.

"Why are you so sure?"

"It's exactly what I'd do if I were them."

The pause was much longer than before. "If you're right . . .?"

"I am. This is the same as what happened on Horlon's Moon, Teegarden's Star, B Luyten, Tau Ceti F, and Brickmoor's World. This is the Flock punching back. Punching back hard. And if we don't do something about it, they're going to smash us flat."

"It can't be that," protested Lulu. "How could the Flock have ever built something like that?"

"Maybe they didn't," said Micah. "Maybe they found it. That's their racket, right? That's their scam—scavenge, repurpose, find new applications for something, and act like it's always been their own."

"But something like this?"

"Yes," said Micah. "We need to stop acting shocked and dazed and stupid and just accept that it's real and figure out how to stop this thing."

Lulu said, "Do you think *they* will be able to help?"

He laughed. "That's a nice dream, but they've been ice cubes for two hundred years. I know I approved the historian's mission, and I'm glad she's out there giving it a shot, but that's a very long shot."

"Which we took anyway?"

"Let's face it, dear heart, we don't have that many shots to fire," he said. "We're out there, we're nicely organized, but don't think that because we're smarter than those birds that we are winning. And now they have this."

"You sound scared, Micah," she said. "You're never scared."

"Oh, I'm scared out of my mind. We were outnumbered and outgunned *before* this."

Micah looked at the burning mega city on the news. The cameraman had cranked up the gain on his mics so that the sounds of people screaming filled the air. Anything for ratings.

"No doubt about it," he said to Lulu. "That's *Juggernaut*."

36

The homeless man at Lexi's doorway was already aware of the problem. He indicated that they needed to take the underground, which meant through the Bottoms. Now that they had two members of King Rat's crew with them, they would be unable to navigate. They all managed to slide through a door into a dank access tunnel a mere moment before security forces came screaming to her apartment in emergency hover vehicles.

Lexie carried Ahab in a pack on her back and wore another pack on her front. She had no weapon other than the stunner in her pocket, but Dubbs, Fire, and Fodder had grabbed what the Flock had dropped as well as the old-fashioned lead thrower that Pickle has brought. It was funny—Lexie had gifted it to him last year but more out of his declared interest in antique firearms than any imagined use. And now it had saved them.

Something needed to be said for coincidence.

Something needed to be said for preparation.

Fire pushed herself to the front. "This is my place down here. Flock won't be coming but that doesn't mean we don't need to be careful."

"What does that mean?" Lexie asked.

"Never underestimate what one human will do to another in the name of survival."

They filed into an old lift, grime and moss climbing up the interior walls. Fire punched a series of numbers too fast for Lexie to follow.

"We need to get to the museum."

Fire shook her head. "Too far."

"You don't understand," she said. "I have a ship waiting for us."

"That was before the Flock found us out. They'll be all over the surface."

"Then let's not go by the surface," Pickle said.

Lexie flashed Fire a look and she gave it back to her. "Listen. We need to get off the rock. I could be fucking dramatic and say that the fate of the world rests on us and it wouldn't be an understatement."

"Everyone thinks they are important," Fodder said. "We'll have to get King Rat involved and he's not just going to let you transit without payment."

"Did you say payment?" Lexie asked. "Pay with what? We're talking about the human race."

"King Rat don't care about no human race," Fire said. "He cares about the Bottoms. Period."

Fodder nodded. "Period."

Lexie hated the idea that more than two hundred years of planning were going to be laid at the feet of a street thug who was going to decide whether or not she deserved to transit his environs. Not for the first time she wondered how easily they would have been taken over by the Flock if humanity had had a unified response. As a species they were too selfish. And without a legacy, was the human race worth trying to save?

The lift lurched and died. Fire and Fodder began to argue in some ghetto patois Lexie couldn't understand.

Fodder punched Fire in the shoulder.

Fire slapped Fodder in the face.

Lexie rolled her eyes and made eye contact with Pickle. He shook his head.

Mugabe stood silently; eyes closed. Dubbs bopped his head to some unknown beat.

The lift suddenly jerked back to life and began to descend again.

Both Fodder and Fire high-fived.

A minute later and the lift slammed into an immovable object.

Presumably the Bottoms.

The door opened halfway, and Fodder was forced to pry it open the rest of the way.

A crew of miscreants awaited them. All had their head shaved like Fire and Fodder. Two had the yellow nostrils of Loopers. They'd be no threat. All had various Basque tattoos indicating they were part of *Arratoiak*. The irony was that even at the bottom of the world living in the detritus and dripped shit from the rookeries, humans found a way to snipe at one another. To give inhumanity a fresh voice. That saddened and angered Lexie. Keeping her frustration off her face took real effort.

A miasma of aromas reached out to engulf the party. Compared to streetside, the stench almost buckled their knees. It was an assault to the senses and she couldn't parse the smells, but she couldn't help but believe it was not only the odor of the unwashed, but disease and probably death.

Lexie took a moment to center herself as the others covered their noses with hands and forearms, then found the strength to be the leader and stepped forward.

"Take us to King Rat."

The two loopers blinked absently and fondled themselves. Drool fell from tattooed lips.

A man whose face had been burned so his nose had all but melted into his face eyed Fire and Fodder. "Thought you two had moved on to a mission for the Rat."

"We did."

"We are."

"We need to move through the Bottoms," Pickle said.

"I don't know you, SunScraper. Keep your lice to yourself."

Pickle was about to say something more, but Lexie shook her head ever so slightly.

"This is Kresh," Fire said. "He's one of King Rat's lieutenants."

"I am Lexie Chow," she said, nodding slowly at the burned man.

"You related to the Alexander Chow from Calliope?"

"The same family. I'm named after him."

"And you have a way to defeat the Flock?"

Lexie shrugged. "It's a better chance than anything else I've heard."

The man looked her up and down. "You don't look like much."

"Neither do you," she snarled.

He grinned and never had she seen anything uglier. "Follow me."

Fire and Fodder took up the front and back. They got more than a few glances when the Bottom-dwellers noted the Flock weapons they carried. But that was as close as anyone got to them.

Lexie passed more squalor than she'd ever imagined could exist. People seemed to live wherever they stopped, forever looking upward and waiting for something to fall as if the Flock weren't throwing away trash but the pipes and conduits that made up the ceiling were some immortal being providing sustenance for them.

Every now and then a piece of something *would* fall and ricochet all the way down, the sound of it hitting metal and composite a precursor to a mini riot. Children dove into the fray, scraping the ground until their already black hands were bloody, then scooting away and licking their fingers to get whatever had mixed with their own blood.

Lexi averted her eyes as she moved past. Those who were more enterprising gardened moss, using their own excrement to feed the free-form algae so that it might grow that much faster. This is what the Flock had reduced them to.

She heard sobbing and glanced over at Dubbs, who couldn't stop the tears from flowing. As bad as life had been for him and everyone he'd known, it could not have been even an inkling as bad as what those on the Bottoms faced. The rumors of their existence didn't come close to the reality.

Thirty minutes of wading through the miasma later, the group entered an enclosed space. In the middle of the room sat a fat man on an old-fashioned lawn chair. Not only were there no lawns so far beneath the city, but there were no fat men. Just as a seeing man was king in the land of the blind, a fat man was king in the land of the starving. By the way he stared imperiously at them and by the deference made by the others, this must have been King Rat.

A man with a missing leg and a homemade prosthetic stood in front of him and both Fodder and Fire approached, exchanging a complicated series of handshakes that seemed to last for a full minute. When they were done, the man turned to the king and nodded as if verifying the pair's authenticity.

It was then that Lexie realized that what she'd seen was more than a handshake, but a language where information was passed silently by the movement of hands and fingers.

The king was more than fat. He had rolls upon rolls to the point where he could barely stand. His eyes were all but hidden in the creases of his face. His hands were like sausages, incapable of closing. Lexie had imagined some sort of great warrior, but this man couldn't defend a hatchery of lice, much less himself. How had be become king? She tried to imagine him walking but even that seemed a stretch.

"We have reports of the Flock looking for you," said King Rat, his voice surprisingly high-pitched and melodious. "Your presence here is problematic."

"We had no choice. Someone informed on us," Lexie said. "We needed a place to hide and a way to get to our ship without the Flock knowing."

King Rat's beady eyes blinked rapidly. "What have you brought me as payment for transiting my space?"

"I am bringing you freedom," she said flatly. "Don't you want to be free of the Flock?"

He laughed, his voice higher still. "Do you think my people could live up top? They would die with the sun. They wouldn't know how to hustle food or harvest moss. It would kill them as surely as a bullet to the head. These two I gave you are from the Bottoms, but they have been sun side more than most." He chuckled. "And look at me. Do you think I care? Do you think I want for anything? *Look* at me. Do I seem underfed to you? Do I lack anything? I am the very epitome of indulgence."

"I see a fat man where everyone else is starving," replied Lexie, her tone cold and hard.

The burned man laughed. The man with one leg grinned.

"You see what I want you to see," said King Rat. "I project power. I have learned what my people require and know what they most desire. I become that so that they might know the possibilities they will never achieve."

"What do you mean?"

King Rat pressed a button secreted in the skin of his left hand and his body deflated with a *whooooosh*. Where an immense fat man had been was now a person in a wrinkled skin suit. He reached back and peeled himself out of it to reveal the body of a woman whose ribs cut painfully at her skin and whose hip bones threatened to carve themselves free. She wore stained panties and no bra, her breasts long ago removed. Her cheeks were hollows so deep that Lexie could make out teeth—what few she had left—pressing against the skin. Her head was shaved like all the rest. The image of the fat man was gone as if it had never existed. If anything, this woman was a victim of malnutrition.

"Do you really think I could be a fat man when my people are starving?" The Rat King's voice was a pure as a child's.

"I . . . I don't know what to think."

"And again, I ask," said the ruler of the Bottoms, "what payment should there be?"

Mugabe stepped forward. "I am a Prophet of Morpheus. Do any of you have dreams?"

"Some of us," the wasted female king said after a pause. "What of it?"

The prophet nodded. "So then you have Travelers among you."

"How is it you know?" the Rat King asked.

"Because it is the traveling that allows one to be part of the greater being you call the universe." He regarded her and said softly. "You, though . . . you don't dream, do you?"

King Rat's eyes were hooded. "I have nightmares, but . . . no. I don't dream. Not like that. If I did, I would want to dream of the end of the Flock, but that is not something my people will ever know."

Mugabe turned to face Lexie. "What do you know about the Mahabharat?"

"Other than it being part of the phage virus?" Lexie shrugged. "Not much. I just know that everyone who has gone through transductive travel has within them the potentiality of the virus. It can be turned on or off, but no one really knows how."

Mugabe nodded and his golden eyes flashed. "It is the universe that turns it on and off. If you haven't been one with the universe, then you can't have the virus."

"Why would anyone want the virus?" Pickle asked.

"Right now, there are those who see it as a bad thing," explained Mugabe. "But what if it is something beneficial? What if it is the thing that links us all? We chose to call it the Mahabharat Phage Virus for good reason. We know that it is a bacteriophage that is awoken, but we are as yet unsure what it does. We also view the Mahabharat as the word that breathed life into the phage. Although it was written eons ago, the epic Sanskrit poem from which it was named reflects our current reality."

"I don't understand," admitted Lexie.

"Let me explain," said the prophet, nodding. "Not only is the Mahabharat one of the most important sources of Hindu moral law, but it is the story of two groups of cousins: the Kauravas and the Pandavas. There is anger between the families and the Pandavas are forced to leave and go into exile. Now, the Kauravas or Kurus worship in a falcon-shaped altar. They are left to rule for a time and form their own society in their own image. One could say that of the falcon. But then the Pandavas return and in a great battle are able to defeat all of the Kurus and restore the people to prosperity. The greatest of the Pandavas is Krishna who became a sort of Jesus figure over time. What is interesting was that until peace once again reigned, sacrifices were made by Pandavas to ensure their rightful return."

"But this Mahabharat was written so long ago," Lexie said.

Mugabe smiled warmly. "Do you believe in coincidence?"

"Sometimes."

"You can't have it only sometimes. Do you believe it or not?"

She adjusted her arms and then crossed them, more a way of keeping them from moving than anything else. "I suppose I do. But I also believe that you can create your own coincidences. Isn't that when planning meets opportunity?"

"The Roman philosopher Seneca said a similar thing," agreed Mugabe. "He said that *luck* is where planning meets opportunity."

"Luck . . . coincidence. I can see where they could be the same." She had her arms crossed and tapped the fingers of one hand on her elbow. "But what you seem to be talking about is destiny."

"What do you know about predeterminism?" Mugabe asked.

"I know enough that I don't believe it."

"Yet you believe in coincidence."

"I plan for it."

"What makes you plan?"

She thought for a moment, then said, "Necessity."

"That view can be attributed to Socrates. Those ideas have been around for millennia."

"It's because as humans we want to explain the unexplainable," countered Lexie.

Mugabe shook his head. "It's human nature to try and create order where chaos exists. Oscar Wilde said that 'without order nothing can exist; without chaos nothing can evolve.'"

"You can't have it both ways," she said.

"Can you not? Have you ever wondered why everyone who travels outside the realm of human ability is infected with MPV? How can the virus appear out of nothing?"

"It can't," she said. "Perhaps it is awoken."

She remembered her speech to the Underground Science Institute when she used Arthur C. Clarke's *2001: A Space Odyssey* as an example. The primates' approach upon seeing the obelisk was to immediately begin to worship the object, even though they did not know what worship was. They could not help themselves as they regarded the advancement among them. In an effort to identify the unidentifiable, their cortical neurons blast and sizzle, creating the need to acknowledge something greater than themselves and in that moment, they realize that they are not alone.

Could it be the same thing as the virus? Could the virus have been implanted in the human physiognomy at the beginning of time only to became awakened when the moment was right? Was that what the Prophet of Morpheus was speaking about? Was this his determinism? Did that mean that there was some sort of divinity at work or was this just something randomly programmed into her genetic puzzle?

She was back to coincidence again.

She laughed and then an alarm went off.

37

"The Flock have come to the Bottoms," the burned man said.

The Rat King was working her way back into her suit. Men and women came from secret doors hidden in the walls. They formed a circle three layers deep around the King as she once again became the fat man everyone believed she was.

The men, women, and children of the Rat King's gang carried all sorts of weapons. Many were single-use lead throwers made from pieces of scrap metal, but there were others that had clearly been stolen from other sources. None were as advanced as those carried by Fire and Fodder, but they could do damage nonetheless.

"I need to get to my ship," Lexie said.

"You brought death to us," the Rat King said.

"Death has always been among you. I just gave you the opportunity to get your own pint of blood."

Mugabe nodded and whispered, "Nice Shakespeare pull."

She ignored the comment. "Well?"

The burned man leaned in and said something to the Rat King, whose lip curled as he shook his head. He gestured for Kresh to speak

"The Flock apparently can track their own weapons. We've checked and the ones you are carrying have transponders that have been accessing our wireless nodes. We've been able to identify which addresses they've been broadcasting to, but it's too late. The Flock has already pinpointed this space and are coming in a wave."

"You have brought the Birds to us," King Rat said.

All eyes went to the new group, anger boiling over.

While Lexie could appreciate their emptions, she forced her voice to be calm, practical, even cold. "While I appreciate your predicament, I do need to get to my ship."

"And before the Flock find us," Pickle said.

Fire stared at one of the weapons. "What about these?"

"Take them with you," Kresh said. "They will follow the trail."

"Which means they might leave our people alone," King Rat said.

"The old two-dimensional film from the twentieth century titled *The Wrath of Khan*," Mugabe began. "The logic alien known as Spock indicated that the needs of the many outweigh the needs of the few."

"You are arguing against your own need," the Rat King said. "There are far more of us than of you."

"But I wasn't talking about just us. I was talking about the entire *human race*. They are the many." Mugabe then pointed at the Rat King. "You are the few."

The Rat King stared at Mugabe and Lexie, then nodded once, quickly. Then she turned to her right-hand man. "Make it happen. Get them to their ship."

"What about the Flock?" the one-legged man asked.

"We disperse," Pickle said. "We hide. We attack if necessary. We are like ghosts. In and out. Take no prisoners. We want them to regret ever coming here."

"What will you do?" Lexie asked the king.

"I will wait here until I know everyone is safe. Then I will blend in as well. No one knows what I really look like except the people in this room. The Flock will be busy looking for a fat man and never find him."

Pickle shook his head. "Crazy like a fox. Who would have guessed it?"

Fire and Fodder made one last complex handshake with the burned man, passing on god only knew what information before joining the group. They had an escort of two teenagers and two women, each with what appeared to be blades of some kind strapped to their backs and holding knives in each hand.

"The call has gone out across the Bottoms," Fire said. "We will have free access to your ship. And the Flock will be harassed every step of the way."

Lexie reconsidered the people of the Bottoms and wished she had more time to get to know them. Her original thesis had been faulty. These were true heroes. They were going to fight so that she and her team might live.

They ran.

Her AI pet sent her a message asking to be let down because of all of the jostling. She declined at first, but as it began to bump and grind against her back, she acquiesced.

Ahab shook himself and wagged his tail like the world was a happy place. He trotted at Lexie's heels, eyes bright, tongue lolling.

They'd gone perhaps a hundred meters before the first Flock spun around the corner. It took aim and shot at them.

One of their escorts went down in a heap.

Fire and Fodder opened fire with their Flock rifles, the result pummeling the bird alien into the ground.

Pickle kicked it as they went by.

Ahab lifted a leg and pretended to pee.

Lexie stepped over the body and the rest followed suit.

More Flock appeared behind them and they began to run, following their remaining escort. Around pipes, past family units huddling in the shadows, through piles of well-sorted trash, they sprinted as best they could, until they were all breathing heavily.

And still the Flock came behind them, occasionally firing a shot that missed, sizzling against the walls next to them.

Lexie paused a moment, turned, and returned fire.

Then she was off again, now everyone in front, racing to freedom.

Suddenly, she was snatched from behind, jerked into an alcove, and slammed into a wall.

"Lexie Chow, you are a traitor," said the Flock.

Her breath in fear, but she managed to stutter, "Not to you."

The Flock ignored her words. It grabbed her by the hair and dragged her deeper into the warrens of the Bottoms, away from her friends.

Didn't the others know she'd been taken? Where were they? Was she on her own? Fear blossomed, exploding in her. She did all she could do at the moment and sagged to the ground, her dead weight causing the Flock to pause. It jerked at her hair hard enough to evince a scream of pain. She swung her arms at the hand that grabbed her, screaming to be let go.

The Flock pulled her painfully to her feet and punched her in the side.

She doubled over.

Then she glimpsed Dubbs running lankily toward her. He lifted his rifle and capped off several rounds.

The Flock grabbed her by a leg and began to pull her with one hand as it fired its weapon with the other.

Dubbs juked and jived and fired again. Then he did

something strange. He stopped. He just stood there and watched Lexie get pulled away as if he didn't have a care in the world. The Flock kept its aim, but didn't fire, just continued deeper into the darkness.

Then the sky fell in.

A pair of teenagers dropped from the pipes above and onto the shoulders of the Flock. The knives in each of their hands worked like pistons as they stabbed and stabbed and stabbed, the Flock unable to even respond from the immediate assault. It dropped its rifle and its grip on Lexie who managed to scoot herself out of the way.

The Flock fell to its knees and still the pair stabbed it, not ceasing until it was lying face down on the ground. Lexi wasn't prepared for what happened next. Both assailants used their knives, leaving the alien where it lay as they absconded with its vestigial wings.

By the time Lexi managed to climb to her feet and catch her breath, the body was gone, taken by someone else. Hunger drove everything and everyone in the Bottoms.

Dubbs ran up to her. "Are you okay?"

She nodded and licked her lips. "Where are the others?"

"Fighting. Come on. They might need our help."

38

As it turned out, they had everything under control. The Flock should have never come to the Bottoms—Lexie doubted that even one of the birds had made it out. It wasn't long before she was able to access the basement levels of the museum and find her way to her ship.

"It looks like a garbage scow," Pickle said.

"It is a garbage scow," Lexie replied, "but with a transductive drive. We essentially have the fastest garbage truck in the known universe."

"And how do you imagine we're going to get off planet?" Dubbs asked. "The Flock have grounded everything coming and going."

"The Resistance has a plan for that," Lexie said. "We have someone in place."

"In science we call that a single point of failure," Dubbs said.

She glanced at him and shrugged.

Mugabe arrived last. His face was covered in Flock blood and feathers but carried no visible weapon except for two lengths of metal, both of which dripped more blood as he held them to his side. The liquid pooling on the ground at his side. His face was implacable, but his golden eyes were wide from the effort of killing and the adrenaline pumping through his system.

She'd only seen him in action once during their flight, but it had been one of those moments where she'd almost stopped to watch. He didn't so much fight as flow, his arms and the metal rods crisscrossing in the air in complex patterns that disengaged weapons, broke arms, cracked beaks, and yet never seemed to slow.

Mugabe had clearly received training from someone somewhere. Were all prophets as proficient as he? With a battalion of them they might be able to take down the entirety of Raptors. Then again, they were also priests who promulgated a universal belief in the phage and the reality of the Sleepers. They had their own mission. Much like the people of the Bottoms, the lives of the Prophets were locked in a specific destiny.

"I saw you attack," she said to Mugabe when he came close.

He stared at her a moment, then said, "I do not attack. I defend."

"I . . . I just wanted to say thank you."

"Do not thank me. We have Sleepers to awaken. We must leave this place. We must move like an interstellar wind."

"Then let's go," she said.

"Pickle, do you want the honor of opening the door?" she asked.

"Sure, sugar," he said, grinning. "You can count on me to open the garbage can for you."

39

Paul Finney had been working for the Flock since he was a child. He'd first been nothing more than a servant, helping where he could, making himself indispensable. He'd started like many other humans had, scraping the shit from the bottom of the rookeries and transplanting it to the fields to help with the growth of grain and corn to feed the hatchlings. Then he'd moved onto farming. Then after having his mental acuities test, they sent him to a carefully monitored school where he was allowed to study one subject.

The Flock controlled their servant species in many ways, but none so carefully as their dispensation of knowledge. Finney was taught a single machine language that allowed him to work with a single finite set of machines. Even sitting strapped into a machine language interface system (MLIS), the man or woman to the right or left of him had no idea what he was doing or what his particular machine language even did. It was a classic case of the left hand not knowing what the right hand was doing.

This was their policy.

This was their method.

The irony was that the Flock didn't do this because they were themselves geniuses. Far from it. Their minds couldn't understand machine languages, and without tech implants, their brains were no match for those of humans when it came to devising, manipulating, following, constructing, or even creating new methods for machines to function. The Flock was entirely dependent upon their servant species except for those few humans assigned to the engineer class who augmented themselves with tech implants and external feed devices.

Finney didn't require such tech. He'd come to discover that he was a prodigious programmer and could create backdoors, dead ends, and multilevel language interfaces that appeared to be nothing more than simple indecipherable jargon. Programmed to be read three-dimensionally, he could perform functions even the most teched Flock engineers had no inkling could be completed.

Finney could have lived and died in his programming chair, plugged in, zoned out, surviving on the binary language of machines that comprised solitary functions. He could have achieved a merging of man and machine, creating a hierarchical representative of the possibilities of language, understanding, and compulsion.

Then he'd met Lexie.

They had little in common except for hatred.

Glorious hatred.

But it was the kind of hatred that was distilled and curated so that the objects of the emotion had little to no idea the depth of their emotions as focused and subsumed as it was. He'd met Lexie when touring the museum, searching for older tech that might help him better understand the incredible horizons of his own skillset. She'd shown him everything from clunky early Apollo 11 machine code to the luxurious code created from the entire crucible of human knowledge by the child prodigy only known as Justice. Born with no arms or legs, he'd been jacked into the world ecomachine system since he could breathe and made it his own.

Even now he had followers who reached out and attempted to determine his location but, like the Flock, were eternally unable to find it. Justice or Just Ice as he loved to be called, using the calling card of a solid block of ice melting into rivers of tears, was more than a man, he was a force of unnatural convention, able to create with machine language ideas that had never seemed possible.

Preceding the object-oriented C++ and the Program Extraction Language of Perl, Assembly was both simple and lost to time. It had even less to do with Java and the first artificial language, also known as Python. But it was able to be manipulated using server-side languages such as Golong.

But the Flock engineers had been studying Justice. They knew the basics of his machine language and shut it down as soon as they discovered even a hint of his personal code. What they didn't bother with, however, was the language of the ancients.

Like Latin was to twentieth century mankind, the Apollo 11 was powered using computer assembly language, or Assembly. The Assembly code was converted to the "machine language" of the computing device being used, ones and zeroes, by a utility program that made conventional sense of the numbers. Although this type of coding was amazingly tedious, it took advantage of the processing capabilities of the computers of the age.

Then came Squid and Jackal + and Oort Frequency Modulation Reaction Code (OOFMERC), based on a combination of the language of Earth-based whales and the ultrasonic sounds of comets hurtling through apace.

And then the Flock, their primitive codes partitioned within their ships to do the simplest tasks.

Finney could have chosen any version or a combination thereof, but instead went back to the beginning.

Assembly.

So simple it had been lost to time.

And now, strapped into his machine language chair, he received the request he'd been hoping for.

Lexie.

Her plan had come together.

She was preparing to leave.

The Flock still had Earth-based and orbital telemetric monitoring systems that would bring down her ship with a simple OOFMERC thought.

And it would have except for his prepared code.

He'd established servers in the Oort cloud that could be accessed only using Assembly. With a few Golong datapoints, his server-side language began its invitation and all telemetric monitoring data was transferred to a host of three hundred servers all empty and waiting to be filled, then encoded. To unlock them would require Assembly which, like Latin, was tense dependent and could be absolutely misconstrued if the Flock handled it incorrectly.

The code words to start the program were *sic semper tyrannus—thus always to tyrants*—purportedly the words of both Brutus when he assassinated Caesar, and John Wilkes Booth when he assassinated President Lincoln.

Finney converted the thought into Assembly and fired it across the bow of every computer in Earth system.

They all went down.

To restart them one must know the new activation code, *oderant dum metuant—let them hate as long as they fear*.

His final moment was to partition his own life-support systems from his computer language interface chair using a 9,999-bit encryption system. While OOFMERC could figure out the code, it wouldn't be before his body ceased to function.

His last moments were filled with a smile and the words *Flock inclinant, sed non obligant*, over and over and over, broadcasted across every screen in every device in every room in every home in the Earth System.

40

"Line?"

"Clear," said Micah.

"Did they get away?" asked Lulu Feng. Her voice was hushed and secretive, but there was plenty of anxiety packed into those four words as well.

"Yes," said Micah.

"And?"

"It got messy."

"How messy?"

"Very."

There was a long pause and he could hear her breathing. Then she asked, "Will this work?"

"God only knows," said Micah. There was just as much anxiety in his voice. "God only knows."

PART THREE
TIN MAN

"All men dream, but not equally. Those who dream by night in the dusty recesses of their minds, wake in the day to find that it was vanity: but the dreamers of the day are dangerous men, for they may act on their dreams with open eyes, to make them possible."

—T. E. Lawrence

"Modern science says: 'The sun is the past, the earth is the present, the moon is the future.' From an incandescent mass we have originated, and into a frozen mass we shall turn. Merciless is the law of nature, and rapidly and irresistibly we are drawn to our doom."

—Nikola Tesla

41

Flock inclinant, sed non obligant appeared on every screen aboard the ship. Although to call it a ship was akin to calling a moon a planet or a child an adult. The optimism of the word was evident, and reality was absolutely in the eye of the beholder. The ship was an antique Fastburner that was literally sitting in the basement of the museum Lexie had been working in. Older by far than a Saturn class, it was closer to a Mercury class but was really a hodgepodge of spare parts thrown together. She tried not to read anything into the fact that it was disguised as a slow-moving garbage scow, but her heart simultaneously sank and soared when she read the words that meant it was safe for her to leave.

Dubbs stared at the words and asked what they meant.

All eyes went to Lexie except for Mugabe's, who was currently checking the displays in the instrument panel.

She closed her eyes a moment because she realized the true value of the words. On one hand, they were going to be free of the planet and begin a mission that would change the fate of everyone and everything they knew. But on the other hand, the words meant that an old friend of hers—a partner in freedom— had taken his own life so that he could never be forced to reveal his secrets.

"Why are we just sitting here?" Pickle asked.

Lexie still had her eyes closed. What she was about to do was irrevocable.

"Seriously," Dubbs asked. "What does that mean? Inclement obligation whatever, whatever?"

Mugabe spoke first. "*Flock inclinant, sed non obligant.* It's old Latin. It means that *the Flock inclines us but they do not bind us.* It's a statement of freedom derived from words uttered long, long ago. It refutes the idea of fatalism. That the Flock will always be our masters. The words revel in their own optimism and hint towards free will."

Fodder snorted. "Free will. Sell that in the Bottoms."

"You can sell it everywhere," Lexie said. She opened her eyes and began the launch process. "Those words mean we are free to take off." Her voice was monotone and tightly controlled. "The words also mean that some else had died to make it happen."

Fire nodded. "Then let's make it worth their while."

"Fuck yes," Fodder said.

Pickle put a gentle hand on her shoulder. "There will be many deaths. But it takes dying to live."

"Who said that?" she asked.

"I think it was part of an old rap song," Pickle said.

"What the hell is rap?" Dubbs asked.

"It was a singing modality wherein people would speak in rhymes about their lives, generally on the street, popularizing the drug culture, the importance of subversive behavior, and the victimization of women," Mugabe said.

Everyone stared at him a moment.

Dubbs was the first to speak. "That sounds terrible."

Mugabe shrugged. "Different times breed different art and science."

The space frame began to shake, rattle, and hum.

Everyone reached for something to hang on to.

Lexie stared at the ancient readouts on her command console. She barely knew what she was looking at—she might have made so many fatal mistakes putting the craft together.

The shaking doubled, then tripled.

"I don't think it's going to make it," Pickle shouted over the screeching of metal.

"It's going to get worse," Lexie said.

She depressed a button that had clearly been affixed to the control panel, something new, something not original to the ship.

From outside and above they heard explosions.

The noise from the ship stopped abruptly and the ship began to rise.

More explosions could be heard and the hull rang with slabs of the roof that had just been remotely destroyed. Debris fell around the ship, filling the space where it had been built.

Lexie sent a silent prayer to the universe.

They rose more and then jerked. The panel indicated that the anti-gravity wells were established. Lexie sighed in relief as she realized they weren't going to immediately explode.

They rose higher but no shaking as the anti-grav wells surrounded the ship. They'd soon engage the micro black hole, which would further insulate them from outside influence, but for now, they had to safely exit the atmosphere without exploding and without interference from the Flock.

"It is unlucky to fly a ship with no name," said Pickle as the old boat lifted through the clouds.

"What did it used to be called?" asked Dubbs.

"Depends on which part," Lexie replied. "There are pieces

of at least twenty ships used to cobble this contraption together. The forward hull is from the *Diplomat,* the cargo bay is from *Bob's Retirement III,* the left thruster is from *Bagram II* and the right thruster is from *Bagram VI.* Some of the solar plating is from a *no-shit* garbage scow named *Frangella.*"

"Got it," said Pickle. He looked around. "Suggestions welcome."

"*Bird-Stomper?*" suggested Fodder.

"That's a bit on the nose," said Lexie.

"*The Omelet?*" said Fire.

"No. And it's disgusting."

"So, *Chicken Tenders* is out then too?" offered Fodder.

"Anyone else?" asked Lexie.

"*The* S.S. *Alarm Clock?*" proposed Pickle.

"Boring," said Lexie. "Next . . ."

"S.S. *Asylum?*" said Dubbs.

"Again, too close to the mark."

"*Seas the Day,*" offered Fodder, and spelled it.

"God. Last thing I want to do is be crew on a flying pun."

"*Bad Dream?*" suggested Dubbs.

"That feels like bad luck," said Lexie, and Mugabe nodded agreement.

Pickle said, "How about *Ragdoll?*"

They all looked at him and then turned away without comment.

"*Tin Can?*" Pickle said hopefully.

Lexie raised an eyebrow.

"Or better yet," said Pickle. "*Tin Man.*"

They all turned back.

"I like that," said Fire. "I read all those books when I was a kid."

"You read books?" asked Fodder.

"Fuck you," Fire said.

"I was joking," Fodder said.

"I like it," said Mugabe. "*Tin Man* has a nobility to it."

"Seriously. I was just joking," insisted Pickle. "This is going to be in history books."

"*Tin Man* it is," Lexie decided.

And *Tin Man* it became.

Pickle gave a philosophic sigh, nodded, and punched some keys. A mechanical voice devoid of any trace of artificial personality said, "*Shipboard vocal interface activated.*"

"Command protocol," said Pickle. "Override previous designation, name, call sign, call numbers, and links to regulatory networks."

"*Confirmed.*"

"New ship designation is *Tin Man*. Confirm."

"*Confirmed,*" said the ship, then added, "*I have a wide selection of languages, voice characteristics, regional dialects, regional vocabularies, and personality subtypes. Would you like me to list them?*"

"No."

"*I am an interactive Cosmo-Dynamics RealPerson A-111-GH model. I require a personality profile in order to be of best service.*"

Pickle looked at Mugabe. "Are you shitting me? Is this for real?"

The prophet shrugged. "All of the older models were like this."

"Oh, for fuck's sake," grumbled Pickle. To the ship he said, "Just frigging pick one."

A few lights on the console flashed and there was a sound suspiciously like someone humming. And then, in a very persnickety middle-aged and very nasal voice, it said, "*Foul language is a sign of low intelligence.*"

Pickle stared at the console. "Wait . . . what?"

"*Just joking,*" said the AI.

"Joking?" echoed Lexie.

"Kind of don't need jokes right now," said Pickle. "The shit is hitting the actual fan."

"*There you go with language again.*"

"Jesus, shut up."

"*My name isn't Jesus,*" said the AI, "*It's Tin Man, or you can call me Tinny. Or Man. Or AI. Or even Ship.*"

"That's a little too much personality," said Dubbs.

"You think?" Pickle snapped. "Okay, *Tin Man*. Dial down the personality. We need you to—"

"*Once personality sub-type has been chosen during an active flight it cannot be reconfigured until touchdown or space dock,*" the ship said officiously.

"Christ."

"*Let's not have profanity either,*" scolded the ship.

Lexie turned to Mugabe. The prophet's eyes were closed, his body shaking with suppressed laughter. Fire and Fodder burst out laughing, shoving each other on the shoulders. Dubbs grinned and shook his head. Pickle glared at them all.

"You know I kind of hate every one of you."

"*Manners,*" said *Tin Man*.

Lexie stroked Ahab's faux fur and tried not to laugh too. In that she failed utterly.

"*Oh, look, we're about to exit the atmosphere. Let's all try to have a lovely trip.*"

Tin Man broke through the skin of the Earth's atmosphere and headed toward the far side of the moon where the least used transduction deck swung in slow geostationary orbit. The anti-grav kicked in and Pickle dialed it to almost Earth normal.

42

They'd had to take off in such a hurry that Mugabe had little time to run an integrity check on the star drive or the EMF field controlling their anti-gravity system. The Xing-Reilly star drive was old, but he'd ensured that they used the newest parts so they could reconstruct it without alarming the Flock. It had worked during ground checks, but the real test was now, as it moved through space.

The same applied to their anti-grav tech. AG had come a long way since initial contact with the Flock all those generations ago. Demonstrating the universality of physics, one of the Flock's previous servant species had already discovered the elements of Hawking radiation first promulgated by a genius in a wheelchair in ancient 1970s Earth. The Hawking Radiation allowed for the lashing of the black holes, and with the fine tuning of an Abraham-Lorenz electromagnetic field, they were able to create the means for the black hole to not only travel with the ship but also provide gravity for those inside. The gravity could be adjusted for more or less of Earth normal. Aboard ship, 60 percent Earth normal seemed to be the most efficient setting and allowed for ease of movement without feeling the unneeded weight.

Establishing gravity in a spaceborne ship was more dangerous than FTL. Any loss of field containment could unleash the power of the black hole and literally eat them from the inside out.

Mugabe had spent several years wrangling black holes near the Oord cloud from ships that had either wrecked, lost cohesion of the EMF fields, or been the victims of a battle. Such efforts were akin to surfing the corona of a star—they weren't for the faint of heart.

"Coming up on our exit in under a couple of hours," said Pickle, who had familiarized himself with the navigation systems over the last several minutes.

"*Two point four hours,*" corrected *Tin Man*.

"That long?" Lexie squatted between the two cockpit chairs. Mugabe seemed to be dozing, or perhaps praying, in the pilot's seat. "I thought transduction was faster."

"Transduction is fast," Pickle said. "But this isn't supposed to be a fast ship."

"So, we're fleeing at a leisurely pace?"

Pickle snorted. "We're going just under the top speed for what's safe."

"We're away from Earth," said Lexie. "Why keep the brakes on now?"

"Look at the forward scanner. Screen three. See that?" Pickle reached over and tapped some green dots on one of the monitors that was positioned where the windscreen of a hovercar would be.

"Birds?" she asked.

"Birds," Pickle replied.

"*Birds is a derogatory term for members of the Flock species,*" said the ship.

"Bite my nutsack."

"*I am unable to perform the command!*" said the AI, and then it fell silent.

To Pickle, Lexie said, "Can you tell what kind of Flock ships they are? They just look like blobs."

She had only a passing familiarity with space-based scanners. She knew that each Deck had a variety of cameras, telescopes, and sensors—even before the Flock commandeered them—because space was big but it wasn't empty. There were uncountable pieces of debris, asteroids of all kinds, wreckage of old satellites, and other space junk. Nav systems on all modern spacecraft could steer around them if they knew about the obstacles, so critical traffic feeds were funneled back through the decks to telemetry satellites at launch points, and also fed to crafts in passage.

Pickle braced himself, teeth gritted, and asked the ship. "*Tin Man*, can you identify the ships on scanner three?"

"*Please?*"

He glared at the speaker, then at Lexie. "Where did you get the command computer?"

"From a third-generation diplomatic training simulator," Lexie said. "It's the only one I had access to."

"So, what you are telling me is that we have a command computer that wants us to maintain our decorum?"

"I think that's the case."

"And words like nutsack?"

"*Is not a proper communication method,*" said the computer.

"Fuck me," Pickle complained.

"*I am unable to perform the command.*"

Pickle seemed to be on the brink of saying something additionally cringe-worthy, but said instead, "*Tin Man*, can you identify the ships on scanner three?"

"*Please?*"

"Please," he said in a way that sounded like it physically hurt to say it.

"*There are three Flock standard patrol vessels,*" said *Tin Man.* "*Each is repurposed from Class C long-range Terran scout craft. Do you want the specifications?*"

"No," said Pickle, then quickly added, "thanks. What about the other five?"

"*They are Flock attack ships rebuilt from Terran Tiger-Shark Mark 22s,*" said the AI. "*Tactical analysis based on incidental log since launch indicates a high probability of either open hostility toward the Flock or criminal activity. I do not judge, of course, but in either case, might I advise taking any course that will not bring you into direct contact with those ships.*"

"You don't say."

"*I literally just did,*" said the AI. "*Though based on your speech patterns and inflection should I assume your comment was meant as sarcasm?*"

Pickle sighed. "Yes."

"*Noted,*" said *Tin Man* waspishly. "*Please, be aware that sarcasm can be misconstrued in mixed company. As for the imminent threat, I recommend a course correction.*"

"That's what I'm doing," Pickle said. "Now hush . . . please."

"What do we do if they catch up to us?" asked Lexie. "Can we fight them?"

Mugabe touched the console. "We have pulse cannons and rocket pods. Some missiles of the kind they use to clear flight-paths through asteroid fields."

"Is that enough?"

The prophet smiled. "I put as many guns on this ship as I could. They'll tax the engine, and the gunports are disguised. We would do well enough in a surprise attack, but we don't have enough of a trained crew to effectively fight the ship. Our best bet is either a hit-and-run, or to pretend we really *are* a cargo ship and try not to get shot at."

"I like the last part of that plan," said Pickle. "Been shot at enough, thank you."

"*Given the weapons arrays I detect on the Flock fighters,*" said *Tin Man,* "I would highly recommend flight or surrender."

"Shut up," said Dubbs, Fodder, Fire, Mugabe, and Pickle at the same time.

"*Shutting up,*" said the AI with a touch of hurt. "*Though verbal abuse is beneath us all.*"

The AI voice went silent.

The AI was silent.

"Mugabe, you got this?"

"Affirmative," said the pilot without opening his eyes.

"Once we land," said Pickle, "there's a real good chance I may take an axe to that thing."

"Oh, I think it's sweet," said Lexie.

His glare could have stripped the paint off a coal barge.

"Seriously, Pickle," said Lexie, "tell me what's going on."

He took a breath, nodded, and said, "The way it works is the birds monitor traffic going both ways. These transduction tunnels were built by our people a couple of hundred years ago. The Flock's tweaked them, but the mechanics are the same. Luckily, we can tap into the scanners and that's why we can see what's waiting for us, follow me?"

"So far," she offered.

He nodded. "Because of all the mining operations in the asteroid belt, there are a bunch of decks out here. That cluster of ships on scanner three is positioned near the exit of the deck most commonly used for Flock or Flock-approved human transport. Our transponder signature lists us as an unmanned scow that collects salvageable debris for analysis and reuse. What they used to call a trash-picker boat."

"That'll look great in a history book," she said.

"Better than in our obituary, sweetie." He pointed at another screen. "Just don't forget that there are sensors in the deck that stretch out along the energetic highway through our whole journey. A ship of our kind is the equivalent of oxen, lumbering along at a steady pace. If we tried to speed things up, that would ring an alarm. It would ring even louder alarms if we exited into real-space too close to any of the moons of Jupiter itself. We're going to use this deck"—he pointed to screen seven, which showed a single green dot—"way over here as our exit point."

"But . . . that's not even close to our trajectory."

"Sure, and that's the idea. It's in a part of the asteroid field that's been pretty well mined out. Space is big as fuck. You can't scan in every direction. Noncritical areas are swept with scanners but not often. Like shining a tiny jeweler's flashlight in an empty building. You see what the light shows you, but that's a miniscule sliver of what's actually there, you dig?"

"Got it," she said, filing the analogy away.

"So," Pickle continued, "a seemingly unmanned ship like ours exiting a deck over there isn't going to raise eyebrows. Do birds have eyebrows? Come to think of it, I don't actually know."

"They don't," she said quietly.

"Anyway, point is that's about the only place we can exit within reasonable distance to Jupiter without tripping so many alarms that the entire Flock would be waiting for us."

"Okay, important safety tip," said Lexie. "But what does that do to overall flight time?"

"It's not great but not horrible. Once we're outside of the deck and no longer being scanned, we can kick things up a bit."

He patted the console again. "Truth is . . . this old crate is actually supposed to be pretty fast. Mugabe had some fun tinkering with it while we were loading."

"I did," said Mugabe, though he still looked asleep.

"Won't our increased speed at that point trip alarms?" asked Lexie. "I mean . . . can we slip past them?"

Pickle gave her a pitying look. "Do you mean are we fast enough? Yes, as long as nothing falls off. Like the stardrive, for instance. This baby is being held together by hopes and prayers, honey. Can't you smell the adhesive holding her joints together? And the old mildew from Terran storage?"

"You really know how to put a gal at ease, Pickle."

"Setting expectations," Pickle said with a shrug.

"We have all the work Finney did as well," said Lexie. "Before he died."

"We're not going to let his death go to waste," Pickle assured her. "Before Mugabe was a prophet of the fortune cookie, he worked on plenty of ships."

"I heard that," murmured the pilot, still not looking at them.

"No offense," said Pickle.

"None taken."

Pickle looked amused. To Lexie, he said, "Evidently you did a great job, Lex. Fast, yes. Strong, yes. The Resistance scavengers must have gotten everything on your shopping list, but those parts came from other old ships. For obvious reasons we were never able to do any test flights or shakedown runs. I know you did the best with what you had, and Mugabe tweaked what he was able to tweak."

"Swell."

"Seriously, though," Pickle said, "even if we could risk going to full speed, we have more to worry about than the ass falling off of this bucket."

As if a reply, a sudden deep shudder rippled through the decking.

"Sorry, old girl," he said, stroking the consoling in a soothing manner. "Didn't mean to offend."

The shudder passed and the ship kept moving along the transduction stream.

Lexie eyed the console dubiously. "Was that the AI sulking or is something wrong with the ship?"

"My guess," said Pickle, "is that it's a bit of both."

"Swell," Lexie repeated. "Whatever it is, it seems to be making our flight path a bit erratic. Isn't that going to attract attention?"

"The key thing to remember," Pickle replied, "is that the birds are paranoid but unimaginative. If we look like a duck and quack like a duck . . ."

"Got it," she said. "But at the risk of more sarcasm, won't the birds pick us up on scanners when we approach the target?"

Eyes closed, Mugabe gave her a devious grin. "Tell her about Screwball."

"What's that?" asked Lexie.

Pickle fished in his shirt pocket and brought out a slender piece of plastic. A data slip.

"This is our version of a secret weapon," he said. "Once we get closer to Jupiter the automated security systems in their satellite network will ping us and ask for ID. That's when we send this. It'll read like a standard ID reply that a boat of the kind we're *supposed* to be would send, but that's only a shell. Written into that data is a screwtape virus that will have a little fun with their systems."

She took the slip and examined it. "How do we even *have* this?"

Pickle grinned. "Hey, you're not the only brainiac the

Resistance has. They have a couple of small cells that are crammed with nerds."

"Geez, man," said Fodder, "do you know where *every* cell is?"

Pickle snorted. "Hardly. But I'm wired in pretty deeply."

"Be a real clusterfuck if you got caught and sent to one of their interrogation camps."

"Yes, thank you," said Pickle. "I wasn't nearly stressed enough before, so that's just the kick in the balls I needed."

"Sorry, man," she said, "just going for a perspective check."

"I can tell you what to do with your perspective," muttered Pickle.

Fodder caught Lexie watching and gave her a sly wink.

"Getting back to an adult conversation," said Pickle. He waggled the data slip. "The cell that made this is mostly computer code-monkeys and a psychopath of a security systems guy. They've been coming up with all kinds of goodies for data sabotage. And, in case you've been sweating it, sugar, another of those super-geeks will be scrubbing our backtrail. We will be officially dead. In fact, you died in that explosion earlier today."

"The rookery on the edge of town?"

"Yup."

"Wait," she cried, alarmed, "are you saying that was ours? That the Resistance did it?"

"What?" Pickle laughed. "God, no. You can blame that on some Dreamer whack-job. But the plan was to take any large-scale industrial accident, reactor explosion, or terrorist attack that happened around the time we got our go-order and use it as cover for our escape. That, along with Finney's efforts, created the perfect story to hide our tracks. We have teams ready to use stuff like that for clean-ups."

"But how will they sell it?"

"Easy-peasy. Remember when they took those DNA samples

when you joined the Resistance? Well, one of our cells is a genetics bio-grow lab. They've cloned you."

"They *what*?"

"Not with consciousness," interjected Mugabe.

"Yeah," agreed Pickle, "Don't look so shocked, Lex. They made a body from another cell so that your remains will be properly identified."

"That's disgusting."

"It's practical."

"But the Flock came to my apartment," protested Lexie. "They were going to arrest me for treason. What about that?"

"By now that will all be cleaned up," said Pickle. "That was unexpected, but we have a lot of people working on contingencies, and action teams ready to roll at the snap of fingers. They'll send in a crew and there will be no traces left. Even the damage from gunfire will be repaired. A bit of fast-drying plaster, some paint, and boom! It'll be up to the Flock to figure out what happened. After all, it'll look like you died shortly after you left work. A heroic but tragic death as a concerned citizen tried to help search through the ruins of that rookery. Don't ask me for specific details, though, because that's something the other cell will figure out *in situ*. We have people in emergency services, so they'll finesse it."

"Your body too?"

"Nah," said Pickle. "I'm easier. I live underground. They cloned me too. They let me choose my own death, so I'll have had a coronary while in bed with a 'bot.'"

"A sex bot?" She rolled her eyes. "Seriously?"

"Oh, stop clutching your pearls. It's a set-up."

Lexie turned and looked at the closed hatch behind them. "What about the others?"

Pickle shook his head. "Fire and Fodder live in the Bottoms.

No one down there matters to the Flock. Besides, no one knows they came up into the sun."

"As for me," said Mugabe, "I'll self-immolate in protest as a religious statement."

"Another clone?"

Pickle nodded. "They're very handy."

Lexie chewed her lip thoughtfully for a moment. "And Dubbs?"

"I was told they'd work something out for him. Same kind of thing." Pickle paused and looked at her. "Look, kiddo, don't sweat it. We have people for that, and they're really good. The fact that you haven't heard of anything like this in the news is proof that they know how to cover their trails, because we've done it a lot. Besides, we have more important fish to fry."

"Yes," she said, "we do."

They sat in silence for a while. There was no video feed to show what the passage through the deck looked like, because it looked like nothing.

43

Fire and Fodder were like a pair of children in the cargo bay. They weren't used to anything close to less than 100 percent of Earth gravity, so the 60 percent Earth normal allowed them to leap and perform complex twists and somersaults over the stacks of crates, laughing every moment they were in motion. It wasn't until they exhausted themselves that they lay back on the deck and stared toward the ceiling.

"Do you believe we're really aboard this ship?" Fodder asked. "It seems like a lifetime from the Bottoms."

Fire turned to her best friend, partner in crime, and lover, propping her head on an elbow. "King Rat wanted us to be part of the liberation. He said that we'd been unknown for so long it was time that the lowest of us do something everyone will know about."

Fodder turned to face Fire, propping her own head up with her hand. Her nails were all black and blue from being slammed and her hands were a discolored a shade of black. "The only way we will become someone who can inspire anyone else is if we survive. Did you see the sunsiders?"

"A squad of Bottom children could take them down."

Fodder chuckled. "A pair of Bottom oldies could do it. These . . . what do you call them . . . team members of ours wouldn't last a day back home."

"Then again, we don't know how to operate in the sun."

"Ain't no sun here anymore. We're in space," Fodder said.

"What I don't understand is where Pickle fits in," said Fire.

"What do you mean? He's the one who hired us."

"Hired would mean we are getting paid." Fire arched an eyebrow.

"Okay then. Recruited us. Is that a better term?"

Fire nodded. "Your eyes get all sparkly when you get mad."

Fodder faked a growl. "I'm not mad. You want to see mad?"

"Maybe," Fire said, glancing back at the closed door. "But back to my question. Lexie is the leader. Mugabe is a pilot and mechanic. Dubbs is important because we can't wake the Sleepers without him. You and I are the muscle."

"I got your muscle," Fodder said, flexing her arm.

Fire lightly shoved her in the shoulder and rolled her eyes. "What about Pickle? What's his specialty?"

"He claims to be a fixer."

"In the Bottoms we're all fixers. King Rat insists that we have more than one skill. We're not just guards and not just combat techs but we also have been trained in every weapon known to man or Flock. Granted, much of that was from VR sims, but because of it we can field strip and use any weapon. Shit, I can field strip an M340 as fast as I can splint a broken leg and bind a sucking chest wound. I don't think Pickle would recognize a sucking chest wound if it hit him between the eyes."

"What is it you're trying to say?" Fodder asked.

Fire rolled onto her back and shook her head. "I don't know what I'm trying to say. It just seemed so easy."

"Which part was easy? Was it the fight in the apartment or in the Bottoms?" Fodder asked.

Fire frowned thoughtfully. "Neither. Both. I don't know. It's just a feeling."

"I'm having a feeling too," Fodder said, sitting up to roll down her suit to expose her breasts.

Fire grinned. "Is that all you think about?"

"I think about killing Flock a lot too. Makes me feel oogy all over."

"Oogy? Is that a technical term?" Fire asked.

"It's Bottoms for 'I want you to get nekkid and touch me all over.'"

"How come I've lived my whole life in the Bottoms and never knew that?" Fire asked.

"Because you've only known me for a few months. Now shut up about Pickle and get over here."

What came next was more spectacular than they could envision. With only 60 percent Earth normal gravity, they could move and do things they couldn't ordinarily do. They enjoyed each other during this moment of privacy, reveling in something they never could have experienced in the Bottoms.

When they were done, they both lay grinning, eyes closed, closer to heaven than they'd ever thought possible. Fodder's head lay in the crux of Fire's shoulder and they both snored gently as dreams of warriors and gods came to life inside of them and a Dreamer whose voice could rattle confidence of a thousand Flock.

44

It moved through the darkness like a shadow, like a thought.

Unseen but not entirely unfelt.

Billions of tons of steel alloys and structural polymers. Engines shielded to hide their heat signatures. Its skin covered with a trillion tiny video panels that took the surrounding vista of stars, planets, and debris and painted them into place so that there was not the slightest distortion. Any eye turned its way saw right through it.

Moving with the grace of a zephyr wind.

Warping space-time with calculated indifference.

It existed in dark space where nothing made a shadow and stars seemed oblivious to its passage.

45

Mugabe looked out into the endless night. The image was distorted, of course, by the combination of the warping effects of the transduction networks and the EMF field, but it was still there. It was impossible not to feel it stretching in all directions forever.

"Something is out there," he said as if in answer to a question no one had asked.

"There are a lot of things out here," said Pickle, keeping one eye on the controls while he used a tiny pair of sonic shears to trim his nails. "Not sure if you heard, holy man, but space isn't exactly empty."

"No, the ship feels very strange," said the prophet, taking no offense. "I can hear it. I can feel it. There's something else out here and I think you know what I mean."

Lexie glanced at the pilot. "What are you talking about."

Mugabe glanced at Pickle. "Tell her."

Pickle gave a long sigh, but then explained that the Resistance astrophysicists had been concerned about some anomalies in terms of gravity. "They think it's either a gravity well or something else. But to make the math work, there would have to be something huge. Smaller than Earth's moon, but bigger than anything else in the solar neighborhood. Which sounds impossible because the moon's mean radius is 1,737.5 kilometers, with a mean diameter of 3,475 kilometers. And its mass is 7.34767309 by 1022 kilograms. Nothing smaller than a fifteenth of that could exert the kind of pull the ship tells me we're feeling."

"*That is correct,*" said *Tin Man*. "*You must have been very good in school.*"

"Please shut up," Pickle said, and the AI voice fell into a palpably sulky silence.

"But there's nothing like that anywhere," Lexie said. "Not on any map of the solar system."

"That we can see," murmured Mugabe. "And yet it might be out there."

"And by 'it,' you mean . . . what exactly?" asked Pickle.

Mugabe looked surprised. "Why . . . *Juggernaut*, of course."

Pickle sighed again. Louder, with drama.

"You say that as if I should know what it is." said Lexie. "So . . . what is this *Juggernaut* thing?"

"It's a myth is what it is," insisted Pickle, tilting his chair back and putting his crossed ankles on the console.

"It's real," said Mugabe.

"What is it?" pressed Lexie.

"The Flock secret weapon," said Mugabe.

"It's horse shit is what it is," scoffed Pickle.

Lexie frowned. "What *kind* of secret weapon?"

"Oh, it's supposed to be this supersecret Flock ship," said Pickle dismissively.

Lexie looked puzzled. "Could a *ship* create a gravity well?"

"If it is a ship of immense power and size with a sufficient enough black hole to power its anti-grav tech," said the prophet.

"It would have to be of unprecedented size. Beyond anything we've ever seen before. Maybe a couple of miles long, with a huge crew. The flagship of a new conquest fleet, perhaps."

"Which is proof that it isn't real," said Pickle. "The birds already conquered everything. They hold the pink slip on the whole galaxy. Where are they going to get such a ship? *Juggernauts-4-Sale*?"

Mugabe gave him a long, steady look. "There are *other* galaxies, my friend."

Lexie began to protest but caught herself. Although no one had ever tried to use transduction tech to bridge the vast gulf between the Milky Way and the closest galaxies, like the Large and Small Magellanic clouds, the Sagittarius Dwarf Elliptical Galaxy, and the Canis Major Dwarf Galaxy, the whole transduction process was difficult enough just going from one star system to another. The first part was sending a ship along a series of established decks and then using a TDSP—a transduction deck ship projector. It was a radical technology build that would send a colony ship laden with engineers and other staff, and with a cargo of parts to build a proper receiver deck.

The science was beyond Lexie's understanding, but a Resistance engineer had explained that the TDSP process used a method that approximated folding space-time. It was incredibly dangerous, and it ruptured enough of the fabric of space around the destination that it could only be used once. Similar ruptures existed everywhere humans had expanded out in the Milky Way. Optimistic projections held that such ruptures would take anywhere from two to fifty thousand years to self-heal.

What this meant was that exploratory ships could be sent via TDSP to uninhabited and unexplored areas that had been found using long-range telescopes. Once the colony ship arrived, the crew—all in protective cryosleep—would be revived and would spend the next couple of years building a proper receiver deck. They would use the equipment brought with them and manufacture the rest using 3D printers. Once completed, more colonists could come through and that part of space would be officially annexed.

It had taken centuries to expand human presence across the Milky Way. Several of these decks had been seized by the Flock because this expansion had crossed into parts of space under their imperial dominion. With those appropriated decks, and using similar tech scavenged from cultures the Flock had conquered, the Birds had been able to replicate it and use the decks to launch their war against mankind.

"So," said Lexie, "this *Juggernaut* thing is a new kind of TDSP colony ship?"

"No," said Pickle. "They don't have that level of sophistication."

"Unless they do," suggested Mugabe. "They've surprised us before."

"Oh, please," said Pickle. He glanced at them, then away.

Mugabe's eyes narrowed at the response, but he seemed to let it go. "But there's more to the *Juggernaut* project," continued Mugabe. "Much more and much worse."

"In what way?" asked Lexie.

"As I said, it seems to be a prototype of a new kind of ship of conquest," said the prophet. "Radical engine design, weapons of unknown power. It's clearly intended to destroy, to smash."

"Nonsense," grumbled Pickle, but Mugabe ignored that.

"The *Juggernaut* was conceived as a weapon for pacification of human populations in rebellion," Mugabe said. "Transporting cargo from the cloud to various parts of the system, we were aware of the possibility of its existence. At first, it was a rumor—almost a legend—but then we began to hear reports of missing space and an immense energy well affecting ships in space."

"There haven't been any large-scale uprisings, though," said Lexie.

"Have there not? Surely, you've heard talk about Brickmoor's World, Horlon's Moon, the Colony Station orbiting Luyten, Teegarden's Star B, and Tau Ceti F."

"I heard about them, sure," said Lexie, "but those weren't rebellions. Luyten colony was wiped out by a solar flare that damaged the terraforming machines and blew out all the satellites. Tau Ceti F was a mutated virus triggered by poor filtration and . . ."

Her voice trailed off. Mugabe, studying her face, nodded.

"You've written about each disaster," he said. "I watch the news. You shared the story the Flock concocted to hide what they have been doing—testing their weapon."

Pickle snorted. "Oh, so now you're saying this *Juggernaut* bullshit can generate solar flares and create plagues?"

"Not at all," said Mugabe, sitting back on his heels. "I think they used some kind of weapon on colonies that had begun uprisings, picking those farthest from any kind of trade routes. The solar flare, virus, volcanoes, and other catastrophes are fiction fed to the public through the office of propaganda. Why do you think those areas are now designated as quarantine zones?" He laughed. "People on Earth and the other colonies only know what they are told."

"Through me and people like me," said Lexie.

Mugabe nodded.

"I'm calling bullshit on all of this," said Pickle. "You're trying to blame Lexie for a conspiracy theory that holds no scientific water."

"Does it not?" asked Mugabe.

"Not sure how else I need to phrase it, holy man," said Pickle with irritation, "but the birds are scavengers. They are not innovators."

"They have had two centuries to study human innovation," said Mugabe.

"Even so."

"No, Pickle," said Lexie, "I think I see where Mugabe is going with this. Not saying I believe in this *Juggernaut* thing, but I can make a case for reasonable doubt."

"Oh, I can't wait to hear this," Pickle said, trying to stand up, then deciding to sit back down.

"Before the HEs were introduced near the end of the war," she explained, "the general public had no clue about how far into developmental and evolutionary genetic manipulation we'd gotten. Alexander included scores of articles written by top molecular biologists about the impossibility of actually *forcing* test subjects to the next level *up* in evolution. But the HEs are proof those top scientists were wrong. It also proved that the black-site Department of Defense labs were farther out on the bleeding edge of technological development. Beyond beyond. What, then, makes it such a stretch that the birds found and expanded upon other kinds of research? After all, they have access to everything of ours."

"They didn't get the HE stuff," countered Pickle.

"As far as we know," said Mugabe. "The Raptors are themselves products of genetic manipulation. If the Flock obtained bulk research from Defense Department Black Clouds, then there could be Flock labs working on the next generation of Raptors. Super Raptors."

Pickle shook his head.

Lexie said, "Most of the HE stuff was restricted from the Flock even after we turned over most of the rest of our infrastructure. But then they conquered us. They own everything now. Since then, they've had fourteen years to mine all of our secrets. Not just the HE science but transduction science and radical new ship and weapons designs."

"Sorry, kiddo," said Pickle, "but I just don't buy it."

She gave him a hard smile that carried with it her dismay of her own part in the possible cover up. "You don't have to believe it for it to be true."

And that was the end of that conversation. Mugabe gave them both an enigmatic smile and faded back to the cargo bay. Lexie and Pickle exchanged a look, eyebrows raised, but neither said another word.

46

"Line?"

"Clear," said Micah. "Day code?"

The voice on the other end of the call was a stranger. A younger female voice with an Austrian accent.

"Sailfish."

"And the other thing?"

"Moonbeam."

"Confirmed," said Micah. He didn't know her, but the codes were right. "Report."

"Deck forty-one has logged the passage of a class-eight cargo ship."

The line went dead.

Lulu looked up from her workstation, which was tucked into a corner of their shared suite. "Who was that?"

"A friend," he said, using the shorthand that meant someone in the Resistance.

"Good news or bad?"

"Good," he said. "I hope."

47

The Eldest entered a small chamber—a private communication egg—that self-sealed behind him. Once he was settled, he used the holographic keyboard to make a series of calls that he did not want all the other Elders to overhear. Those who needed to know already knew. Those who were far less important to his own agenda would find out just a little too late.

The first call was to an admiral belonging to his own Privilege who was an old and trusted friend as well as a blood cousin. The admiral had a beak disfigured by scars won in combat, and one eye that was milky and blind.

After the brief formal and familial greetings, the Eldest said, "Some of your senior staff are still in the Paris Metroplex."

"Yes," said the admiral.

"Will they remain there?"

The admiral nodded. "Most, yes."

"They are disposable?"

"Almost all. A few are less so, but we need to be seen taking heavy losses, do we not?"

The Eldest twitched his crest feathers. "We have always

understood each other so well. We might as well have come from the same clutch of eggs."

"In spirit, we have," agreed the admiral.

"When will you leave Paris?" asked the Eldest.

"Very soon, actually. I have a shuttle on its way here to take my command staff offworld."

"And is your fleet massed?"

"Nearly all," said the officer. "A few more ships are inbound."

"What story have you told your captains?"

"Combat exercises in variable gravity. Moving ships and crew in various formations between Earth, Luna, and the space stations, using that new navigational software package. That will justify the number of ships being in orbit. And it gives us some extra fighters as well."

"That's excellent," said the Eldest. "We may well need those fighters."

"You've said that before, cousin," said the admiral, "but you've never explained why. The report I just read said that the historian and her crew made off with an old boat from a museum. A Mercury FastBurner used as a cargo ship, as I understand. Minimal shielding, minimal armament, and a small crew. No ship that size carries its own fighters."

The Eldest nodded. "We will leave that ship to my firstborn and his crew," he said. "As for your fighters . . . we have intelligence that the Resistance has several squadrons of their own. Old and new."

"And given a few days' notice we can bring fifty thousand fighters through the decks." He paused and studied the Eldest with his one good eye. "Ah . . . you really don't want them dead, do you?"

"The Resistance squadrons? Yes. The crew of the historian's ship? No."

"Are you really going to let her find and wake the HEs?"

"Yes."

"Is that wise?"

"For what we might potentially gain?" asked the Eldest. "Yes."

"A lot of Flock will die to see your plan come to fruition."

The old statesman spread his hands. "And what is that when measured against the greater Glory of the Flock? We have lived in fear of the HEs' return for too long. Better to force them into the open and then tear the secrets of their power from them."

"And what of the Dreamers?" asked the admiral. "The rumors are that it is those same HEs who are sending those dreams to terrorists across the galaxy."

"All the more reason to capture them and let our best scientists do their work."

The admiral nodded slowly and, perhaps, a bit reluctantly. But he was family and the Eldest trusted him.

"My fleet will be ready," said the officer. "Always ready."

The Eldest ended the call. He sat in contemplative silence for several minutes, and then made another call. And another.

48

Much later, Pickle and Lexie were alone in the cockpit. He was in his copilot's chair with the controls switched over while Lexie sprawled in Mugabe's chair. Ahab sat in her lap on calming mode and she absentmindedly scratched it behind an ear.

Pickle leaned back in his seat and watched the flowing lines of transduction energy flow past. "Hey, kiddo," he said, "about that *Juggernaut* thing."

"Yes?" said Lexie, pulling away from her thoughts of the last twelve hours.

"You don't actually buy that stuff, do you?"

"I don't know. Mugabe believes it, and as strange as he is, he's pretty sharp."

Pickle glanced over his shoulder to make sure the cockpit door was closed. "He's spooky."

"Doesn't make him wrong."

"Look, kiddo," said Pickle. "We have enough shit to worry about without adding conspiracy theory doom and gloom to the soup."

"Okay, but what if he's right?"

"What if pigs could fly out of my ass?"

She shook her head. "You're an idiot."

"Possibly true. A case could be made," he said, grinning. "But I'm not wrong about *Juggernaut*."

"What makes you so sure?"

"Because I'm a fixer, remember? That's what I do for the Resistance. I find shit out. I'm in a lot of loops. I know most of what goes on. It's what makes me valuable."

"I know, but . . ."

"If there was something like *Juggernaut* actually out here," said Pickle, "don't you think the big brains at the Resistance would have let me know? Especially since they knew I was going with you on this crazy mission. It's impossible to believe that they would send me without clueing me in. Absolutely impossible."

Lexie nodded, taking some comfort from that.

Tin Man flew on and on and on.

"How are your folks doing?" asked Pickle, the question coming out of the blue.

"Good, I hope," said Lexie. "Though I'll feel better if the Resistance in Seoul gets them somewhere safe."

"That's the plan. But I meant . . . how's their health?"

"Oh, you know them. Mom walks five miles a day and Dad's doing Tai Chi all the time. They'll outlive me."

The small joke seemed to hang there between them. Lexie quickly changed the subject.

"How's your family? You have, what, four kids now? Has Millie gotten them out of the Bottoms? I didn't see them when we were there."

"They're being taken care of," said Pickle, though he avoided her eyes.

"Is everything okay at home?"

"Sure," said Pickle. "Life's a freaking peach. My wife and kids, my mom, my two sisters . . . they're all back there. By now they probably think I'm dead."

"Won't someone from the Resistance tell them you're okay?"

"Look," said Pickle, "can we change the subject? Really. Anything else."

"Okaaaay . . ." she asked, drawing it out. "Mind if I ask you a personal question?"

"Sure. Go for it."

"Have you had any dreams?"

He stared at the screens for nearly half a minute before he answered. "Everyone has dreams."

"That's not what I mean."

"I know what you mean, sister," he said, not looking at her. "And I'll say it again. Everyone has dreams."

And that was exactly as far as he would go.

Tin Man flew on.

Mugabe reentered the cockpit and Lexie moved into the jump seat behind him. She watched as he checked the controls and mapped their telemetry. Her thoughts were all over the place, but always seemed to end up back on the mission at hand. Occasionally she'd take surreptitious glances at Pickle. Despite his offhand comments and easygoing patter, he looked like a frightened kid trying to put up a stoic front. He was faking it until he really felt relaxed again.

Good luck with that, thought Lexie.

She stroked Ahab's back and the robot dog snuggled closer.

The rest of the team was no better, she decided. They were all in varying degrees of shock. Savvy and streetwise as Fire and Fodder were, they'd lived in the shadows of the Bottoms these last years. Both were only a little younger than she was—in their early twenties—so their memory of the world before would be limited. She wondered if they had been born into one of the lower rungs of the leisure class or actually belonged to that much smaller population of actual poverty. Despite the pervasive comfort afforded to humans as humble servants when the Flock ran everything, there was still crime, still substance abuse, and—somehow—still poverty. Lexie's own family had been affluent because they were important as teachers, historians, and cultural sophisticates. Before now, Lexie had never quite felt as acutely the gulf between social castes. Her awareness of it made her feel ugly and snobbish and clueless.

She shifted away from that and considered Dubbs. He had an understanding of science and the pragmatism that engendered, but he seemed more at ease around Fire and Fodder. And he looked as freaked out as the others by what had happened.

Even Mugabe looked rattled, and Lexie did not think that was a common thing for the prophet. They were notoriously stoic, but stoicism hardly prepared one for shocking violence or desperate flight.

All of them had risked everything. Maybe at the outset it had seemed like a game to them. A thrilling adventure. But she didn't think that's how they felt about it now. Fire and Fodder, all through the trip to the warehouse, had been talking too much and too fast. Breaking legs for the Rat King was one thing; killing a Flock official and two Raptors was another. If they were ever caught and identified, then the Flock would round up everyone they knew and loved and put them against a wall.

Lexie worried about her parents for that same reason. It would be months or longer before Lexie knew if the Resistance was able to keep her family safe. That gnawed on her heart.

"*Tin Man*," she said, "how much longer before we're in real-space?"

"*One hour and forty-six minutes*," came the prompt reply.

"Thank you."

"*Now you see*," mused the AI, clearly directing its comment to Pickle. "*That's how manners are used.*"

"Fuck off," growled Pickle. "Or would you like me to start tearing wires out of this console."

"*Okay then,*" said *Tin Man*, actually saying the word. "*This is me fucking off now.*"

There was a frigid silence.

Lexie touched Mugabe's arm. "Is it safe to put the ship on autopilot?"

"I'd rather not," he said. "Why?"

"Because I think it's time we had a proper council of war."

"I'd rather not let Tin Maniac drive the boat." Pickle looked around. "Better see if the others can all squeeze in here."

Mugabe grumbled, "It's going to be a tight fit."

"We're all friendly here," Pickle said. "Might as well get to know each other."

49

Lincoln Pohl stood in front of a painting older than most of human history on the cultivated worlds of the system. At least, older than any of the occupation.

The picture had been painted by the artist Titian in 1548. The subject was Sisyphus, who'd been the king of Corinth. Sisyphus had very cleverly tricked the gods numerous times, managing to escape death twice through magnificent deception. In order to prevent him from evading death entirely, Zeus obliged Sisyphus to carry a boulder to the top of a mountain, but it always fell down just before he reached the top.

As far as Lincoln was concerned, Sisyphus represented humanity. They had come close so many times. They had been masters of their own destiny too often. Then they decided to become masters of the universe. Had they stayed in their own little corner, they might not have had an issue. But they'd wanted more. They'd wanted to be greater than they had been, as if they were racing themselves and trying to be taller than a mirror image.

As the Prime Minister of the Parliament of Humans in Exile, Lincoln certainly had the worst—and best—job in the known universe. The planet Leto was similar to Earth, but a quarter of the size. As such, almost all the land mass had been taken over by what was left of humanity. From the bottoms of the cities to the tops, people were eager to return to a way of life they'd only learned about in history vids. As long as the Flock existed, however, they had little chance of succeeding.

The problem with the human race was that they didn't know how to play the long game. Short-term wish fulfillment was the mantra of every living and breathing person of the species. Both their greatest success and the moment of their downfall occurred in 2095 with the discovery of the transduction tunnel, allowing for faster-than-light travel without a propulsion system. Humanity could suddenly origami space into different places rather than swans and tigers and bears.

Decks were created—self-assembling receivers that provided fixed points in space for transduction travel from one point to another. These were sent to over 21,900 planets in the first year alone, with more than 900 of those in the so-called Goldilocks zones, the areas where life as humanity knew it could most easily exist.

And still no contact.

Humans were alone in the universe.

Colonists began to follow the decks.

The Great Expansion had begun.

Then Dr. Kyra Cho invented and patented the first gateway-based communications system. A planet was named after her and the Cho Corporation dominated all communications for the next forty years with their Vox Stellarcom Systems.

Religions were created to explain the unexplainable. The Church of the Endless Spiral, also known as Spiralism, supported that each galaxy had its own deity, all of them revisionist versions of the Judeo-Christian god, with sacred texts appearing that said Earth was the Garden of Eden and angels were from different worlds.

Eighty years later, in 2291, a moon, Fuego, was discovered orbiting an exoplanet "hot-Earth" on which were several bizarre cities and wrecked spacecraft. It was evident that the inhabitants had perished tens of thousands of years ago. Evidence suggested they were insectoid. However, bones were also uncovered from a totally different species—large creatures about the size of ostriches, but with more powerful skeletons and two opposable thumbs on the "hands" at the end of what anatomists conferred must have been wings. The cities and the remains demonstrated evidence of catastrophic damage, and it was hypothesized that the two races came into conflict in a way that destroyed the planet's atmosphere and destabilized its core. It was determined that this damage ultimately led to the destruction of the planet's solitary moon.

By then, the human race had established settlements on 16,022 planets and worlds. Earth had become a leisure planet, with sectors set aside for administrations, stellar courts, museums, and universities. Earth's moon becomes the headquarters of the StarCorps, the branch of the military whose job it was to patrol the settled galaxy via Burners—ultra-fast ships that used the Xing-Reilly Stardrive—a revolutionary form of FTL travel that allowed a ship to create a limited transduction bubble. It wasn't used to go from star to star, but to patrol with great speed between planets within any visited star system.

It was a time of human exceptionalism—an endless summer of content with humans alone in the galaxy.

And then in 2231, the colony of Pharos went dark.

After a brief investigation and the first pitched battle against an alien species, the Flock War began. Whole worlds were dev-astated, but with 3D printing technology, the human race was able to make new battleships at an alarming rate. A draft was established, and human/AI interfaces downloaded knowledge of combat to those just preparing. SpaceCorps staged a massive invasion of what was believed to be the Flock home system but were beat back in what was the largest human defeat in history. The war had turned and the Flock surged forth, taking planet after planet. They appropriated worlds, interrogated prisoners, and learned more about humans than we knew about them.

Then the Flock created their own super warrior called Raptor. Stronger, better, faster, smarter, it could kill humans at an alarming rate.

Humanity was desperate not to become like the skeletal remains of those unknown and unnamed insectoid species on Fuego. Dr. Ingrid Teller, daughter of Chimera Project founder Hans Teller, gave a secret presentation to the Stellar Council's Department of Strategic Planning. She and her team had devel-oped a gene-editing and gene-therapy process to greatly enhance muscle density, intelligence, reaction time, and the brain's ability to process information from the five senses. This enhancement project was kept under wraps because the volunteer subjects were so radically altered that they could no longer be accurately described as *Homo sapiens.*

They were the first generation of forced evolution or *Homo eximius.* She suggested an immediate sanction by the council to apply this tech—along with requisite AI-enhanced sleep learning—to create enhanced soldiers capable of engaging in direct combat with the Flock's Raptors.

She likened the result as being similar to the 300 Spartans versus the Persian Immortals—only in this case, the Raptors were the Spartans and the *Homo eximius* were the Immortals.

After thirty years and two generations of warfare with the Earth systems under constant attack and the likelihood of a ground invasion of Earth, the first teams of *Homo eximius* were deployed against a Raptor ground invasion of the planet Hecate. Hecate was chosen for many reasons, none less important than it had been used as an orphanage for children of soldiers killed in combat. It was a Red Cross world, with few defenses. Three Teams of HE soldiers were sent against several brigades of Raptors. It would go down in history as the Battle of Red World, with the press emphasizing the red of alien blood on the Red Cross world.

Two hundred and eleven Raptors were killed, fifteen of their ships taken, and fifty-four dropships destroyed. Every single Raptor was killed in the battle, except one small scout ship, whose one Raptor crew was allowed to flee in order to carry the news of the battle back to the Nest—the pop culture term for the Flock homeworld.

Only one HE soldier was killed.

Over the next three years, in eleven ground battles against the Raptors, the HE soldiers were victorious. The level of destruction they brought to any battle was so intense that even human news agencies pondered if it wasn't too much. HE pilots proved equally deadly because of implanted AI-learning software that synced with their enhanced reflexes and sensory processing. Within thirteen months the Flock was beaten back from forty-two star systems. The Teller Group's Chimera program was now in constant production, with dozens more of these teams being prepared for a counterattack on the Nest. There were protests against genocide, but the push from the public after the deaths of nine billion humans across that end of the galaxy shouted them down.

Then inexplicably, in 2266, on the first day of the new year the Flock sued for peace.

They claimed that their attacks were both justified and culturally mandated. Humans had incurred into worlds sacred to the Flock and the aliens were only doing what any race would have done to protect their culture.

Their ambassador apologized for all previous enmity and indicated that it had taken this long for them to be able to translate human language and get a perspective on mankind's ethics, religions, customs, etc.

They offered a complete and unconditional surrender.

They offered reparations for the damage done.

Their principal offer was to become a kind of indentured service race for humanity, helping to rebuild, sharing their medical knowledge, etc. They said that they would take on any task that would help humanity rebuild, prosper, and forgive. They'd seen and finally understood that they needed to live side by side with the other living beings of the universe.

And like suckers, humanity fell for it.

Thus began the long process during which the Flock became willing servants to humanity. They disarmed completely. Over the next several decades, they took on every menial job from garbage disposal to boring clerical work. Now that they'd mastered the human language using Vox technology, they became an indispensable and tireless workforce.

A very long time of guarded suspicion and oversight by humans passed without any adverse actions. Because of the loss of threat, the Flock became a mainstay in human everyday existence and became a presence in virtually every aspect of human infrastructure. They never complained, they suffered abuse without protest, and they performed exceptional work.

Then in 2268, during the Treaty of Orion, because there was no more perceived threat, the human government agreed to put its HE program on standby. Then in 2269, after several violent incidents on the part of HE soldiers, the teams of enhanced humans were put into cryosleep. This was done quietly, as part of the armistice between humanity and the Flock. For safety and security's sake, each HE team was put to sleep in facilities scattered throughout the settled worlds. The locations of these were a secret guarded from everyone.

After two centuries, the Flock were so dedicated to managing all aspects of the interstellar infrastructure that mankind didn't need to lift a finger to help themselves. The Flock handled everything. If some new issue arose, they insisted on handling it. Since their appearance and social engagement, the human race had experienced no war. The peace dividend was paid to everyone in the form of enforced leisure, as the necessity to do nothing spread throughout the thousand human worlds and moons.

The only issue was the location of the Sleeper Teams.

The Flock insisted on knowing where they were located, but the Sleepers had vanished from computer databanks. The Flock couldn't find them—the actual locations were protected by unbreakable codes—so the Flock used tapeworms and other software to make database searches for Sleeper/HE information impossible. But it was unnecessary, because by then the public had long forgotten about the Sleepers.

Then in 2466, on the 200th anniversary of the surrender, the long game came to its foregone conclusions.

The Flock rose again. They shut down all decks, wiped out the human fleets, locked all of humanity out of the computer databases, and took down the Vox communication system. A fleet of new Flock Raptor ships swarmed through the settled systems. In the space of eleven days humanity fell and the Flock now ruled all.

Their long game worked.

Humans had become helpless and enslaved.

And they deserved it.

The humans were allowed a Government in Exile on Earth, but with no connection to the rest of the galaxy, it was a laughable construct. The entire idea of a human government was a joke and the Flock allowed it, laughing all the way to their Nest.

"Excuse me, sir?"

Lincoln broke from his reverie. He could still feel the weight of the boulder on his shoulders.

"Yes, Nguyen. What is it?"

"The Flock ambassador is on the line and wants to speak with you."

"About what?"

"He says you have a secret mission to unlock Sleepers. He's not happy about it."

Lincoln turned and regarded his political czar. "I've done nothing of the sort."

"He wants you to know that if the Sleepers are allowed to awaken, then he will have no choice but to destroy the home world."

"Doesn't he know that we aren't involved?"

"I don't think he cares."

Lincoln closed his eyes as he imagined the boulder tumbling back down the hill to the bottom. "Tell him we will stop the awakening."

"How will we do that, sir?"

"We'll send in Special Unit Nine."

"Nine, sir? After our own? Aren't they all crazy?"

"Of course, they are," he snapped. "And of course, I will. I can't have the home world threatened."

Sanchez Nguyen shrunk back and nodded. Then he bowed and hurried out of the room.

Lincoln returned his attention to the painting and willed the man at the bottom of the painted hill to once again pick up the boulder.

50

"What do you know about what we're doing?" Lexie Chow faced her ragtag crew. "I mean about this mission?"

The cargo bay of the old Mercury FastBurner was crammed with all the crates of supplies Mugabe had managed to steal. Weapons—should the HEs actually wake up and not have their own gear. Extra space suits. Weapons for the *Tin Man* crew, including automated sentry guns, small surveillance drones, and even crates of mines that could be deployed via a re-rigged garbage disposal chute to hamper pursuit. There was more stuff than they could possibly use, though its presence was a comfort. The downside was that the cargo bay was crowded, and this mission was intended to find, thaw, and bring back as many as two dozen HEs. The ship already felt claustrophobically cramped.

She looked around at the crew. There were seven, counting herself. Ahab, though he didn't take up very much room. Eight counting *Tin Man*, but Pickle patently refused to include the AI in the conversation.

"We've been briefed," said Dubbs.

Lexie caught Pickle giving a small shake of his head. She replied with the tiniest of nods.

"Tell me what you were told," suggested Lexie.

Dubbs said, "We're going to an unknown location in our system to find one of the teams of HEs in the hopes of waking them and getting them to help us fight the birds."

"Which I personally think is sketchy," said Fire. "I mean, they've been on ice for two hundred years, give or take a decade. How do we know they aren't dead?"

"They speak to us in dreams," said Mugabe.

Fire shook her head. "Oh, come on, don't give me that magic mumbo jumbo crap, man."

"You're not a believer?" Mugabe asked mildly.

"I spent the last fourteen years in the Bottoms," snapped Fire. "If there was a godMorpheus or whateverthen why the fuck didn't he help any of us out?"

Mugabe spread his arms to indicate the ship and crew. "I would say he is."

"Really? After two centuries? What was the All-freaking-Mighty doing all this time? Working on his golf game?"

"Morpheus moves at his own pace and according to his own truths."

"Oh, please," said Fire, making a face.

"Children, behave," scolded Lexie. "Last thing we need is an ideological debate. And that goes double for theological discussions."

"I second that," muttered Fodder. Fire shot her a withering look.

Mugabe nodded but said nothing.

"The abiding theory," said Lexie into the icy silence, "is that the HE teams put into cryosleep are somehow reaching out to people and causing dreams. No, we don't know how or why. Maybe it's some telepathy, maybe it's some tech we don't know about. Hell, maybe it *is* religion. All I know is that it's happening. Dubbs, you're the cryogenics expert, do you have any thoughts?"

Dubbs took a moment on that. "I believe in what I can see and measure," he said carefully. "That said, we don't actually know what the effects of extended cryosleep are. The longest sleep on record prior to the war was three years and forty-six days. That was before the development of transduction decks, when we were sending crews to Neptune and Uranus. And, before you ask, there were no reported incidents of weird dreams. The crew did not recall having dreamed at all, and no one associated with the project reported having dreams of an unusual nature. So, all of this . . .? Well, it's totally uncharted territory. Frankly, I'm not sold on the idea that people in cryosleep can dream, let alone transmit their dreams across space. Show me the science and maybe I'll bite, but so far? I'm leaning toward some other—*any* other—explanation."

"How do you explain the Dreamers, then?" asked Pickle.

"I don't," said Dubbs. "I only know what I see on the news, and there are a lot of wild theories."

"Like it's god's plan," said Fire under her breath.

Mugabe offered her a small smile and said, "God moves in mysterious ways, haven't you heard?"

It was as close to a joke as he had made so far made.

"Then let's add this to the mix and see where it takes us," said Lexie. "The HEs are not ordinary people by any reasonable definition. They were cybernetically and genetically enhanced. It's likely their brain chemistry was altered to accept all those modifications as normal."

"Well," said Fodder, "that's not creepy at all."

"I'd go as far as appalling," said Dubbs under his breath.

"I won't argue with either assessment," said Lexie. "Now here's something you guys don't know. My ancestor, Dr. Alexander Chow, met the same team we're hoping to find. He spoke with them, and also overheard some conversations about them. It was his personal belief that the scientists who accomplished those enhancements may have done a lot more than making the XEs stronger and faster. He believed that they may have forced Jason Horse and the others along the pathway to the next stage of human evolution. After all, that's what the Chimera Project was all about."

"Whoa," said Dubbs. "That's not what I heard. I thought the Chimera Project was for adapting people to terraformed worlds."

"Must be nice to be that naïve," murmured Pickle. Fodder shot him the finger and got an amused wink in reply.

Lexie said, "Yes and no. Adaptive biological restructuring was the public face of Chimera."

Fire raised her hand. "Back up. I don't know what that camera thing is."

"Chimera," corrected Lexie. "In Greek mythology it was an amalgam creature. A fire-breathing monster with a lion's head, a goat's body, and a serpent's tail."

"Cute," said Pickle. "And to think I asked for a pony for Christmas."

Lexie ignored him. "The Chimera Project, launched in 2308, was a highly controversial genetic, surgical, and biomechanical enhancement process developed by Dr. Hans Teller to physically alter colonists to make them better suited to life on the different exoplanets. So, yes, as I said, that much is true. But, like a lot of radical technology, there was another agenda in play. More so after the Flock War began. In 2311, Teller's daughter, Ingrid, gave a secret presentation to the Department of Galactic Defense's Strategic Planning Group. She and her team had developed a gene-editing and gene-therapy process to greatly enhance muscle density, intelligence, reaction time, and the brain's ability to process information from the five senses. They even pioneered a way to radically increase the speed with which the body's muscular functions reacted to nerve conduction, resulting in reflexes that were, for all practical purposes, lightning fast. This enhancement project was kept under wraps because the volunteer subjects were so radically altered that they could no longer be accurately described as *Homo sapiens sapiens*. They were the first generation of "forced evolution" *Homo eximius*Exceptional Human. HEs. Ingrid Teller urged the council to apply this techalong with the AI-enhanced sleep learning— to create soldiers capable of engaging in direct combat with the Flock's Raptors. She likens it to the 300 Spartans and the Persian Immortals."

"I have no idea who either of those last two are," said Fodder. "Spartans? Immortals? Are we back to religious stuff again?"

"Ancient Greek history," explained Pickle. "Stop there and you won't have to sit through Lexie giving you a five-hour lecture on the subject. The shorthand is that the Persians had a big fucking army and should have been able to win any battle through sheer numbers. To make it worse their king had this group of badasses known as the Immortals who basically killed everyone they met. Until, that is, they ran into a group of just three hundred soldiers from Sparta. Those Spartans were trained from birth to be the best of the best of the best, and they handed the Immortals their own asses."

"So . . . they beat the Persian army?" asked Dubbs.

"No. They were eventually slaughtered."

"Well, as pep talks go, that sucks balls," said Fire.

"You're missing the point," said Pickle. "The Spartans were

so fierce that they killed a hell of lot of Persia's top soldiers, and that scared the piss out of the king. Demoralized his whole damn army. And it wound up rallying the rest of the Greek states and they, collectively, won the war."

Lexie beamed at him. "So, you *did* listen?"

"I did," Pickle said. "But, honey bun, you could try and summarize every once in a while."

"There's an old Greek quote," said Lexie with a charming smile. "It goes, 'kiss my ass.'"

Pickle rapped the console. "*Tin Man* would be so disappointed in your language." Then he gave her a grand gesture. "Pray continue."

"Sadly, much of Dr. Teller's notes are missing, eradicated by the Flock before the uprising," said Lexie. "My ancestor was able to somehow obtain bits and pieces, but there are major holes in the body of knowledge. So much so that we can't make any kind of accurate guess as to what has happened to the Sleepers. Most of the senior members of the Resistance seem to think those HEs are either in some kind of semi-waking state despite being frozen"

"Which is impossible," cut in Dubbs. "According to all current understanding of how cryogenics works."

"Noted," she said. "But it doesn't change the fact that several Dreamers have had dreams about the XEs in combat, even to the point of knowing their real names. Not their combat call signs, mind you, but the actual names of some of the Sleepers."

"But people know some of their names," said Fire. "Horse, Short Dog, Pryss . . ."

"As I said, I don't understand how that works," said Lexie.

"How'd *you* find out?" asked Fodder.

Lexie explained about word of mouth handed down generationally in her family, and even then, only to select members who earned great trust. Alexander Chow's caution had become something close to a mania for secrecy, and he wanted future generations to safeguard the knowledge. He had not trusted the Flock at all, and time had proven him right. Lexie told the crew how she'd meticulously pieced together information from within her family legacy and used that to locate the crystal data core in Alexander's snow globe. They all listened, fascinated.

"As far as I have been able to establish," Lexie finished, "that data core is the *only* source of information that has some of the real names of the Sleepers. I know because I've spent the last eleven years going through the Flock computer systems. As a historian I have a remarkable amount of freedom. Covering my tracks was the tricky part, and the Resistance computer experts have been useful in that."

"And you're 100 percent sure the Flock doesn't know where Alpha Wave is?" asked Fodder.

"Yes," said Lexie with more confidence than she felt. "It's one reason I haven't even told you. Also, the Flock may not be brilliant, but they are diligent. It's what made them such excellent civil servants."

"Besides," said Pickle, "you know how those birds like their propaganda. They *know* that people are dreaming of the Sleepers the same way they know names like 'Alpha Wave' and 'Jason Horse' are rallying cries. People are painting them on buildings." He was clearly a happy pickle. "It has to be driving them batshit. If the Flock knew where that team was, they'd have the Sleepers dead and on display on every news cycle, guaranteed."

"I tend to agree," said Mugabe, and Dubbs nodded.

"When are you going to tell us where we are going?" Pickle asked.

Lexie took a deep breath. There was a reason she had waited until they were spaceborne, and Pickle's revealing that the Resistance had been breached by Flock spies proved her carefulness. But now was the time to tell them, so she merely said, "We're going to Io."

Everyone glanced at each other.

"So close," Mugabe all but whispered.

"Sure," said Lexie. "The Flock spent a long time and a lot of effort to expunge all other records, so the fact that any information about the Sleepers is in the public conversation hurts their credibility. So, to answer your question, Fodder, I think we can be reasonably sure that the only people who know the location of Alpha Wave are the two senior members of the Resistance and the six of us right here."

"You can count on it," said Pickle, smiling to himself like a kid who had just received his most wanted present.

"One really good piece of news," added Lexie, "is that the locations of any of the HE teams was *not* in any computer. My ancestor managed to somehow verify where Alpha Wave is, and that's why we're going to Io. But the other teams are missing. We *hope* that if we can revive Alpha Wave, then they'll know where the other teams are placed."

"None of which explains the dreams people are having," insisted Fire.

"We don't have those answers," said Lexie. "So . . . your guess is as good as mine as to how this is happening."

Everyone glanced at Mugabe, who briefly pressed his hands together in a prayerful manner but said nothing. His golden eyes were completely unreadable.

"The bottom line," continued Lexie, "is that something is happening that involves the Sleepers. The people setting off bombs are Dreamers. The few who have left notes behind confirm that they had dreams that inspired them to do what they did."

"Freaky shit," said Fire.

"Even I think so," admitted Mugabe.

"Dreams and all that weird stuff aside," said Fodder, "have you thought past first contact?"

Lexie said, "You mean after we awaken the Sleepers?"

"Yeah."

"I'm sure they'll be happy to be awake," she said.

"Why are you so sure?" Fodder asked. "I mean . . . they live in a dreamland where the truth of the universe is unknown to them, right? Far as they know, they won the war and the rest of humanity lived happily ever after. They have no idea that everything they fought for was for shit."

Lexie opened her mouth to argue, then shut it as she realized Fodder might be right. She'd been so convinced that what she had been doing was right, she hadn't considered another outcome—a sin committed by close-minded historians.

She felt a flush of shame. She'd made the mistake of approaching the Sleepers as prisoners needing to be rescued. Living under the Flock's heavy heel had convinced her that the HEs would bring down the Flock as quickly and efficiently as they had two centuries before. That was sloppy, wishful thinking on her part.

Fuck.

"You make a good point," she said weakly, barely able to meet anyone's eyes. "We don't really know how they'll react."

"Well, that's just frigging swell," sighed Fire.

"But we have to try," insisted Lexie. "What other options do we have?"

The skepticism and disappointment in their eyes after her concession was now overwritten by the naked truth of her question. Everyone looked at one another as an uncomfortable silence grew heavy around them.

"I have another question," Fodder said. "Can you promise us that if we do this, we'll see the Flock gone?"

Pickle winced but said nothing. Mugabe and Dubbs exchanged a look but also remained silent.

Lexie squared her shoulders. "I can't promise anything, Fodder. And to your earlier point, no . . . I don't know if the Sleepers want to be awakened."

"Well hell," said Fodder glumly, "that's not the answer I wanted to hear."

"Oh, for fuck's sake," complained Fire.

"They *do* want to wake," Mugabe said. "They have told me in my dreams."

Pickle closed his eyes for a moment. He seemed to be biting back several different sarcastic comments.

Lexie studied the prophet. "Have they told you what they'll do once they're awake?"

Mugabe nodded. "They said they will finish what they started before they were forced to stop."

Lexie sighed. "I wish I could trust that this is real, that it's the truth."

Mugabe spread his hands but said nothing more.

"Back to first contact," Dubbs pressed. "What will you *say* when they wake? I mean, the news is going to hit them pretty hard, don't you think? They thought they were going to sleep for a year at best, right? Now they'll be waking up in a world where everyone they knew is dead. Family, friends . . . everyone. And everything they fought for was for nothing. We *handed* the galaxy over to the Flock. We disbanded the military, and once the Flock rebelled, they shut down the Vox system and commandeered the decks. They'll be waking up with no real chain of command, no support or logistics. Just us and who the fuck are we? Two leg-breakers, a prophet, a cryogenics tech, a book nerd, and whatever the hell Pickle is. They'll probably get pissed that we woke them up to what has to be the worst odds in the history of armed combat. What will you do, Lexie? How will that make any sense to them? Do you at least have a plan?"

Lexie felt trapped by the logic of Dubbs's questions. She felt her face burn. But she knew that everyone was counting on her, so she took an extra moment to make sure that her voice did not betray her own doubts.

"The plan is to wake Jason Horse first," said Lexie levelly. "He was—*is*—the leader of Alpha Wave. We'll explain things to him and ease him down from any emotional reactions. Once he's up to speed, most likely he'll know best how to deal with the rest of his team."

"That will be badass," said Fodder, breaking the tension of the moment. "Jason Horse and his superhuman team of Flock killers. That'll be epic. Ever since the first Dreamers started talking, Horse and the others have been legend. They're rock stars. Even at the bottom of the cities in the deepest holes in the ghettos, kids know about Alpha Wave. You see kids playing them."

Dubbs nodded. "Don't forget that the Flock knows too."

"They know and they're *afraid*," agreed Lexie, leaning on it. "It means that they see this as a real threat. Maybe more so than we do."

"It also means they'll be coming for us," Dubbs said.

"Sure," said Pickle, stepping in. "Eventually, yes. But the Resistance isn't going to make that easy for them. As of right now, the Flock thinks that each of us is dead. The team that went to Lexie's apartment will never be found. And the birds we killed at the warehouse can't tell anyone anything." He cut a look at Fire. "Before you ask, one of our geeks uploaded a virus to the security cams at the warehouse. All the birds are going to get in playback is forty minutes of static and a high-pitched squeal that'll give them migraines."

"That's comforting," said Dubbs, meaning it.

"We still have to get past the Flock out here," said Fire. "And get to Io, wake those icicles, and then get the hell out of there." She waved her hands around. "And we're driving an antique piece of crap that's slower than my grandmother."

Mugabe placed his hand on the console. "Oh ye of little faith."

"What if we get into a dogfight?" asked Fire. "I didn't see any cannons. What are we going to use? Harsh language?"

"Just because you did not see guns, little sister," said Mugabe, "it doesn't mean they are not there. We needed to *look* the part, and so that's how I built her. But, trust me, she's faster than anything bigger, and bigger than anything faster. And I think she will surprise you."

"For real?" asked Fodder. "*This* . . . boat?"

"This ship is blessed," he said. "Perhaps you could all try to have a little bit of faith in her."

No one said a word to that. Mugabe smiled anyway.

51

Io was one of those moons where you'd never hide a thing, Lexie mused. It was too open. Too noticeable. Too close to Earth.

It had been discovered by Galileo over eight hundred years ago. That moon had been in the night sky and in the mind of humans for centuries along with its sisters, Calisto, Europa, and Ganymede. Io was the least habitable of them all, also known as the Volcano Moon.

"And we're headed right there," she murmured.

"What was that?" asked Dubbs.

"Nothing."

On the big viewscreen, the moon rose from a colorless dot to a yellow globe. Its surface was dotted with shadowy caves, jagged mountains, and the angry red of active volcanoes. There were no known human settlements, only automated stations for gathering data and relaying comms signals to the other moons and the thousands of satellites that ringed the gas giant.

Fire and Fodder were in the hold, helping Pickle with the gear they'd need to trek through that hostile atmosphere. Dubbs had lingered in the cockpit and leaned past Lexie and Mugabe to peer at Io on the screen. "Well, it certainly looks charming. Fiery volcanoes. Very comforting."

"It gets better," said Lexie. "The atmosphere is 90 percent sulfur dioxide."

"Very charming. Great vacation spot."

Dubbs had a very, very nice smile, and it was in a very nice face, mused Lexie. She also took note of the fact that he seemed very aware of that smile and used it a bit too much.

Her love life was, at the best of times, hit or miss. Mostly miss. The number of times she had been taken in by a handsome face, a nice body, and boyish charm was dishearteningly high. Scoundrels seemed able to find her no matter how much she tried to hide behind books and artifacts. Dubbs was exactly the kind of man—good looking *and* a scientist—that she usually fell for. Despite a track record of being wined, dined, bedded, and abandoned, she could feel her hormones overriding the safety protocols her logical brain tried to enforce. It pissed her off. A lot.

And yet, those eyes. And dimples. Why the hell did that son of a bitch have to have dimples?

Tin Man's waspish voice interrupted her thoughts.

"*We are approaching the atmosphere.*"

"I understand," said Mugabe.

"*Severe turbulence is certain.*"

"We *know*," growled Pickle, poking his head into the command center. "Why are you telling us this?"

"*Well . . .*" said the AI, drawing it out. "*I was just wondering if you wanted the rest of the crew to die, or at the very least sustain traumatic injuries.*"

"What?"

"*They are in the cargo hold moving supplies,*" said *Tin Man*. "*Given the G-forces we will be—*"

"Fuck," cried Pickle as he sat down in the navigation chair beside Mugabe.

"*Given the circumstances,*" said *Tin Man*, "*I'll overlook that expletive.*"

Pickle punched the comms button. "It's going to be a little bit bumpy. Shipboard gravity is going to zero out, so activate mag-boots if you got 'em, and then strap in and hold on. I don't need you lot bouncing around. Mugabe . . . maybe now's a good time for some prayers."

Mugabe nodded and switched off the autopilot, talking the controls in both hands. Lexie's stomach seemed to grab hold of her spine as the Gs increased as they approached the gravity well that was Io. "The problem with Mercury Class was that they're not really planet-hoppers. Once we hit atmo this is going to get really entertaining."

"How many times have you done this?" asked Dubbs.

Pickle gritted his teeth. "What? Landed on an alien world?"

"Yes."

"For real?"

"Yes."

"Never, genius. I've never been offworld before," confessed Pickle. "Logged a shit ton of hours in simulators. Fourteenth in my class."

Dubbs's face blanched beneath his tan.

Pickle looked over his shoulder. "You'd better strap in too, surfer-boy. Anyway, we have Mugabe at the helm. I'm just backup."

"I already told you I'm not a . . . oh, the hell with it." Dubbs hurried out of the cockpit.

Pickle glanced at Lexie. "Your boyfriend's cute."

"Don't start," she warned. Pickle laughed.

"Anything down there?" Lexie asked. "Any Flock scout ships?"

"Wish I could tell you for sure, sweetie," he said. "This close to Io, the gravity well is blocking any topological folding and our own ions are in the way."

"Meaning?"

"We can't see shit in terms of what might be hidden behind a ridge or in a canyon."

"Well, that's just . . . just . . ."

Pickle laughed. "Oh, shit . . . your face."

She gave him a very cold look. "You know, Pickle, you can be a real asshole at times."

"My mom used to say the same thing," Pickle said. "Look, don't worry. If there was anything hiding down there, we'd have scanned it before we entered the atmosphere."

"You'd better be right about that."

"Guess we'll both find out."

The ship began to judder and shake.

"Okay, Lexie, input the coordinates."

Lexie fished a blue data slip from her shirt pocket and slid it into a slit on the control panel. It took her several tries because the ship was already bumping like crazy. She managed it on the third attempt and the specific location preserved by Alexander Chow flashed onto the main viewscreen. The data was blanketed over a geodetic survey map of a cluster of small, angry-looking volcanoes.

"*This is probably not the best time to tell you,*" said the ship's AI, "*but the changes of hull integrity remaining intact is 42.337 percent. If we explode, I just want to say that's it been a moderate pleasure getting to know you.*"

Pickle, for no good reason at all, burst out laughing.

Tin Man hit the thin envelope of sulfur gasses. Everything that could rattle did so. A lot. The whole cockpit seemed to try and tear itself loose. Lexie clutched Ahab with one hand and she clamped a death-grip on the arm rest with the other. The hull groaned as if in terrible pain. Lexie's heart kept throwing desperate punches against the inside of her chest.

Against the massive G-forces, Pickle turned his head toward her. He was grinning like a ghoul.

"This. Is. *Awesome*," he gasped.

Mugabe finally said a prayer.

The troubled little moon got very big and very ugly, and it did so very fast.

52

"You know what they say," Pickle announced. "Any landing you can walk away from . . ."

Tin Man squatted at a forty-degree angle. Smoke in three different colors curled upward from various parts of the controls. Two of the scanners had gone dark, and two others were twisted so far off true that the only images they sent to the screens were of one another. Another scanner gave a highly detailed image of sand. Although the ship was on the ground, the hull still gave an occasional long and weary groan.

Ahab stared wildly around, his AI clearly unable to select a useful canine response, especially since it had long since been unleashed from its WIF tether. The dog merely looked shocked, and its hair stood out in all directions.

Lexie looked at Pickle. Her hair was as wild as Ahab's, and her eyes kept twitching uncontrollably.

"I hate you," she said. It took three tries to make her mouth work.

Pickle merely smiled. But it was lopsided and there was a flutter in a little muscle in his cheek.

He punched the comms. "Any survivors back there?"

There was a long silence filled only by faint static. Then Fire spoke.

"Fuck you," she said.

Pickle reached over and patted Lexie's arm. "You good?"

"Not in any way that word can be defined."

"*I'm doing tolerably well*," said *Tin Man*. "*Although you didn't ask.*"

"And don't care," said Pickle.

Mugabe loomed beside them as he stood. He clung to the frame to compensate for the moon's miniscule gravity. Sweat beaded on his face. "What have you done to my ship?" he wheezed.

"Could you have done better?" asked Pickle.

The prophet pointed to Ahab. "*He* could have done better."

They paused as an important-looking piece of the console floated serenely by.

"Go check the ship," said Pickle.

Mugabe growled something in a language Pickle could not understand and vanished back into the hold.

"*Tin Man*," snapped Pickle. "Run a full diagnostic analysis."

"*What do you think I'm doing?*" the ship answered tartly.

"Are we okay?" asked Lexie.

Pickle glanced back to make sure no one else was within earshot. Then he leaned toward her. "I sure as hell hope so. Frankly, I'm surprised we didn't explode."

"Gosh," said Lexie, "that's comforting."

Ahab began struggling as his software adjusted to the new reality. Lexie released the straps and let the little robot bounce gently around the cockpit. As soon as she undid her own belts, she felt herself beginning to float. It was not the same as the zero gravity gyms she'd enjoyed as a kid, or the Hi-Fly lounge at the bar she frequented with her friends. That was artificial, and both were designed to simulate the weightlessness of deep space. Here she had some of her actual weight, but so little of it that any movement tended to push her up. It was unsettling, and the *Tin Man*'s tilt made it worse.

"How sure are you that we're in the right place?" she asked.

"Hey, babe, you input the coordinates." Pickle tapped one the remaining active screens. It showed the slopes of a large volcano rising from a relatively flat plane where *Tin Man* sat. Steam rose from fissures in the ground, and a dull, sluggish crosswinds pushed the noxious fumes this way and that. The color palette was in a tone of sickly yellow, poisonous green, and countless shades of gray.

"*If* we found the right volcano," Lexie muttered.

"If we didn't, we'd be sinking into the molten floor as we speak," Pickle said with a touch of asperity. "There're only a few volcanos on all of Io that aren't active."

"How do we know we aren't sinking?" Fire asked, appearing in the hatchway. Dubbs was behind her.

"Because you aren't dead yet," said Pickle.

"We could be, and that," said Fire, pointing to the boiling clouds of smoke outside, "could be hell."

"Am I the only one who packed his optimism?" Pickle wondered aloud.

"Hey, guys," said Dubbs, "what's that over there. Looks metallic."

Lexie leaned forward so sharply that the micro-grav nearly pulled her face-forward into the console. She braced a hand against it and stabbed a finger at the screen. "Can you zoom in?"

Pickle played with a control. The image flickered a few times and once vanished entirely for four disheartening seconds, but then it came back. As the exterior camera tightened its focus they stopped talking. Lexie even stopped breathing.

Set in the dreadful landscape of Io, draped in shadows by the towering volcano, was a hump of rock, and set into that was an airlock. The acid winds had scoured and pitted it, but it was there.

"You have lights?" asked Dubbs in a ghostly whisper.

Pickle turned on the exterior lights and swiveled them toward the airlock.

"There," said Lexie. "See it? There's something above the door. Zoom in."

Mugabe and Fodder joined them, and everyone clustered together, peering through the blowing dust at a metal plate bolted to the steel face. Two letters, one number.

HE-1

"Well fuck me blind and move the furniture," gasped Fodder.

"*That is both disgusting and, frankly, unlikely to help in this—*"

"Shut up!" yelled everyone. Even Ahab barked sharply.

The shipboard AI fell silent.

They sat for a long count of seconds, staring at the airlock.

"Well," said Lexie, "no time like the present."

PART FOUR
WHEN THE SLEEPERS WAKE

"A single event can awaken within us a stranger totally unknown to us. To live is to be slowly born."

—Antoine de Saint-Exupéry

"People sleep peaceably in their beds at night only because rough men stand ready to do violence on their behalf."

—George Orwell

53

Micah Fontenot stood looking out the window of his office high in the Tower 584. It was an old high-rise that had once housed the offices of many of the top designers in the Paris fashion scene. But that was before the Uprising. Now the building was mostly empty, the rooms filled with dusty memories of times that would never come again.

Unless a hell of a lot of dicey things all went well, and those were odds he wouldn't have bet a bent penny on.

Except that he had.

Somewhere above the cloudy blue-white-gray sky, out in the endless black, a handful of lowlife criminals, a state propagandist, a holy man, a rogue scientist with some smudges in his background, and one of his own third-tier fixers were trying to save the world. Except, instead of a quiet exit on a patchwork ship, they were now the most wanted criminals in the solar system.

Hardly the plan.

Hardly something that skewed the odds any way but toward the shit.

And yet . . .

He sipped from a glass of Croizet Cognac Leonie 1858—the most expensive and rarest brandy known to still exist—and tried to look through the sky and into the future.

"You're a million miles away," said a voice behind him.

"A lot farther than that, Lulu."

Lulu Feng came over, leaned a shoulder against the window and studied him. She wore a thin white robe, unbelted, the luxe fabric hanging open so that weak sunlight and gray shadows painted her naked stomach and thighs, darkening the smudge of precisely trimmed pubic hair.

Their bed, reflected in the glass, was a rumpled mess. All of his own clothes lay where they had fallen, and he stood naked, enjoying the cool radiating from the window.

"Don't take this the wrong way, love," said Lulu, tilting her head toward the bed, "but you were pretty far away back there too."

"Yeah," said Micah. "Sorry."

"No, I get it."

He offered her his glass. The brandy was warm from his palms and she leaned her nose into the balloon to inhale the heady vapors. Then she took a small sip to prepare her palate, paused, and took a larger one, letting different parts of her tongue explore the subtleties. She gave him a small nod of approval and handed the glass back.

"That's the good stuff," she said. "What are we celebrating?"

Micah sipped and said, "We know there are spies in the Resistance. We caught eleven of them in the last forty-eight hours."

"Yes, and . . .?"

"I'm not in jail yet. Or on the Flock's gallows."

"And what do you infer from that? That the spies don't know who you are?"

He shook his head. "Either we got them all before they could do more damage . . ."

"Or . . ."

"They're buried deeper than a wood tick and our screeners looked right through them."

Lulu took the cognac back and sipped. A longer sip this time. "So . . . again . . . why are we celebrating?"

"Same reason they played nice music on the deck of the Titanic."

"Titanic?" she asked, giving a small shake of her head.

"Old cruise ship. Water, not space," he said. "They said it was unsinkable, but it hit an iceberg and went down on its first run."

"So this is a celebration of us sinking?"

Micah leaned his forehead against the glass and closed his eyes. "It was a solo pity party before you woke up."

"And you're usually Mr. Optimism."

Lulu came over and laid her cheek on his bare shoulder, looking out at the sky above the Paris Metroplex. Huge cargo ships were lifting into the air beyond a row of Rookeries. Taking tons of furniture out of the city and into the mountains. Leaving more newly built Flock towers empty.

"I don't understand that at all," she said.

Micah opened his eyes, and they watched as one cargo ship after another floated west in utter silence.

"I didn't used to understand it," he said quietly. "I think I do now."

He leaned back and took another sip. It was only then Lulu noticed how badly his hands were shaking.

54

The crew gathered in the cargo bay. Mugabe sealed the interior doors and showed everyone how to put on the bulky space suit. He took pains to familiarize everyone with the various fittings and functions. He was the only one of them who had ever been offworld.

He said, "These are newer models. Good quality. We did not have access to the kind of suits used in exploration EVAs and—"

"What's an EVA?" asked Fodder.

"Extra vehicular activity," explained the mechanic. "What you'd wear if you were going outside while the ship is in space, or on the surface of a planet with no breathable atmosphere."

"Like, say, a moon with nothing to breathe but sulfur dioxide?" Dubbs mused aloud.

Mugabe shrugged. "We work with what we have. Ship parts are hard enough to scavenge, but space suits are more difficult. Remember, most exterior repairs or mining operations are done by robots. The idea was to avoid having to put people in danger. So, I managed to get some older suits. They're bulky and we did not have the kind with large-capacity oxygen tanks. Instead, we have a type of rebreather that will allow your suits to manufacture enough oxygen for about thirty minutes. That should be enough time . . . if we can get that airlock open. If your O2 runs low, then you'll need either to return to the ship, or find an alternate oxygen source."

Lexie nodded. "If this is truly an old HE station, then somewhere inside will be a system for flooding the place with breathable atmosphere."

"Right," agreed Mugabe, "and we can refill the suit tanks from that."

"That's a big 'maybe,'" said Fire.

"You knew the risks before we left, kiddo," said Pickle. He looked around. "Anyone else want to bitch about stuff we can't change? No? Good."

"Dubbs," said Lexie, "do you have all the tools you need to wake the HEs?"

He patted the two heavy pouches on his hips. "And I have the software to help me get access."

"Good."

"Still the same plan," added Dubbs. "Only wake Jason Horse? Or all of them at once?"

Lexie thought about it. "I'll make that decision when we get into that cryo-bay."

"Speaking of that," said Pickle. "Maybe we need to take a moment on that."

"On what?"

"On whether we wake *any* of them," he answered.

"What are you talking about? It's literally why we came here."

"I know, kiddo," said Pickle, "but what if Mugabe's right and the dreams people have been having really are connected to these Sleepers. How do we know it's safe to wake them? What if this mind control thing shouldn't be abruptly cut? Face it,

Lexie, we don't know what will happen if they wake."

"Well, we're going to find out," she said with real force. Then she turned abruptly away.

"Maybe we should take a vote on it," suggested Pickle, his tone more than half sarcastic.

Lexie wheeled and marched right up to him. He was eight inches taller and she had to look up, but she looked with heat. Her jaw jutted out and her eyes blazed. "Listen to me, Pickle. You're the fixer, you put this all together and that's great. But that job ended once we left orbit and hit the first deck. You know who's in charge now? Me. This mission was mine from the beginning. I brought this to the Resistance. I got us all the security data and intel that we needed. I found the location of the first Sleeper facility. And, as chief historian, I am the only person qualified to liaise with people two centuries out of their time. This is my mission and I call the shots."

She stepped back and looked around.

"Does anyone else have am issue with that?"

Fodder folded her arms and shrugged, then shook her head. Dubbs spread his hand, saying in essence that this was never his to decide. Mugabe smiled and bowed his leonine head. Fire looked Lexie up and down and nodded. Lexie turned to Pickle and raised her eyebrows.

He looked at the floor, at the wall, at the door, and at the ceiling. Then he sighed and shook his head. "Sure. Fine. Whatever. It's your show, Lexie."

There was a moment that stretched and stretched, and then, as if there had been no big semi-blowout, dropped right back into the conversation with Mugabe.

"What about guns?" she asked. "Pulse or bullet?"

"Both," said Mugabe. "Take your pick."

"Bring both," said Lexie. "Bring everything you can carry.

And plenty of ammunition."

"If the Flock was anywhere near," said Pickle, "don't you think they'd have put their claws in us by now?"

"Unless they're tracking us somehow in hopes of finding the HEs."

"To what end?" asked Dubbs.

"Propaganda, what else?" replied Lexie. "But the safest version of that is to let us find the place, let us get in, and then swarm us before we can wake the Sleepers. That way they can keep the HEs dormant for transport back to Earth. Then imagine a big public event, broadcast via the Vox network in real time as the HEs—apparently dead, because they'll be frozen in their coffins—are displayed to the public."

"Yeah," said Fire. "Those pigeons would do that."

"And worse," said Lexie. "Once out of the public eye and, essentially *to* the public, then the Sleepers would be whisked away to a black site lab somewhere. For experimentation, dissection, replication through adaptive medicine to create an HE version of Flock." She smiled very prettily. "So, bring *all* the guns. Bring everything that goes boom."

"It's duck-hunting season on Io," said Fire.

"Hell yeah," said Fodder, offering her fist and taking the bump.

"Another thing," said Mubabe. "Since they were military, it's possible there may be an armory in the facility. If so, we can arm the Sleepers."

"Sure," muttered Pickle, "'cause that sounds safe."

Mugabe tapped a pair of stacked cases with his toe. "We'll take these. Sentry guns. Old school, but in good shape. I strip-cleaned them; new coils and software. Full ammo packs, so they'll be heavy to carry."

"I can manage," said Fodder, flexing her huge biceps.

"Besides, gravity isn't much out there."

Mugabe nodded to the crates. "You know how to use them?"

"If it goes *bang*," said Fire, "we know how to use them."

"Excellent," said the prophet. He opened another crate and invited the others to look inside. Pickle peered in and smiled. "Party favors."

The crate was filled with grenades of various kinds, from shock-and-awe stunners to limited range fragmentation—critical in firefights where metal walls were the only thing between life and death—and starbursts, which created a cyclone of fire in a limited area. Fire, Fodder, Pickle, and Mugabe filled pouches with them. Dubbs shook his head.

"Not my thing," said the scientist. "I mean, I can pull a trigger. I've been to laser-tag ranges and all, but stuff like that in my hands just makes me a danger to everyone. No thanks."

Lexie took two of each of the grenades, mostly to have extra supplies in case more experienced fighters needed them. In terms of skill, she was on Dubbs's team.

Mugabe filled two shoulder bags with canary drones and gave one satchel to Fodder. "More to carry."

"I'll manage," said Fodder.

Lexie considered leaving Ahab behind, but the robot dog had a surveillance package known as Mouse in the House, or MH. Ostensibly it was to hunt vermin in a family domicile, but Lexie thought it might have other uses.

"Okay," she said once everyone was sagging under the weight of weapons and equipment.

Mugabe said, "Keep an eye on your O2. Sixty percent is the point of no return. You hit that and you turn around and make your way back to *Tin Man*. Follow your beacons and it'll bring you home."

They all nodded.

"Once you're out of the airlock," Mugabe added. "Visibility will drop to 50 percent. Always keep someone else in sight."

They nodded again, as prim and observant as good children in school.

Lexie smiled. "Then let's go."

55

They passed through *Tin Man*'s airlock and onto the surface of Io.

Pickle launched a pair of surveillance canary drones—re-purposed from old mining models—and hoped their durable polymer shells would last in the caustic atmosphere. The drones sent their video feeds to the holo-screens inside the face shields of the suits.

Because they weren't sure of the metal content of the surface, they disengaged their boots and activated the electronic ballast belts above their utility belts. The gravity of Io was about one eighth that of Earth and they needed to ensure they had enough useful weight to grip the ground. Still, they cheated and each of them only dialed in about 75 percent of earth gravity, making them lighter, leaner, and more agile in the event they needed the advantage.

The HE entrance was a hundred yards away and inside the cone of a volcano that had burned itself out. The steep walls curved around it like the arms of a sleeping giant, with the airlock pressed against the chest. The interior of the volcano was as large as a parade ground and had been flattened long ago by the constant acid wind.

Movement was easy from their ship to the airlock, with each of them skipping several feet at a time above the ground.

"This is kind of wild," said Fodder. "We're not on Earth. I mean . . . it's kind of just catching up to me."

"If you want to prove you're on an alien world, girl," said Pickle, "take your mask off. But be sure to tell us first where to ship the remains."

"You can't possibly be talking to me," said Fodder.

"Tell you what," said Dubbs, managing the conversation, "but even with the wind, it's a lot less difficult than I thought it'd be."

"Yeah," said Fire. "Look, there's that steel wall already."

They hurried to it. The wall in which it was set was curved, the wings acting like natural barriers to slow the wind, and so they all huddled close. Fodder and Fire faced outward, guns ready.

"Mugabe," said Pickle, "you're up. Get us inside."

The prophet stuck his magnetic tool kit to the wall. The exposed steel was three meters tall and four wide. Mugabe quickly removed heavy cables, a highly illegal VaultCracker zetaBOMB designed over a century ago for bank jobs. It came with a sophisticated little scanner. Mugabe did not bother to explain what he was doing. The clock was ticking and the O2 meter on his suit was already shifting toward the two-thirds mark. No one interfered with him, though they each became antsy and nervous as the minutes burned off.

Lexie kept looking around at the bleak and barren nightmare landscape. She tried not to look at the impossible massive arc that cut the throat of the night from side to side. It was the belly of Jupiter. Second largest object in the system after the sun. Thirteen hundred Earths could fit into that giant blob of gas.

Pickle had warned her not to spend too much time looking

at it. It was the biggest thing any human could hope to see from a safe distance, at least in the solar system. The scale was un-imaginable. The mind wasn't wired to process that kind of data. It offended nature as far as the human brain could interpret. It could not be allowed.

It made her feel so small. Not merely in actual proportion, but in relative size. Her power and its. Her significance to the Great All, and its. Her lifespan and its. There was nothing with which to relate.

Lexie stood looking for as long as she could and then turned away, closing her eyes to the soothing and empty darkness.

"Got it," said Mugabe, stepping back and holding his arms wide to clear the others away. The airlock swung outward with no drama, no hissing release of gasses, and no surprises leaping out at them. Fodder, the strongest of the team, grabbed the edge of the thick panel and pulled until there was enough room for their bulky suits to fit in.

"Go, go, go," said Pickle.

They crowded into the inner chamber and Mugabe and Fodder pulled the door shut, shrouding them all in absolute blackness. Everyone switched on their exterior lights. They were in a holding area that was three cubic meters a side.

"There's a panel over here," said Fire, pointing to an old-fashioned computer terminal set into the metal wall next to the inner airlock door.

Lexie was mildly surprised that everything was so pristine. She expected dust and cobwebs, but except for some debris that had blown inside with them, the walls and floor were spotless. Somehow that wasn't as much of a comfort as it should have been. It was like standing inside a newly constructed steel tomb.

Pickle positioned himself in front of the computer terminal and fiddled with the keys. "Man, this stuff is old."

"Can you make it work?" asked Lexie.

"Gimme a sec . . ."

He bent over the terminal, and Lexie had the idea that, despite all the preparations, he wasn't really as savvy about antique computers as he had claimed. But suddenly a row of little lights popped on. He turned to Lexie.

"Okay, babe, let's have the goods."

Lexie opened a stomach pouch and removed *it*. The device. It, too, looked old, but was actually cutting edge. However, it was configured to work with ancient systems like this. Resistance code-writers had spent more than two years on the software that would wake up a military computer system that had been above top secret and proprietary to a covert division of the Department of Galactic Defense.

"If your god is listening, Mugabe," she said, "now would be the time to ask him for a big favor."

"You may take comfort in knowing that I have been saying prayers ever since before we landed on this rock," Mugabe assured her.

The software inside the device connected and uploaded as fast as the old-fashioned terminal would allow. Nine digital numerical displays appeared, but they were all stationary at zero.

"What's it doing?" asked Fodder.

Lexie didn't answer. She, too, was praying. There was a long, ponderously heavy silence as the stationary zeros flickered and flashed. Then suddenly one of them began cycling through all ten digits, in order at first and then randomly. They all watched, transfixed. It took nearly thirty seconds before that first counter stopped on number seven. Immediately the second counter began cycling.

"It's working," said Pickle, sounding both surprised and astounded.

The second counter stopped at four.

The process began to speed up.

Two.

Seven.

Six.

Six.

Lexie held her breath as each number in the facility's security code appeared.

The tenth number—a four—locked into place and immediately lights came on, and then there was a sharp hissing sound above them.

Mugabe held up a hand scanner. His stoic face suddenly split into a huge grin.

"It's oxygenated," he cried, and everyone cheered. Pickle leaned his head against the wall and closed his eyes.

A small display on the terminal counted upward from zero as the O2 filled the cube. When it reached 100 percent, the inner airlock door opened.

Mugabe took a single step out of the airlock, his arm extended with the atmo scanner. Then he lowered it, exhaled a heavy sigh, clipped the scanner onto his belt, and removed his helmet. Everyone watched as he took a few tentative breaths.

"It's safe," he said.

They all shut off their rebreathers, removed their helmets and stood there, panting from nerves and relief. Lexie sniffed the air. It was stale but breathable.

"We're here," she said softly. "It's real, we found it, and we're here."

Tears broke from the corners of her eyes and rolled down her cheeks.

"Thank God," she said. And in that moment, she meant it.

56

They removed their masks and attached them to their utility belts. They all wore modern Level 4 antiballistic body armor: full articulated body suits that could withstand assaults from most projectiles but were susceptible to laser or plasma devices. They'd been modified using technology from previous Terran companies that had arisen during the Great Expansion, such as EZSkinz, ExoMeds, and X-O-Sport technologies with all the applicable benefits.

They were antiques, but they were antiques with character, and given the creative malaise that set in over the last two centuries, there was nothing better. Not even a little.

Each set of armor also had a Personal Acoustic Armor Link Systems, or PAALS, augmentation, which provided them personal acoustic shields that could be attuned to specific frequencies to allow only attacks to penetrate at slower speeds, thus giving the wearer the chance to deflect or move out of the way. By dialing down the ballast belts, they were able to wear the additional armor without being overburdened, something that Dubbs had read about in old Special Operations Field Manuals.

Mugabe and Fodder removed handfuls of canary drones, activated them, and let them fly. The machines went off in all directions. Taking a cue from that, Lexie pulled Ahab from her suit, switched him on, and initiated the Mouse in the House protocol. The little dog switched from happy tail wagging to crouching alertness. She sent it ahead of them. Being larger than the canaries, Ahab had a more sophisticated sensor package.

Almost immediately an alarm went off on Pickle's belt. His face went dead pale. "Oooooooh shit."

"What?" demanded Lexie as everyone clustered around him.

Pickle held up his forearm and tapped the *Mon Tout's* 3D holo-projector. It showed a view of *Tin Man* squatting amid the clouds of abrasive dust. "There goes our way off this moon," he said.

"I don't see anything," said Fodder.

Pickle turned the hologram 180 degrees.

Ingwae Mugabe growled. Fire and Dubbs looked stricken. Fodder's eyes went wide.

A second ship sat just beyond it. Not as big, but strange and dangerous-looking. A fighter of some kind with stealth paneling covering every inch of its hull.

"What *is* that?" Lexie gasped.

Pickle nodded to the display below the hologram. "Has to be Flock," he said.

"I've never seen that hull design," said Mugabe.

"Yeah, well," said Pickle, "it says that our ship's been breached."

"How are they even here?"

"She must have been ghosting us," said Dubbs. "Look at it, that's some new kind of stealth ship, right? He must have landed right behind us."

"So soon?" Lexie asked, panic rising in her chest.

Fire shook her head. "No, no, no. I mean, how'd they know where we were going?"

"Too late to worry about that shit now," said Fodder.

"You're right, kid," said Pickle. "They're here and they're on our ship. Which means we are well and truly fucked."

"No," snapped Lexie despite a dry mouth and the feeling that the room was spinning around her. "We still have a chance."

As they watched, a second Flock ship was landing behind the first. It was bulky, heavy, and had gun ports everywhere.

"A chance?" asked Fire bitterly, pointing. "Really?"

Mugabe growled again. "That's a Flock fast troop transport, the kind with an intersystem ion propulsion drive. Holds up to forty regular Flock or thirty Raptors in full kit."

"Shit on my shoes," groaned Fodder.

"They didn't waste any goddamned time," Fire complained. She added something in mangled English and Spanish. Lexie caught only some of it, but it was foul, painful, and physically improbable and involved whichever Flock laid the eggs of the pilot of that stealth craft.

"Preach it," agreed Fodder.

Lexie cursed, but she knew her words held no force. They were just epithets shouted into the unforgiving winds of circumstance. She shook her head clear and wheeled on the others.

"We can't worry about that now," she barked. "We're out of time. We need to find a way to the cryo-chamber. Dubbs?"

"On it," he said.

"Wait," said Lexie. "We don't have codes for the cryo-chamber."

Dubbs nodded. "You might need to blow it."

"Sure," said Fire, looking happy about it.

"With *small* charges, surfer-boy," warned Pickle. "Let's not blow ourselves off this moon just yet."

"Don't kill us all. Important safety tip. Got it," murmured Fire.

Dubbs unclipped a thermal scanner from his belt, held it up, and turned in a slow circle. "It's this way."

With that he was off, running down a shadowy corridor, with Ahab racing ahead. His movement triggered small lights that popped on as he ran.

Lexie said, "Fire and Fodder, do whatever you can to jam the hatches. Set up the sentry guns. Do it fast. There're a lot of crates around, maybe use some to block the inside of one of the airlocks. That should trigger the atmo failsafe and keep the outer one from opening. Go!"

The two Bottoms enforcers unslung their Super B Shotguns and swapped out the standard magazines for ones marked with a red circle. The rounds in those contained Satan's Toothpicks—tungsten flechettes that looked like tiny pitchforks. They slapped them in hard. Fire clapped Fodder hard on the shoulder.

Fire grinned. "Party time, big girl."

"You know it." Her lover grinned back. They laughed like a couple of juvenile delinquents.

"Pickle and Mugabe, you're with me," Lexie rapped. "Dubbs will need us to guard his back while he works. Let's go. Speed is our friend."

Lexie and the others ran to catch up to the cryogenics expert. But they made it only about fifty meters down the main hall before a heavy explosion rocked the whole facility.

57

Lexie screamed as she was plucked off the ground and hurled farther down the hall. Mugabe grabbed Pickle and pulled him down close to the base of the wall, sheltering his friend with a broad back.

Lexie landed hard but did not allow herself to be confused. She *knew* what was happening. She rolled onto her knees and drew her pistol—an old-fashioned firearm with an extended magazine holding sixty micro-rounds. The gun trembled in her hands. The explosion had sent swirls of dust dancing down in the corridor, obscuring her view.

A recorded voice began shouting.

"There has been a hull breach at airlock one."

"Well, no shit," snarled Pickle. The voice kept repeating it, and then the message abruptly changed.

"Emergency atmo seals engaged."

All Lexie could see was the smoke, but deep within it there was a shimmer. The force shield used to protect the station from explosive decompression, and to keep the lethal atmosphere from the moon from entering.

"That's a huge power drain," said Mugabe desperately. "If there isn't a hard seal, then we're really fighting the clock."

On the other side of the veil of smoke, the two hoodlums opened up, sending molten slugs down the length of the hall. The sound of the sentry guns whirring to life made Lexie feel marginally better. At least this was a fight and not a slaughter.

She staggered to her feet and helped Mugabe pull Pickle upright. The young man's face was streaked with blood that ran from several scalp wounds torn by flying debris.

"You okay?" she asked.

Pickle shook his head like a befuddled dog. "I am not okay in so many ways we don't have time for a summary."

"Can you walk?"

Pickle pushed the others back and stood swaying. He nodded. "Yeah. I think so."

"Can you run?" demanded Lexie.

A stray pulse blast fired by a Flock gun punched through the smoke and struck the wall inches from Pickle's face.

"Fuck right I can run," he said, and proved it. Lexie and Mugabe had to sprint to catch up.

Rounds rang like sideways hail down the corridor behind them. She was gratified to hear the death screeches of some Flock, but then another sound answered the first. A weapon with a higher rate of fire.

They reached a corner around which Dubbs had vanished, and Lexie paused for one moment to look back. The dust was clearing and there, as if showcased by stage lighting, was Fire. She had guns in each hand and was firing. Her face was gray with grit and dust, but she was grinning wildly as she fought.

Suddenly Ahab began barking wildly.

And a split second later Fire's chest *exploded*.

Lexie could not see the Flock soldier who fired it, but the

pulse must have struck her between the shoulder blades. Fire's body arched backward, and her head snapped back as both arms went wide. The blast tore through back and front body armor, melting skin and bone, but the sheer force of it splashed the wall with a gallon of bright blood. Fire's eyes were wide and filed with too much fury to even recognize that she was dead. Her fingers kept twitching on the triggers, filling the corridor with bullets. Even as she fell, one of those rounds found a target—maybe even the Raptor who'd killed her—and its death scream rose above the sirens and the din of battle.

Then the smoke closed around her as she fell.

Fodder's voice—a ghostly wail from within the cloud—rose sharply and then was overwhelmed by the sound of her guns.

Firing.

Firing.

Firing.

"Nooooooo," wailed Fodder. She shifted her gun to one hand and knotted the other around the back collar of Fire's suit. Her eyes burned with pain, and tears rolled down her face. "No, no, no, god no . . ."

But Fire was gone. Fodder held her lover with that one hand, but in every way that mattered, Fire was infinitely beyond her reach. Even so, Fodder did not let go . . . could not let go.

The rest of the team was crouched in relative safety, and she ran backward, firing, stumbling, weeping, cursing, dragging Fire as the pulse rounds burned the air around her. A Rorschach of Fire's blood spattered across her chest, neck, and left cheek.

Mugabe reached out and grabbed Fodder by the shoulder and collar and hauled her to safety, then pivoted and lobbed a grenade down the hall. The world was filled with flames and thunder, and for a moment the alien gunfire slowed.

Lexie knelt beside Fire, hoping that what they all knew was

somehow wrong. But it wasn't. Fire's bright eyes stared back at her, and through her, and through the walls, and deep into eternity.

She realized she'd never seen a dead human before in real life. On news feeds, sure, but not close up. Not in the actual flesh. Fire had been pretty once, before disease and starvation had caused her skin to gray and her teeth to fall out, replaced by ill-fitting dentures. She looked forty but was really twenty. She'd worn silver teeth replacements, something that would have made her popular in the ghetto but indicated her fate in the upper world. The Flock had killed her long ago . . . it had only taken until now for their bullets to arrive.

It stunned her. It hurt Lexie's heart and her mind. With all the death around her in the Paris Metropol—the Flock death squads, public executions, the Dreamers and their bombs—this death somehow made it all more real than it had ever been. This was someone she knew and liked. This was a young woman who should have had her future ahead of her, but now everything that made Fire the person she was had come to a full stop. Over. And with a permanence that terrified Lexie to her core. Fire was not a name in a news story or a historical account. She was not a "hero" mentioned with all the shiniest superlatives on *Radio Free Earth* or the other pirate networks.

This was death. Actual death. It was real. It was ugly. There was blood and snot and entrails and excrement, and all of the other crudities not mentioned in news reports.

"God save my soul," she whispered. "God save us all . . ."

Mugabe drew a strange sign in the air and bowed his head for a moment. "Sleep, sister," he said, "and drift upward to dreamland where the gods and heroes will welcome you with songs of your glory."

Lexie turned away to try and stifle a sob. Dubbs pawed tears from his eyes.

Pickle stood over her and touched Fodder's wrist. "Let her go, sister," he said gently.

Fodder looked at Fire and then at her own bloody fist. It cost her a lot to release that grip, and Lexie's heart broke for her.

Lead bullets slammed and pinged along the corridor walls.

Lexie, momentarily confused, said, "*What*? Who's shooting?"

"Sentry guns," Fodder explained, pounding her bloody fist into her forehead. Her voice was thick with grief. "Deployed both at the entrance, remember?"

"Oh," said Lexie distantly. "Right."

Pickle ducked as pulse blasts sizzled past where they crouched. "Will the PAALS stop them?"

"No idea," said Fodder. "Maybe. Who the fuck cares now?"

"It would be unfortunate if our own sentry guns cut us down," said Mugabe.

Lexie shook her head like a wet dog and blinked her eyes clear. "Fodder . . . how many Flock are there?"

Fodder slowly stared at her bloody hand, then wiped it on her chest. "Lots. Too many, maybe. All of them big-ass Raptors. Different house colors, but a lot of red, and that's scary as fuck. But here's the weird shit—the bird that seems to be calling the shots back there is dressed in white. Not even sure he's a Raptor, though he's pretty big. Something about him . . . I dunno . . . just looking at him scared the piss out of me. I set the sentry guns for full auto, grabbed . . . Fire . . . and hightailed it."

The sentry guns, much like Lexie's handgun, did not fire heavy caliber rounds, but instead used the smaller micro-rounds, which were hollow points with tiny explosive charges. They were less than a fifth the size of a standard round and would not do much damage to walls and airlocks, but anything organic caught in their sights would be torn to pieces. And with such small ammunition, the guns would not run dry anytime soon. Their continuous roar was comforting.

"Those guns will keep them back for a bit," he said. "And they know we have grenades, so even with their grease-shields they'll be cautious as fuck."

"Good work," said Mugabe, touching Fodder's chest over her heart. "Fire would be proud."

Fodder made a gesture as if she was about to slap the prophet's hand away, but then she paused and looked into Mugabe's eyes.

"Yeah," she said. "Thanks."

Lexie turned to the scientist, who was looking at a 3D holo that rotated slowly above his forearm. "Dubbs?" she said. "Anything?"

"Maybe," he replied. "I have old schematics of what the facilities were supposed to look like, but when the engineers arrived on site, they had to build to conform to the limitations of the environment. That said, I'm getting readings on a massive power load several floors down and to the left. Can't be anything else but the mainframes and the cryogenic machinery using that much juice. So, that should be the place where Alpha is, if it's anywhere at all here."

"We saw that sign," Pickle said. "*Homo eximius.* That has to be it, right?"

Dubbs shrugged. "Sure. Maybe. Probably. But I'll believe it when I actually see it."

"What the fuck are we waiting for, then?" asked Fodder as she reached down to grab full magazines from Fire's body. "Those birds are coming."

"If it's not and you are wrong," said Lexie, directing it at Dubbs, "then we'll have to fight through the Flock to get back. And even then, if they're already on *Tin Man* . . ."

"The gods of dreams will grant us passage," Mugabe said.

Fodder snorted. "Then the gods need to give us some damn reinforcements."

Lexie looked at the hologram. "The only reinforcements around are asleep. We need to wake them up."

"Hey," said Pickle, who stood with his head cocked, "the sentry guns are slowing down. Does that mean we won?"

Fodder gave him a pitying look. "They've been firing non-stop. The software's probably just conserving ammunition."

"Hey, guys," called Dubbs urgently, "I think I tricked out the best route. C'mon, we're good."

As if in rebuke to his statement, pale-purple pulse blasts filled the hallway around the bend. The sentry guns barked in protest, but then they fell silent.

"Oh . . . *shit*," breathed Pickle.

"Go," yelled Fodder. "I'll secure the hall. I dare them to come at me now." She flexed her massive arms and let the tears run free. "I need to hunt some fucking birds. For Fire. For her. Goddamn."

"I have your back," said Mugabe.

"You know how to use cornering rounds?" asked Fodder, tapping the rifle the prophet held.

"In theory, yes."

"Then let's entertain these fuckers for a bit." Despite everything, Fodder gave Lexie, Pickle and Dubbs a wild grin. "Haul ass."

The others hauled ass.

58

Hell walked without haste through the complex. Two lieutenants flanked him. Scores of Raptors ran past them, moving in squads of four, all of them heavily armed.

"The second troop ship has landed," said Kig'Ngo-Kepler, one of the lieutenants.

"Send a squad to reinforce the captured ship," said Hell. "Bring the others in. This is a larger complex than we were led to believe. I want every inch of it covered."

"At once," said the officer.

59

Fodder made an adjustment on her rifle and showed the setting to Mugabe, who nodded and did the same. Then Fodder knelt, leaned around the corner, and opened fire. Rounds burst from the muzzle, but instead of firing straight, they took a sudden hard left down the perpendicular hallway. The cornering rounds were amazing. There were screams of pain and surprise from the Flock.

"That's for Fire, you ostrich-looking sons of bitches," roared Fodder.

Lexie had given the Resistance lists of what to steal from the museums, and the cells had manufactured the ammunition somehow. The cornering rounds worked like magic, and they were able to remain in relative safety while they sent death along the facility's corridors searching for flesh. More cries of pain and more screeches filled the smoky air.

"I love this shit," laughed Fodder, her voice still rough with emotion.

But then two small bird-shaped machines came soaring down the hall and Fodder gaped at them. She'd seen them in museums too, but none had been part of Pickle's haul from the museum.

Drone grenades.

The tiny machines had prisms in false eyes, and these shot out scores of narrow targeting lasers. The drones were basically flying proximity mines. It only took one point of contact with something that fit the targeting software and then the target would be painted, and then the drones would chase the target until they closed to an acceptable and lethal blast radius.

"*Fucking run!*" she screamed. She scrambled backward, trying to kill the drones with a quick burst, knowing it would fail, slipping, skidding, turning, running, shoving Mugabe ahead of her.

They ran like hell.

The rest of the team had gone down a flight of stairs that hit a T-junction and split. Fodder hadn't checked to see which turn to make and, in that moment, did not care. She jumped down the last three steps, whirled and took up a firing position to cover Mugabe. They crouched in the shadows and together fired up, praying that the narrow confines of the stairwell would allow them to take out the drones.

60

Lexie and the others ran down halls, around corners, smashing their way through closed doors, found more stairs, and kept descending into the heart of Io.

Lexie was already out of breath. She was so out of her element. Because of her family connection and her ownership of the legendary hard drives of Alexander Chow, she was essentially the savior of humanity. If this all worked. It was a staggering thought that towered miles higher than her ego could perceive. Deep down she knew she wasn't ready for it. Who would be? Who *could* be?

And yet . . . she'd never felt so alive. She felt like that primate with the bone.

As she ran, she couldn't help but grin at the possible glory, of the humanity of it all.

Dubbs raced ahead, holding his forearm with the hovering hologram ahead of him like a beacon of hope. Pickle brought up the rear, casting terrified glances over his shoulder.

"Fodder and Mugabe will hold them off," she panted.

"God, I hope you're right," said Dubbs. "We've been weirdly lucky so far."

"Lucky?" blurted Pickle. "You call *this* lucky?"

Dubbs didn't answer until they reached another door. He initiated a wireless interface with the security scanner and began cycling through the codes.

"Yes," he said coldly, "I think we've been very lucky."

"*How?*" demanded Pickle, dragging a forearm across his brow to mop away sweat.

"Think about it," said the scientist. "We got all of those weapons and equipment from the museum. Mugabe managed to cobble together enough parts—and just the *right* parts—to build *Tin Man* and to retrofit it with guns and missiles and all that stuff. We got off planet without being caught, ran through a deck without being stopped, got here, and got into this facility. And who the hell are we? A book nerd, a mystic, two thugs, me, and whatever the hell you are."

"Utility infielder," said Pickle.

Dubbs didn't smile. "My point is that the statistical probability of a group like ours doing all of this is some really iffy math."

"Maybe Mugabe's gods are really on our side," suggested Pickle.

"Or maybe there's something else in play here," countered Dubbs. He looked at Lexie. "You're the brains behind all of this . . . what do you think?"

But Lexie did not answer. She didn't want to because the same thoughts had been very quietly whispering in her head.

When she didn't reply, Pickle said, "Give me another explanation."

"The birds let us do it," he said.

"What? Oh, come on. That's bullshit. Why in the swirling freaking stars would *they* let us steal a ship, sacrifice a shit load of their top fighters, and risk us finding and waking up the Sleepers?"

Dubbs spent a few minutes studying the scanner. He made no reply.

It was Lexie who spoke.

"I get it," she said.

Both men looked at her.

Pickle said, "Then please enlighten the rest of us. How does anything surfer boy here says makes sense?"

The truth hit her like a missile, and suddenly it was too big to stuff down into the shadows of her mind.

"They wanted us to find the Sleepers," she said.

"Bullshit," protested Pickle.

"No, think about it . . . if you look at it from their perspective, suddenly all of this makes a weird kind of sense. They know the HEs have been hidden somewhere but *they* could never find them. They have spies in the Resistance, so now they know that we *have* found them. Or at least we had a plan."

"Then why didn't they just arrest you straight out?" asked Pickle.

"They had to be sure," said Lexie. "I never shared everything from Alexander Chow's data files with the Resistance. I kept key elements on the device, remember? I never shared it with my cell, or even with you, Pickle. I kept it hidden and I told the Resistance leaders that only I could access the data. That if anyone else tried the device would self-erase, right?"

"Okay, fair enough. That was a smart plan. So what, though?"

"So, they had to let Lexie go find it," said Dubbs. "Which she did."

"Which I did," said Lexie.

"Again, so what?" demanded Pickle. "Why would they risk us waking the Sleepers at all? Those HEs kicked a lot of bird ass back in the day. Wouldn't it be a smarter plan to follow us here and just bomb the fuck out of Io? Once they knew the actual location—this moon—they could use ground penetrating radar to find this place. They could drop a few fusion-3 bombs and turn the base, the Sleepers, and us into little floating particles of who gives a shit?"

Lexie was shaking her head before he finished. "No. They need to *take* the Sleepers. They need this base intact, and maybe they need me alive. They absolutely need the device."

"Why?"

"Figure it out, man," said Dubbs. "There were a whole bunch of HE teams. Even Lexie doesn't know exactly how many. If they kill her and destroy the base, the Sleepers, and the device, then they'll never know where to find the other teams. The Dreamers will keep dreaming—"

"And blowing things up," added Lexie. "He's right, Pickle."

"But we've killed so many of their kind," insisted Pickle.

"So?" asked Dubbs coldly. "Cannon fodder. Acceptable losses. The cost of doing business."

"A battle worth the blood . . ." said Lexie.

"What's that?"

"It's actually part of a quote," she said. "One of the presidents of the old United States said it once. Dwight D. Eisenhower, I think. The full quote has a different meaning. It goes, 'There is no glory in battle worth the blood it costs.' It's a concept the Flock could never embrace because their minds are more like insects than humans. The old histories of the Flock War talked about it all the time. They sacrificed thousands of their own to ensure every victory. In most of those battles we actually killed more of them than they did of us, but they won through sheer numbers and the determination to win at any cost."

"Shit."

"Eisenhower's view is closer to that of most humans. There is a certain point at which the number of deaths makes the victory hollow. You see, we care about morale and the birds don't. Or can't."

"You literally work for their propaganda department," said Pickle. "You sanitize history for them as much as for us."

"Sure, they want to save face, want to be regarded highly. They're vain far more than they're compassionate. They'd have to be since their entire culture and empire is built on what they've scavenged or stolen. They have no real pride, so they construct it, they demand it of us and any other race they've conquered. To get there, though, they endured two centuries of what amounts to slavery. Self-imposed, sure, but slavery nonetheless. All those generations of Flock who lived, worked hard, and died without ever seeing the rewards of what happened after the Uprising. Think about that level of sacrifice—of the government sacrificing their own to win the long game. Now, dial it down to us right here. The three we killed at my apartment, the ones we killed stealing the ship, and however many we killed here on Io. What's that? A couple of dozen? And for what? To stamp out the Sleepers and the Dreamers. To find and destroy the HEs, and maybe take down the Resistance with it. History tells us that we compassionate humans have spent the lives of many, many more of *our* kind in order to win. In the grand scheme of things, the Flock letting us wipe out some Raptors is nothing."

Pickle stared at her, unable to speak.

Dubbs said, "And—no disrespect to Fire or those guys upstairs—but given how easily we've won these different little fights, I'm inclined to think that the Raptors we've encountered are hardly the A-team."

Pickle shook his head. "No, this is nuts. You two are out of your damn minds."

Lexie looked back the way they came. "I hope so," she said, but her tone said something else entirely.

Ahab ran ahead of her, hunting for birds rather than mice.

61

Fodder and Mugabe burned through two magazines each.

But it was a single shot that did the trick. Impossible to say whose shot it was, but a bullet struck a drone in the throat. Maybe one of the flashing lasers had somehow—impossibly—painted the bullet. Maybe it was luck. Maybe it was the Dreaming Gods doling out a splinter of mercy.

The drone exploded into a massive orange fireball. A microsecond later, that blast detonated the other drone. The combined explosion sent shock waves both up and down the stairs, knocking Fodder and Mugabe forty feet down the left corridor. The main force of the blast—and the entire fireball—went up and struck a group of Raptors the second they stepped into the entrance at the top of the stairs. The timing was tragic for the birds. Their grease-shields melted away and the flames consumed five Raptors.

Their screams were the loudest thing Mugabe had ever heard.

He lay there, his body dazed, flash-burned, and hurting; and yet his mind seemed oddly calm and introspective. For a moment he wondered if this was what people meant when they said their entire lives flashed before their eyes.

His did.

Ingwae Mugabe didn't mind being called Prophet or a Child of Morpheus. He *was* one and was proud of it. The entire Mugabe Clan were prophets. When praying, although it had been a little over two hundred years, he could see the *Human Extremis* had evolved into something even more glorious than their initial certification.

It wasn't until he was seven that he was visited in his dreams. At first, he was terrified. He'd heard of the nightmares. They'd make you dream and the evil in the dreams would come true, which was like being possessed. He wanted anything but to lose his individuality with the exception of his clan.

Clan was everything.

And his clan were all prophets.

They left Mars when he was nine and became refugee smugglers in the Oort cloud, ensuring that those being searched for by the Flock could never be found.

He'd prayed aboard ship and his Dreaming God had promised him he would survive this day. Not that he'd ever seen his Dreaming God; that wasn't how it worked. But it gave him visions. It assuaged the eternal fear he held close like a cybernetic pet they give children to manipulate and deconstruct. He'd seen himself on a different ship and sleeping—a future yet to be—which meant that they would succeed in this mission.

Still, he knew he had to do for himself. The Dreaming God was only direction. So, when the others ran, he ran. When the others ducked, he ducked. He was from Mars and a pacifist. He never would have sought the group out except for a dream, and even now he felt that he didn't belong.

The thing was that his loyalty lay with the Dreaming God.

His prophets were known to attack both Flock and human fa-cilities, the decision solely dependent on the vicissitudes of a decision made by a super soldier sending dreams across the galaxy at the speed of dream.

Like the dream he'd had on his naming day. It showed a visiting Earth Human Dignitary evaporating in a spontaneous cloud of DNA. He'd studied all the weapons, both new and old and had determined that he needed to do what had been done back on Earth toward the end of the twentieth century.

The ruling humans on the planet during those dark days had been fond of war, spending most of the money that should have gone to science and discovery on better ways to kill their fellow human beings. Those who had the most money had the tendency to win all the battles, but those they attacked, like many of the downtrodden and forgotten across the known breadth of human space, developed ways to fight against the overwhelming odds.

They couldn't wipe out those who came after them, but they could dissuade them from further assaults. An ancient human race known as the Chinese had long since popularized and de-veloped *Lingchi*—or death from a thousand cuts. Although used for torturing captured enemy soldiers and those who had dis-graced the emperor, *lingchi* could also be a tactic for a smaller force to use against a larger more determined foe.

The thing about those who felt themselves superior was that they felt death by an inferior force was an insult to their pre-supposed destiny. When the Americans first invaded what was then called Iraq, they learned as much when the roads began to explode beneath them. The same events occurred in the then country Afghanistan.

The Russians experienced it in Ukraine and later Poland.

As did the Lunar colonialists when they tried to take Mars.

The death of one soldier, two soldiers, even ten soldiers could be forgotten. But the continual loss of life from the invisible hands of explosive experts became too much for the invaders to accept. They soon discovered reasons not to fight and left the places they had invaded, believing that it was their choice to leave, when in truth, it was the practice of *lingchi* and the unsuitability of those being forced to continually deal with the loss of their soldiers.

Using lessons learned and the knowledge provided by the Dreaming Gods, Mugabe secreted a row of explosives beneath the Martian surface, keyed to specific DNA profiles. It wasn't long before the first of a thousand cuts was sliced, resulting in the explosion of the visiting dignitary.

He had yet to do it again, but if he was to dream it, then he would be forced to do it.

Even if it was one of his companions.

For what the Dreaming Gods shared was more important than any friendship or law.

It was truth and it was universal.

Without knowing he was going to speak, he asked, "Am I dying?"

That question was like a rheostat on his perception, abruptly dialing down the inward reflection and slamming him back into the moment. Into the screams of the burning Flock. That was still happening. All those thoughts that had flashed through his mind had to have consumed no more than a microsecond.

He felt himself return fully to his body. He felt the pain, but it was merely *there.* It was not traumatic enough to define him, which told him that he was not dying.

"F-Fodder?" he called, stammering with shock.

There was a groan, and something moved. Mugabe realized that Fodder was sprawled across him, pinning him to the deck.

The big enforcer pushed away, got to her knees. Then Mugabe saw Fodder's savage face looking down at him. There was blood and grime and burned skin, but there was also a weird joy in the young woman's eyes.

"Tell me you ain't dead," said Fodder.

"I . . . live . . ."

Fodder got to her feet and stood there, huge and indominable against the fire glow on the ceiling. She reached down a blistered hand.

"You just gonna lay there all day or are you gonna help me get more revenge for Fire?"

Mugabe laughed and took the proffered hand.

62

Hell stood at the top of the ruined stairway, capricious breezes funneling the dust up past him. Raptors and parts of Raptors lay everywhere. The walls had become art installations of mayhem, with garish patterns of blood and chunks of unspeakable matter.

Each riser of the staircase was shattered, some completely obliterated. No one of any species could have survived that blast if they were even on the fringes of the blast radius. Not after the detonation of two pigeon drones.

He wondered if the humans had gotten clear or if they were part of the gallery display of grotesque destruction.

A lieutenant of the Raptor detail he had conscripted for this part of his hunt lurked nearby. He was one of the Red House clan, his tunic and cuirass redder still with the blood of his fellows. Hell searched his feelings and decided that he did not care one slender damn.

"Should I send more troops down there?" asked the lieutenant. His deference was forced, and he clearly struggled to keep contempt out of his voice. Hell was amused at his discomfiture.

If all the red clan Raptors were ground to paste during this mission, then he would not shed a single tear.

"Not yet," said Hell.

"But they'll get away—"

"No," said the Flock in white. "They will not."

He touched the comms unit affixed to his cheek.

"Now," he said.

Immediately, the sounds of furious gunfire erupted—distant but potent. They did not come from his milling troops. They were not on that level of the facility at all. This new barrage was somewhere else. Somewhere down there, beyond the shattered stairs, beyond whatever human survivors waited in ambush in the dusty darkness. Those battle sounds came from farther down and deeper inside the facility.

Flock cannot smile, but when they are happy the feathers on their head crests rippled with an unseen wind.

As Hell's did now.

63

Fodder and Mugabe stood together, slapping dust from their clothes, legs shaky, ears half-deafened, faces smeared with blood and grit.

"Weapons check," suggested Fodder, and they did a quick appraisal of the status of their guns and their remaining ammunition. The guns were functional but battered.

Mugabe found his shock rods among the debris. One was bent at a ten-degree angle, the other had a crack running a third of way down its polymer housing. But when he thumbed the controls, the business ends sparked and glowed.

"That's something," said the prophet as he slid them into their thigh holsters. He patted his pockets. "Low on ammunition. Two magazines left."

"Yeah, I've only got one mag left," said Fodder.

They swapped out the partial magazines from their guns with full ones, each putting the partial in the same slot on their belts so they'd remember that one was low.

"One grenade left," said Mugabe.

Fodder shook her head. "I'm out."

They very carefully peered around the corner and up the ruin of the stairs—and immediately pulled back. There were Flock soldiers up there.

"The one in white," said Fodder, keeping her voice down. "What the hell? I thought white was the one color those birds never used."

"I don't know," agreed Mugabe. "Something strange is happening."

The sound of gunfire made them both stiffen and turn. The corridors were dark except for small service lights. From somewhere far along those metal hallways the clear sounds of a battle came rolling toward them.

"Lexie . . ." breathed Fodder.

"The birds found another way in," cried Mugabe.

They glanced once more up the stairs, and then they ran like hell toward the noise of violence and death.

64

Lexie felt panic rising inside her.

They were so close now. So close. But the Flock was already inside the facility. If they disabled *Tin Man*, or worse, destroyed it, then what good could come of awakening the Sleepers? They would be trapped on Io, with the Flock fully aware that they were here and awake.

And what if Jason Horse and his team were damaged from that extended cryosleep? What then?

She fought the tears back as forcefully as she squashed down the scream that tried to tear its way out of her chest. The plan had gone so well that she'd allowed herself to be fooled into thinking it was good luck. But Dubbs was totally right when he suggested that it was part of a subtle Flock plan.

Now she was certain Dubbs was right and that everything she believed in and hoped for was wrong. Worse, one of the people who believed enough in her to risk everything—Fire—was dead. And maybe Fodder and Mugabe too.

Odds were that none of them were going to make it.

And now this.

A second team of Raptors had crawled out of an air vent down on this level. Ahab had sniffed them out in time to give Lexie a few quick barks of warning as the birds opened fire. Pickle looped an arm around Lexie's waist and dragged her down behind a stack of crates. Now she and Pickle were laying down fire from this new threat while Dubbs tried to break into the room where he'd detected the heavy power usage.

None of them were soldiers, but Lexie understood enough about military history to form a basic strategy. One of them would switch on their PAALS so that the other could get ready. Then in between enemy fire, the other would open fire with their M600s and throw thirty or so rounds down the hall, then switch back again. All the while protecting the back of Dubbs, who wasn't working fast enough but working as fast as he could.

The cacophony was deafening. The *ka-sizzles* from the Raptors' plasma guns, and the percussion from their own case-less ammo rifles made the single hallway a sound chamber of impending death. Their principal problem was that every few moments, the Raptors would creep closer, using other stacks of crates as cover as well as their own grease-shields. It was a game of slow chess and Lexie knew she was losing ground and time. She judged that in two more minutes, they'd be on top of each other and then it would be hand-to-hand with three humans against a dozen highly trained and incredibly powerful birdmen stacked up in the corridor.

"Almost there," said Dubbs in a tight voice.

"I'd be fine with you hurrying the hell up," growled Pickles as he swapped out a spent magazine.

"Give me thirty more seconds," begged Dubbs.

Lexie fired at the birds.

"We might not *have* thirty seconds," she said, but the sounds of the pulse rifles drowned her out.

All but one of the Raptors were out of the air duct now. The last lingered there and fired what Lexie thought might be the Flock equivalent of a sniper rifle. Instead of filling the air with pulse blasts, he fired several spaced shots. Each one struck a key stress point on the stacked crates behind which she and Pickle crouched. That was its own frequency of terror.

But then something occurred to Lexie. She paused in her own shooting and looked at the air duct, following its course above and along the ceiling. It ran the entire length of the hallway and branched out to follow side corridors.

"Hey, sweetie," snapped Pickle, "maybe you forgot but we're in an actual firefight. Maybe you want to stop daydreaming and, oh . . . I don't know . . . maybe *fight*?"

"The ducts," she said.

"Yes," he said, "I see the frigging bird in the frigging duct."

"No," she said, pointing upward. "Those ducts go all the way across."

Pickle leaned out, fired several shots, and ducked back quickly as the Flock hammered back with a fusillade. "So what?"

"Why did they come out of the duct all the way over there," she asked. "Why didn't they come out on *both* sides of us?"

"How the hell should I know?"

"But it's—" she began, but a voice cut her off.

"*We're in!*" came Dubbs's cry.

Lexie and Pickle spun to see the door to the HE chamber swinging open.

"Run!" bellowed Dubbs. He rose up, unslinging his rifle. He activated his PAALS and began laying down cover fire.

Pickles bolted and ran and actually dove through the doorway like someone going off a diving board. Flock pulse blasts slammed into the doorframe and two shots chased Pickle inside.

Lexie lingered one moment longer, looking again at the airducts. Something was definitely wrong. She was certain of it.

The Flock poured on the firepower and that drove everything from her head except stark terror.

Lexie Chow activated her PAALS, jammed her rifle against her shoulder as she rose up, burned through an entire magazine that sent the birds ducking for cover, whirled, and ran for the door to where the Sleepers lay waiting.

65

Lexie was the last one in and locked the door behind her. She placed her back to it as her breathing began to return to normal. And stopped.

Her expectations and all her hopes and fears washed up hard against a sea wall of reality. This was it. This was the actual *it*.

The room was big, but failed lighting draped so much of it in dense shadows that it felt close, tight, as claustrophobic as some ancient tomb. Was this what Howard Carter felt when he first entered the tomb of Tutankhamun? Was this the same awe and fear and sense of surreal wonder Omar Habib experienced when he rappelled down into the palace of some alien king on a world so old and distant that even the Flock had no records of it?

The sleep capsules were laid in a long row, like the sarcophagi of priest kings. The crystals and rare metals used in construction gleamed like precious jewels and polished gold. The air scrubbers had not managed to remove all the dust particles, and so these swirled and danced in the air like sprites.

"I . . ." she began, but there were no words in the vast library of her mind with which to construct a thought adequate to the moment.

Lexie walked forward as if floating in the soft rivers of a dream.

The capsules were each ten feet long bolted at one end to a huge central cryogenic control bank. Cables, wires, and hoses of various sizes and incomprehensible purpose snaked from the capsules and tangled along the cold concrete floor. Monitors leaned out over each of the sleepers, their faces filling with streams of data in old fashioned formats—flat digital readouts rather than 3D holographic text models. Somewhere—behind the walls or deep underground—massive engines chugged and whined and hummed. But softly. Very softly, as if they did not want to wake these sleepers.

She stopped by the closest of the capsules. There was a strip of white tape affixed to the curved metal shell just below the glass screen. Her lips moved silently as she read what had been stenciled there.

FIRST SERGEANT JASON HORSE

ALPHA WAVE

Lexie took another half step and stood looking down through the frosted crystal at the man's face. Alexander Chow had written so much about him, even to the point of describing this man, and the account from his diary came back to her with perfect clarity.

"Jason Horse had a powerful face. By that I mean his bone structure was very heavy, with high ledges of cheekbone, a broad and very clear brow, and what a poet might have called a hero's chin or a lantern jaw. Heavy eyebrows over eyes that were unafraid, unconvinced, skeptical, and

*intelligent. I suppose a face like that tends to evoke po-
etic phrasing, and I'm no poet. It's hard in description
to do justice to a face like that. From the moment I first
saw him in the nursery, I knew instantly that here was
someone whose level of personal power dwarfed my own.
In subsequent encounters, it was clear he was likely to
command any room in which he stood, even when in the
presence of his military superiors. But superiority of rank
is subjective; superiority of personality is not."*

None of that really prepared her for actually seeing him. For years Lexie had tried to construct that face in her mind. In other references, Alexander had noted that Horse had a mostly Polynesian face, with the rich complexity of genetics—drawn from various Austronesian backgrounds but with small hints of Western European tumbled into that mix by conqueror-explorers and immigrants. Alexander said that he also felt there was some North American indigenous aspects, though this was pure speculation.

Lexie thought he was the most beautiful man she had ever seen. Regal without doubt, and she wondered if there were, indeed, kings in his ancestral tree. His eyes were almost but not quite closed, and she could see the bottom curve of his irises. Even with the frost on the inside of the glass they were a black so dense it was as if they were polished obsidian.

Her heart was racing nearly out of control because this was the face she saw in her dreams. This was the face she *wore* in her dreams. Like the one she'd dreamed the night before she and her companions fled Earth. Was that only forty hours ago? That seemed impossible.

More impossible still was the fact that *she* had dreamed of being inside the skin, inside the mind, of Jason Horse. Inside the flesh of this killer king, this superhuman thing that had no longer been truly *Homo sapiens sapiens* before he went into the ice. She had no idea what it meant to be *Homo eximius*.

"How did I dream of you?" she murmured.

"What's that?" asked Pickle. His words jolted her, and she turned to see him standing directly behind her.

"What?" she said quickly. "Oh, nothing. Just . . . I mean . . . this is incredible."

Pickle gave her a strange look. "You said something about dreams . . ."

"Did I?" Lexie shook her head. "No. It's nothing."

She moved on to the next tube and saw the name.

PAULA O'NEIL

"Pryss," said Lexie.

Dubbs was further down the line, and he sharply called out, "Oh no!"

Lexie and Pickle hurried over. Even before they reached the scientist, they could see what alarmed him. The digital display above the capsule was black and blank, and there were no ice crystals on the inside of the crystal window. Inside, inside, was a withered husk of a face, all the moisture leeched away over the years. Since the chamber was free of parasites, the flesh was intact, but it had turned to a yellowish parchment stretched tight over a skull shape, the lips peeled back from white teeth.

"What happened?" cried Lexie.

Dubbs shook his head. "I don't know. Some kind of malfunction. Maybe a faulty gasket. The glass cover did not seal properly. Poor bastard died in his sleep."

The name on the capsule was:

ANDRE GASTINEAU

"There's another," said Pickle, pointing to a tube shrouded in shadows beneath a burned-out light.

LEJAN DE WINDT

The corpse was that of a woman, evident from the relative delicacy of the skull, though otherwise it looked barely human.

They moved quickly up and down the row and saw that of the twenty-one capsules, all but seven were dark. Panic rose up inside Lexie's chest. She, Dubbs, and Pickle ran to one after another after another. Seeing dead faces. Withered to terrible caricatures of people, like displays in a museum—mummies or bog people. Not the super soldiers they had once been.

One capsule stopped the three of them and trapped them in a long moment of absolute horror. The name on the capsule was Hiram Gomez, a staff sergeant. But that information barely registered on any of them. Instead, they stared at his face. At what was left of his face. Desiccated hands with fingers curled into claws. Flesh clawed and torn from the cheeks and brow, revealing bone that was likewise gouged. And the eyes . . . they were gone. Ripped to ribbons, burst, destroyed, gouged out of the sockets.

But even that was not the worst thing.

Written on the inside of the crystal in brown letters that had to have once been bright blood were words. They were in reverse, but readable.

Sadly, dreadfully readable.

I AM GOD

GOD IS DEAD

I AM IN HELL

66

Lexie blinked tears from her eyes but was otherwise unable to move.

The horror was a vise that held her fast.

The thought of what that soldier—Hiram Gomez—had gone through. The sheer hell of it. The unimaginable horror. Not only of waking up trapped in the capsule, but of clearly going mad.

I am in hell.

"What *happened* here?" gasped Pickle.

Dubbs stood on the far side of the capsule, looking almost blankly down into the dead man's eyeless face.

"I . . . I don't . . ."

And then he threw back his head and screamed.

It was so abrupt, so sudden, so shockingly loud that it tore cries from Pickle and Lexie. It staggered them both. But Dubbs stood stock still, his legs wide, fists knotted at the end of his outthrust arms, every muscle in his body taut. His mouth was open so wide the skin at the corners split and blood ran down his jaw and along his heaving throat. Veins stood out on his neck and forehead and temples. Blood erupted from his nose and ears. Red tears boiled from his eyes.

The scream was not brief. It endured. It rose and filled the world. It went on and on.

Dubbs's legs buckled, and he dropped down hard onto his knees, still screaming.

Lexie tried to lunge over the capsule and grab him, but she felt herself falling. Falling.

But she did not hit the curved metal of the capsule. Instead she kept on falling, through it, through the floor, through the miles of rock that made up Io. Through absolute darkness and searing lava and then into the airless coldness of space itself.

She fell through forever.

The fact that she could still breathe was of no consequence. She was not even aware of it. All she felt was that plummet. Falling through an eternity of space. Jupiter filled her vision but it whirled away from her, and Lexie continued to hurtle through the void faster and faster. The other planets of the solar system whipped by. Suns flashed into view, and she flew right toward them, passing through their hearts, burning with the impossible heat, and then cooling to ice again as she emerged from the other side.

Time lost all meaning for her. She fell for an hour, a year, centuries. Distance was an equally irrelevant concept. Lexie could feel herself accelerate as if she was a ship traversing a high-speed deck. But it was just her body.

And then she felt herself slowing.

Slowing.

As a world blossomed in front of her.

Huge. Shrouded in clouds that glowed with poisons and radiation. A dying world. She punched through the clouds, her senses flooded with their chemical stink. Below there were vast mountain ranges of jagged rocks—gray and green and black—with diseased jungles below in the clefts. Hairy vines choked the trees and mottled ferns with leaves as long as whales hanging pendulously. Insects whose bodies were warped by the polluted atmosphere, crawled painfully along, chewing on toxic leaves or on the corpses of creatures who lay rotting in the reeds sprouting from rancid swamps.

Her movement slowed, slowed, then stopped, and for a long time Lexie hung there in the sky, tasting the vile air and yet not choking on it. As if her own body and all her senses were overlayed on something else, something *able* to endure this.

Then she saw something move just below her.

It was an animal, but its color was faded, blended with the ugly swirl of browns and greens of the landscape. A limb raised up, trying to reach for the air. For cleaner air. Long taloned fingers scratched at the sky as if somehow it could pull itself from the muck. The arm was muscular but not in any healthy way—with stringy sinews and running sores mottled and distorting it.

Then another limb reached up alongside it, and for a moment Lexie thought it was a second creature—a smaller or younger one. But the limb was not the same. This was stunted, with withered protrusions along one side. They were like long brush bristles and . . .

No.

With a start she realized that this was not a second creature, nor was it a second arm.

It was a *wing.*

And in that moment of understanding, Lexie knew with perfect clarity where she was.

This broken planet, this destroyed place, was the Flock homeworld.

She looked all around, and her perception sharpened so

that the broken mountain peaks revealed themselves as the burned-out shells of titanic towers. Rookeries vastly larger than anything they had built on Earth. Some had to be miles high. Thousands upon thousands of them. And yet every single one was crumbling, their walls pocked with uncountable divots from every kind of gunfire. The slopes of each were littered with bones. Millions upon millions of Flock dead. Crushed and shattered, lying where they had fallen.

Lexie knew it with absolute certainty; just as she knew that this was not where the Flock now lived. This was where they had come from. This was their true place of origin, and it was completely ruined, wrecked . . . destroyed.

By them.

None of the bones below her belonged to any other species.

"They killed themselves," she said aloud, though the voice was not her own. It was a woman's voice, but one she had never heard before. And yet the thought was in her brain, as if she and the stranger within shared the same idea at the same moment. "This is who the Flock are. They overpopulated their world, squandered it, ruined it, and fought to the death over the scraps. This defines them."

Lexie felt her heart twisting in her chest. Part of her—perhaps the real part—felt a bottomless sadness for these creatures. And at the same time there was a loathing for what they had done to one another. For what they had done since survivors of this self-inflicted catastrophe somehow escaped into space. To other worlds.

To Earth.

"This is the future," said her voice. "The future of Earth and all of the worlds on which we live. We are nothing to them but another field of wheat before a plague of locusts."

The arm and wing that clawed at the sky trembled and fell back, exhausted or dead.

Lexie wept.

For them. For Earth. For everything in the path of the Flock.

"You have no idea what's coming," said her voice, and this time it did not mirror a thought in her mind. The voice changed, more fully becoming another consciousness. More stern, deeply bitter.

"Who are you?" begged Lexie.

The voice laughed. So very cold. So angry.

"I am the daughter of Morpheus," said the voice. "I am the wind of war blowing through the stars."

"Are you a Sleeper?" asked Lexie. "Are you Pryss?"

"I . . ." began the voice and it faltered for a moment. "No. I was . . . was . . . Lejan. Yes. That was my name. A long time ago. Before . . . before . . . before I died."

A wave of emotions flooded through Lexie, and in the space of one moment, she felt everything that Lejan de Windt had felt since she lay down in the capsule two hundred and fourteen years ago. She heard the hydraulics of the lid closing. She heard and felt the hiss of chemicals flooding into the capsule. Then the cold. And the dark.

The long dark.

Only . . . not dark enough. The cryogenics had taken her down, but something happened. There were years of nothingness, and Lexie actually felt them too. But even in the darkest, coldest places she could feel. The five senses had not shut down along with the motor cortex. In the tomb of frozen blackness, Lejan had been fully alive, fully sensate.

For *centuries*.

There had been a time of silent screaming. Of praying. Of a waking nightmare beyond what anyone had ever experienced before. Each moment was an eternity; there was an eternity of sensation in every moment.

Since time was meaningless, Lejan did not know when that waking nightmare had become actual dreams.

Those dreams had filled her, consumed her, *become* her.

Even after she died.

Then—only then—did her mind escape the capsule and go roving. Wildly, madly, in all directions at once. The *Homo eximius* transformations increased her cognitive abilities by orders of magnitude, but the ability to process all that incalculable data was beyond what any sane mind could endure.

And so sanity—by any normal definition—was discarded. It was shucked like a chrysalis as something else emerged. The Sleeper giving birth to its higher self. Unnamed and unnameable.

Lexie's mind was inundated by that. It slammed into her as hard as a fist. Like an asteroid striking the earth, it destroyed her. Scattered who she was to the winds. Then gathered up the pieces and crammed them back into Lexie's human mind.

All in one fractured second.

"You have no idea what's coming," whispered Lejan again. "Pray for your soul, Alexandria Chow. Pray that the gods of sleep have mercy for you. For they had none for me."

The world around her exploded.

Every sun in the galaxy exploded.

Every molecule in every fragment of rock and flesh and tree exploded.

Lexie tumbled through the destruction.

Back into her real body. Into the moment. Into the chamber of the Sleepers. She struck the floor and lay there.

And lay there, clawing at her face.

Screaming.

Screaming.

Screaming.

67

In the corridors outside, above . . . closer to the Flock invaders, Mugabe and Fodder sprawled as if dead. Their weapons lay where they had fallen from nerveless fingers. Gun smoke hung in the air, but the echoes of battle had all stopped.

Silence surrounded the two men. But it was an exterior thing. There was no silence in their minds.

Mugabe stood on the crest of a hill that rose above a series of deep valleys. Everywhere he looked, no matter which direction he turned, he saw death. Uncountable bodies were tangled with such extreme ferocity it was clear they had died in terrible pain. In agony that was physical and emotional and spiritual.

He had witnessed it all.

Every shocked twitch of nerve conduction, every wound, every laceration to body and mind. Witnessed it, felt it.

The difference was that he was doomed to watch and *experience. To* know. *To be the witness to the utter and complete fall of mankind and be able to do nothing.*

Nothing.

Except scream.

Forever.

Fodder knelt in blood that was rising like a slow tide. It pumped from Fire's chest in absurd amounts. Not liters, but kiloliters. Impossible amounts of it. The red bubbled from her torn chest, but also spread out from under her, from the entrance wound, and she lay in a lake of it.

The blood filled the corridor from side to side and along its length. Fodder knew this was insane. The blood of fifty elephants wouldn't generate that much volume. Fire kept bleeding, though. Nothing she could do—not bandages or hand compression—could stop it or even slow it. It geysered up between Fodder's fingers and sprayed her face, blinding her. She shook her head to clear her eyes and saw to her horror that the blood was now as high as the tops of her thighs. Fire's entire body was submerged.

"No!" she screamed.

Over and over again.

One floor above, at the top of a flight of stairs, seven Raptors were draped over the steps, over each other. An eighth, slightly smaller, dressed in white, sat with his back to the wall, arms and wings hanging slack, eyes open but without focus or signs of life.

Hell was in hell.

It was not the Flock hell. It was not the lightless underground where their primitive bodies had once wriggled like worms. It was not the bowels of their homeworld. There were no snapping lice or spider-mites. There was no fetid fungi growing on the rotting flesh of five million years of evolutionary muck.

No.

He stood in a church of human design. Vast, though, with Gothic windows arching upward many hundreds of feet.

Larger than anything humans had ever built. Impossibly vast, as if constructed by their gods. No such beings were visible, but Hell felt the ponderous weight of their judgment. He felt the unseen lash of their scorn.

And in the presence of that, he stood small and weak. Helpless. Not forcibly disempowered, but in every way that it could be interpreted, his power simply did not matter. Like the energetic potential of a pebble matched against the weight of a black hole. The scales that calculated each were not even part of the same mathematics.

He turned in a slow circle, looking at the images locked into forever within the stained glass. They were not of Jesus or any figures from Judeo-Christian theology. They were not Hindu gods or aspects of Buddha. There was no formal religion whose saints were depicted there.

Instead, each of the countless stained-glass windows was a soldier. Not human by any stretch. These were giants. Hugely muscular, sinister in aspect, with grim and haughty faces that leered down at him. Specifically, at him. At the scion of a disgraced and colorless Privilege.

At Hell.

Despite being made from colored glass, the figures moved as he moved, turned as he turned, watching him. Smiling with bitter coldness.

Hell looked up and saw that the ceiling was not complete. There was an opening. Small, but large enough for escape.

If only his wings could lift him that far.

If only the Flock were true birds.

If only he had that power.

If only . . .

Beside where Hell sat dreaming, one of the Raptors—a seasoned fighter who had earned his colors—broke free from the talons of the dreams.

Free in a way.

His eyes flicked and danced in their sockets as he struggled to his feet. Blood ran from the corners of his beak from where his teeth had gnawed his tongue to rags. It took every last bit of strength he possessed, and that was a considerable amount. His muscles bulged and strained as he fought to stand.

Once he was on his feet, he looked around in horror at the others. They lay as if dead, and it took concentration for him to see the subtle rise and fall of each chest. Alive, yes, but . . .

Something had done this.

This was some trick of the humans. Or of the HEs who slept away the centuries in this forgotten place.

"No," he said, snarling the word. Making it both a statement of his shock and a vow.

No. He would not let this stand. He would not allow this to go unanswered.

With a trembling hand, he clawed at his pistol and dragged it free from the holster. He checked that the power pack was full.

"No," he growled, casting a baleful look around.

The gun was a comforting weight in his fist.

"No," he said with certainty, with all the dignity of his Privilege, with the surety of his legion, with the force of his own history as a warrior and killer. "No."

With all that certainty and determination burning in his chest and mind, the Flock raised the pistol.

And shot himself in the face.

The Eldest leaned back in his chair and clutched his chest, fearing that one or both of his hearts was failing. He had suffered heart attacks before. Twice. The tiny pacemakers with their fifty-year battery had saved him then, and he prayed that they would save him now.

He punched a button on the arm of his chair, sending a medical alert to his secretary.

No answer came.

Not then.

The secretary was under his desk. Weeping. Lost in the dark webs of a terrible dream.

68

Lexie fought her way back to her feet. Even with the diminished gravity on Io it was like lifting fifty tons. As soon as she was upright the room took a sickening turn, and she grabbed the closest sleep capsule for support.

Pickle and Dubbs were awake but dazed. Dubbs crawled up the side of the neighboring capsule and leaned against it, gasping, staring goggle-eyed at nothing. Pickle was the last to get up and he thumped back against a wall, mouth opening and closing like a boated trout.

He looked around and saw the others. "What—and I mean this with my whole heart—the fuck?"

Dubbs shook his head.

Lexie said, "I had a dream."

"So did I," groaned Dubbs.

"Has to be them," said Lexie, touching the glass plate over the frozen HE.

But Dubbs kept shaking his head. "You can't dream in cryosleep. It's impossible. Brain tissue, nerves, all of it is literally frozen."

"Well, I'm open to alternate goddamn theories," snapped Lexie. Her tone was so sharp and bitter that it froze Dubbs.

"I . . . I don't have any," he confessed. "All along, since long before I got involved with you people, I've been telling the truth as I know it. The science is thorough on this. It's specific."

"You didn't say it like that on the way here, surfer boy," said Pickle.

"Because I thought that maybe some of the HEs were literally awake. Resuscitated. But . . . the survivors are all frozen solid. The readouts confirm they've been on ice, in deep freeze, all this time. So . . . there's simply no way there can be brain activity of any kind. That's the whole point of cryosleep. It's like time travel. One minute you're in the now, and then you wake in the future. No dreams, no aging."

Pickle came over and stood between the two capsules where his shipmates stood. He looked down at the face of one of the HEs. The stenciled name was:

DARREN BURRIS

"Alexander mentioned him," murmured Lexie. "Combat specialist. Combat callsign was Skyboy."

"This cat's a popsicle," said Pickle, "but damn if he wasn't in my head."

"He was?" asked Lexie. "You saw him?"

"Saw him? Shit. For the last three frigging hours he was chasing me through the house I grew up in. I watched him tear apart my family and everyone I knew. Literally tore them apart." He shivered and avoided their eyes for a moment. "Maybe don't wake him, okay?"

"The system is set to wake them all," said Dubbs. He turned to Pickle. "Three hours? You sure?"

"At least. Maybe longer."

Dubbs looked at the digital display. "It's been less than twenty minutes."

The others gaped at him.

"That's impossible," insisted Lexie. "It was hours. Longer."

"I know how it felt," agreed Dubbs. "It was days for me. Or at least that's how it felt. I have no explanations. Psychic phenomenon wasn't in the curriculum I studied. I'm hard science all day long."

Lexie looked around, her gaze lingering on the door. Ahab stood there, his mechanical eyes completely vacant. She snatched him up and fumbled for the reset button. It seemed to take longer than it should for the hard reboot, but then Ahab yipped as if in recognition. She hugged him to her chest, but the ferocity of it was less about the robot and more her need for comfort after what just happened.

"They stopped," she said after a few moments, her voice hushed. "No gunfire. Nothing. I wonder . . . did it affect *everyone*?"

That was a sobering thought. Pickle touched his comms unit. "Mugabe, report."

They all listened to the feeds from their earbuds.

"Nothing," said Pickle. "Shit."

"Fodder, report," said Lexie.

Nothing.

"We don't know if they're alive and just out of it or dead," said Dubbs.

"If they're dead, then what kept the Flock from breaking in here? Twenty minutes is a lot of time. Dubbs, could what happened to us also have affected the birds?"

"I know next to nothing about Flock biology," said Dubbs, "but thoughts are nerve conduction in every species. If there was some kind of attack across the entire facility, then . . . maybe yes? I'm guessing."

"I—" began Pickle, but his words were drowned out by a fresh burst of gunfire. Sporadic at first and then growing into a more focused barrage.

"Shit," said Dubbs.

"It's closer too," said Lexie. "Dubbs, I know you're as freaked out as the rest of us, but you have to focus. You have to wake the remaining HEs up."

The young scientist closed his eyes for a moment. He took a deep, steadying breath, exhaled, nodded, opened his eyes, and set to work.

"Hurry," begged Lexie.

"It's not an off and on switch," said Dubbs as he worked. "The process takes time. And even though it's supposed to be a synchronized process of group resuscitation, after a certain point it comes down to individual biology. They might wake one at a time, and likely will. And the process of awakening conscious-ness is different for everyone. When we all got iced in college, I was the fifth out of twenty to wake up. So . . . we need time. It's not like they're going to spring out of the tubes ready to join the fight. Takes the average person a couple of hours to shake it off, and that's with short-duration cryo. These guys? Hell, it might be all day."

"We don't *have* all day," Lexie said. "We need to speed it up somehow."

"Can't be done," said Dubbs.

The words were barely out before the sound of furious ham-mering filled the chamber. Lexie hurried over and touched the steel door. It looked impenetrable but her heart sank as she felt the whole thing shuddering in its frame.

"Work faster," she begged.

"Then come over here and help me," yelled Dubbs. He di-rected her to the other side of Milo Burris's capsule. "See those cables? Check them. The whole length from that board to where they socket in. Let me know when they start getting warm. That'll give us some idea of where this guy is in the process."

"They're already warm," said Lexie. "What does that mean?"

"I—"

A row of bright red lights mounted above the row of capsules suddenly began to flash and a shrill alarm started screaming like a banshee.

"What's happening?" cried Lexie.

"Fucking hell," yelled Dubbs. "The system is failing. Shit, shit, shit. Look at those numbers." On the digital display the readouts were changing with hysterical speed. Temperature numbers shooting up and dropping down, biometrics giving contradictory readings. Life signs flatlining and then spiking.

"What'd you do?" accused Pickle.

"I didn't do anything," snapped Dubbs. "It's the system. Christ, I think this Sleeper is dying. I need to get him out. I know CPR. Pickle, get my bag. There's a case with syringes. I need adrenaline and the stuff marked as G-11. It's a stabilizer. Come on—*move!*"

The hammering on the door was much louder and concrete dust was puffing out all around the frame.

I'm going to die here, Lexie thought. *We're all going to die.*

She did not dare to say it aloud. That would be as deadly as if she turned her own guns on her companions.

Dubbs punched a sequence of buttons. A hissing noise came as the canopy lifted and gasses were released. The chemical smell was mixed with a dreadful organic stink of sweat, testosterone, excrement, and blood.

"That's not possible," he said, speaking to himself. "Not in deep freeze. No, no, no . . ."

He grabbed the glass cover and threw his weight against it,

forcing it up. Mist boiled out, obscuring the Sleeper inside and sending tendrils creeping down to the floor.

A series of huge, spaced blows struck the door.

"They're using breaching charges," said Pickle. "We're fucked."

Lexie waved at the mist to try and see Burris's face. "Is he alive? God, tell me he's alive."

"I don't know," said Dubbs, working furiously to raise the entire steel cover of the cryo-tube. "We have to get him out. And the board says that Jason Horse is starting to wake too."

"Dubbs," yelped Lexie. "Your nose . . ."

Blood had begun flowing from the scientist's nose and ears. His eyes were jumpy with stress and pain.

"I know," he snarled, but he kept working. "Lexie . . . check on Horse. I need to stay here with Burris. Pickle, *where are those fucking meds?*"

Lexie ran around to Jason Horse's tube, but his face was completely obscured by mist. The crystal visor was still shut, and Lexie began pulling at it.

Pickle ran over to Dubbs with the syringes. Dubbs snatched one and moved to where he could stab it down into the dying Sleeper's chest.

"He's bottoming out. He—"

With shocking, hideous speed a huge hand shot out of the mist and clamped like a crushing vise around Dubbs's throat. The young scientist was lifted to his toes and then completely off the floor as something huge and dark and immeasurably powerful rose from the capsule. It looked around—eyes wild, mouth twisted into a snarl of bottomless hate. The Sleeper threw back his head and let loose with a roar that no human throat could ever have made. Fireballs exploded inside the digital display boards, bursting them apart. Glass-fronted cabinets all along the far wall shattered, their contents flying everywhere with poltergeist frenzy. As the roar filled every space, every corner of that chamber, cracks whipsawed down the walls. The other capsules groaned and dented as if struck by blows. Three of them flew upward, twisted, and crashed to the floor, spilling out the corpses of dead HEs.

The thing that had been Darren Burris stepped out onto the floor. Naked, immensely powerful, inhuman in every way that mattered. Snakes of electricity rippled along his skin. His eyes glowed with a hellish red. He looked at the man he held and then flung him away like garbage. Dubbs hit the wall and puddled down, unconscious or dead.

Lexie screamed, but the roaring giant drowned her out.

The floor rippled as if with earthquake tremors.

The Sleeper had awakened.

In every possible nightmare way.

69

Fodder and Mugabe moved through a series of service corridors, brailing their way through darkness to avoid the Raptors. After shaking off the awful effects of the dream ambush—and ambush was the only word that seemed to fit—they had somehow managed to elude the bands of Raptors.

Their ammo seemed barely enough. Not with dozens of the birds in the facility. Fodder had reckoned that there were as few as thirty and as many as a hundred of the hunters. Mugabe put the number even higher. Considering that it took upward of a full magazine to bring one down—what with the grease-shield and cutting-edge body armor—they did not want to waste the ammunition they had left.

Mugabe followed Fodder, watching her in the infrequent glow of small utility lights. The young enforcer from the Bottoms was a cat in the darkness. Her boots made hardly a sound, and despite her bulk, Fodder moved with the oiled grace of a leopard. The prophet was impressed and did his best to imitate the woman.

All kinds of echoes found them, though. Not theirs, but

the hum-chatter of pulse weapons, the staccato chatter of sentry guns, the *whump* of breaching charges, all punctuated by the occasional scream.

It was the screams that worried Mugabe the most. Some were bird, but some were human. Kind of. There were screams that seemed impossibly loud and lasted improbably long.

"What the hell is that?" whispered Fodder the first time they heard it.

They paused, crouching in shadows, guns ready, listening to that cry go on and on.

When it stopped, they thought they caught a snatch of speech. The same timbre as the scream, but it was not any voice that was familiar to them.

"You reckon that's a Sleeper?" asked Fodder.

"Who else could it be?" replied Mugabe.

"Someone woke up cranky," quipped Fodder, but the joke fell flat.

"Something is wrong," said Mugabe. "We need to get to the cryo-bay."

"And we need to get back into this fight," agreed Fodder. "I need some serious-ass payback for what they did to Fire."

They moved off.

70

As Darren Burris rose from the cryo-chamber his hand clamped around Lexie's throat, raising her first to her feet, then the tips of her toes, and as the Sleeper stood, he held her completely off the floor.

The grip was so tight. Lexie could not drag in even a spoonful of air. Black poppies seemed to form in the air in front of her eyes, the petals spreading so fast and so wide they blocked the light. She clawed at his hand, scratching him, beating at the iron-hard fist that held her. She kicked, hitting him every single time in his stomach and chest and hip. It did no good at all. It was like fighting a statue of stone, of steel.

Burris looked around, his eyes wild. Fires seemed to ignite in those eyes and his lips peeled back in a snarl every bit as feral as a wolf or tiger's.

Pickle and Dubbs rushed at him. Pickle grabbed Lexie around the waist and tried to pull her free. Dubbs shouted and pleaded as he tried to pry the man's fingers open. With his free hand, Burris swatted both men away. One, two. Appallingly fast; deeply savage. Pickle spun around and slammed into the wall, the impact splitting his lips and cracking his nose, a splash-pattern of blood staining the wall.

Dubbs went flying, his big and muscular body plucked off the deck as if he were a scarecrow filled lightly with straw. His caterwaul rose and then ended abruptly as he struck the side of Jason Horse's chamber. The impact doubled Dubbs over and he slid bonelessly to the floor.

All of it in a single second. Time itself seemed to slow, nearly to stop.

As Darren Burris continued to scream like something from hell itself.

"*I am alive!*" he roared in a voice so loud that it seemed no human throat could have ever managed. Impossibility defined the moment more than anything else.

Lexie heard that scream on a level beyond human hearing. It was louder than that. And she saw everything through a veil of red-tinged black that seemed to have dropped over everything. There were so many things she wanted to tell this man, this HE. This Sleeper. She wanted to prove to him that she and her friends were here to help. She wanted to warn him about the Raptors trying to break in. Even as he slowly killed her, Lexie wanted to assure him that she was not his enemy.

She felt herself moving through space and realized—dimly with her oxygen-starved brain—that Burris was bringing her around so he could look at her. More than that, she could feel him invading her, violating her. Not her flesh, but her mind. Intertwining with her thoughts. Obscuring her dreams. Raping her very idea of self.

There was no logic to how she knew this. There was no science to explain it; nothing from history to define it. He was just there; inside her; violating her.

The pounding on the door became louder, sharper, imminent.

Burris ignored it and stared into Lexie's eyes. His irises were a fierce and icy blue encircled by gold rings; the sclera was bloodshot, veins as red and jagged as summer lightning. Lexie searched those alien eyes for some trace of humanity, something with which she could connect before she died.

Her death was there, behind the glowing orbs, whispering in her ear. Her death, her failure. The end of all dreams and plans.

Except . . .

Except that it was not the end of dreams.

As the darkness wrapped itself around her, Lexie's mind tumbled out of that moment and back into the dreamscape. Into a new and terrible place. All at once, and with complete truth she *was* Darren Burris. She was in his mind. She could even see herself as he saw her—not as a human woman, but as a cringing, snarling, twisted caricature of a bird. Of a Raptor. And she knew with complete certainty this was what Burris saw. Somehow he, too, was trapped inside a distorted dream. This was not the Sleeper facility on Io. The floors and walls were curved, and there were huge windows beyond which antique human and Flock ships were embroiled in a deadly dogfight against the vastness of deep space. Despite the soundlessness of space and the intervening glass, she could hear cannons fire, engines roar, and ships explode. Buried in the midst of those sounds was another—higher, thinner, sharper, and more urgent.

The screams of children. Of infants. Hundreds. Thousands. Babies screaming and not understanding.

And she knew where Burris's maniac dream had taken her.

They were on Calliope Station. The fractured flow of time allowed Burris to drag her two hundred and fourteen years into the past. And yet, farther away, she was dimly aware of the cryogenic chamber and the door that was buckling beneath the Raptor's assault. Both realities were blended. What little integrity time possessed was leaking out of the moment as another second ticked by.

No, she tried to say. Her physical voice was gone, clamped to silence by his hand, but she was in his head, in his dream. And there, at least, she could speak.

"*No! I'm human. I'm here to save you. Please . . .*"

Another second ticked by. How long had she been in his grip? Five seconds? Six? A thousand years? Time was meaningless.

The pounding on the door seemed to be in sync with her heart—growing louder as her heart faded and failed.

The Flock is coming, her dreaming voice yelled.

And everything flickered. For just a moment. The walls of reality faded, came back sharper, faded again. Burris held her in his mind, in that dream, the Flock in the memory dream were much more real than the twisted version that was Lexie in the Sleeper's dream. Lexie turned her head—*their* heads—and saw that bodies were lying all around them. Jason Horse, Pryss . . . others. All the Sleepers that had rescued Calliope Station lay dead, their bodies sprawled like broken toys, their eyes empty of all light, limbs twisted at impossible angles. Darren Burris stood above them as the Flock's elite killers closed in on him.

"*I live,*" he roared, and Lexie felt herself saying those words. She could feel every muscular movement of throat and tongue and lips. She could even feel the exhalation of breath from deep in their shared lungs.

And then a massive explosion changed everything.

It was not on Calliope Station. It was right there on Io.

As the Raptors breached the door and flooded into the room, grease-shields glowing, pulse rifles firing.

71

And that saved Lexie Chow's life.

For the moment.

With a grunt of savage effort, Burris flung her away and Lexie could feel herself being physically torn from the dream and from their shared consciousness. It was a truly awful feeling. A kind of mental rape in reverse. A rejection of everything she was. Ugly, violative, painful on too many levels to catalog. It also hurt her emotionally, because the action broke a level of contact, of inclusion, that—despite its horrors—was the deepest connection she had ever felt. It was even more powerful that what she'd felt in her dreams of Jason Horse. In that moment, with that action, she was nothing at all, nothing of worth to the thing that was Darren Burris. That rejection struck her harder than the floor on which she landed. Despite what had been done to her, she wanted to return.

Lexie hit the deck and slid twenty feet, her body spinning and spinning until she came to rest on her side in the cleft between two of the capsules. It was only chance that positioned her to see the Raptors pouring in even as the steel door twirled on a corner and then crashed to the floor with a ringing *clang*.

Darren Burris stood and waited for them. Ahab darted in and nipped at his naked ankle. Lexie screamed for him to get back, but Burris simply kicked the dog the length of the chamber. Ahab hit a wall, rebounded, and lay on his side, feet moving weakly.

The pulse blasts filled the air and yet none of them seemed to hit the Sleeper. Lexie could not understand it. They were firing from point blank range and Burris had no grease-shield, no PAALS, not even body armor. He stood stark naked.

And yet . . .

There was something unreal about it. Wild energy crackled around him as if he were a lightning rod. His huge hands opened and closed, and when he smiled it was the most terrifying thing Lexie had ever seen.

"*Mine!*" declared the Sleeper. That single word was packed with a crackling malevolence.

He waded into the knot of Raptors.

The first one to reach him—a burly creature with a dark blue Mohawk and matching colors on his armor and clothes—was the unlucky first victim. Burris snaked a hand out and caught the alien by the throat. Just as he had grabbed Lexie. The bird jammed his pistol against Burris's chest and fired. The pulse blasts flashed purple, but the energy seemed to do nothing. Absolutely nothing.

Burris pulled the Raptor very close and with a howl of wicked delight, he bent and buried his teeth in the creature's throat. Blood geysered, splashing Burris's face and the wall behind him. The other Raptors froze mid-stride as the Sleeper tore their companion's throat completely away. It was all very immediate and messy.

Burris tossed the dying Raptor away as if it were trash. He chewed the torn flesh and swallowed it, then grinned with bloody teeth from which strands of skin hung.

"*Lexie!*"

Lexie turned to see Dubbs on his hands and knees, blood running down his face.

"Wake the others," she screeched.

He gaped at her. "Are you out of your fucking mind?"

"Does it matter? We're dead anyway!" she yelled back. "Wake them up. Wake them all up."

The young scientist pulled himself painfully to his feet and hunched over the controls as, ten feet away, Burris was literally tearing the Raptors apart. He ripped an arm from one and, holding it like a club, plowed into the others, beating down their guns, smashing their faces, brutalizing them as they screamed.

For a moment that image flickered, and it was like watching two vid channels playing at the same time. She saw what was really happening there in the room, but once again she shared Burris's inner vision and it was clear he was not seeing the same reality. In his mind he was in full HE battle kit—body armor, with weapons in holsters and sheaths and clipped to crisscrossing web-belts. In that version of reality, Burris was ten feet tall and the Raptors nearly as big. In that reality they were different, more like medium-sized therapod dinosaurs than birds; like *deinonychus* or *austroraptor cabazai*. More overtly reptilian in aspect, with feathers the same color as their real-world clothing. They shrieked and chirped and howled with a more primitive fury. Lexie wondered if this was an older—much, much older—version of the Flock. Their preconquest days from a million years ago.

Even with their more ferocious aspect, Burris moved among the Raptors like a storm, twisting and spinning like a tornado. Wherever his hands moved, blood filled the air. With every turn and swing, something died. He was a moving disaster and everything in his path was consumed by it.

Six Raptors had breached the room.

Two lay dead. Two others were in ruins, and Lexie knew that they were aware that death was the only option left in their futures. Not even the best surgeons of the Greater Flock could repair what one HE had done to them. The other two tried to fight the man, but really all they could do was prolong their own deaths.

All of this made little sense to Lexie. She'd read everything Alexander had written about the fighting skills of the HEs. They were far stronger than an ordinary human being, but . . . not like this. Nothing like this.

Whatever Darren Burris was, he was no longer human. Not by any metric.

He was a monster, and the Raptors were nothing to him but objects to remove from his reality.

For fun.

For an almost erotic satisfaction.

Movement to her left made Lexie turn and she saw Pickle on his feet. He held a pistol in trembling hands and kept moving the barrel back and forth as if totally uncertain if he should shoot . . . and if so, who?

72

Fodder and Mugabe exited the service tunnels and found themselves around a corner from the cryogenics bay. They reached the turning and peered around just as the Raptors blew the heavy steel door off its hinges and rushed in through the smoke.

There was more gunfire and they grinned at each other, ready to join this fight and—with any luck—catch the damn birds in a crossfire. They swapped their partial magazines for full ones, shared a nod, and moved.

Which is when the screaming started.

Fodder wished Fire were with her, but the prophet knew how to more than hold his own.

Exchanging glances, they waded in.

73

One hundred and fifty yards down the hall, Hell observed his soldiers die.

He had deployed several hummingbird drones and their tiny eyes sent him high-res 3D images of one of the HEs tearing apart some of the finest soldiers the Flock had to offer.

And doing it in ways that made no sense to the order of the known universe.

This man—if man he still was—moved too fast; he was too strong. Sophisticated firearms meant nothing to him. That would be disturbing enough if the HE wore some version of a grease-shield, or even the experimental frictionless body armor that Flock scientists were developing. But he was naked.

And unarmed.

Hell leaned against a wall, his head still throbbing from the forced dreams that had nearly killed him ten minutes ago. A dozen Raptors clustered behind him, waiting for orders but peering over his shoulders at the 3D horror unfolding in the hologram.

"What do we do?" asked one of his lieutenants. "Do we attack?"

Hell did not answer; could not answer.

He watched. He could *feel* the fear of his Raptors. No one sane could watch such bestial mayhem without deep terror. In the hologram another Raptor died in a very bad way, screaming for its mother, screaming for the safety of the nest.

The HE roared like a creature resurrected from his most feared nightmare and attacked the last of the advance team.

Hell found it at once interesting and terrifying. The microcomputer built into his gauntlet recorded every bit of telemetry from the drones. Every single detail.

"Sir," urged the lieutenant.

"Not yet," said Hell. And then repeated it to himself. "Not quite yet."

He was waiting for the perfect moment.

Or was he merely too scared to advance?

He closed his eyes a moment, then opened them.

He couldn't let the humans get the best of them no matter what their weapons.

He had to be ready.

74

"Back, back," warned Fodder. "Something weird's going on in there. Hear those screams?"

"Hear them? Hell, woman. People back on Earth can hear them," said Mugabe.

"The shit's happening in there?"

The prophet's expression seemed to vacillate between dread and hope. "I think the Sleepers are awake."

Fodder looked at him. "You think that's what happened to us back there?"

"Of course," said Mugabe. "What else?"

"I don't like it."

Mugabe said nothing.

They moved, hugging the wall as they crept along the corridor toward the sound of agony and destruction.

75

The Sleeper stared down at the sea of red that covered the floor. Bodies—and parts of bodies—formed islands and archipelagos all around him. He saw it and smiled, well pleased.

Then he seemed to notice Lexie again. For a moment his face flickered into a nearly normal expression, and she saw doubt and confusion there, a heartbreaking vulnerability. He opened his mouth in an attempt to speak, but nothing came. He tried several more times, then finally was able to make his mouth work, if barely.

"I . . . I . . ." said Burris, and in that brief respite his voice was not thunderous. It was almost that of a child, high-pitched and seemingly helpless.

Lexie got to her feet and took a small step toward him, hand outstretched.

"Don't," warned Pickle, who was on the other side of the Sleeper.

"Mr. Burris," said Lexie gently, "it's okay. We're here to help you. We—"

"*I ate their souls,*" roared the Sleeper, his voice like a road grater chewing rocks.

Burris hurled Lexie back against Pryss's capsule, rocking it. Behind the Sleeper, two figures appeared in the doorway. Fodder and Mugabe.

The young enforcer raised her shotgun and was about to send fifty Satan's toothpicks into the back of Burris's head. But Mugabe touched her arm.

"No," said the prophet very quietly.

Burris looked around the room, his strange eyes rimmed with unshed tears. Even with all of his rage and power filling the room, there was fear there that was almost childlike. A terror of the dark. A dread of something unseen. A profound confusion.

"I am alive," Burris whispered. The difference in his tone was heartbreaking. It was nearly a question. Plaintive, needing validation of that simple truth.

"Darren Burris," said Lexie, raising her hands, palms outward. "It's okay. You were asleep for a long time, but you're okay now. We woke you."

Those blue-red eyes snapped toward her. Stared into and through her.

Then they came into focus once more. The red veins flared as if lava and not blood ran through them. The doubt burned away to be replaced with a fiery blend of outrage and anger.

"You . . . *woke* . . . me?" growled Burris. "It was you? *You?* You tore me from my slumbers . . . my dreams." He inhaled deeply. "You have no idea what you've done," he said, each word a sigh.

He took a threatening step toward Lexie, fists knotting so tightly the knuckles cracked. Tendons flexed all over his huge body. He gripped the edge of one of the capsules and tore it free from its fastenings. It was Jason Horse's unit, and the still slumbering team leader bounced around inside, his head striking the crystal cover. Bolts snapped as loud as gunshots, pieces of metal and plastic flew everywhere as Burris raised the hundreds of kilos of the capsule as if it was nothing. With a yowl he flung it behind him. The cryo-tube spun and crashed onto the cold floor, tearing loose from the wires that connected it to the resuscitation computers.

"I will rip you apart and wash myself in your blood," said the Sleeper, his voice rising once more to the level of thunder. All along the row of sleeping HEs electrical shorts began blowing apart the telemetric monitors. Flashes of color detonated in the air, born of nothing, pulled into reality by the inexplicable power of the Sleeper's mind. Three of the dead Raptors rose into the air, their bodies twisting, bones snapping audibly, blood and feathers filling the air as Burris raged. The raging monster reached for Lexie once more, this time with both hands, fingers clutching in anticipation of crushing the life from her.

"I will drag you to hell and live in your mind and—"

And his head exploded.

Blood and bits of brain and bone slapped Lexie's face, but she stood stock still, absolutely unable to move, mouth agape, eyes unblinking. The Sleeper towered above her, but his grasping hands lost their precision; his next step was a wandering sideways failure and Darren Burris dropped to his knees. Even with most of the top of his head gone, his eyes still blazed. His lips still moved as if he needed to say something else, to reclaim dominion over this moment.

Then he fell.

His body lost all rigidity and flopped onto that broad chest, arms grasping nothing. The Raptors that had hovered without support in the air, collapsed down too.

None of this made sense. Lexie's mind felt like it was

tumbling too, but she fought for control. For understanding.

A thin thread of sense was slowly stitched into the fabric of reality.

Behind Burris, behind the dead Raptors, standing in the doorway, were two figures. One held a pair of glowing shock rods. The other had a combat shotgun in filthy hands. A thin wisp of smoke curled up from the barrel.

Fodder lowered the gun very slowly. Her eyes were bright with shock, mouth open and lips slack. Beside her, Mugabe stared in absolute horror.

Pickle and Dubbs, both bruised and bleeding, stared at the corpse, then raised their eyes.

"What have you . . . *done?*"

The voice was deep, rich, filled with unfiltered anger. They all turned as something rose from behind the wreckage Burris had created. It was massive, even bigger than Burris. Electricity crackled all around it, and in its dark eyes dangerous fires burned with inferno heat.

It was another Sleeper.

Awake.

Aware.

Standing over the corpse of one of his own.

Lexie's heart sank all the way through the floor, but she was frozen as Jason Horse reached for her.

76

Fodder cocked the shotgun and was about to send fifty Satan's toothpicks into the immense head of the second Sleeper, when a hand reached up, pulled down the barrel and commanded, "No."

At least, it felt as if that's what happened.

But there was no hand actually touching the barrel. Not even Mugabe, who stood beside him in the doorway.

No.

The word echoed in the room. Or . . . maybe in her head. Just that. One word.

No.

Spoken aloud or inside her mind, Fodder did not know. The only thing she was certain of was that it was the voice of this Sleeper, and that somehow the man—thing?—had touched her, had moved her gun barrel.

Fodder could have fought it. She could have easily pulled the trigger, but the voice of the Sleeper was so heavy with emotion that it stopped her. There was such *need* in that single word that Fodder almost cried. That a single word could bring a woman like her to tears was almost beyond comprehension, but hundreds of forgotten years fueled those two letters and created a perfect expression of frustration, love, hate, confusion, and resignation.

And of life.

These Sleepers were the reason she had followed Lexie here on her bizarre quest. They were the hope of humanity. Maybe the only hope. Fodder knew—as did the others—that the power of the human resistance was far short of what was needed. They could hurt the birds, but the Flock was too big, too powerful, too well-placed for anyone to take them down.

Anyone *normal*, that was. Anyone human.

The Sleepers were neither. Fodder looked at Lexie and saw her give the tiniest shake of the head. Her eyes were bright with too many emotions to catalog, but the one emotion she looked for seemed suddenly absent.

Fear.

Despite every reason to be completely terrified, there was a strange sense of peace in Lexie's eyes. Of acceptance. Of . . .

Hope.

Instead of firing, Fodder pointed her shotgun barrel to the ceiling so it wouldn't do any accidental damage, and watched the gigantic man, ready to help him but ready to kill him just as easily.

Lexie drew a deep breath and then took a step forward. Her hands were still up and out in a no-threat gesture. He was just like in her dreams, if not more majestic.

"We are not here to hurt you," she said.

Jason Horse watched her. The arcs of electricity snapped and crackled along his arms and in his eyes.

"My name is Lexie Chow," she said to the Sleeper. "Alexandra Chow."

Jason's eyes flickered for a moment and deep vertical lines appeared between his brows. He said nothing. Waiting. Watching her.

"You knew the person I was named after," she said. "Alexander Chow."

Jason's lips shaped the syllables of that name, but there was no sound.

"My family has known about you for generations," continued Lexie. "We've been the keepers of your secret. I've come here with my friends to awaken you because the human race needs your help."

Jason licked his lips, then echoed one of her words. "Generations?"

Mugabe couldn't take his eyes off the giant of a man. The look on the prophet's face was both peaceful and needful. Pickle and Dubbs merely looked stunned. Beside him, Fodder's eyes were narrowed with doubt.

Lexie stopped less than a yard from Jason Horse. Waiting.

She knew he had an active AI in his head, created using the height of technology from two hundred years ago, that allowed him leaps of logic. That along with the workings of the phage virus had made him beyond ordinary.

Jason glanced around the room at the other cryomachines and seemed to nod at each one. Finally, he spoke. "You're here to wake us up. You want us to help you fight the Flock." He sighed. "Again."

"Yes," she said softly.

"You want us to help the same human race who put us to sleep?"

Lexie's heart was hammering painfully inside her chest. "Yes," she said again. "The same."

Jason Horse smiled at her. It was a faint, wondering smile. "Why should we even consider helping you?"

That question was actually something she'd spent a lot of time preparing to answer. She had five or six separate replies. Each logical, each couched in politics and social understanding and humanism. Her whole adult life had prepared her—uniquely her—to answer on behalf of the human race.

She cast her eyes down feeling like an utter failure, unable to speak because she knew in that moment that anything she said would be an insult packed with idealistic hope and half-truths. The Sleeper was more intelligent than all his rescuers put together. Combined with his AI, he could disassemble any lie or argument to its DNA and juxtapose her arguments back to her.

Disappointment and anger flickered on Jason's face.

Fodder stepped forward. "Hey, brother," she said, lowering the shotgun. "Yeah, people fucked up. The military bent all you cats over a barrel and took you hard. It sucks. It sucks so bad that actual books will be written about it. But here's the thing, sport, you're a tool, just like me."

"Who are you?" asked the Sleeper, eyes still burning hot.

"Me? I'm nothing?" said Fodder. "I was born in a small town near the Paris Metropol—and I guess you don't even know what that is. After your time. Now, I live in the Bottoms. Think of the worst ghetto you ever saw and the stinkiest, shittiest, darkest sewer you can imagine, then double it and that's where I've been living since I was ten. People like me are what topsiders scrape off their shoes. We're less than nothing to fucking suped-up heroes like you." She took a step forward. "But you know what? Lowest of the low and all that . . . I still fight."

The Sleeper turned to her.

"I'm a tool, a weapon," said Fodder. "Like you, I guess. Different scale, but still the same. I may not like it, but it's what it is. And here's another thing, man, tools are meant to be used. When they lie about, they break down or oxidize. They're no longer able to function as a tool. Is that what you want? To be useless?"

The Sleeper regarded her, but it apparently didn't faze Fodder. It was clear the man was listening. Considering.

"You were purposefully made," said Fodder. "Your purpose was to destroy the goddamn Flock. And you did that. Damn if you didn't. You and your other suped-up super-goddamn-soldiers. HEs. Better than the best of the best. Who knows, maybe you're not human anymore, but you're human enough. You were made for war and we are ass-deep in a war right now. We're losing the war. Dr. Chow here . . . Lexie . . . she's not even a fighter. Not like you and me. She's a bookworm who risked everything to come all the hell the way here from Earth to be your alarm clock. Shit is bad, brother, and she came here to find you. To wake you up. To use you like the tool you are. Just as she uses me. I get why. That's why I came with her. That's why these other guys are here too. We lost everything by coming here. You, though . . . you were *made* for this."

"We won the war," said the Sleeper. "We won and we saved the galaxy from killing itself. That's what we were made for."

"Well, bravo, motherfucker," said Fodder, grinning. "Sorry they didn't give you a parade, the key to the city, and a blow job. Life sucks like that. But the thing is . . . the war ain't over. I guess it never really was. The military fucked you but good. But the birds fucked all of us a million times worse. We're here to get you back into the game. To let you do what you were made for."

"Made for?" mused Jason. He stared at the ceiling as his voice came out ponderously. "Yes. They changed us, modified us in every possible way. We agreed to it; we allowed them to perform all the surgeries and bury their implants and rewrite our DNA. Why? Because we believed in the cause, we believed the mission, and worse . . . we believed the government.

Then, after we did what they wanted, they put us away. Like *tools*." He loaded that word with tons of sarcasm and accusation and hurt.

"Well," said Fodder, "welcome to the real world where humans are assholes and assholes are a dime a dozen. I guess you never had the chance to stand and salute the flag and sing the anthems and be Joe Citizen of Earth, spotless hero. And you know what? Fuck that noise. As I understand it, human beings were losing the fight and there was no Plan B. It was using you or getting wiped out. Does it suck? Sure. But try growing up in the Bottoms, with the Flock always ready to stamp you flat."

Lexie did not dare interrupt Fodder. The young enforcer was speaking from the heart. Raw, unfiltered, but seething with truth. And Jason seemed to be listening. Whatever had driven Burris mad did not seem to control Horse.

Fodder said, "You think it was bad before? Well, it's worse now. There's no army left, no marines or navy. No space rangers, no fleet. There's nothing but a few idiots like us trying to do what we can." She paused, then added. "You know how they have fire axes inside glass boxes on the wall? *Break in Case of Emergency*? We came a long damn way to break that glass. I guess what I'm saying is that we need you. We're the axe and you are behind the glass. Guess what? We broke the glass so it's now your turn."

The Sleeper regarded Fodder without comment. He looked around at the five strangers in the room. Then he walked over to where Darren Burris sprawled. He knelt and touched the dead Sleeper's chest, long fingers brushing across the man's heart.

"You came here to wake us up," murmured Jason. "To enlist our help. And yet—"

"We had no choice," said Lexie, stepping closer.

"Choice." Jason repeated the word, tasting it as if it was something new.

"Your friend . . . he woke up . . . wrong," said Lexie. "He wasn't . . . wasn't . . ."

"Human?" mused the Sleeper. "No. How could he be?"

He pivoted on the balls of his feet and looked up at her with his strange eyes.

"How could *we* be human?" he asked. "We weren't really human when they brought us here. We haven't been human for a long time." He paused. "Alexander knew that."

"Yes," said Lexie. "He knew."

She knelt slowly, with Burris's body between her and Jason.

"I'm sorry for the loss of your friend," she said. "Whatever happened in cryosleep changed him."

"Yes."

"It warped him."

"Yes."

"He was going to kill us."

"Oh yes," said Jason. "And can you blame him?"

Lexie felt the impact of Jason's stare. It was so very much like Burris's. It flowed past her defenses and probed at the gates of her mind.

But it stopped there.

She knew he could push through those gates, that she possessed no defenses that could keep him out if he wanted to invade her mind. Lexie felt incredibly helpless in that moment. And yet . . .

She braced herself and said, "I think you can read my mind. I . . . don't know if you always could. Alexander never mentioned anything about that in his journals. Maybe it's something he never knew about. Maybe it's something new, even to you. I don't know. Can't stop you. But I can give you permission, Jason. If you need to do that to me, if it will help you understand, then . . . do what you have to do."

"Lexie, no," cried Dubbs, but she ignored him. Out of the corner of her eye, she saw Fodder's gun barrel jerk as if Fodder was fighting to keep the weapon from rising.

Lexie focused on Jason Horse. They were so close that he could touch her. Grab her. Kill her. The level of power he had was incalculable by any metric she understood.

The Sleeper's dark light-filled eyes searched her face. She could feel him leaning close to those internal gates. There was a strange sensation as if his fingers were actually touching her skin. The hair on her arms stood up. The energy that still rippled along his skin jumped, forming small arcs between her and him. These did not crack or pop like static energy, but instead merely *were*. She felt them but without pain. Without . . .

Threat.

Jason Horse smiled at her. It was the saddest thing Lexie had ever seen.

"I dreamed of you," he said. "Alexandra Chow."

Her eyes widened.

"I dreamed that we were inside of a glass globe and it was eternally snowing."

Across the room, in a corner where no one was looking, one of the Raptors stirred. It was on the edge of death, of collapse, but it still lived. The creature was the daughter of an ancient house of high Privilege, and the pistol that lay an inch from her hand had been handed down from parent to offspring for seventy years. That gun had taken the lives of fifty-four humans. It was beautifully made, the epitome of the gunmaker's craft.

The Raptor reached for it with infinite slowness. Her taloned fingers curled around the grip. It took effort to lift it. Not because it was heavy but because there was so little life left in her. She knew she was dying. Nothing could prevent it now.

The gun was the gun, though. It only required that she aim and then to exert the smallest pressure on the trigger.

The Raptor pointed the barrel at the back of Lexie Chow's head.

And pulled the trigger.

77

Hell watched everything.

He saw everything.

The terrible dreams he had endured were still in his mind. Haunting him, challenging him, but filtering a reality that was perhaps magnifications worse.

He turned and glanced at his group of battle-hardened Raptors clustered about him. Short of the ambush tactics used when Chow's team stole the ship and again here in this facility, any one of his soldiers was normally a match for four to six humans. Even with the high attrition from Chow's surprise strategies and the presence of more sophisticated weapons and armor than the Eldest said would be available, Hell knew that given time his forces would overwhelm these humans.

Until now, Hell's only concern was following Chow until she found all the Sleeper cells. Hell had even allowed her crew to kill more Raptors than they might have in a standard fight. That collateral damage was, as he saw it, the fee that would pay for the greatest win in Flock history. The HEs had given the Flock one of its few defeats in the uncounted years of their campaign of conquest. Hell expected to lose no more than two or three hundred Raptors by the time they found the last HE cell. And what was that when measured against the enormity of the potential victory?

After all, the Flock had bodies to spare. There were millions of Raptors—armed and trained—throughout the galaxy. It was the largest group of special forces known to have existed in any culture going back fourteen thousand centuries.

Their only threat were the HEs. Like the Raptors, they could be replicated, their numbers expanded exponentially as long as humanity reclaimed the technology and found willing recruits. Though, that in itself was a limit because humans relied on volunteerism rather than conscription. One of their many, many failings.

But now . . .

Two HEs had been resuscitated. Both seemed—somehow—to possess abilities that could not be explained away by what the Flock knew of human genetics, surgical, and cybernetic enhancements.

It confirmed the rumors that the Dreamers who were such a problem on star systems across the galaxy, were somehow connected to these *Homo eximius* monsters.

And if merely two had such power, what of multiples?

What would happen if they all awoke?

An unlikely end for the Raptors and the Flock might be on the horizon.

The dream assault here in this facility proved that, as far as Hell was concerned.

Hell watched, and he waited. And he learned so very much . . . hopefully enough to stop what the humans believed was inevitable.

78

The dying Raptor pulled the trigger. The glowing purple plasma blast ripped across the room toward Lexie and exploded. Harmlessly. Missing her by a full meter.

Lexie screamed anyway.

The Raptor howled in shock and confusion.

There was a hole in the wall exactly where her target stood. Had stood. Should have still stood. She blinked, trying to understand what just happened.

Lexie was equally confused and shocked.

One moment she stood talking with Jason Horse and the next she was in his arms, grabbed as he moved.

A second pulse blast tried to chase them, but it struck a computer console and blew it to fiery pieces. Fodder grabbed Dubbs and Pickle and bore them down to the floor. Mugabe dove for cover between two capsules.

The Raptor kept firing, trying to hit the human carrying the woman, but as soon as her taloned finger depressed the trigger, the big HE moved. It was as if the man could read her mind and move at the precise moment of trigger-pull.

Lexie clawed at Jason's iron grip but was unable to free herself.

She tried to climb up and over him and out of the line of fire and failed.

She screamed for him to put her down. He ignored her.

A dazed Ahab tried to bite him and failed. Instead, the robot fell over again, and this time did not move.

Jason held her as he moved, zigging and zagging, slipping the pulse blasts as easily as if the Raptor was throwing slow softballs.

Jason reached the Raptor and kicked the rifle out of the alien's hands. It spun away, clattered to the ground, and skittered away under a row of cabinets. With no pause or slackening of his lightning pace, Jason pivoted on the ball of one bare foot and thrust out with the heel of the other. Once, twice. The Raptor sagged back, her chest punched inward and the shape of her head entirely wrong.

And the room fell silent.

The big HE stood there for several seconds and then set Lexie down, doing it with surprising gentleness considering he had just killed a bird with brutal efficiency.

Lexie staggered backward, arms pinwheeling for balance. She crouched, steadied herself, arms still out, and then straightened slowly.

"That was . . . that was . . ."

"Are you hurt?" asked the HE, sounding uncertain, distant, as if his mind was in a much different and lower gear than the body that had performed those shockingly efficient combat moves were not connected in any meaningful way. He towered above her, naked, brawny, glistening with melted ice, chest heaving, fists balled. His eyes were jumpy and unblinking.

"What? No. No, I'm . . . I'm good." She shook her head. "How did you *do* that? It was so fast. He should have killed . . ."

Her voice trailed off before she said "me."

"It's what we were trained for," he said, his voice still sounding as if the words came from far away, down a long hallway. "It's what we were . . . *made* for."

Lexie stared into those eyes. She looked deep. Seeing him. Allowing him to see her.

There was no invasion of her thoughts. No force, no violation. In that moment it was two people examining each other.

She wanted him to *see* her. To know her as well as she knew him from a dozen dreams. The combat ones, and the others. The deeply private ones and she hoped like hell that Jason had not somehow been aware of them.

And yet . . .

The connection was there. Waiting. Softer than she expected. There was no pain, no sense of attack.

"Jason . . ." she said very softly. "I dreamed about you too."

The big HE was still as a statue, and Lexie saw that the electricity no longer rippled over his skin. Somehow, though, its absence did not make the man seem more human.

Jason turned in a slow circle, taking in everything. He stalked past Dubbs and looked down into each of the capsules. He touched them, one after the other. Pryss, Trig, Sushi, Short Dog, Girlie . . .

Then he moved deeper into the room, pausing by each of the darkened capsules . . . the dead ones. Even in the poor light, Lexie could see the silver of tears as they ran down his cheeks. When he got to the last one, Jason bent forward as if stabbed in the stomach. He caved in on himself and rested his forehead against the cracked glass of the last . . . what was the right word for it now? Coffin?

Lexie felt tears burn in her own eyes. She scooped up Ahab's still little body and once more hugged it to her own.

No one spoke. Not a word.

Then, incrementally and as if with great personal pain, Jason Horse raised his head. He looked at them.

"Tell me everything," he said, lips curling back from white teeth. "Goddamn it, tell me what the *fuck* is going on."

79

Lexie told him.

She told him every single thing.

How the Flock had manipulated human psyche by making them believe that the Flock needed to be saved. She detailed the horrors reaped upon the Flock, then how it was decided that the HEs needed to be put to rest . . . tossed into the back of a faraway place to gather dust in the off chance that they might be needed.

Then the uprising.

How the Flock had placed their soldiers in all of the most strategic locations so that when humanity's greatest weapon was shelved, they were left with nothing other than the ability to capitulate.

What happened after the surrender. The Flock's devious long game to gain control over every single aspect of human society and its critical infrastructure. The uprising. The domination.

Then she told them about the subjugation. About the rookeries and the Bottoms and the incremental reduction of humanity until all that was left was a servant species.

She told him about the Dreamers and even her own dreams. Much of that was personal, embarrassing, far too private. She told him anyway, knowing the four people left in her team were listening and heard every intimate word.

Fodder watched the door, shotgun in her hands. Mugabe stood nearby, head bowed, lips moving in silent prayer as he listed to the tale and heard the subtle acknowledgements of the Dreamer. Pickle stood helplessly behind Lexie, a gun hanging slack in his hand. Dubbs waited by the row of capsules, his eyes wide with shock and his face bathed in fear sweat.

As she spoke, she kept hitting Ahab's reset button. It failed and failed and then . . . the dog opened its eyes, looked around, curled its tail between its legs, and tried to burrow into Lexie's chest.

As he listened, Jason Horse opened a cabinet and removed clothes. His own. Sealed in plastic too many years ago. Once he was finished dressing, he sat down cross-legged on the floor and said nothing as Lexie spoke. He did not interrupt her even once.

His face was impassive. Not a twitch of mouth, not a furrow of brow.

His eyes, though, they were his tell. With each new bit of news, each twist, each betrayal on both sides of the war, his reactions were there in those eyes.

When Lexie was finished, Jason put his face in his cupped palms and sat there in silence for a very long time. The only movement in the room was the soft shudder of his shoulders as he wept.

Whether he wept for himself, his lost soldiers, or humanity in general, it didn't matter. All that mattered were the tears and the emotion and the groans he released that were increasingly turning from sadness to rage.

80

Then the big HE rose and walked over to Pryss's capsule. He placed his palm on the curved lid as he looked down the row. Lexie and the others stood by, helpless, awkward, hushed to a cemetery silence.

"It might be kinder to let them sleep on," Jason said after a long moment.

"For now, you mean?" asked Lexie.

"No," said Jason. "Forever."

There was a heavy beat of shock.

"Really?" asked Dubbs, horrified.

The big soldier closed his eyes. As powerful as he was, Lexie could see how the weight of knowledge pressed down on him.

"No," he said, raising his head and looking at the *Tin Man*'s crew. "Wake them."

Dubbs hesitated.

"Now," ordered Jason.

The young scientist turned away quickly and set to work.

Pickle cleared his throat. "Permission to, um . . . speak?"

Jason snorted. "I'm not your commanding officer. You don't need my go-ahead."

"Or mine," said Lexie.

"Well, okay then," said Pickle. "What about the other HE teams?"

"What about them?" asked Jason.

"We know there are more of them out there, but that's pretty much all we know." Pickle flapped his arms to indicate all of space. "How many teams are there? *Where* are they? And shouldn't we go and wake the rest up?"

"I agree," said Mugabe, opening his eyes and getting to his feet. "We need to find and awaken all of the sacred Sleepers."

"'*Sacred*,'" echoed Jason faintly, shaking his head. "God Almighty."

"That doesn't sound like a smart plan," said Dubbs quickly. "I mean, after what happened. We woke two of them . . . I mean *you*, Mr. Horse—"

"Call me Jason."

"Okay, Jason," said Dubbs, looking very uncomfortable. "We resuscitated you and Darren Burris. One of you tried to kill us."

"Jason did not," Lexie said.

"Sure, but the math is still iffy. Fifty percent of the HEs revived tried to kill us. At least one other member of Alpha Wave had a mental breakdown in the tube." He gestured to the capsule where *I am God, God is Dead,* and *I am in Hell* were written in blood on the crystal cover. And we know that the HEs have been dreaming during their cryosleep, which was always believed to be a physical impossibility. Just as we know that somehow their dreams have reached out across space, and in some case thousands of light-years of space, to—hell, what do I call it? Infect? Inspire?—influence the dreams of human beings. Many of *those* people, those Dreamers, have committed acts of violence."

"Against the birds," snapped Fodder over her shoulder.

"Okay, sure," agreed Dubbs, "but you know as well as I do that a lot of humans were killed in some of those incidents. And not just collaborators. Innocent people too. Personally, I don't want to hear about 'collateral damage.'"

"There's nothing we could have done to save those people," said Pickle.

"Maybe," said Dubbs, "but if we wake up all of the HEs and some of them go ape-shit like Burris did, we could be unleashing a huge threat to *human* life across the galaxy." He looked up into Jason's eyes. "You have to know that you're not the same as you were when they froze you. You can't stand there and tell me that something inexplicable and demonstrably dangerous didn't happened to you all while you slept."

"Oh, no," said Jason, "you're right. We're different."

Ahab tottered over to him and sniffed the big man's calves, which was as high as he could reach. His little tail wagged for a moment, and then he scampered back to his mistress.

Lexie touched Jason's arm very tentatively. "Can you tell us how you're different? Do you understand it?"

"Understand it?" Jason laughed. "You have to be out of your mind. I've been awake for—what?—half an hour. Lexie . . . I dreamed about you and you dreamed about me. In some of your dreams you *were* me. How does that make any damn sense? What happened with Burris is . . . is . . . well, shit, I don't even know if there are any verbs for it." He held out his hands and residual flickers of electricity danced between his fingertips. "Don't even get me started on stuff like this. My head is a puzzle box. I have memories in here that I know for *sure* aren't mine. Maybe some are ordinary dreams, but like you said, Dubbs, I shouldn't have been able to dream at all. I can remember walking on the surface of worlds I've never been to. I remember flying through space as a thought . . . without a physical form. And there are big shadows in my mind that I can see and almost touch, and I think that they are blocking me from knowing more about what I dreamed. All of that scares the living hell out of me. I'm totally freaked the fuck out. Frankly, I don't know how I'm keeping my shit together."

Everyone simply stared at him.

Pickle nodded. "I feel better knowing you don't know what the fuck is going on either."

Jason ignored him. "So, yeah, the looks on your faces? That's what I'm going to have to get used to. It was bad enough when they rolled our HE teams out. Even while people were celebrating our victories, they were looking at us like we were the boogeymen come out from under the beds. Maybe we are. Maybe more so now after that long sleep. I mean, best case scenario is that we're freaks. Dangerous freaks."

"Worst case scenario is what, then?" asked Dubbs.

"Worst case scenario is that," said Jason, pointing to Darren Burris's corpse.

"No," said Pickle, "worst case scenario is that there are other HEs like him and they don't get put down."

Jason turned to him, his eyes going cold. "'Put down' is a questionable choice of words, son. You want to say that again?"

Pickle went pale. "N-no . . . that's not what I meant."

"It was," said Jason. "I can tell. I can see it in your eyes. Maybe I can feel it on some *other* level that doesn't yet have a name. You think we should all be put down. You don't think any of us should be revived."

"That's not true," said Pickle, straightening a little, showing some defiance. "You can read my mind all day long, man, but you're reading it wrong. I think we need to be careful with how we go about it. Take our time. Examine each HE as they wake. See who or what they are *when* they wake."

Jason considered that for a moment, then shrugged. "Okay, so maybe I'm not really a mind reader. Not like that, anyway. But I can feel your resistance. I can taste your fear."

"Well, no shit," said Pickle. "Of *course* I'm afraid, and of *course* I'm not eager to see what might happen. You were still asleep when Burris was trying to kill all of us. Look at the bruises on Lexie's throat. He did that. And he *ate* some of the birds."

Lexie said, "Let me put this into the mix. Some or all of the HEs have been dreaming. We know that. Some or all of them have projected their dreams to people on Earth and elsewhere. Some of those dreams have sparked people to act as suicide bombers against the Flock."

"I—" began Pickle, but she cut him off.

"Let me finish. Some of the HEs, though, have communicated with us in other ways."

"Like getting jiggy?" suggested Dubbs.

Lexie flushed. Jason looked down at the floor for a moment.

"My point," said Lexie, standing her ground, "is that the connection I had with Jason didn't make me want to strap explosives to myself and walk into a rookery. And I bet there are plenty of other Dreamers who didn't commit acts of violence."

No one commented.

"I say we find them all," said Pickle. "That's why we came all this way. That's what the resistance needs. It's what we all need."

"At any cost?" asked Dubbs.

"Yes," said Pickle firmly. "So, again I ask you, Jason . . . how many teams are there and *where* are they?"

"And if they wake up like Burris and try to kill us?" demanded Dubbs.

"Then God help us all," said Lexie.

"It's not like we'll be worse off than we are now," insisted Pickle.

"You willing to bet your life on that?" asked the scientist. "Are you willing to bet all of our lives?"

Jason Horse nodded at him. "Wake them up," he said. "Now."

81

Dubbs, resigned and reluctant, went to work.

The Sleepers woke.

Paula "Pryss" O'Neil was the first to wake. She was tall and had the long muscles of an athlete, and the high cheekbones and red hair of her Irish heritage.

Then Lamont "Short Dog" Hammond came next. A fireplug of a man, he rose only to Pryss's chest, but his muscles were five times the size, as was his side-cracking smile.

Fatima "Girlie" had religious tattoos over almost all her body, including one of the Virgin Mary on her neck. Her black hair was matted and twisted from two hundred years of uneasy slumber. Her eyes were still heavy with sleep.

Billy "Trig" Hollister slipped soundlessly to the floor. Where Short Dog was short and wide, Trig was as tall as Jason but lacked the mass of the HE leader. Trig's eyes were constantly narrowed as if he were always examining his universe. His nose was thin, his lips almost nonexistent.

Finally came Hiro "Sushi" Suzuki. His head had been shaved and other than a black goatee he was completely hairless.

He wore nothing but a jock strap, revealing skin that was tattooed like a Yakuza.

Jason stood ready with their clothes.

None of them awoke like Darren Burris had. Not one.

But none of the Sleepers woke up the way they had gone to sleep. Even though Lexie did not know what special gifts they each might now possess, she could read the awareness of being different—of being alien—in their eyes. It was a terrible thing to see.

As each Sleeper looked around, frightened and confused, Jason Horse calmed them down, hugging each one, looking into their eyes to get his own read on the people who shared the long, strange trip with him from a black-site Department of Defense genetics lab to this cold moon on the wrong side of the solar system.

Only when they were all awake did he offer any explanation.

However, before he could tell his tale, the revived HEs saw the darkened capsules. There were cries of pain, shouts of denial. There were tears and prayers and curses. Not only for the loss of their own, but the capriciousness of a universe that had decided who would live or die.

Jason gathered the survivors around him, and they all sat on the hard concrete floor. It was then that he related to them everything Lexie had told him.

It was a hard thing to say.

It was a hard thing to hear.

Lexie and her team sat on the floor as well, set slightly aside from the circle that had formed around Jason.

After the briefing was over, the HEs sat in stunned silence. Their fear was palpable.

It was a long, long time before anyone spoke. Then Pryss broke the silence.

"What *are* we?" she asked. Begged. Pleaded.

Jason Horse shook his head. "I don't think there is anyone in the galaxy who can answer that question."

It was a horrible answer.

But it was the absolute truth.

82

There were two rows of lockers lining the wall of the cryo-genics lab. One held the personal gear for the HEs. The other held never-used atmosphere suits. Granted they were two centuries old, but still sealed in plastic. A tank recharger was built into the wall. Their cryogenic clothes lay in piles on the floor.

Alpha Team stood in a cluster a few yards away from Lexie and her associates. The narrow strip of floor separating the two groups might as well have been ten thousand miles wide.

"Well," said Pickle quietly, "this is awkward."

"Of course it is," said Lexie as she began fastening the seals on her suit. "How would *you* feel if you woke up one day and everyone you ever knew was dead? And you found out that your government had betrayed you?"

"I'd probably shoot myself," said Pickle, and when Lexie glanced at his eyes, she realized it wasn't a joke.

Mugabe patted his shoulder. "I can understand that, brother. You don't believe in anything. Hope does not grow in the absence of faith."

"I don't know about that," said Fodder, "but anger sure as shit does. I'm not big on church either, but being royally pissed has kept me going all this time." She paused. "These chicken fuckers killed my best friend. They killed Fire. So, there's no way I'm taking a dirt nap any time soon. In fact, I think I'll start collecting Flock scalps. Those Mohawks? Yeah, I think I need a hundred of those to lay on Fire's grave."

"That's disgusting," said Dubbs.

"Didn't ask you, surfer boy. Don't give a shit if you approve."

Lexie kept cutting looks at the HEs, and each time she did she caught Jason looking at her.

Pickle leaned close. "How do we know we can trust those freaks?"

"Dude," said Dubbs, "they got mad superpowers. I'm pretty sure they can hear you."

"Want me to say it louder?"

"Enough," said Lexie. She fastened the last seal, then turned to the HEs. "Okay, elephant in the room time. We're all scared to death of you. How do we get past that? Because otherwise our operational efficiency is going to suffer."

The Sleepers stared at her, their expressions ranging from surprise to hostility to amusement.

"That took balls to even ask," said Pryss, pitching it loud enough for everyone to hear.

"For the record," began Trig, "I think we're a lot more freaked out than you are."

"How do you reckon that?" asked Fodder.

"You're all afraid of monsters," the soldier replied. "We just woke up and found out we *are* the monsters."

The silence followed that remark was crushing. Trig walked over to the capsules in which the dead Sleepers lay. He stopped there and placed his palms on one with a woman's name on it.

MONIQUE ST. PIERRE

Trig closed his eyes and stood there, still as a statue.

"I mean," said Short Dog, breaking the silence, "do you clowns have even a *clue* as to how we're all feeling?"

Lexie walked over to him. "No," she said. "We don't. We can't. How could we? Sure, we have sympathy, but empathy is likely beyond us all. Now, for sure, and maybe always."

Short Dog blinked. "Ummm . . . okay. That's fair. I guess. Changes nothing. You're a bunch of Norms. We've been through worse shit than you ever heard of."

"Norms. Normals," said Lexie, dryly. "I get it."

A couple of the other HEs chuckled. Lexie kept her gaze locked on the HE. He was shorter than Jason, but massively muscled, with the chest, shoulders, and arms that would have been better suited to a silverback gorilla. His energy and attitude matched.

"But let me ask you a different question, Short Dog. That's your combat call sign, right? Short Dog. Well, not to measure dicks here, but do *you* have even a clue as to how we are feeling?"

"You? Why should I care?"

"Why," mused Lexie. "Why indeed. I get it. You won your war. You saved the human race. You took the Flock empire down and then went to sleep. Dreams and all that. We, on the other hand, lived through the Flock uprising. We lived through the pogroms where whole populations were forced below ground to live in shadows. We witnessed the mass slaughter of more than half of the human population, on Earth and across the galaxy. There's not one person on my team who didn't bury family and friends. We've lived as slaves for 214 years, and if we can't do something to fight back, we'll die as slaves. Actually, all of us are outed as members of the Resistance, so there is no safe place— no world, no moon, nor space station—where we can go and be safe. We risked everything to find you and wake you up. The only thing that kept us going was the knowledge that you were out here. Sleeping. Waiting. And friends of ours died helping us get offworld. One of our friends died today. One of yours too."

She took a step forward so that she and Short Dog were nearly chest to chest. His mass was three times hers, but Lexie held her ground and stared up into his intelligent pointy face.

"We don't have superpowers," she said coldly. "*You* do. Even before whatever happened to you while you slept. You're bigger, better, faster, more than all of us put together. We're a Bottom dweller, a smart-ass fixer, a surfer boy scientist, a Martian prophet, and a history nerd with an unlikely inheritance, and we came halfway across the solar system with the most dangerous killers in the Flock fleet on our trail. We came here, to this moon, to this facility that no one could even prove existed, in the thin hope that you and your friends were still alive. On the thinner hope that we could wake you up. And on the tissue-thin hope that you, after all that was done to you, might— *might*—help us. Knowing full well that there were more ways we could fail than succeed. And when we wake one of you up, he's out of his mind and tries to kill us. The rest of you wake up understandably hurt and pissed and confused. You're angry at us because we represent the culture that used you and threw you away. You terrify us. You terrify me. My parents are still on Earth. I'd built a cover story for them, but I'm pretty sure that was blown when the birds figured out who we were. That means my family is either in prison or dead. I will probably never know. And if I found out, what could *I* do about it? I'm not a soldier. I'm not like you."

There was no sound at all in the room.

"So, yes, I get that you're fucked up about all this. But you've been awake for less than an hour. We've been *living* this. I'm surprised, astounded really, that only one of my team died getting this far. I don't expect to survive whatever is coming next. Pretty sure none of my friends do either. But you . . . god . . . there's nothing like you in the whole galaxy. Not on any world. You might as well be gods or, at the very least, demi-gods. Even just the few of you here are what the Flock has been terrified of for two hundred years. *You're* the reason they surrendered. *You're* the reason they pretended to be our friends and acted like slaves all these years. *You're* the reason they played this long game. And *you* are the reason so many people have died. You're the heroes and the villains of this drama. So, yes . . . we're afraid of you. Even as we try to understand your experience, we're caught up in our own, and the odds are that if this comes to a war . . . and even if we win, some or all of you will be still standing while my friends and I will be bones in the dirt."

She looked at him for five hard seconds, then at Pryss, Girlie, Short Dog, Sushi, and finally Jason.

"And none of you probably gave any of that a second's thought," she said. "None of you even said that you're going to help. You don't have to. You can take our ship and fly off, wake your friends up, and go conquer a world that the Flock won't dare try and take back. You owe us nothing. I get that. But don't you dare ever mock us."

With that she turned her back on Trig and all the HEs, walked over to the recharger, and began fiddling with the oxygen hose.

"Well, hell . . . I . . . I didn't mean . . ." said Short Dog.

"Maybe you ought to shut the fuck up," suggested Pryss.

Shaking her head, she came over and stood behind Lexie. "Turn around."

Lexie finished connecting the hose, trying her best not to bungle it with her trembling fingers. Only when the hose was tight and the gasses hissing through the hose did she turn. Pryss was inches away.

"That was quite some speech," said the soldier.

Lexie looked into the woman's eyes. They were green, rimmed now with the same gold that encircled all the Sleeper's eyes.

"I need to say this and make sure I'm heard loud and clear," said Pryss.

Lexie braced for it, hands balling into icy fists.

"No one ever talks to us like that. Even our commanding officers soft-soaped it. Ordinary people just don't talk to people like us."

Lexie did not trust herself to speak.

"We're not even human. You know that," continued Pryss. "We're HEs. *Homo eximius.* Super soldiers built using ultra top-tier shooters as clay. You said it, we're bigger, better, faster, more. Any one of us could wipe the five of you out without breaking much of a sweat. We could snap your necks and leave you here and go find a planet to make our home."

Lexie looked into those bottomless green eyes. Alien eyes.

"I can't speak for my team," said Pryss. "Certainly not for Short Dog. Not for any of us. We're not even part of the army anymore. I don't know where we belong. That script's unwritten. But right now? At this moment?"

Lexie said, "Y-yes?"

"Right now, Miss Lexie Chow," said the Sleeper, "I think I'd follow you to the gates of hell."

"What?"

Pryss held out a hand and after a long pause, Lexie took it. That hand was hard and strong, and the fingers were still cold. But it felt human to Lexie.

It felt wonderful.

A shadow fell across her and she turned to see Short Dog standing there. He held out his hand.

"Never had my mouth washed out with that much soap," he said. "I got you, Miss Chow."

"It's Lexie."

"No, ma'am," said Short Dog. "I'll call you that when I earn it."

Pryss clapped him on the shoulder.

Then they were all there. The Sleepers and her team of misfits. Shaking hands. Hugging. Laughing. Weeping. Except for Trig, who was still by the darkened capsules, eyes closed, head bowed.

Jason Horse was the last one to offer his hand to Lexie. That grip lingered a few ticks longer than it should have. His hand was warmer than the others.

"That was some speech," he said. "Now . . . let's go start a war."

83

Jason and his remaining team began scouring the chamber for supplies. There wasn't much, but Mugabe insisted that there was more than enough of everything they could use back on *Tin Man*.

"Which, as I believe," said Jason, "has been taken by the birds."

"Well . . . yes."

Jason nodded. "Just noting it."

"Adding it to the to-do list," said Pryss.

"You guys have cooked some birds getting to us, right?" said Girlie. "Then we can take whatever they were carrying."

"Pulse rifles, mostly," said Fodder.

"Works for me."

"New models, though," said Mugabe. "You won't be familiar with them."

That just made the HEs laugh, and Mugabe said nothing more.

"Let's go," said Jason and Lexie at the same moment. They looked at one another, smiled, nodded, and then Lexie waved a hand toward the door.

"I'm a book nerd," she said. "I'm totally fine with you being the one to shoot things."

"Works for me too," said the big HE.

As they moved out into the hall, stepping over the bodies of dead Raptors, Pickle lagged behind and tugged on Lexie's sleeve. She lingered with him.

"What's up?" she asked.

Pickle nodded at the retreating backs of the HEs. "How much do you trust them?"

Lexie chewed her lip for a moment, the shrugged. "I don't know."

"That's not a comforting answer, kiddo."

"I guess it wasn't meant to be."

She ran to catch up with the others. Pickle lingered a moment longer, looking at the corpses on the floor.

"Well . . . shit," he said, and followed.

84

Micah Fontenot pressed the medial epicondyle of his left arm, holding the pressure steady until his forearm opened. The skin around the long, slim slot was mostly real, though Micah had paid a lot of money to a top body-mod doc to make sure the organic plastics meshed completely with his own flesh. He had similar slots in each thigh, and unless one knew where they were, only an autopsy would ever reveal them. Expensive but useful, and they made good use of old scar tissue left over from some pre-Uprising exploits.

He removed a crystal-blue data slip, closed the port on his arm, and inserted the slip into a slot on the conference table. Then he told his AI to resume normal viewing, which caused the charcoal-colored bubble around him to vanish. Selling that kind of tech to corporate bigwigs, corrupt politicians, and drug lords had made him very rich once upon a time. Now it foiled birds and scan-bugs, and even temporarily blocked the eyesight of the other Resistance members at his table.

Each of the others had their own ways of transporting data and masking themselves as need. It amused Micah that some of the best advancements in this kind of technology had not come from any government lab, because they were all too busy doing nothing for the last two centuries. No, the best stuff was made in pirate labs that moved around and catered to a clientele whose business never hit a slump, even in the calmest of days during the Flock occupation.

Now that tech was doing for humanity what the military simply could not do—protecting the people involved in a war against an alien occupation. Life was funny like that.

The computer built into the table read the files and launched the presentation. The lights dimmed as hundreds of tiny holographic projectors clicked on, filling the space above the table with images so dense with micropixels that it looked real enough to touch.

They stared at a ship of a kind none of them had ever seen before.

"This is it?" asked Junko, a Serbian who ran arms for the cells in Eastern Europe.

"That's it," said Micah.

The board room held the table, ten chairs, a sideboard, and the presentation tech. Nothing else. All four walls, the floor and ceiling were layered with Soothe-H5, a fabric developed nearly eighty years ago for lining the walls of recording studios. A bomb could go off in the next room and they wouldn't hear it—the nanites in the fabric absorbed all sound and remixed it into white noise.

"What's the scale?" asked Guimarães, a Brazilian chemist who manufactured illegal drugs for Loopers in the Bottoms.

"Accurate down to millimeters." Micah tapped the holo-keys projected by his *Mon Tout.* Two other ships appeared and immediately a network of pale-blue lines appeared, offering dozens of measurements to compare and contrast.

"A pair of Falcon fighters and a surveillance photo of a ship of completely alien design. We think this is *Juggernaut*."

"Not sure I follow this," said Shimada, a Japanese smuggler who helped move key cell members around the globe and occasionally off world. "I was expecting something bigger."

"Much, much bigger," agreed Lucius, the author of the Resistance's most influential and highly illegal Net posters.

"That's the thing," said Micah, "it's not the monstrous miles-long ship we were expecting. Rumors have value but they often distort. Now, we are pretty sure the ship is the size shown here. Big enough, but actually smaller than a standard space carrier and even smaller than most battleships. So, it isn't the size that concerns me. No. It's the damn thing's *mass*. 6.67970281 x 10^21. Approximately 1/11th the mass of the moon. Calculated based on the gravitation influence it exerts. You've all seen news stories recently about tidal surges and unexpected weather changes. Abrupt stuff that doesn't fit forecast models? I saw that stuff too and didn't pay much attention because it didn't seem to play into anything we're doing. Now I get it, and I think that the bizarrely dense mass of *Juggernaut* *is* the culprit."

"No way," said Junko. "Those numbers have to be wrong. No ship ever built has mass like that. The fuel needed to propel it through solar and planetary gravity would be astounding. No, Micah, you're wrong. This is impossible."

"Yes," said Micah, "it pretty much is."

The three ships turned slowly above the table. The fighter and the carrier from the old war. And *Juggernaut*.

"We don't understand it," Micah conceded. "There is nothing our geek-squad has so far come up with that explains that mass. Or how it can maneuver dragging that weight."

"The design is so strange," said Shimada. "I keep thinking

'alien,' and I don't mean Flock. The birds are scavengers, though . . ."

"Right," agreed Micah. "Which means this might be tech they scavenged from some other race."

"If so, that means *other* science, *other* approaches to physics and engineering."

Micah nodded gravely. "And other levels of threat."

They all leaned in to study the strange ship. It was sleek and elegant and, in terms of overall design, called to mind the head of a striking viper.

"Do we have anyone who can get onboard?" asked Quinnayuak, an Inuit logistics fixer.

Micah picked up his coffee cup and sipped. "We're working on that."

They were silent a long time as *Juggernaut* turned slowly, slowly, slowly above the table.

PART FIVE
SWORN TO ACTION

Soldiers are citizens of death's grey land,
Drawing no dividend from time's to-morrows.
In the great hour of destiny they stand,
Each with his feuds, and jealousies, and sorrows.
Soldiers are sworn to action; they must win
Some flaming, fatal climax with their lives.

—Sigfried Sassoon
"Dreamers"

Out of the night that covers me,
Black as the pit from pole to pole,
I thank whatever gods may be
For my unconquerable soul.
It matters not how strait the gate,
How charged with punishments the scroll,
I am the master of my fate,
I am the captain of my soul.

—William Ernest Henley
"Invictus"

85

Lexie, as a historian, pragmatist, cynic, and citizen under the rule of the Flock knew full well that bad times could get worse.

What she hated was being proved right. Over and over again.

Some would love the idea that their theses were accurate.

She'd rather have been wrong.

86

As they left the cryogenics lab, Jason sent Girlie ahead to take point and assigned Short Dog to watch their backs. The big woman named Fodder gave them two sets of PAALs to be used and explained how they worked. Neat gadgets designed for primarily close combat. They made sure that Girlie had one and Short Dog wore the PAALs that had so recently been on the dead woman named Fire. He didn't know the history behind the relationships of the new crew yet, but he couldn't help but recognize the longing in Fodder's eyes as she passed the system to Short Dog.

The HEs moved like oiled shadows—very fast and so silent that Lexie found it both impressive and creepy. It reinforced the fact that these people really weren't human. Even without whatever happened to them in cryosleep, they were everything Alexander had said, and more.

It also made her aware of how much noise *she* made. Her breath, the rustle of her clothes. Even her light footfalls in Io's reduced gravity seemed to pound the floor like a rhinoceros. She glanced around nervously and saw that the rest of her friends wore similar expressions of comparison and self-awareness. Even Mugabe, though he seemed amused. Fodder, she noticed, was doing her best to imitate Jason's movements, and wasn't doing too badly, but it called to mind a puppy doing its best to imitate its dad.

Her attention was torn away from that speculation to the immediate when they moved through a section where Fodder and Mugabe had clearly done some real damage. There was blood splashed high on the walls, and the floor was littered with raw pieces of flesh that did not seem to add up to anything that could ever have lived.

Trig, who was midway through the line, seemed to nod his approval.

"You?" he asked very quietly.

"Me and Mugabe," said Fodder.

"Rock and roll."

That firefight had done a lot of damage to the walls and floors, too. A couple of storage rooms stood with their doors ripped to pieces. Short Dog checked them out. The first was stacked floor to ceiling with field rations of a kind soldiers called "horse shit on toast." High protein and vitamins, but incredibly awful taste. Mugabe touched his arm.

"We have much better stuff on the ship."

"Actual horse shit would taste better than this stuff."

When he poked his head into the next closet, he broke into a huge grin.

"Boss," he yelled, "check this out."

They all gathered inside except for Sushi left to guard their backs. The closet was larger than the other, and it was filled with three kinds of crates. One stack was marked *Ice Rigs*, which was exactly that—protective garments and supplies for work on frozen moons, where the Flock often hid their own supply depots. The second was marked parts, each box stenciled with complex codes. When they opened a few, they found arcane pieces of machinery that even Mugabe had a hard time identifying.

The third stack, though, made Jason smile too. He tore off a lid and they all leaned in for a look.

"At a guess," said Pickle, "these are the worst space suits I've ever seen."

Fodder poked at one. "Why are they so damned big?"

"They're something special," said Jason. "These are breaching pods." He explained how they worked, and Lexie snapped her fingers.

"I remember Alexander writing about those," she said excitedly. "It's how Alpha Wave got into Calliope Station to attack the Raptors."

"Exactly," said Jason, but then he looked wistful. "Hate to leave them here, but they're nothing we need for what we're doing, though." He put the cover back and went back into the hall.

"Maybe we'll find something else," said Sushi. "A couple of mech suits would be nice. Maybe a mech-tank suit. Always wanted one of those."

"I'd like a cold beer and a plate of fish tacos," said Short Dog. "Don't think we'll find those either."

They left the closet.

The HEs carried the Flock pulse rifles retrieved from the dead birds in the cryo-lab. But there were more guns at this ambush site, and they took those too. One of the dead Raptors had three grenades on what was left of his belt. Jason took these and gave one each to Girlie, Trig, and Pryss.

They moved on.

As they stalked up the corridor, Lexie overheard a hushed conversation between Pryss and Trig.

"I can't tell shit from Horse," said Trig. "That goddamned stone face of his never gives anything away. But . . . how are *you* doing with all this? The rest of the team back there? That weird dream shit. Burris going all ape-shit. And . . . let's face it, sister, we woke up wrong. Weird. I don't know what else to call it."

Pryss walked a few steps before she replied. "It's freaking me out, is how I'm taking it. Not sure what's hitting me hardest. Maybe the time. Two hundred years? Shit."

"No joke." He cut her a look. "You dreamed too, right?"

Lexie had the feeling Pryss didn't want to answer, but she eventually nodded.

"What did you dream about?" asked Trig.

"I don't know how to describe it," said Pryss pounding a fist into her other hand. "It's jumbled. Like I watched fifty vid-screens all at once. It's hard to separate it all out."

"Same," said Trig. "I remember some stuff, though. It was like waking up in someone else's body. I was me, but I wasn't. I was even speaking French, which is weird 'cause I only know English and a little Spanish. That's it. But I was speaking French like I was born to it. So was my . . ." He paused.

"Your what?"

"My wife."

"You're not married. Or . . . *weren't* married."

"I know. But I was in one of my dreams. The most recent one. I was some kind of construction worker. I remember talking to my wife before bed, and then I remember getting up, going to work, going into a shed where they had demolition charges, rigging a vest, and . . . and . . . well, I blew myself up. Took a whole bunch of birds with me."

Pryss looked at him and then away. "I had dreams like that too. Maybe we all did."

Trig indicated Jason with an uptick of his chin. "Even him?"

"Yeah, I overheard him and the Korean chick talking. She was dreaming of him and he was dreaming of her. Not sure if they were in the same dream and interacting, but . . ." She shrugged.

"This is so fucked up," said Trig.

They walked.

Pryss said, "I wonder what really happened to the others. You saw what Gomez wrote on the inside of his capsule cover. *I Am God* and all that."

"Yeah," said Trig, "that was some crazy shit."

"You think it means anything?" asked Pryss.

"Fuck if I know."

The group climbed a flight of steps and turned into another long and empty hall.

"Pryss," said Trig, "they said that Burris was different. That he had some kind of—I don't know—superpowers or some shit. Jason too. Electricity all over him. Us too."

"Yeah."

"Do you . . . I mean, do you think we're *different* somehow? Changed, I mean."

Pryss didn't answer. Which, to Lexie, was answer enough.

87

The stairwells and corridors seemed longer, colder, darker than Lexie remembered. And as she gradually and deliberately silenced the sounds she made, she could hear odd noises sneaking toward her. The scuff-scrape of a clawed bird foot. A clink of metal. Dripping water. And with each new sound, Jason turned his head slightly in that direction. She tried to read his expression, to guess his thoughts, but there was a wall between them in every meaningful way.

What's he thinking? she wondered. *How is he taking all of this?*

As if she could hear Lexie's thoughts, Pryss turned to look at her. But the woman said nothing, and after a moment turned away again.

"Airlock's ahead," said Girlie, speaking quietly. The S-sounds of whispering carried farther than low conversation, and she was very careful. Lexie remembered reading that somewhere. One more thing that filled the chasm between what she knew firsthand and what these HEs already knew. That difference was both frustrating and comforting.

A few moments later Girlie raised her fist, and Lexie copied the HEs as they immediately knelt—silent, weapons up and covering all possible directions, eyes tracking along with their gun barrels. Jason moved up and crouched beside Girlie.

Lexie was close enough to hear them speak.

"If there's going to be a trap, boss," said Girlie, "it'll be here. It's what I'd do. Those pigeons might as well hang a sign."

"Yeah, well, let's have a little fun," said Jason. He pivoted on the balls of his feet and gestured for Trig to advance. Jason used quick combat hand signs and the two soldiers moved off at once, slipping along the walls carefully and taking up positions on either side of the open airlock. Jason unslung his helmet, showed it to the others, and put it on. They all followed suit.

Sushi moved up to kneel beside Jason, who waved him on, and the man ran low and fast to a position on one side of the airlock. Girlie broke left and took her spot on the other side.

Jason waved the whole team back and to the side, using the curve of the hall as a shield.

The two HEs on point took the grenades in hand, grinned at each other like school kids, whipped them into the airlock, and scrambled back. Lexie clapped her palms over her ears and squeezed her eyes shut.

There was a dreadful pause of about one full second and then four Raptors tried to cram out of the airlock together. They fired their rifles wildly, filling the corridors with purple fire.

Lexie opened her eyes, sure that the grenades had misfired. She saw Girlie and Sushi rise up in perfect harmony. Girlie shot one Raptor in the face from six inches away, and grabbed the barrel of a second's rifle, jerking the bird forward with such shocking force that Lexie heard something audibly break in the Raptor's arm. Sushi did not use his rifle, but instead had gas knives in both hands. He leapt up, slashing down with one blade, shearing through muscle and bone on a third Raptor's forearm, and driving the point of the other up under the fourth bird's beak.

The screams were terrible.

High-pitched, laden with awful pain, polluted with fear, desperate and helpless.

It was all over in seconds.

One Raptor was down with a hole burned through its face. The third and fourth seemed to disintegrate inside a net of silver woven by Sushi's blades.

The second one, though, pitched forward, losing its grip on the rifle Girlie had grabbed. It fell hard and badly, tried to roll sideways as it fumbled for a holstered pistol. Girlie dropped down, pinning the reaching hand with one knee. Lexie heard those bones break too. Girlie plunged her other knee into the bird's stomach, her suit's gas jets firing to push her downward, amplifying the apparent weight of the woman many times. All of the air whooshed out of the Raptor's lungs. Faster than Lexie could comprehend, the bird was flipped over onto its stomach with a rifle barrel pressed into the back of its neck.

Sushi darted into the airlock and there was a flash of pulse fire and a fifth Raptor staggered out, eyes bulging, hands and vestigial wings clamped over a huge hole in its midsection. It tried to keep its guts in place, but that was no longer possible. The creature sagged down to the floor in a red and sloshing heap.

Suddenly the rest of the HEs were moving. They swarmed forward. Pryss and Trig ran ahead, past the airlock, weapons moving back and forth in overlapping patterns as they made sure the corridor was empty. Short Dog and Sushi immediately began dragging the dead birds out of the way and then set to stripping them of every useful item.

Fodder was on her knees, gun hanging forgotten in his hands, staring at the HEs with a mixture of fear and absolute worship. Mugabe drew a sign against evil in the air, and Lexie was unsure whether it was against the Raptors or the HEs.

Pickle got slowly to his feet, helped by Dubbs. Both men looked dazed. Lexie got up more cautiously.

"The grenades . . ." she said.

Sushi laughed, walked into the airlock again, and came out with both grenades in his hand. The arming triggers were in place, and Lexie suddenly understood. They had never intended to detonate two high explosives in the airlock. But the Flock could never have known that. The highly trained Raptors had seen the danger and rushed out to save their lives and confront the enemy. It was a trap to spring a trap.

"Jesus fucking hell," gasped Pickle.

88

They clustered around the wounded Raptor. The bird's eyes were glazed with fear and pain, and his beak twitched as small high-pitched chirps escaped him.

"He's a red cloak," said Mugabe. "Dark red, from an important family."

"No rank markings," said Trig.

"They do that when they're on special missions," said Pickle. "That way if they mess up, or fail, it doesn't land on a particular Privilege."

"Privilege?" queried Sushi.

"That's what they call their family groups. Extended families, really, way out to like fiftieth cousins and such. There are eight of them, each with a different color. Smaller family groups within each Privilege are ID'd by the shade of color. The darker the color, the higher the rank."

"Got it."

"When something like this happens," continued Pickle, "the whole clan takes the blame for the defeat, but without specific identifying rank or family crest, that blame is diffused, and the

Reds are the ones no one dares spit at. A single bird who fucks up can just be edited out of the Privilege records."

"Got to love the family sentimentality," said Pryss.

"Birds are birds," said Fodder.

"We didn't know that stuff when we went into the ice," said Jason. "Once we're off this rock, I'm going to need you folks to give us a briefing."

"Of course," said Lexie.

Pryss glanced at Jason. "He's hurt but he's not dead, boss."

Jason smiled thinly. "Sucks to be him, then. You're better at this than I am. See if you can have a meaningful conversation." He looked around. "Who here speaks Flock?"

"Don't need to," said Lexie. "They all have translators on that collar thing. He can hear us, and we'll be able to understand him."

The bird glared at her and tried to look away, as if that action meant he could neither hear nor speak. No one was fooled.

"Sushi, Short Dog," said Jason, "move him over to the wall. Someone go through the gear on those other birds. See if there's a first aid pouch. He's going to be in a lot of pain and we don't want it to be so bad he can't talk."

"On it," said Fodder, and by the time the wounded Raptor was positioned in a seated position against the wall, she'd returned with a slender pouch which contained a series of syrettes. She handed it to Lexie, who selected one filled with pale golden liquid. After a brief consideration, she removed a second that had a green fluid.

She held up the gold. "This is their painkiller. Works fast and lasts long. Given how bad he looks, I think maybe a third of it would be enough. Any more than that and he'll pass out. Works like a narcotic."

"What's the other?"

"A stimulant. If he *does* pass out, this will wake him up."

Jason nodded and took both. He administered the pain-killer, and they waited as the obvious pain from the injuries eased visibly.

Pryss knelt beside it. Lexie shifted so she could study the Raptor's face.

"I know you can hear me," Pryss said to the Raptor. "I know you can understand me. Don't pretend that you can't. It's pointless and there will be consequences."

The bird said nothing.

"I'm going to ask some questions," continued Pryss. "You will answer them. I'll know if you're lying and, again . . . there will be consequences."

She leaned closer.

"I know you're bred for war. I know you come from a noble house and are highly respected. We both know that this means you've been fed a lot of propaganda about how tough you are, how much pain you can endure, how unlikely it is that you'll ever be made to talk. Well, I'm military too, and I'm stronger than you are. I'm *Homo eximius*."

The Raptor flinched.

"You know what that means. Go ahead, nod. Agreeing to the truth is no betrayal."

After a moment, the Raptor gave a single tiny nod.

Lexie was impressed. She understood the tactic of manipulation. By making a statement that was both inarguable and noncontroversial, the Flock could agree without danger. However, that agreement, that nod, was itself a win. Pryss was teaching the bird to agree, to respond.

"How many of you are in this facility?" asked Pryss.

No answer.

"How many ships brought your team here?"

No answer.

"What is your mission?"

No answer.

"You're not here just to kill us. If you were, you'd have bombed this base from space. What do you want?"

No answer.

From the look on Pryss's face, she expected this, and it was part of some strategy. Before she could continue, though, Short Dog spoke up.

"Hey, this one's not dead." He crouched over one of the pair that Sushi had slashed to ribbons. "He's circling the drain, but he still has a pulse."

"Bring him over," said Pryss.

Short Dog squatted, sliding his arms under the bulky Raptor. He braced himself to lift but stood up so fast he lost his balance. Jason caught his arm and steadied him.

"Lower gravity," suggested Dubbs.

But Short Dog had a puzzled look on his face. "Nah . . . it's not that. It's like he doesn't weigh anything. It's weird. Like my bag."

"What do you mean?" asked Dubbs.

"My gear bag. Even at this level of G-force the bag had to be thirty pounds. But it weighed nothing at all. This bird's like that. Here." He handed the wounded Raptor to Dubbs, but the beefy scientist staggered under the weight.

"What are you talking about? He weighs a ton."

Frowning, Short Dog took him back. Then he bounced the injured bird up and down in his hands. "Doesn't weigh shit."

Jason went over. "Give him to me."

Short Dog handed the bird over. Jason grunted. "Feels like normal weight."

They stared at one another.

Lexie said, "Short Dog . . . see that barrel over there?" A big fifty-five-gallon drum of coolant sat in a niche. "See if you can lift it."

The soldier shrugged, set the wounded Raptor down next to the one in the red cloak, walked over, took hold of the handles mounted on either side of the barrel, braced himself and hauled. It sprang up off the floor. "Feels empty."

"Let me try," said Fodder and tried to take it from him. The barrel crashed down to the floor. "Holy jeez. Must weigh a hundred pounds or more."

"You're outta your mind," laughed Short Dog. He gripped the barrel by one of its two handles and lifted it one-armed without straining. After a moment he realized everyone was staring at him. He set the barrel down slowly. It made a heavy thump on the floor. Short Dog looked around. "I . . . shit, I got nothing."

Jason walked over to him. The team leader was several inches taller and much broader. He held his hand out as if offering to arm wrestle. Short Dog shrugged and gripped his hand. Jason pushed. Hard. Very hard. Short Dog just stood there, keeping his arm in place. Veins stood out on Jason's arm and neck. Sweat burst from his pores. Then he let go and stepped back, gasping.

"Someone's been taking his vitamins," said Pickle.

"Wait, wait," said Short Dog to Jason, "are you saying I'm *stronger* than you?"

"Quite a lot."

"But . . . how?"

No one tried to answer that.

"Curiouser and curiouser," murmured Pickle.

Jason turned to Pryss. "Get on with it."

89

"When you say we have *fighters*," began Micah, "are we talking more roughnecks from the Bottoms, or . . ."

"Fighters," said Lulu, "as in armed multifunction air or space craft. So . . . yes, fighters."

"You're shitting me."

He was alone in his conference room, feet up on the table, a very tall glass of black tea-infused gin resting on his belly between steepled fingers. A weird synth-jazz take on the Goldberg Variation filling the room. Outside the sky was a dreary gray from which a heavy, leaden rain fell hour after hour.

"I'm telling you the truth," said Lulu.

"What kind of fighters? I mean, what class? How old? Where? What condition?"

Lulu laughed. "The *how* is complicated. Deep salvage teams have been grabbing wrecks of space junk out of the orbits of half a dozen planets. There was some stuff here on Earth in a collapsed military base in Colorado. Everyone thought the collapse was total, but a scavenger team digging for parts for the black market cracked open a cavern where there's a whole slew of stuff. And a lot of tools and parts."

"Are we talking stuff that will actually fly?"

"Not as such," she said carefully. "Right now, it's a mixed bag of older Mercury- and Saturn-class fast-burners. A couple of really, really old Stingrays and Tiger Sharks—those are the ones in the cavern. Condition ranges from not-too-horrible to it'll-make-you-cry."

"I'm suddenly less excited," sighed Micah and drained two fingers of the gin.

"Don't get depressed," she said. "Everything we have is fixable. Well, nearly everything. Mostly fixable. It's a work in progress."

"When you say 'fixable,' what kind of time frame are we looking at?"

When she didn't answer, Micah's heart sank.

Finally, Lulu said, "Four, five years. Some of the key replacement parts need to be milled or manufactured. We need to get updated computers to the various shops. We need diagnostic stuff—Japan is the best right now because their hover-rail system uses a lot of the same basic anti-grav tech. We need armament because one of our teams tried to fire an old molecular fusion gun—you know what that is?"

"Yes. What happened?"

"Well, we lost that team. And four acres around the base."

"Shit on toast."

Lulu said, "It's a lot of work."

"Four or five years?" breathed Micah. "Goddamn."

"That's four or five years and then we'll have a bunch of combat-ready ships."

Micah sipped his drink.

"Thanks, Lulu. This is . . . um . . . great. Keep me posted."

He ended the call, took a sip, crunched an ice cube, and thought about everything she'd said and all that it meant.

That had been just under five years ago.

90

The focus shifted back to the elite Raptor. Pryss asked him the same questions as before, and once more the bird stonewalled her.

"You're not going to get anything," said Pickle. "We're wasting time here."

Pryss ignored him.

"Who commands your team?" she asked.

"Be damned," said the Raptor. It was a human expression, since the Flock did not have a concept of damnation. What it told Lexie was that this creature was very familiar with humans and their culture. Not all of them were.

Pryss smiled and drew her sidearm. She tapped the Raptor on the beak with it, making a *tik-tik* sound. The bird went nearly cross-eyed trying to look at the barrel. Then his big eyes moved as Pryss slowly swung the gun away from it and pointed it at the other Raptor who lay in a semi-daze, blood leaking from a dozen cuts.

"What is this Flock's name?" she asked.

After a pause to consider, the Raptor said, "Thel'Igo-Antares"

"No," said Pryss. And she pulled the trigger. Her sidearm

was a standard model with lead hollow-point rounds. It blew the back of the wounded Raptor's head off and splashed the wall—and the senior Raptor—with blood and gore. "Now he is nothing. Now he is dead on a foreign world. No one from the Flock or from his Privilege will ever know how or why he died. If anyone comes to this rock to investigate, they will find bodies with no clan markings, no weapons, no heads. They will find spoiled meat that belongs to no family." She leaned close but did not raise her voice. "The question is whether they will find your body—just as naked and stripped of family colors—as this one."

Lexie stared in horror. So did Dubbs. The others watched impassively.

"Tell me *your* name, bird," ordered Pryss, touching the hot barrel to the creature's reptilian skin.

"*Kig'Ngo-Kepler.*" The Raptor officer said his name with defiance and a show of pride.

Pryss repeated the name slowly. Lexie shifted so she could see the woman's eyes. They blazed with strange lights. As she spoke the Flock's name, it suddenly opened its mouth and cried out, but not in words. Only in sounds.

Suddenly reeling back, Pryss squeezed her eyes shut, hissing as if in sudden and terrible pain. Her teammates moved in, but she stopped them with a raised hand.

"No," she said sharply. Then, more quietly as the pain passed, "No. It's okay. I'm okay."

"What the hell was that?" demanded Jason.

Pryss looked surprised. "Just him cursing at me."

"What?"

"You heard him."

"No," said Jason. "He didn't say anything. Just groaned."

She turned and looked at him and then the others. "He was

clearly cursing. He called me a coyote, a fox. Bunch of others—bobcat, weasel, raccoon, opossum, skunk . . ."

"Pryss," said Jason quietly, "he didn't say any of that."

"Sure he did. Clear as day. Weren't you listening?"

"We all were," said Lexie. "And, yes, the Flock use the name of any egg-thief animal as curse words. But he didn't say those words just now."

The moment stretched. Pryss looked down at Kig'Ngo-Kepler.

"He's still fucking speaking, guys. H-how can you not hear it. He's telling me that he'll never talk. That Hell is coming. That . . . that . . ."

She trailed off.

"He's not speaking," said Lexie.

Mugabe leaned in. "He's not speaking out loud."

"What?" asked Pryss, confused and disturbed. "I can *hear* him."

"You can, sister," said the prophet. "We cannot."

"But that—"

"This is some spooky shit right here," said Short Dog.

"Sushi," said Jason, "keep this asshole bird here. He doesn't move." Then he took Pryss by the arm, raised her to her feet, and led her a dozen feet down the hall, out of the bird's earshot. Lexie trailed along to listen.

"Boss," said Pryss, "I don't—"

"Listen up," said Jason. "I think I know what's happening here. It's freaky and, frankly, it scares the crap out of me, but I get it."

"Get *what*?"

"From what Lexie told us, Darren woke up changed. You saw Short Dog pick up that barrel like it weighed nothing. *He* could do that; none of the rest of us could. And now you're hearing what that bird is thinking. There's a pattern here."

Pryss's eyes grew very big and very round. "Holy . . . shit . . ."

"He's right, Pryss," said Lexie. "You're changing. All of you are. I don't know how. Maybe it was the long cryosleep . . . maybe it's something else. We already know that some, or maybe *all* of you have been able to communicate with people on Earth and throughout the galaxy. You entered our dreams and shaped them. Sometimes in good ways, and sometimes in bad. You saw what Hiram Gomez wrote on the inside of his capsule. He must have become aware of some new power, some new ability. His consciousness went beyond the capsule and it drove him insane. But the five of you survived. Maybe Hiram's power wasn't something useless or easily understood like Short Dog's strength. Maybe he went as crazy as Burris did but the cryosleep kept him trapped. Now you can hear the thoughts of that Raptor. It's a pattern."

Pryss looked like someone had punched her in the face.

"Are you talking telepathy?"

"Or something like it," said Jason, nodding.

"This is freaky as shit," said Pryss. She laughed, but it was fake. Her eyes were jittery, and the gold rims seemed to flare. "Have to tell you, boss, that this is scaring the piss out of me."

"Welcome to the club." He cut a look over to where the rest of Alpha Wave were huddled around the Raptor. "Scaring me worse to think of what other *abilities* might emerge. What other changes."

"Listen," said Lexie, "I can't even begin to understand what you're all feeling. I mean, with *everything* that's happened. But we have an opportunity here."

"Yes," said Jason slowly. "We damn well do." He put his hand on Pryss's shoulder. "Are you up for it?"

"Up for . . ." She stopped and considered. "I mean, okay, maybe I've been rewired but it's not like it comes with an instruction manual."

"Figure it out on the fly."

Pryss straightened slowly and took a couple of steadying breaths, and then she went back to Kig'Ngo-Kepler. Lexie saw the others—even the other HEs—edge away from her.

They're afraid of her too, she thought. *Maybe they're afraid she'll read their minds.*

Pryss knelt once more. The Raptor looked terrified, and it seemed to be trying to look anywhere but at Pryss.

"Let's have a chat," said Pryss. "Just you and me."

After which she said nothing at all.

The Raptor understood. Somehow—maybe because he had already felt Pryss in his mind, Lexie thought—he knew that his thoughts were no longer sacred, no longer safe. He squirmed and fought against the soldiers who held him. He cried out in a dozen alien languages. He even tried to shout meaningless phrases of old Flock poetry as if somehow filling his conscious mind with nonsense could block her.

Pryss sat leaning forward, her hands lightly touching the sides of the bird's face, her eyes nearly closed, unfocused. Sweat beaded on her face and ran down her cheeks. Two very small trickles of blood seeped from her nostrils. She didn't speak.

It did not take long before Kig'Ngo-Kepler began screaming. But by then, Pryss had it all.

When she was done, when there was no more to take, when the inner mind of the Raptor had ceased to speak and was reduced to a constant, howling scream . . . she stopped. It took sheer force of will to tear herself loose before she, too, began to scream.

She was seconds too late.

The shriek rose from the molten pit of her being, rose up like lava and punched its way out. Pryss reeled back, thrashing, hitting, and clawing at the distorted monster things clustered around her. They were nightmare images composed of leering faces, gaping maws, ripping claws, and voices so shrill they were like knife cuts to her mind. She broke away from them, stumble-staggering down the corridor, holding onto the wall to keep her from falling off the edge of reality. She was back in the realm of dreams once more. Nothing was real. It was all created by a fractured mind whiling away eternity in a capsule of ice.

Kig'Ngo-Kepler's eyes were wide and unblinking and totally vacant. A slow, soft rattle of escaping air seeped from between its throat as the bird's lungs deflated into perpetual stillness.

Electricity crackled along her arms and up to her head, making her hair stand up like a fright wig. Lightning danced in her eyes and then the snapping arcs leapt from her to the walls, seeking grounding but finding wild conductivity. Several of the recessed lights on the ceiling exploded, showering them all with sparks that glowed in strange shades of blue and orange and red.

Pryss staggered to her feet, eyes filled with madness. Then she bolted and ran.

Trig ran, faster than the others, catching up to her, calling her name. Calling her back.

Pryss whirled, her hand scrabbling for the pistol, drawing it, thumbing off the safety only to have the monster shape swat it from her grip. Then hands were on her upper arms. Holding her. Steadying her.

Bringing her down to the surface.

"*Pryss!*"

The voice came from ten thousand miles away. The echoes of it were like blows. The hands were iron, but hot . . . burning her down to the bone.

"Pryss," cried Trig.

And it was Trig.

Not a monster. Him. Really there.

"Pryss," he said again. Infinitely gentle. "I got you, babe. It's me. I got you."

The swirl of uncountable images—her own and those of the Raptor and his Flock—swirled and swirled and slowed.

Down.

To.

Stillness.

The bizarre electrical discharge dissipated. Pryss felt her legs tremble. Her knees refused to perform any useful function and they buckled, but Trig caught her, held her as he knelt with her. Steadying her. Drawing her close.

"It's okay," he said.

She looked at him, her heart swelling with love.

Trig. Her friend.

He had found her in all that endless madness. He saved her.

"Trig . . ." she gasped.

"I'm right here, sis," he said. "I'm here."

Thank you.

Only she didn't say it. She wanted to and needed him to understand how much what he had done mattered. She ached to tell him how much it mattered.

Thank you.

Those words rose to her lips.

But a tide of vomit rose faster, and she threw up all over him. On his face and throat and chest.

91

"Well," said Trig, his body frozen in place, eyes wide, face dripping, "that was charming."

92

Jason picked Pryss up and carried her into the airlock, setting her down with a gentleness that surprised Lexie. The HE leader used his sleeve to clean her up and then gave her some water to drink. Pryss's eyes gradually cleared, and her breathing slowed. Except for Short Dog and Fodder, who were patrolling the halls to make sure there were no surprises, the rest of the mingled teams gathered together, each face marked with concern.

Trig was the last to join the group, needing time to clean up. Midway through that process, the nausea caught up to him and he, too, vomited. And cleaned up again. Pale, trembling, his skin a ghastly gray-green, he finally staggered into the airlock.

"Pryss," said Jason gently, "are you okay? Are you back with us?"

She blinked wet eyes for a few moments longer, then nodded. "That was . . . was . . ."

"Take it slow," said Jason.

"We don't have time for slow," said Sushi under his breath, but Jason ignored him.

Pryss nodded again. "It was so strange," she said, her voice hoarse from the burn of bile. "It wasn't like talking. It wasn't him there and me here. It was . . . I don't know . . . like we were the same person." She paused, considered that, then shook her head. "No. Not that either. It was like we were sharing the same mind. I don't know how else to explain it. I was there, and he was there, and . . . I was me and I was Flock."

She looked around, searching for understanding in each face.

In a voice filled with wonder, Mugabe touched his face just below his golden eyes. "I *saw* you. You were not you. You were . . . transcendent. You were a thing of fire. It was beautiful and terrible and glorious."

Lexie saw how those words hit Pryss. She expected the woman to flinch away from such a description, but instead Pryss nodded in mute acceptance.

"Ticktock, boss," said Trig quietly. Jason nodded.

"Pryss," he said, "did you learn anything? Did he tell you how many of them are here on Io? How many ships? Any of that?"

Her eyes were still jumpy, but she nodded. "He didn't actually *tell* me. Not in the way you mean, but . . . yes. In a way I can't explain, yes."

"Then you have to tell us, Pryss. We need to know."

Pryss nodded, drank more of the water, and tried to put it all into words.

"I stood for a while on the Flock homeworld," she said, and flicked a glance at Lexie. "You think you've *seen* that world—in stories and vidcaps—but you haven't. It's a dead place. All of its resources used up, its seas murdered by pollution, the skies gray with poison. Nothing lives there now except bacteria and fungus. That was where they came from, and when they used it up, they went looking for new worlds. They found many worlds. Uncountable places where other races had evolved. Some were dead too, lost to time. But most of them had populations, cultures.

The Flock is more like a swarm . . . they took each world, finding ways to ingratiate themselves into each alien society. That's one of their strengths, a kind of pernicious empathy. I *felt* it. I felt their hungers, their driving forces, their need to take and take and take and . . ."

"Whoa," said Jason gently, "ease down, girl. Take a breath."

She did and nodded, and when she was able, Pryss continued.

"They are one of the oldest surviving races in the galaxy. Millions of years old. With each world they conquered, they stripped it of every bit of technology, every useful resource, and when they had taken all they could, they . . . they . . . slaughtered the survivors. God, Jason, it was awful. I could feel it. And it wasn't even hate. They have no ideology or theology, nothing that inspires them. They just destroy what they don't need. Without malice or passion. And they move on."

"Jesus," gasped Dubbs.

"The thing is . . . they never really grow," continued Pryss. "They don't have a central set of ethics. There's no real imagination, no sense of art. Their clothes, their decorations, their rookeries, even their caste-system of Privileges are borrowed—stolen—from other races. But that's their strength as well. No sentimentality, no sense of purpose to do anything but survive. Until . . ."

"Until what?" prodded Jason.

"Until they met us," said Pryss. "We have something they hadn't encountered before. Or . . . something they had not encountered in a way with which they could connect."

"What is that?"

She looked almost surprised to say it. "Emotion. I mean . . . the *range* of human emotion. They understand things like pride, guilt, fear, shame, and avarice, but exposure to us forced them into collision with other feelings that disrupt their way of thinking. Love and compassion, romance and anxiety, joy and desire . . . all of it. They encountered the feelings in parts, but not as a whole. So much of that is unique to *their* experience. Other races they've encountered have either been at the end of their growth, or too early in it. Or, maybe it's that the Flock mind has more similarities to us than to them. I don't know because *they* don't know."

"Maybe they'll develop an understanding of shame and back the fuck off," said Trig.

It was a joke, but Pryss shook her head. "It's more complex than that. Exposure to us has taught them something bad. Something really dangerous."

"What? Our tech?" asked Girlie.

"No," said Pryss, fear glittering in her eyes, "hate."

"I'd have thought they always understood that," said Dubbs. "They've killed billions . . ."

"No. That was expediency, to sustain and expand their feeding grounds and territory. They always understood anger and brutality, but from a perspective of expansionism and efficiency. Hate was never part of their emotional makeup."

"But it is now?" asked Lexie.

"Oh yes," said Pryss. "They hate us with an intensity that words can't describe. It is the emotion more powerful than fear, and they have feared us since . . . well . . . since *us*." She looked at her fellow HEs. "Knowing that someone who worked for them—you, Lexie—has discovered where we are and plans to wake us and use us as a weapon against them has driven that hate to a level they've never known before. It's warping their decisions, driving them to a kind of madness."

"Shit," said Pickle.

"It explains a lot," said Lexie. "You all showed them that

they could be beat. That even with their stolen tech, there was a power more dangerous than their own. An attack on their efficiency. That made them afraid. Further contact with us made them resentful and hateful."

"It's worse than that," said Pryss. "If they didn't still need human slave labor and the resources we have, they would have wiped us out long before this. They have a plan, a timeline, and we are endangering it. But they foresaw it. They knew that we . . . *Sleepers* . . . were out here, but the dreams have terrified them. Their greatest fear is that enough humans will have those dreams, and that there will be an uprising across the galaxy."

"I wish," said Dubbs.

"No," said Pryss sharply. "You don't. And it has something to do with the phage. The virus we all have in us. They have it too. It links us. It links us all."

"What do you mean, Pryss?" asked Jason. "What else did you see?"

"Three things." Fresh fear sweat beaded her face. "First, the Flock has a dual purpose in hunting us. They want to kill us, of course, but not right away. They want to *capture* us. At least one or two of us."

"Why?" asked Lexie. "To make some public political statement about how powerful they are? To crush the hero worship and hope people have felt since those dreams started?"

"That's only part of it," said Pryss. "They want to study us. Dissect us. Learn from what the science teams did to us so they can create a Flock version of us. Not just to create a far stronger group of Raptors, but to force their own evolution. They want to create versions of Flock that have *all* of our strengths—including our emotions. Instead of trying to quash human emotions from the Flock, they want to embrace them, *build* on them. Think about it—within a single generation they can take the best of what we have and give it to an elite new generation of Flock."

"You're talking eugenics," said Lexie.

"Oh yes. But it gets worse."

"Fuck," said Pickle. "I don't know if I can do worse."

"First," said Pryss, "there is already a different kind of Raptor out there. And I mean literally out there." She pointed to the airlock door. "His name is Ren'Mgo-Hell. He calls himself Hell. Just that, bringing with it the human interpretations."

"Since when do the birds believe in hell?" asked Pickle.

"I just told you," said Pryss. "They're changing. This Raptor—Hell—he's a step ahead, I think. He's Flock but he thinks like us. He's a strategist and maybe something of a psychologist. He *gets* who we are."

"That's scary," said Lexie.

"Why him?" asked Jason. "What makes him so special?"

"Because he is a direct descendant of the Raptor we captured, boss. The one we patched up and sent back to the Flock with our threat."

She explained how that Raptor was made to bear the weight of Flock versions of guilt and shame; that his family had been forced to be "colorless," and that one of those descendants had gone to extraordinary lengths to push back against his species' scorn.

"Hell is vicious, powerful, and as I said, he's clearly embraced human emotions. He feels hate. Very much so. He's also smart, devious, and subtle. The Flock Elders put him in charge of finding us, and he has. These birds are his, and he is somewhere in this facility."

"Hell?" mused Girlie. "Well, to hell with him. A bird's a bird, and if he gets in our way, we'll send *him* back to the Flock. In pieces this time."

Pryss shook her head.

"I said there were three things, guys. The last is bad."

"How bad?" asked Jason.

"I . . . don't even know how to quantify it," admitted Pryss. "What's worse than awful? Apocalyptic? Yeah, that fits."

"If you're trying to scare us, miss," said Dubbs, "you're doing a pretty good job."

"Christ, you look like you're going to scream or faint, Pryss," said Trig. "What's so big and bad that it's freaking you out like this?"

She licked her lips before answering. "It's a weapon," she said. "Not something built on any kind of human technology. Nothing based on anything the Flock ever developed. And nothing *we've* ever seen. This is completely alien."

Mugabe suddenly stiffened. "No," he gasped.

Pryss looked at him, studied his face. "You know, don't you?"

"I have prayed with all my heart that I was wrong," said the prophet. "Please tell me I'm wrong."

But Pryss shook her head. "It's real."

"*What's* real?" Jason demanded.

"It's a weapon," repeated Pryss. "A ship. It's called—"

Lexie finished it for her.

"*Juggernaut*," she said.

93

The Eldest entered a small communications egg adjacent to his office. The door hissed shut behind him and a chair rose from the floor. The lights dimmed to their preset levels as he settled into the gelfoam cushions and a holo-screen flickered to life.

The ancient Flock leader spoke a few key words that brought up a satellite image of a dark ship silhouetted against the dusty red disc of Mars. Dozens of small Kestral two-Flock fighters moved with the ship in close orbit.

The Eldest spoke a name and immediately the image switched from the exterior view to that of the ship's captain, who sat on an ornate chair of unusual design. The captain, like all of his crew, wore dark hues of the red Privilege, the captain's darkest of all.

"My lord," said the captain, bowing.

"Are you current with the intelligence reports?"

"Yes. And I concur that the Resistance is making its move. We tracked them on the way to Io but lagged back to keep their sensors from detecting the gravitational fluctuations." The captain paused. "Do you think they will succeed in reviving the HEs?"

"I do," said the Eldest.

"Is it your belief that they will bring them to Earth? Or, as General Gub'Sgo-Wasp believes, that they will continue on to find and revive the other groups of Sleepers?"

"What is *your* opinion?" asked the Eldest, turning it around.

The captain nodded. "I think they will continue on. There's too great a risk to the entire Resistance operation for them to return to Earth. They made too visible a mess when they left."

"I agree," said the Eldest. "Therefore, we need to make sure they return to Earth."

The captain looked very interested. "And how shall we accomplish this?"

"Not 'we,'" said the Eldest. "You."

"Tell me and I will see it done."

"Our spies have provided us with the location of key metroplexes where Resistance cells are located. Three in particular pose the greatest threats to us. Chicago, Lisbon, and Paris."

"You are in Paris," said the captain. "And the admirals of the fleet have rookeries in Chicago." He paused. "And Lisbon . . . there are many hundreds of thousands of Flock living there. The evacuations to the countryside have been, as I understand it, slow."

"Yes," said the Eldest. "Some of our fellow Flock have become too comfortable in the metroplexes. They were warned to move their key family members to the country. There is a concern that the Resistance might learn of our plan because of the movement."

"Have Lisbon rookeries been told why?"

"No."

"May I ask the reason?"

The Eldest crossed his thin legs and settled deeper into the seat. "We have come to believe that there have been communications between some Flock and the Resistance."

"Communication? I don't understand?" said the captain, and then he stiffened as understanding blossomed. "No. Traitors? I've heard those stories, but I can't credit them. There hasn't been a rogue Flock in . . . in . . ."

"You are an excellent captain," said the Eldest, "and your loyalty to the Flock is spoken of across the galaxy. I fear, though, that your absolute dedication may blind you to the possibility of discontent in others of lesser station and fortune."

"But . . . traitors among the Flock? The very thought is unbearable, it's—"

"The word you are looking for is intolerable, and in the purest sense of that word. It cannot be tolerated."

The captain looked physically stricken, as if the thought of Flock dissidents was making him ill. His hands, though, clenched slowly into fists of pure rage.

"There is a rather disgusting and yet appropriate human expression that fits the moment," said the Eldest coldly. "'Killing two birds with one stone.'"

"How does that relate to . . ." and again the captain grasped the answer to his own question. That understanding seemed to steady him, replacing tension with anticipation. "And these dissidents are in one of those three metroplexes?"

"Yes. But only some. Many are here in Paris. Which is why our quiet evacuation is much further along, at least in terms of those Flock who are inarguably loyal, and those officials who are necessary for the next stages of the Grand Plan."

"What is my target?"

The old Flock leaned forward and murmured, "Lisbon."

The caption nodded, digesting that.

"Do this, then move out to orbit around Luna. Your presence, and the implied threat to the other metroplexes, should draw the HEs and their human rescuers back to Earth. It will make your ship their target. We have worked through the statistical probability of their coming back here rather than seeking the other Sleepers and even the most conservative estimates is an 87 percent probability. Human sympathy, loyalty, and their tendency to make sentimental rather than pragmatic decisions will be their downfall."

"How heavy a blow will it take to draw them here? Selected targeting of Resistance cells?"

"Oh, no," said the Eldest. "The humans love their dramas as much as they worship their martyrs, so let us give them something spectacular."

"And the loss of Flock lives?"

"We have use for our own martyrs," said the Eldest. "Just as we have use for examples made. Now go. Lisbon is yours."

The captain bowed his head. "For the glory of the Flock, father."

"For the glory of the Flock, my son," said the Eldest.

94

"That's total bullshit," laughed Pickle.

Startled, everyone looked at him.

"*Juggernaut* is a myth," insisted Pickle. "It's the Flock version of the boogeyman. Everyone knows that."

"Unless it isn't," said Mugabe. "It has been seen in dreams."

"Enough with the spiritual mumbo jumbo. *Juggernaut* isn't real."

"And how would you know?" asked Jason sharply.

"Because I have common goddamned sense," Pickle fired back.

"What *is Juggernaut*?" asked Girlie, perplexed. "What kind of ship are we talking? Battleship? Carrier?"

"It is a ship that exceeds any possible description," said Mugabe. "Supposed to be a mile or two long. A crew of many thousands."

"Maybe," said Pryss. "Except we're guessing. Rumors say that *Juggernaut* is *miles* long and a correspondingly huge crew. But I'd have to see it to believe it. Something like that would change interstellar warfare forever."

"Holy fuck," said Girlie.

"Total horse shit," said Pickle.

"That Flock," said Pryss, nodding to officer who lay dead outside, "has seen it, which means *I* saw it. I was *on* it. It's real."

That silenced them all, though Pickle kept shaking his head.

"We felt it, I think," said Lexie, and she explained the gravitational disturbance that made their flight from Earth so erratic.

"Yes," said Pryss. "But that effect is not just because of its size and mass. There's something about its engine that Kig'Ngo-Kepler did not know. It's way above his pay grade."

"What are they going to use it for?" asked Dubbs. "They already conquered everything."

"Yes," said Sushi. "And why a ship that big? Even if it was primarily used to launch fighters and anchor a fleet, it's weirdly huge. At that size it might be fast in a straight run, but it would have to steer like an elephant. Feels like overkill."

"There are other galaxies to conquer," said Mugabe, repeating what he'd said to Lexie and Pickle earlier.

"Do we care about that?" asked Trig. "I mean, sucks to be anyone that far out who has that show up in their sky, but we have our own fish to fry."

"Kig'Ngo-Kepler didn't know anything about that," said Pryss. She paused and pressed her hands against her temples. "My head feels like it's splitting."

They waited in a cloud of nervous tension for a few moments until Pryss soldiered on.

"Before he was seconded to Hell, Kig'Ngo-Kepler was working with a Flock group focused on urban pacification. The dreams we've . . . um . . . *inspired* . . . have them worried— terrified, really—about a galaxy-wide uprising and *Juggernaut* is their response."

"Uprising? Ha!" scoffed Pickle. "How exactly are we

supposed to be doing that?"

"You're part of the Resistance," said Trig. "Uprisings kind of go with that whole thing, or am I wrong?"

"We're a thorn in their sides," protested Pickle. "We've been hoping *you* guys would handle the actual uprising."

"Pussy," said Sushi under his breath.

"Hey, fuck you," Pickle fired back. "Excuse the living hell out of me for not being someone's science experiment. Excuse me for actually being *human*."

"Pickle, stop," cried Lexie.

"Why? Just because I'm not one of Frankenstein's monsters doesn't mean I can't have an opinion." To Sushi and the other HEs, he said, "You heard Lexie's speech back there. We risked everything to come find you because you're *trained* for this. You're literally *built* for it. The Flock hasn't needed any super weapon crap to keep us in check because your generation handed the fucking universe to those birds. Now you want me to believe that there's this big ass super weapon that they built to keep *us* in line? I mean, really. That fucking chicken out there was trying to scare you, Pryss. He was lying to you."

"He couldn't lie to me," said Pryss, and for a moment the electricity crackled again in her eyes. Her voice was quiet, cold, certain.

"Christ," said Dubbs.

"Is there anything else you can tell us, Pryss?" asked Jason. "Anything more about this *Juggernaut* weapon?"

She looked troubled. "That Raptor didn't know too much. Just bits and pieces. He was only in one of the docking bays with his group leader, Hell. He heard some things, but they were scuttlebutt stuff. Nothing he was certain about."

"Give it to us anyway."

She nodded. "The ship has an engine that no one is allowed

to see. Highest possible security clearance. Something based on alien tech, but that's all. It's tied to the transduction network, though. Not sure how, but I think that its engines *are* transduction decks. It's the first of its kind, the flagship of a new fleet. They've been using it to suppress human resistance groups. Tau Ceti F, Teegarden's Star B, and some others. There were other names there that I can't recall. I think they were places built after we went into the ice. It doesn't blow up planets . . . it does surgical strikes to cities or regions. And now that . . . *thing* . . . is here in this solar system. I think . . . I think they're going to hit four mega-cities where the Resistance is strongest. London, Atlanta, Shanghai, Lisbon . . . and the Paris Metroplex."

"That makes no sense," argued Pickle. "There are hundreds of thousands of Flock living in each of those places."

"Less than you think," said Mugabe. "You've seen how many rookeries are empty, how many Flock families have been moving out to the country. Do you think that's because they like the scenery?"

"Even so," said Dubbs. "I'm with Pickle on this one. Would they kill some of their own just to shut down some Resistance cells?"

"If people from those cells are working to find the Sleepers and wake them up?" asked Mugabe. "Do you really need an answer to that?"

"Then we need to find our other teams and wake them the fuck up," said Girlie. "If they have a super weapon, then we need more of *our* boots on the ground. Otherwise this is a slaughter and we're spectators."

They looked at Jason, who was staring into the middle distance. Lexie could almost hear wheels turning in his head.

"No," he said. "We don't have time to find the other teams of Sleepers."

Dubbs stared at him. "And do what instead? Watch Earth

burn?"

"That ship is already there," said Jason, pointing out the air-lock. "It's already near Earth. The next closest team is a long way from here. We don't have the time to get them, even if any have survived. We need to warn the Resistance. We need to get the hell out of here, find your ship, take it back from the birds . . ."

"And then what?" asked Lexie.

"Then we need to go find that ship."

Pickle looked at him as if he was insane "And do what? We have a crappy little cargo ship with popguns and a total crew of ten. Eleven if you count Lexie's robot dog. If *Juggernaut* even exists, which I doubt, it's a monster and we're . . . hell, we're nothing."

"Sure," said Jason. "It's a monster. So am I. So are all the Sleepers."

Lexie smiled. "Then let's go monster hunting."

95

Hell did not hear this conversation.

He did not see anything after one of the HEs—a female—did something to Kig'Ngo-Kepler.

He disliked losing someone as valuable as Kepler, but that Flock's death was useful in what it had revealed about the HEs. Hell had already seen one of them hoist a heavy barrel as if it weighed nothing. And the electrical discharge around each of them at various times was fascinating. All the data feeds from the drones had been forwarded to *Tartarus* and were being run through sophisticated analytical software.

He wished he knew what actually occurred, though. The female HE had done something to Kepler. That she killed him with her mind was interesting enough, but the process had taken some time and had begun with a verbal interrogation. Had something happened on a different level? Hell had read about theories on mind transference, telepathy, and forced empathy. Was that what he had seen?

There was no way to know for sure, but his instincts told him *yes*.

There was a soft scuff of a footfall behind him and he half turned to see another officer and two of the remaining Raptors.

"Mon'Pgo-Trenton," he said, "the enemy is leaving the station. They are all near or in the airlock."

"Should I send the rest of the team to intercept them?"

"No," said Hell. "Let them leave. We are tracking them. In the meantime, I want you to send Flock to the cryogenics chamber. Recover the bodies of the dead HEs. Disconnect four capsules—two of the damaged ones and two that were functioning. Then sweep the complex for all software and hardware related to the cryogenics and, if you can find it, the HE program itself. Take everything that will fit in one ship and return with it to Earth."

"Are you not coming with us?" asked Mon'Pgo-Trenton.

"No," said Hell. "I have other work to do."

96

They began suiting up, and then Jason stopped and looked back the way they'd come.

"What's up, boss?" asked Pryss.

"I'm having a thought."

"Uh oh," laughed Girlie. "Nothing good ever comes of that."

Pryss said, "What're you thinking?"

"This ship you saw . . . this *Juggernaut* thing . . ."

"What about it?"

"Be nice if we could somehow get aboard her."

Lexie, who stood near, said, "But why? It's supposed to be a couple of miles long with a crew of a couple hundred thousand."

Pryss shook her head. "I don't think so. What I saw in that bird's mind was nothing like that. Big, sure. Dangerous and powerful, sure, but not that."

"Okay . . . but even so . . ."

"Pryss," said Jason, "how many ships have we breached?"

She shrugged. "Eight. No, nine. Not counting Calliope."

"Right." He turned to Short Dog. "Hey, how strong do you actually feel?"

Short Dog gave him a huge grin. "Fuck, boss, I don't even know."

Jason pointed down the hall. "You think you could go grab some of those breaching pods?"

Short Dog looked momentarily confused, and then he got it. "Damn right I can. How many?"

"One for each. Six."

"Wait," said Fodder, "what about us?"

But Jason shook his head. "They were designed for us, miss. They're complicated to drive and using them involves body stress that is way above human norms."

"I'm willing to try," she insisted.

"I'm not willing to let you," countered Jason. He nodded to Short Dog. "Take whoever you need. Get them and haul ass back here. They're heavy, but this facility's artificial gravity won't matter once we're outside. On the surface, any one of us or any two of Lexie's team can carry them. Now move."

Short Dog ran off, with Girlie, Sushi, Trig, Fodder, and Mugabe running to catch up. They returned in under ten minutes. Short dog carried two of the heavy crates. The others managed the other four.

They suited up and went out into the howling hellscape that was Io.

The crew of *Tin Man* huddled together in a bunch, with the HEs of Alpha Wave spread around them in a wide circle. Short Dog was on point and was amusing himself by doing fantastic leaps and hurling boulders, reveling in his newfound power. Jason had to bark at him to stop fucking around.

"Sorry, boss," said Short Dog over the comms, though he did not sound at all contrite.

They paused at an outcropping of volcanic rock fifty yards

from *Tin Man*. Mugabe came up beside Jason and reminded him of the multi-spectrum capabilities of his artificial golden eyes.

"You have thermal scans?" Jason asked, impressed.

"I do," said the prophet, "and I can see three heat signatures ahead. One in the airlock and two more in—I think—the cargo bay."

"What do we need to know in order to enter the ship with the best chance of taking the birds without shooting up the place?"

Mugabe used his finger to draw a diagram in the crystalline sand at their feet. "There is a hatch past the port stabilizer. It's used for EVAs. There's a plate on the outer hull with a pressure pad at three o'clock. Press and hold it for two seconds and it will slide back to reveal a keypad. The entry code is 4-5-2-2-star. That will allow you to enter the ship. It's a smaller airlock, so only one of you can enter at a time, but there is a kind of vestibule directly beyond it. One can wait while others come in. This is just behind the bulkhead separating the suit storage closet and the cargo bay. The door is quiet but not silent, so the birds may hear it open."

"Got it," said Jason. He considered for a moment and then signaled to Girlie. "You heard all that? Good. You up for it? Pistol on lowest setting, but if possible, use your knife. Quick and quiet. No damage to hull or instruments, feel me?"

"Copy that, boss."

"What about the one in the airlock?" asked Sushi.

"He's yours if you want him. But don't make a fuss."

Sushi grinned through the faceplate. "When have I ever?"

He tapped Girlie and they moved off together, circling the clearing where *Tin Man* sat.

Lexie, having heard all of this, sidled up to Jason. "You're only sending two of them?"

"Overkill, I know," said Jason, and gave her a wink.

They all fell silent and waited.

Fifty-nine seconds later Girlie's voice broke the silence via the comms.

"You guys planning to stay out there all day? Sushi and I are one beer ahead already. Shag it."

Jason laughed.

They shagged it.

97

They all squeezed into *Tin Man*. With the six breaching pod cases it was an even tighter fit.

"Not exactly roomy, is she?" Short Dog commented.

"Needs must when the devil drives," said Lexie.

"What now?"

"Old expression."

"She means suck it up, buttercup," said Girlie. "And maybe lose a few pounds while you're at it."

Short Dog patted his gut. "That's 100 percent rock-hard man-flesh."

"Synonym for fat fuck," said Sushi, who was still removing his gear.

"What's a synonym for 'blow me?'"

A sharp little *yap-yap* interrupted the conversation as Ahab came bounding into the cargo bay, his tail wagging back and forth like crazy. Lexie knelt and gathered him up, cuddling the tiny body to her chest as Ahab's self-lubricating tongue licked every inch of her face.

"Is that a real dog?" asked Trig.

"Robot," said Pickle. "And don't get me started. She treats it like it's real. She treats it like it's her firstborn child."

"Ahab is cuter, neater, nicer, and better groomed than any human I know," said Lexie.

"But . . . it runs on software, right?" asked Trig. "I mean, there's not some weird thing like an actual dog brain implanted or anything?"

"No," said Lexie. "And . . . ewwww."

Jason cut into the conversation. "Lexie, Mugabe . . . does this this rust-bucket have guns?"

The prophet spread his hands. "Defensive weapons only, and some countermeasures."

"Not good enough."

"Why not just take one of the Flock ships?" asked Short Dog. "We killed most or all of the damn crew. Hate to leave good ships go to waste."

"It's too risky to try," said Mugabe.

"Riskier than taking this one?" asked Girlie with a challenging smile.

Mugabe, however, nodded. "Quite a bit. One of the many side effects of you folks sending a Raptor back in his own ship all those years ago is that all Flock combat ship pilot controls are biometrically coded to bird DNA. And *only* to the pilots and officers. If we try to hijack one of their craft, it will explode."

"Shame you guys killed that Raptor officer," Girlie said.

"Fuck off," said Short Dog.

Lexie turned to Mugabe. "Do you think you can disarm those systems?"

Mugabe sucked a tooth for a moment, then shook his head. "If I had a dozen top Resistance code-monkeys, sure. And even then, I'd need six to eight days."

"What about their computer systems? Can we access those? All we need are the recognition codes."

"Not sure what a code-monkey is," said Trig, "but I never met a computer I couldn't sweet talk."

"No need," said Pryss. "I have all of Kig'Ngo-Kepler's security information in my head. I know the codes, but that still won't let us take their ship. And don't think about going back to get his hand either. Their biometrics read living tissue. Wrong pulse, wrong body temperature, and boom."

"What about their heavy weapons?" asked Short Dog. "How long would it take to switch the cannons from the Raptor ships?"

"Too long," said Mugabe.

"Let's deep six all that," said Jason. "Even if we were able to get their cannons installed on *Tin Man,* look around. You really think we can take this boat into a dogfight? No, we need to be fast and sneaky. Get in quick and dirty and see what mischief we can get up to." He pointed at Mugabe. "You're the pilot, yes? Good. Trig, I want you in the copilot's chair."

"Hey," said Pickle, offended. "I'm the damn copilot."

"No offense," said Jason, "but Trig's our computer guy. Nav, scans, weapons, comms, all of it. If you don't like it, file a complaint."

"In triplicate," said Girlie.

"This is bullshit," groused Pickle, but there was nothing he could do.

Jason looked past him at Lexie. "I know this started out as your show, but you did your part. You got to Io and woke us up. Now it's a military op, and that's us."

She shook her head. "I'm fine with that. I'm a scholar, not a fighter."

"From what I gather, you seem to do all right both ways." Jason smiled, and it transformed his face from something resembling a carving of a Polynesian god to a man. A very handsome man. Lexie felt herself flush and buried her nose in Ahab's ruff to hide it.

Girlie and Pryss exchanged a glance, and both rolled their eyes.

Two minutes later, *Tin Man* shuddered as it lifted its aching bones away from the surface of the volcanic moon.

98

Hell made it back to *Tartarus* alone. A pouch was slung around his waist in which were the hummingbird drones.

His remaining Raptors were still in the facility gathering all the science and tech. Waiting for them wasn't necessary. Moreover, he wanted to be alone with his thoughts.

The day had become something more than anything he—or the Elders, for that matter—could have ever expected. Actually finding the HEs was monumental. That alone was something he knew he could leverage to return color to his family. Perhaps even to be invited into the red Privilege. That was something he had dreamed of as a bitter young hatchling. Thoughts of restoring his family's honor were like coals burning in his mind, even when he pretended that he was too aloof for that kind of ambitious sentimentality.

Now, though, he had more political currency. As the Eldest had suggested, there was a connection between the HEs and the Dreamers. That was no longer a theory. The data cores of each drone had true-res video and audio files. The psychic and physical changes of the *Homo eximius* were beautifully and irrefutably documented. Hell made sure that he, and only he, had that data.

The physical materials currently being gathered were a big enough prize—sending them back to the Elders was a sufficient statement. As he shucked off his space suit, Hell mentally composed the message he would send, roughing out the details and making sure the credit fell to him without appearing to be self-aggrandizing. Kig'Ngo-Kepler would be a messenger only. What was the old Earth expression for that? Messenger pigeon? Something like that. The point was that the arrival of the tech would follow the message, thereby reducing the role of the messenger to simply that.

Movement out of the corner of his eye made him half turn as Worm entered the hold. The robot was not built to resemble a Flock. That would have been an unforgivable insult. Instead, Worm was built like a centipede, with dozens of small legs and as many little clutching hands.

"I trust you are well, Flock," said the machine as it accepted the space suit and put it in a cabinet that would sterilize it and recharge the many small servos built into it.

Hell ignored the pleasantry. "Where is the human ship?"

"It is three kilometers to the southeast."

"Have they fired engines yet?"

"Yes, Flock. The ship is prepped for liftoff." Worm stopped and cocked its nub of a head, antennae twitching. "Update. It has lifted off."

"And the tracker?"

"Active, Flock. The signal is coded but strong."

"Spin up our engines."

"Destination, Flock?"

"Flightplan Hell 22. Execute."

"As you command, Flock."

Hell grunted and stalked into the cockpit. *Tartarus* had not been designed for Flock luxury, but whoever had redesigned the ship had put in some useful touches. The seats were gelfoam that accommodated his body as he sat back. Temperature sensors cooled him in areas that were overheated from exertion and warmed him where heat would be the most soothing. The telemetric sensors of the chair were synced with the environmental controls, and as the system read the EKG of both hearts and the wavelengths of his EEG they adjusted lights, ambient temperature, and noise by playing music just loud enough to soften the edges of engine noise. The music was not Flock, which was good. Hell had a strong dislike of what passed for music among his own people. His preference, after years of experimentation, was from ancient Earth—Gregorian chant. Plainchant, as it was sometimes called. It was sung in Latin and sometimes Greek, languages he had never cared to learn because he had no interest in the religious themes inherent in that style. It was the tone, the pace, the monophonic approach without musical accompaniment. Quite soothing.

He needed to be soothed more than the chair could manage. Hell's mind raced at light speed. The psychic and other abilities demonstrated by the HEs was astounding. Frightening in their implications, but also encouraging because this was clearly a bug rather than a feature. Was it a dormant gene called to action by the enforced evolution of the HEs? After all, the entire science used to create those super soldiers was developed too quickly and with such desperation. There was no chance at all that the humans had been able to fully test the HEs to do more than measure their immediate skill set.

Hell took comfort in that. Evolution was a radical, violative, transgressive thing. It took all sorts of leaps and shot off in unexpected directions that could not always be explained away by natural selection. Abilities like HE Darren Burris demonstrated could not have been even predicted by the designers. The physical strength and speed—above even HE levels—were one thing. But the ability to send out what amounted to shockwaves of psychic energy that forced everyone—human and Flock—to plunge into ugly dreams . . . no, that could not have been anticipated. Nothing in human physiology could account for it.

As far as Hell know. As far as the exhaustive studies of human behavior could explain.

Then seeing what the other one—the HE they called Pryss—tear secrets from Kig'Ngo-Kepler's mind. Yes . . . that was very, very interesting. It was an invasion and domination of that Flock's mind. The cost of doing that was significant—it killed the Flock and nearly killed Pryss.

What if that could be controlled? Refined and adapted to a Flock mind . . . to his. So that no mind, whether it be human or the Elders themselves, would be able to hide anything from him. Ideally in a way that left no damage and therefore no evidence of the intrusion.

The engines rumbled and then steadied as *Tartarus* lifted off from the surface of Io.

It did not follow the human ship. No. They would use the same utility decks they'd used when coming here. He, on the other hand, with the credentials afforded him by the Elders would take the high-speed deck. If they were going where he thought they might go, then he would get there first.

"I might even help them," he murmured.

"What was that, Flock?" asked Worm.

But he ignored the robot.

Hell settled back into the gelfoam, semi-aware of the chanting music that filled the cockpit, but mostly getting lost in a whole new species of thought that proliferated in his mind.

The Flock had spent two centuries planning their overthrow of humanity. A typical Flock long game.

Hell, on the other hand, did not want to initiate a program that his descendants would have to complete. That was inefficient.

That was no fun.

That held no glory.

99

Exhaustion caught up with Lexie and she realized that it had been two days since she'd had any sleep. Adrenaline was great, but when the glands were no longer pumping, the body went into shut-down mode. Even in limited-G now that *Tin Man* was offworld, her body felt oddly heavy and also empty.

She foraged in cabinets in the cargo bay, being careful not to step on anyone in that crowded room. Her search yielded a water bottle with a sippy straw and some high-protein paste that looked like it belonged in the diaper of a very sick child and did not taste much better.

She ate it anyway, making sure not to actually look at what she shoveled into her mouth. Lexie's nest was a cramped niche between a stack of crates strapped to bolts inset in the deck and an exterior wall. She was the only person aboard who could have fit into that slot. Ahab came with her, but he did not take up much room at all. And he was a comfort to her.

Another casualty of the cessation of adrenaline was her courage. All of it melted away, and she felt very small, helpless, and terrified.

At the same time, she marveled at the things she'd done . . . but they felt strange, as if she had witnessed someone else do them. Combat was something she read about in books. But ever since the Raptors came to arrest her at her apartment and she'd used the stunner on them, she had become a different person. More confident, aggressive, violent, even ruthless.

Is that me? she wondered.

Ahab, seeming to sense that she was upset, nuzzled closer. Lexie gathered him up and held him to her chest. Holding on for dear life.

PART SIX
JUGGERNAUT

"A strong man cannot help a weaker unless the weaker is willing to be helped, and even then the weak man must become strong of himself; he must, by his own efforts, develop the strength which he admires in another. None but himself can alter his condition."

—James Allen
As a Man Thinketh

"It is not in the stars to hold our destiny but in ourselves."

—William Shakespeare
Julius Caesar

100

Trig settled into the pilot seat and spent some quiet moments scanning *Tin Man*'s controls. The prophet sat in the copilot's chair, with Jason resting his hands on the backs of both chairs. Lexie peered past him, silent and alert. Ahab sat obediently at her feet.

"I would be happy to explain the systems to you," offered Mugabe.

"It's cool," said Trig. "I got this."

"No, a lot of this is new," said the mechanic politely. "Way after your time. And what this ship lacks in fire power, she more than makes up for in software. The scanners are second to none, and I mean that. Better than anything on any ship in the sky. Some of that software was written weeks ago."

Trig looked at him for a long moment. Lexie saw that his eyes were strange. The gold rims around the irises seemed brighter, hotter. But otherwise, his face was incredibly serene, calling to mind mystics when they are deep in meditative trances.

"Believe me," Trig said quietly. "I got this."

His fingers flowed across the controls as if he had always

flown the ship. Within seconds even the ambient noise of the artificial gravity and air vents slowed and smoothed out. A shudder that had been constant since they first left Earth was still there. Mugabe had said it was something from a fuel regulator. But Trig leaned close to the console and whispered, "Shhhhh."

And by perceptible degrees the shudder faded, faded, and was gone.

Mugabe's face registered both shock and confusion, but he said nothing. It was clear he was in awe of all the HEs but Trig most of all.

"*Welcome*," said the AI. It was the only thing the computer voice said. Lexie thought that was rather odd, given how chatty it normally was.

Jason backed away, nodding for Lexie to follow. He closed the cockpit door behind him. They stood together in a cramped hall.

In very low tones, Jason said, "I felt you flinch. Tell me what you saw."

She glanced at the cockpit door. "Has Trig always been like this?"

"You mean his eyes? You know the answer to that."

"That's not what I meant," she said. "It's how he is with the machines, with the ship."

Jason leaned against the opposite wall, folded his arms across his broad chest, lips pursed. "Trig's always been able to sweet talk machines."

"Like that? He told it to calm down and it did. That's not normal."

"Not sure I have a bead on what's normal," said Jason. "That concept was vague before we went into the ice and it's fuzzier now. And . . . as for Trig . . . he's changing. Like Pryss and Short Dog. Like Darren, I guess."

"That's obvious," said Lexie. "Any insight into these new skills?"

"Insight? No. But, I mean, except for what happened to Darren, they're useful as hell."

"That's a weirdly pragmatic view, given everything."

He merely shrugged.

Lexie studied his eyes. "What about you? Are you feeling anything?"

Jason gave her a rueful smile. "You mean have I developed superpowers?"

"Not how I'd phrase it, but . . . yeah. I guess that says it."

"If so," he said, "I'm not yet aware of it."

"Even with all that weird static electricity that was crawling all over you back there on Io?"

"Yeah, about that," said Jason, and she could see uncertainty flicker on his face. "I have no idea what that was. I had no control over it and did not cause it to start or stop. Actually, even though I saw it on my arms and such, I'm not sure I actually felt it." He shook his head. "Kind of hard to explain. It was there, but it wasn't like I felt any shocks. No static electricity snaps. Only a little skin-crawly thing. Like goosebumps."

"What about the stuff you dreamed? And, no, I'm not talking about *those* dreams. I mean other dreams. The combat dreams."

He shook his head. "Far as I can remember, even though you and I were sometimes sharing my head in them, what I was able to do was all HE-level. I didn't dream about being able to fly or set things on fire with my mind or anything else like that."

Lexie considered that. "I wonder if the dreams Short Dog, Pryss, and Trig had were different, then. I want to talk to them about it, but there hasn't been time."

"Same here. I need to sit down with Alpha Team and hash

it all out. Alone, if you can understand that. Just us. But there's no real privacy on this little tub."

"Right," said Lexie. Ahab was rubbing against her, demanding attention and she picked him up. "What I want to know is if the others dream of being powerful like they are now? If so, then we could use that to help figure out which of Alpha Wave will manifest unusual skills."

"Worth a shot," he agreed. "And if someone had those kinds of dreams but hasn't gone all superhero already, then we can watch for it."

"Exactly." Lexie stroked the robot dog's fur and Ahab close his eyes and wagged his little tail. "Do you have theories about these new abilities? Any insights into what's happening? Any clue as to whether it's something from the unusually long cryosleep or from the HE program? I mean, the point of the HE program was to force you up the evolutionary scale. Could this be something inadvertently unlocked from some unused DNA? Or maybe an accidental alteration in the way some genes code?"

He nodded. "As of this minute, Ms. Chow—"

"Lexie, please."

"As of this minute, *Lexie* . . . it's my considered opinion that it beats the living hell out of me."

"Does it scare you?"

Jason fiddled with the closure on his jacket collar. "I don't know enough about it to be scared," he said thoughtfully. "I'm weird, Lexie, but my emotions are still human, enhancements notwithstanding. If I seem calm, then credit that to a life spent in the military, not on some deep awareness of cosmic matters."

"That's comforting."

He looked a little bitter, however. "At least we have some human left in us."

"What about the dreams? I told you about the Dreamers

and the legend of the Sleepers. The religion built around dreams from the HEs. How much of that are you aware of?"

His gaze seemed to turn inward for a moment. Doubt clouded his expression. "Some of it. Not as much as I'd like to know. And, yes, before you ask . . . that scares me too. Quite a lot."

"What do you think happened?"

"Ha! As if I'm qualified to even make a guess. Though, in my more paranoid moments, I wonder if this was something built into us. Mind you, I've only had a couple of hours to suss this out, and I haven't had nearly enough time to work it through. If the mad scientists at the DoD built something into us that both kept us awake or triggered those dreams, then I'm going to find where they're buried and piss on their graves."

Lexie laughed. "I can see your point. Has to be weird beyond words."

"That's the understatement of the millennia." He paused. "There are a lot of variations on that, none of which offer much comfort. For example, if the DoD boys didn't program this in, then is it something new about extended cryosleep that no one ever knew."

"Which is why Dubbs looks so dazed," she said, nodding. "It's shaken everything he thought was hard, solved science. Personally, I think that's the real reason he came along. He needs to know."

"I got that impression." Jason reached out and scratched Ahab's ruff.

"Jason . . . how much do you remember of the dreams *you* were in?"

He touched her chin very gently and turned her face up toward his. "Do you mean the times we shared a body while we were fighting? Or are you asking about the *other* dreams. Where there was no fighting going on at all?"

Lexie wished an airlock would spring open and whisk her into space right then and there.

"Y-yes," she mumbled. "The, um, other ones."

Jason's stern mouth softened and slowly blossomed into a smile of surprising warmth. His eyes, strange as they were, lost their drama and a different kind of light seemed to shine from them. Softer, kinder, and . . . something else. Another frequency of light she had only seen before.

In dreams.

In those dreams.

"I remember everything, Lexie," he said gently.

"Why me?" she said, and shocked herself by asking, amazed she even got the words out.

Jason stopped petting Ahab. "I . . . don't know."

"Do I look like your wife or girlfriend?"

That question seemed to change Jason's face. His mouth tightened and, for a moment, shutters dropped behind his eyes. He said, "My wife died a year after I completed basic training. Car accident. She was four months pregnant. I never remarried."

"Oh God, I'm sorry . . ."

"Thanks. She was a good woman. High school sweetheart. We bought into the whole storybook romance thing. Actually believed 'happily ever after' was written into the marriage contract. Stupid kids."

"Believing in that is beautiful, though."

"Doesn't make it hurt less."

"But doesn't it make the good memories even sweeter?"

Jason looked away, thinking about it. She watched the tension in his jaw. Saw it tighten. Then saw it soften. "I guess maybe it does. Damn, though."

Lexie set Ahab down.

After a few moments of silence that was more companionable

than Lexie expected, Jason said, "No girlfriend. At least not lately. Or, I guess, not after we completed the HE upgrade."

"No office romance?"

He snorted. "Nothing that lasted."

"Okay," she said, then took a breath. "And before you ask, I've never been able to make anything work. Short term, sure. Flings, yeah. But most of the guys I meet work for the Flock and *want* to. So . . ."

"I get it," said Jason. "That could make for awkward pillow talk. No, let me put that a better way. Could make for tension. You can't be real with them."

"Exactly."

"What about Dubbs?"

"Dubbs?" She laughed. "No. He's pretty, but . . ."

"But what?"

"Besides the fact there is zero chemistry, I try not to mix work with pleasure."

"Do you consider me work?" Jason asked.

She stared at him a moment, unable to answer. She remembered her dream of him and her in the snow globe.

"At the risk of you kicking me real hard where it would hurt most," Jason continued, "you were pretty romantic in those dreams."

Lexie felt her skin grow hot. She dared not look into his eyes.

"Those were only dreams," she managed to utter.

"Were they?"

Lexie fumbled for an answer.

Then Jason bent forward and kissed her. It was not aggressive or forceful. It violated nothing because, as he bent, she raised her mouth to his.

That kiss. Lexie's first real kiss in two years, and the first kiss with Jason outside of the realm of dreams, was exquisite.

So gentle. Tentative at first—a soft brushing of lips. Almost shy, almost innocent. And then the pressure increased. A little at a time. He took her in his arms and held her close. He touched her lips with the tip of his tongue, and she parted her lips in a way that was both an invitation and a welcome.

Then the kiss became intense. It happened in the space of three heartbeats.

The corridor in which they stood, the ship that carried them through space, the war with the Flock, the strangeness of those dreams, the forced evolution within him, and her own insecurities all melted away.

There was only that kiss.

101

Hell sent a coded report back to the Flock Eldest.

He explained nearly everything that had happened on Io. He reported the highlights of the conversations he'd listened in on thanks to the hummingbird drones, and that the team of HEs was not headed to find the other Sleepers but instead headed back to Earth.

"I have scanned their ship, inside and out," he said. "The tracker is in place. Everything you need to know is in the data file I am sending now."

He closed the report and sat back in his chair to consider the very great risk he had just taken. His report included everything he wanted the Eldest and the rest of the Elders of the Flock to know. It did not, however, include everything Hell had learned on that troubled little moon the humans had dubbed Io.

There were many things he wanted to keep entirely to himself.

Worm swiveled his metal head toward him from the pilot's chair. "My sensors tell me that you are troubled, lord. Do you wish a sedative? Something to relieve stress?"

"No," said Hell.

"Some soothing music perhaps?"

Hell nodded and soon the soft, moody drone of Gregorian monks filled the ship—the sound the humans had gotten right, for it had the tone and somberness of a Flock funeral dirge. He pressed a button in his chair and a needle shot into the base of his spine, delivering much needed sustenance.

102

Hell's message was not the only one sent to the Elders.

Another, traveling along a special frequency, flashed out from *Tin Man*.

This was replayed a dozen times, with every iteration causing more and more excitement.

103

Lexie did not realize that she had fallen asleep until voices woke her up.

She lay snugged into her niche, with Ahab tucked into the open vee of her coveralls. For a long time, all she did was remain there and think about those kisses with Jason Horse. His gentleness had surprised her. Greatly so.

The moment had lasted until the clatter of feet on a companion ladder made Jason step back. By the time Pickle climbed into view, Jason and Lexie stood ten feet apart—all the short hall allowed—and were talking about . . . well, Lexie couldn't really remember anything about that conversation. From the look on Pickle's face, though, she was pretty sure he'd seen through the chitchat. Pickle had given her a knowing glance and the tiniest of winks.

That's when Lexie had slunk off to find a very private space to sleep. Or die. Whichever came first.

Now she was awake. From the taste in her mouth and the ache in her muscles she guessed she'd slept for hours.

There was a hushed conversation on the other side of the

stack of crates. Two women's voices—Pryss and Girlie—and two men—Sushi and Short Dog. Lexie had no idea where the rest of the crew was.

"—about you," said Girlie, "but this shit has me freaked out."

"I kind of dig it," said Short Dog. "I'm superhero guy. Did you see me lift that barrel? It was nothing. Look at this. See this half-inch long-bolt? It's grade 4 dura-steel. Now, watch."

There was a faint sound of protesting metal.

"I can bend it like licorice. How cool is that?"

"It's great," said Girlie, "but it's scary."

"Tell me about it," said Pryss. Lexie could hear raw tension in her voice.

"Yeah, okay," said Short Dog. "What happened sucked but look how much you got out of it. A team of intelligence spooks couldn't have gotten a tenth of that much under torture."

"It *was* torture," Pryss said sternly. "I tore his mind apart and killed him."

A beat, then Short Dog said, "Okay, yeah . . . there's that part. But big picture here, sis, we're way ahead of the game. So a bird got cooked. Big whoop. We killed a dozen of those fuckers."

"It's not the same," said Pryss. "I was inside his head. It was like *being* one of them. And . . . I saw all of him. His childhood. Taking his first step. His first little flight. I saw the joy in his parents' eyes. I saw him grow and learn. I felt his love of his people, his patriotism, his devotion. His honor. I felt his fear and his hopelessness. I felt when his last faith in his own survival—his own existence—failed him. It was horrible."

Lexie waited for the sound of a sob, but if there was one, she didn't hear it. The other members of Alpha Team were silent for a long while.

Then Sushi said, "I'm sorry."

"Yeah," said Short Dog.

Silence.

After nearly a minute, Girlie said, "I don't feel different. I—like—tested myself. No super strength. I can't see through walls. No laser beam eyes. Nothing like that."

"Me neither," said Sushi. "Trig seems normal too."

"And the boss," said Short Dog.

"I don't think so," said Pryss. "Jason's different but I don't know how. Don't ask me either. Just a feeling."

"You weren't in *his* head too, were you?" asked Girlie.

"No," said Pryss flatly.

"Maybe these powers, these changes are hit or miss," said Short Dog. "Some people get them and some don't."

"Or," said Sushi, "maybe each one's going to happen when it happens."

"Yeah, well either way," said Short Dog, "they're useful as fuck."

"They're scary," said Girlie.

No one answered that.

After a few minutes the group broke up, heading either to the cockpit or the engine room, which is where Mugabe and Fodder had used a bunch of cargo nets to rig hammocks.

When she was sure she was alone, Lexie stood up.

And froze.

Pryss was standing on the other side of the crates. Staring at her.

"I . . . I wasn't snooping," said Lexie hurriedly. "I was sleeping, and you all woke me up."

"I know," said Pryss.

"But . . . I didn't make a sound."

"I know."

Pryss stared at her with eyes that seemed to swirl with colored lights. Then she smiled faintly and turned away.

104

She was Flock but she seldom used that name. Instead, she used only the nickname some humans had given her.

Monster.

A name she very much enjoyed. A name she knew that she had earned many times over.

Monster.

The first time someone called her that, long ago and on another world, had been in one of the interrogation camps established before the Flock rose up and took back the galaxy that was already theirs. There were many such camps and humanity had no idea. None. To them, the many thousands of men and women, boys and girls who went missing every single year were either runaways or victims of accidents and simply unable to be found. Or something. But there was never a real theory. Never much of an effort to look. Leave finding those missing to the Flock. They took care of such things.

Yes.

Some of those people were returned from the camps. They looked and acted the same, but the Flock was inside their heads.

The Flock would always be inside their heads. The conditioning at the camps—particularly in the labs and surgery bays—insured that.

Yet, Monster was not part of any behavioral modification group. No. Her brief, her service to the Flock was in acquiring information. Part of that involved knowing who to target. Her success rate in eliciting information from humans was 92 percent. Far, far higher than her most talented colleagues; far higher than the 61 percent rate that was the Flock average.

Monster was an artist. Everyone knew it. There were special Flock schools where her methods were taught. Some of her proteges were climbing past 80 percent, with a few looking even more promising.

Monster loved that.

Monster loved her job.

She was not a Raptor. Monster was almost frail in appearance—something she cultivated, a bit of theater to keep her victims off balance. She was not a fighter. She had her Green One Hundred—elite and brutal Raptors from various families of her own Privilege. Family loyalty adhered them to her, and she loved them all.

Now, on a cloudy afternoon in the Paris Metroplex, she and ten of those devoted Raptors waited in a stairwell on the 68th floor of a skyscraper devoted to human-based design firms. Benign stuff—packages and bottles, food supplements, diet plans, tourism software. Nothing outwardly offensive at all.

But Monster knew better.

She wore a small circlet on her head, tapered to allow her crest to stand tall, with a slender comms wire curling down to the side of her head. A voice suddenly spoke on her private channel.

"They are all in the room," said a scout, voice low and discrete.

"Perfect," she replied, then tapped the circlet to put her on the full team channel. "All units prepare to move. Minimal casualties. For the Glory of the Flock—*go*."

It happened very fast.

Two Flock leapt from the room—each fitted with harnesses that augmented their wings so they could do jumping flights of short but precise duration. They swooped down and then sharply in, fired entry-nets that struck the so-called shatterproof glass of the big picture windows of the office in which a Resistance cell was meeting. The nets hit the glass, covering each pane completely, and at each cross-knot in the netting was a micro charge. They detonated as one with vibro-shocks rather than high explosives. The glass shuddered, shimmered, and then disintegrated into fragments that fell like rain—down, rather than inward—timed to the entry of the Flock through those windows and the doors.

Monster lingered in the hall as her team smashed their way in. They swarmed the humans, firing stunners or using powerful blows with spring-truncheons.

"Run!" screamed one of the Resistance leaders, a bald man with terror in his eyes. A slender woman next to him tried to pull a small and very illegal Snellig Ultra-D gas dart pistol from a concealed shoulder holster. But a Raptor slammed his truncheon across her arm just above the elbow. The humerus snapped with a dry-stick sharpness that was immediately buried beneath a shriek of agony.

"My god," cried someone else—a burly man with artificial eyes. "That's *her!*"

He was pointing past the Raptors to the figure who stood in the doorway. Pointing at her.

Monster raised her own stunner and shot the man down.

The Raptors laughed and laid into the other Resistance members with an enthusiasm that bordered on mania. Blood seeded the air. Bones broke. Humans screamed for their mothers. They screamed for mercy. They screamed for their god.

Monster watched it all with a heart filled with great joy.

105

Lexie went in search of Jason.

She heard a soft sound from deep inside the cargo hold and crept that way, wanting to know what caused it without disturbing anyone. Ahab trotted along and Lexie used her *Mon Tout* to switch the little robot to silent mode.

Lexie peered around the corner of a stack of crates and saw Fodder sitting cross-legged on the deck, facing away. The enforcer had her own *Mon Tout* activated and a hologram of Fire turned slowly in the air. It was a more persuasively feminine picture of Fire, in camo pants and a bikini top, her tattoos visible, curves clearly on display for whomever took the picture. She smiled a lover's smile. Fodder's broad back twitched with nearly silent sobs.

"Goddamn, babe," murmured Fodder. "Why'd you leave me?"

Lexie, her own heart breaking, backed silently away, carrying a cloud of grief with her. As she headed back to the exit, she passed Girlie and Sushi in the corner of the hold. Sushi was staring at a small crate, fingers pressed to his temples, squinting, face screwed up.

"Keep trying," urged Girlie.

"I *am* trying." Sushi's face was flushing red with effort. Then he spotted her and straightened quickly, looking embarrassed.

"Sorry," she said. "I didn't mean to interrupt."

The two HEs looked like school kids caught smoking.

"What are you doing?" Lexie asked.

Girlie shifted to hide the crate with her body.

"Are . . . are you trying to lift that crate with your mind?" asked Lexie.

Sushi sniffed. "Maybe. What's it to you?"

"No, it's cool," said Lexie, fighting back a grin. "I get it."

"You get *what*, exactly?" demanded Girlie.

Lexie shrugged. "You're trying to find out if you have powers."

They said nothing.

"What else have you tried? Maybe turning invisible? Super speed? No, it's too cramped in here for that. What else?"

They just stared at her.

"Look, guys," said Lexie, "it's really okay. I'm not making fun. If I woke up like you did and my friends were able to do things like Trig, Pryss and Short Dog, I'd be trying *anything*."

Nothing.

"Just a thought, though," she continued. "When the others manifested those abilities, it was during moments of intense stress. Short Dog realized he was strong when we were in the corridors with the Raptors gunning for us. Pryss had the emotional stress of interrogating the Raptor officer. And Trig was processing the deaths of your other friends when his power emerged. So . . . maybe that's the trigger." She shrugged again. "Only a thought."

They remained silent. She smiled, nodded, and turned away. As she reached the door to the corridor, she overheard Girlie speaking quietly to Sushi.

". . . stress, huh? Maybe if I, y'know, threatened you with a knife?"

"Worth a try," said Sushi.

"Overhand or underhand?"

"I'm not sure. Maybe both?" mused Sushi.

Lexie stifled a laugh and exited the cargo bay.

106

Monster did not transport her victims to the ships that always waited for offworld transportation of intelligence assets or special prisoners. There was no time for that.

Instead, she had her Raptors bind them to chairs. They were gagged, but not so comprehensively that they could not scream. Oh no. Screams were useful. Screams were tools that helped her in this important work.

She laid out her tools atop the conference table. The drills and saws, the scalpels and neuro-stims, the flaying knives and tweezers. Some of those items were for window dressing only, she knew. But a bit of theater always helped.

Monster set a tiny holo-projector on the table and let the prisoners watch a five-minute video file. It showed highlights—key moments from some of her most dramatic interrogations. The volume was always high, the holographic definition scaled to the maximum, clearest level.

That video file was edited to include interrogations with known members of the Resistance. Faces some of these captives would recognize. People who were still active in the Resistance, with the clear implication that they now served the Flock. And, more to the point, that they survived moments just like this. Survived intact, unmarred, with all limbs and organs intact.

That was the kind of thing that kept her from having to use the most extreme measures. Though she missed the fun she used to have with those tweezers. It was amazing the things such a small tool could do to human flesh if applied here . . . and there . . .

When the video was finished, Monster allowed for ten seconds of contemplative silence. She watched the faces of each person. She watched their eyes. Telemetry from discrete scanners sent information to the contact lenses she wore over one eye. Heart rate, blood pressure, hormone levels. Many useful things.

Then she walked over to the person whose level of fear was the most acute. A weak-looking man with a soft chin and no trace of authority in his features.

"We'll start with you," said Monster. Her voice was so calm, so pleasant, that it in itself was her sharpest knife. The man's bladder released without her having to touch him at all. And she knew that she owned this one.

Body and soul.

107

In its prison, the thing wept.

As it had wept since time uncountable.

In that prison it fought against its chains. Against the cables and sensors, against the devices built by cold and uncaring hands to inflict pain. It felt the scars of the parts of itself that had been carved away. Those wounds did not heal.

Not in ten thousand millennia.

They could not.

The devices that held it made sure of that. Ages of raw, untreated, sustained wounds.

It huddled there, its body containing all that pain because even screams were prevented, stifled by systems that took such outbursts and funneled them elsewhere.

It wanted to scream.

How it needed to scream.

108

The Eldest was conducting a meeting with his propaganda team to finesse the fallout that still lingered from the disaster at the museum. He only listened with half of his attention while the rest of him was feeling the passage of every second, waiting for a call that mattered very much more to him and to the Flock than human outrage.

When the call came, he rapped his knuckles on the table, and when silence fell, he ordered them all out of the room. Only the other senior Flock remained, as was their right.

When the room was sealed, he tapped a key on the table and a hologram appeared of a small, bent, threadbare-looking Flock. She wore dark green and there was a spray of arterial blood spattered across her tunic.

"Do you have an answer?" he said.

The figure nodded. "I do."

"And?"

"Lisbon," said Monster.

"You are sure?"

"I am absolutely certain, Eldest. And the other two are London and Paris."

The Eldest settled back in his chair.

"Excellent work," he said. "You may continue. Forward any additional information this way." He paused. "Do you have family in Lisbon?"

Monster shrugged. "My family serve the Glory of the Flock. It does not matter where they are. And, besides, there are eggs in other rookeries."

"You have our gratitude," said the Eldest and ended the call.

109

Lexie showered off as much of the last few days as she could. The stall was cramped, even for so small a person as her. She could not imagine Jason fitting in it. Though she would love to have seen him try. All of that muscle and size, dripping with suds . . .

"Stop it," she scolded herself, and felt her face flush even though she was alone.

Alone, except for Ahab, who was nipping at the falling water. Lexie thought that was strange because that kind of play wasn't in his programming. She figured it was his learning software, but even so, the little robot was more genuinely doglike every day.

"And I love you, you little furball," she cooed.

Ahab danced and wagged and dripped and looked very happy.

When she was dried and dressed, she went looking for the HE leader and found him in the galley with Pryss. They stood with fresh cups of coffee.

"Am I interrupting?" she asked nervously.

"Not at all," said Pryss, looking faintly amused. "Coffee?"

"Please," said Lexie. She accepted a mug and buried her nose in the aromatic steam.

Jason said, "We've been talking about this other bird. Hell."

"What do you know about him?" asked Lexie, leaning a hip against the sink.

"Well," said Pryss, "for one thing his name really is Hell. Ren'Mgo-Hell. Every Raptor who has met him fears him. He is relentless, ruthless, smart, and dangerous." She paused, then added, "I only have Kig'Ngo-Kepler's impression of him, but Hell seems to live up to his name. His mind is a furnace."

"Damn," said Lexie.

"Okay, so he's tough," said Jason. "So are we."

"I think he is different in some other way, boss," said Pryss, looking troubled. "From what I learned from Kepler is that he was cognizant of the fact that his commander doesn't think like the rest of the Flock. He thinks like us."

Jason narrowed his eyes. "So, he's gone human?"

"No, boss," insisted Pryss. "He thinks like *us*. Like an HE."

"How's that even possible?" asked Lexie.

"I don't know," admitted Pryss. "But that's the assessment that was in the mind of the officer. He hated Hell, but he feared him too. Not for any political reason, but because Hell was *too* different. He's faster, stronger, more creative, more innovative. His reflexes are not ordinary, even for the top-tier Raptors, and he is not supposed to be on that level. He's not even as big as the average combat Raptor. Frankly, boss, I'm scared of him too."

"What's that? Bleed-through from that bird officer?"

She shook her head. "No. I have his memories stored up here, and I can access his feelings. But this . . . this is what *I* feel. He scares me really bad."

They all considered the truth of that statement.

After a moment, Jason said, "Then we're going to have to teach him what fear really means."

110

Micah Fontenot was getting laid when the phone rang.

Lulu sat astride him, her lean body running with sweat, eyes filled with magic, lips parted as she climbed that steep slope upward toward the precipice. Micah was right there with her, forcing his mind to focus on her and their rhythm and not the phone.

It kept ringing.

His left hand twitched.

Lulu leaned forward and took him by the throat.

"Answer that and I'll kill you."

He believed her.

The bed was a MoodFlexer 4000 that made thousands of tiny micro-adjustments to enhance angle and pressure. The friction was maddening, and Micah felt like his brain was going to explode.

He wished he had a hammer so he could smash his phone.

Then suddenly he wasn't thinking about the phone at all. Or the room, the day, the weather, the Flock, or the Resistance. He and Lulu were caught in a tidal surge as their shared passion rose to a towering, shrieking pinnacle and they, rising together and then pausing in a soundless, motionless fragment of a second, plunged over the edge, screaming all the way.

Later—a few minutes, a year—Micah recalled the concept of "phone."

It took a little longer to care, and longer still to frisk the tangled sheets until he found the device. It was an old-school model, an actual handheld phone with pre-Uprising software for screening and scrambling.

He fumbled it to the side of his face, pressing the right button on the fifth try.

The person at the other end answered with, "Line?"

He said, "Fuck you."

"Line?"

"And the horse you rode in on."

"Line?"

"Clear, clear, clear. Kiss my hairy ass. Clear. What in the worlds is so goddamned important that you—"

"It's Lisbon."

"What *about* Lisbon? And who cares anyway?"

"It's gone."

Micah took a moment with that. "What do you mean *gone?*"

"Gone," repeated the voice.

"Gone how?"

"Like Horlon's Moon."

"No . . ."

"Like B Luyten and Teegarden's Star. It's happening *here* now."

Micah sat up sharply, the motion nearly knocking Lulu off the bed. He switched to speaker.

"Tell me everything."

"Our people were hacked into the Flock security satellite.

They had a three-minute warning that a ship was approaching Earth. It was causing massive disruptions in weather patterns."

"Jesus . . ."

"They tried to warn the cells there, but there was no time."

"How bad?" Asked Micah, pushing the words out through a dry, constricted throat.

"It's all gone," said the voice, breaking with a heavy sob. "The entire Lisbon Metroplex."

"Sixteen million people live there, goddamn," snarled Micah. "They can't all be gone."

There was no answer. Much, much worse, there was no rebuttal.

111

Trig tapped the shipboard comms. "Buckle up, kids, we're entering the deck."

He sat back and took the controls back from the autopilot.

The AI voice came said, "*I assure you, sir, that I am fully capable of piloting the ship along the transduction network. It's no problem at all.*"

"Thanks, but I got it," said Trig.

"*If I may make a personal comment?*"

"Sure."

"*You are remarkably polite for a human.*"

"Thanks, but I'm not quite human anymore."

"*Ah,*" said the voice of *Tin Man*. "*That must account for it.*"

Trig laughed and steered the ship into the commercial transduction deck. The energies of the pathway made the craft shudder, but Trig laid his palm flat on the console.

"It's okay," he murmured.

Mugabe, nearly forgotten in the copilot's chair, watched this and filed it away, nodding to himself.

The cockpit door opened, and Jason entered with Lexie behind him.

"There's a good chance they know we're coming," said the commander of Alpha Wave. "You boys need to stay sharp."

"It's okay, boss," said Trig. "There's nothing ahead."

Jason leaned past him to look at the controls. "How do you know? What scanner are you looking at?"

Trig turned and gave him a long look, his eyes unfocused. "It's not a scanner thing."

"Then how do you know?"

"I just do."

Jason and Lexie shared a look. Mugabe took a strand of beads from his shirt pocket and began to count them, murmuring silent prayers.

Tin Man flew on.

112

Tartarus was at the mouth of the high-speed transduction deck, coordinates locked in for the next leg of his mission, when Worm turned to him and said, "Lord, there is a vid-call coming through on secure channel six."

Hell roused himself from a pool of deep thoughts. "Who is it?"

The robot said, "The caller's signature is merely an integer. One."

Hell sat up in his chair. "The Eldest. Engage all scramblers, set the engines to station-keeping, and put him through."

"As you wish, lord."

The engine noise changed, and a holographic screen appeared, hovering inches in front of the view-screen. The Eldest was in the same chair and at the same table as when Hell had met him all those months ago. Now, however, he was alone. None of the other Elders were present.

"This is an honor," said Hell. He only partly meant it. The rest of him was wary that the Elder was calling to deliver a personal rebuke. Hell felt a flash of guilt and nervousness because of the details he had withheld from his report.

The Eldest, wrapped in his dark red cloak, studied him with ancient eyes. There was a cruel, unforgiving set to his beak, and even the crest of color feathers on his head seemed hostile. However, when the old Flock spoke, his voice was mild, even kindly.

"You have done very well, Ren'Mgo-Hell," he said. "Your actions on Io have gone a long way to encouraging faith in the other members of the council."

Hell, startled, managed a bow. "Thank you, Eldest. It is my pleasure to serve the Flock and to amplify its glory."

The Eldest waved that away. "What is your next move?"

"I was about to take a deck back to Earth and intercept the HEs when they arrive."

But the Eldest shook his head. "No. The Sleepers and the Resistance terrorists will be dealt with by other Flock."

Hell considered this, rapidly calculating the politics, the prestige pros and cons, and his options. The variables were too many, though, for him to make a reliable guess.

"In what way, then, may I serve the will of the Flock?"

"Your mission remains the same," said the Eldest calmly. "It was and is your task to find *all* of the Sleepers. That is your focus."

"Eldest, you saw the video files I sent. The HEs have developed extraordinary abilities of a kind unknown to us. Or, it appears, to them. Do you think ordinary Raptors are sufficiently capable of arresting these HEs?"

The old Flock's face was unreadable. "I agree that arresting them is risky and likely impossible. We will not allow them to set foot on Earth. Not with tensions running this high. Our castigation of the Resistance in the Lisbon Metroplex has resulted in many protests, bombings, and murders of local Flock."

"I think it is unwise to believe that the humans can be so easily cowed," said Hell. "The fact that we conquered them speaks more to our position within the infrastructure than actual dominance. The Dreamers have already been a spark to ignite rebellion. The attack on Lisbon was—"

"Be very careful with what you say, Ren'Mgo-Hell," interrupted Eldest icily. "I am tolerant of your frankness, but not infinitely so."

Hell said, "Am I a free agent or a puppet, Eldest? Did you engage my services to polish your heel claws or to get results?"

The words seemed to hit the Eldest, and Hell felt he might have scored a point. Or crossed a line.

"You are dangerous, Ren'Mgo-Hell," said the Eldest after a moment. "To our enemies and, if you are not careful, to yourself. Even a son of so low a house can still yet fall."

"Eldest," said Hell firmly, "you've chosen me as a scalpel . . . is it your wish to blunt my edge or let me cut? I know what I risk by asking this, but despite your assessment, there *is* no farther down I can fall. Let me show you want I can do. Let me arrest the HEs and interrogate them."

"We are not planning an arrest, Ren'Mgo-Hell," said the Eldest smoothly. "We will feed them to the *Juggernaut*."

"Eldest," protested Hell, "how will that help me accomplish the task you set for me? It was my plan to capture and interrogate them to discover where the other cryogenic facilities are located."

"We have our reasons," said the Eldest and in a way that left no door open for dispute.

Hell wondered if fear was the answer. To kill the HEs rather than risk discovering how deep their new abilities went. He did not dare say so to the Eldest, but he was sure he was right. It disgusted him. Fear should never play into any strategy. Only minds of limited vision allowed what they were afraid of to cloud their universal view of things. Hell feared nothing. Even his response to the Eldest was not fear but a sensible management of the Flock that suited his own ends.

Disappointment, though . . . that was something he did feel, and felt it rather intensely. Anger lurked in that part of his mind too.

"Then what is it you require of me, Eldest?" he asked, careful to keep his resentment out of his voice.

"You have that facility on Io, Ren'Mgo-Hell," said the old Flock. "Return there. We believe that the answers you seek are there. It is a human military facility after all, and as we have learned, humans float on a sea of paperwork. That is how we conquered them. Go back to that base. Tear it down to the last screw and nut if you have to. Find those other teams."

"And if that information is not there?"

"Then the deaths of Alpha Wave and Lexie Chow will put an end to the immediate threat. Once they are dealt with, we will continue building the *Juggernaut* fleet, and with whatever science you can scavenge—genetics, cybernetics, biochemical— we will continue our work on the next generation of Raptors. Then it will not matter if the other Sleepers ever awake. After we promulgate our own next evolutionary step, there will be no stopping us. With *Juggernaut* as a model for a new fleet, we will be ready. We are poised to attack the future and bend it to our will. Your task is to help us get there."

Hell noted that the Eldest used the word "scavenge." It was an ugly word seldom used by Flock unless as an insult. In this case it was the old Flock trying to subtly put him in his place. He kept all reaction from his face.

"As you wish, Eldest," he said.

The ancient Flock studied him in silence for several seconds and then the hologram ended.

Hell sat there as still in his chair as his ship was in space, letting his mind and ambitions perform an autopsy on that conversation. As he chewed on it, he tapped a button on the console and a shallow concealed drawer slid noiselessly out. Inside, resting in foam slots, was a line of hypo-sprays, each with a vial of fluid socketed into the barrel. The fluid glowed with blue-white bioluminescent light. Hell reached for one and paused for a moment, studying the way his hand trembled. Then he took one hypo and pressed it against his narrow thigh.

"Worm," he said after a very long time, "take us back to Io."

"*At once, lord.*"

Hell pressed the trigger and leaned back as more biochemical stimulant shot into his system. It felt like acid eating away at his insides, but he needed it to merge with the grown enhancement he had injected earlier. Separate they were useless. Combined they were magic. But magic had its price.

There were no Flock aboard to hear him scream. Only Worm, and the robot's plastic eyes were dispassionate and without judgment.

113

Short Dog leaned his head into the cargo bay.

"Boss," he yelled, "you better see this. Maybe everyone should."

"What is it?" demanded Jason, rising from a metal case he'd been using as a cot.

"Newscast. Mugabe's got it up on the screens."

Lexie looked up from a holographic obstacle she was teaching Ahab to navigate. "There's a projector in here," she said. "Which network is it on?"

Short Dog gave her a strange, worried look. "All of them," he said.

114

Micah and Lulu sat at the conference table watching the news unfold on the holo-screen. Faces gray and streaked with tears. Their eyes wide with shock and horror and disbelief.

"It's my fault," he said.

He kept saying it. Over and over. When he wasn't screaming. When he wasn't curled into a ball on the floor.

His right hand was wrapped in a bloody towel. There was a red splash on the wall where he had punched it. Ten blows before his knuckles broke. Then three more after that.

Lisbon was gone.

It was—had *been*—the second most important center for Resistance planning and development. Fifty-three cells. Nineteen hundred affiliated agents.

Gone.

And sharing that grave were sixteen million people.

Punishment for the action of the Dreamers.

Worse still, punishment for the actions of the Resistance.

His Resistance.

His.

Him.

"Oh god," he cried as he slid from the chair and onto the floor.

115

It moved away from Earth, taking with it the disruptive force of its presence.

The tidal surges gradually settled down, granting some measure of peace to the battered coastlines of the Tagus River and, further west, the churning Atlantic. Everything from Peniche to Evora, from Pointe de Sor to Sesimbra was gone, a charred wasteland. Burning—all burning—except where towering tides had been shoved inland by the gravitational violations of *Juggernaut*'s passing.

Nothing lived in the river south of Vila Franca de Xira, and there were hundreds of square miles of the ocean in which fish— boiled gray by the hellish temperature—floated blind-eyed, rotting in the summer heat.

Juggernaut moved off in utter silence like the stealthy predator it was. Only when it came close to one of the satellites did its cloaking shield flicker. The onboard jammers kept those satellites from recording its passage, and every camera that might have been turned its way went blind until it was beyond range.

A desultory rain began to fall across the Iberian Peninsula, turning the ash to muck. In the endless swamps of ash, soot, charred flesh, and burned rubble, things crawled with painful slowness. Only at the fringes of the impact points, though. Nothing at all lived in the four massive craters grouped together in the center of what had been the Lisbon Metroplex.

On the outer rim, though, burned and sightless wrecks of animals and men groped in their mad despair for a clean spot on which to die.

Juggernaut turned its snout toward Luna, gouging its way through space-time, skimming on the endless flow of unseen transduction energies.

116

The crew of *Tin Man* stood or sat in stunned silence. They filled the cargo bay, each of them heartsick, angry, frightened, and lost.

Pryss said, "My god . . . all those people." Her voice was pale as a ghost, her face paler still.

Mugabe wiped at his eyes. "So many souls called to the Great Dream."

"Are we sure this is *Juggernaut*?" asked Fodder.

"*Juggernaut* is a goddamn myth," insisted Pickle, though his voice was filled with cracks. His eyes were red from weeping, and shudders tore through his body. "*Juggernaut*'s not real."

"You're an idiot if you think that," said Fodder, her face flushing with anger.

They fell silent again, watching the feeds from news drones. All the beauty and history, art and culture of an ancient city turned to ash.

The HEs had seen the devastation of battlefields firsthand. Lexie had read countless books about warfare going back to the Battle of Megiddo. The rest of the human crew had heard news reports from Radio Free Galaxy about other suspected

Juggernaut attacks. So far, the Flock propaganda machine had managed to cast serious doubt on those, at least as far as the general population went.

And even now, the standard news reports were all shouting about Dreamers detonating terrorist bombs.

Short Dog shook his head in disgust. "You people," he said.

"Which people?" asked Dubbs.

"You lot," said Short Dog. "I mean . . . how are you even surprised?"

"What the hell's *that* supposed to mean?" demanded the scientist.

"You have to know this is because of you."

"Easy, brother," said Sushi, but Short Dog ignored him.

"How is it on us?" pursued Dubbs.

Short Dog rolled his eyes. "You cats told us the story of how you got to Io. You have a massive Resistance network that spans the Galaxy. You've done fifty kinds of sabotage. Those Dreamers—or whatever—are setting off bombs and killed birds by the score. You killed a Flock officer and two Raptors. You racked up more kills getting this tub in the air. You're openly trying to find a group of soldiers who helped end the last war. Did you think the birds *wouldn't* punch back?"

"We're fighting a war," said Lexie with asperity. "I would have thought you'd understand."

"I understand all right," countered Short Dog. "It's just I think you're going about it in a sloppy damn way. Besides, what do you lot know of war? You've never seen one. You're playing at being heroes but all you're doing is making things worse."

"And you're very welcome for us waking you up," snapped Dubbs. "Or was rescuing you from sleeping away the rest of eternity another example of us being sloppy?"

"Hey, asshole, I'm just—"

"Secure that shit right now, Short Dog," growled Jason. "All of you. Nobody's wrong here. And Lexie's right, this is a war. We're on the same damn side, so that's the last bickering I want to hear. Is that clear?"

The others nodded, except Short Dog. He got to his feet and gave Jason a hard look.

"I got no problem following orders," he said slowly. "But it seems to me none of us are actually active military anymore. Pretty sure our terms of service have expired. Which makes me question why you're still giving orders, Jason."

The cargo bay went dead silent.

Jason was several inches taller than Short Dog, but the other HE was broader and almost overdeveloped with corded muscle. The fact of Short Dog's newly enhanced strength seemed to hang in the air.

However, Jason Horse took a step toward the man so that they were chest to chest, eyes locked and hard. The team leader smiled in a way that made Lexie glad it was not aimed at her. Pryss stood up too, but she kept her distance. No one else moved.

"Son," said Jason quietly, "I'm going to give you one pass here. I don't give a cold, wet shit if the Earth military is dead. I don't care if you're pissed because everyone you used to know who's not in this room is dead. I don't care if you're scared of what's happening to you. Or what happened to our friends back on Io. That's the thing, Short Dog, I don't care. You're a grown man, so you can settle your own emotional issues. But hear me on this . . . we *are* at war. *I* am at war. The people who woke us up are at war. The Flock just murdered millions of people. Civilians, not soldiers. For whatever fucked up reason, there is no military left. All that stands between humanity and the Flock are people like Lexie, the crew of this ship, and the Resistance.

You think they played things wrong? Well, here's the news—who cares? None of us can change that. We are where we are."

"That's not my goddamned point and—" began Short Dog, but Jason cut in.

"It's going to be so much better if you shut up right now, private," he said. "If you want off this boat, then we'll drop you at our first port of call. You know where that is? *Juggernaut*. And if you want to opt out of the chain of command, do it when and if you're back on Earth. If there's anything left of Earth. On this boat, though? You're still under my command."

"You think you can slap me down?" said Short Dog, flexing his shoulders. Small arcs of electricity began crackling along his arms.

"Try me," said Jason, his smile still in place.

Lexie was terrified of what might happen next, and she quietly, surreptitiously moved her hand to rest on the pocket in which she carried her stunner. Short Dog was literally superhumanly strong. Jason had so far demonstrated no special abilities beyond what all HEs had.

Short Dog held his place. So did Jason. The expressions on the faces of the other HEs ranged from shock to fright to anger.

The moment stretched so tightly that Lexie thought she could hear it humming.

Then Short Dog said, "This is all fucked up, man. It's not right what they did. It's not right."

It was not an apology in words, but it immediately changed everything about the moment. Jason cupped the back of Short Dog's neck and pulled him forward until they stood with their foreheads touching.

"I got you, my brother," Jason said. "I got you."

Lexie turned away, not wanting anyone to see the tears in her eyes. She was not the only one.

117

Micah Fontenot had found a calm in the eye of the storm that what was his rage. Or if not calm, then perhaps acknowledgement that the face of his planet had been forever scarred. He and Lulu Feng stood watching the news updates on the holo-screen.

A senior member of the Flock stood in ominous and eloquent silence behind the news anchor. The anchor, a Swede with very pale skin and blue, terrified eyes, did his best to read the prepared statement as if it was any other day.

"A shocked world mourns after terrorists stormed the De Sousa Nuclear Power Complex near Lisbon and caused what officials are calling the worst nuclear disaster in history," he said, eyes flicking back and forth as the teleprompter feed on his contact lenses scrolled up. "Because bombs were set off in all twenty of the facilities' active reactors and all sixteen fission reactors, the resulting explosion was of unprecedented size and scope. More than twenty-six million people are believed to have been killed in the first minutes, with another thirty million exposed to potentially lethal levels of radiation. Authorities warn that these estimates might be low. Because of the benevolence and quick action of the Flock," he continued, "resources are being sent from all over the globe, as well as some from colonies in space."

He paused, and Micah watched him fight for control. The Flock officer behind him was as still and silent as a statue.

"At the same time, human and Flock agencies are working together to root out the terrorist network known as the Dreamers, and arrests are being made on a global scale. Senior safety minister, Elko'Pgo-Luna, has issued this statement."

The reporter took a breath. Lulu tapped Micah's shoulder and pointed to a faint distortion on the video feed.

"They're editing out the sweat running down his face," she said.

Micah nodded as he threw himself into his seat.

The reporter continued to read the prepared statement.

"The Dreamers are a terrorist organization composed of dissidents who do not want their fellow humans to live in peace and comfort. They are rabble-rousers and violent extremists who spit on two centuries of peace and shared prosperity. The tragedy in Lisbon only proves that they are a worse threat to humanity than they are to the Flock. That level of species self-hatred is unknown in the history of the Flock and rises above the worst of what humanity in its pre-unification history has inflicted upon itself. We members of the Flock love our human brothers and sisters. We are appalled beyond adequate words at this monstrous and cowardly act. And we assure you—all of you, human and Flock—that these criminals will be hunted down and brought to swift and certain judgment."

A pause.

"We extend our heartfelt thoughts and prayers to our human family for this terrible and inexcusable loss. We share in your grief as we share in your outrage. With you we raise our voices in mourning and as a call for justice. May the peace and mercy of the Flock be with you all."

There was more, but Micah looked away. He and Lulu sat in silence, each of them looking into the middle distance.

When Micah eventually spoke, his bitterness was as cold and raw as flayed skin. "Now we know the stakes. All of us."

"A lot of people will watch that and praise the Flock for their compassion and concern," said Lulu.

"A lot of people are sheep," said Micah. "A lot of people are afraid to embrace the truth. This will wake some of them up. We have counter-messages going out on Radio Free Earth and Radio Free Galaxy."

"And what percentage of the population pay attention to those? Five percent? Three?"

"It doesn't matter. The message is out, and Lisbon is still burning. It's a war now. More and more people are waking up."

"We know they have spies within the Resistance," said Lulu. "We know that there were a lot of them in Lisbon because of the Nine."

There had been nine murders in that metroplex over the last few weeks.

"Two of those Nine had some knowledge about Lexie Chow and her mission."

"I know."

Lulu got up and walked across the room and stood looking out the window. "What if they hit us next? After all, Lexie's ship was launched from right here."

"They won't," said Micah.

She turned. "Won't they? And why not?"

"There are too many important Flock offices here."

"There were Flock offices in Lisbon. There were a hundred thousand Flock living there."

"Some moved out."

"Some, Micah, sure," she countered, "but not all of them. And look how many rookeries are empty right here. How do we know if any of the key Flock officials are still in Paris? They could have all been moved to the mountains or even offworld. Just because we don't know for sure doesn't mean that hasn't happened."

She came back over, knelt, and took both his hands in hers.

"Micah, how can you—*you*—of all people not realize that the Flock has no limits to what they are willing to do in order to win?" she asked, squeezing his hands. "They went into two centuries of indentured servitude—generation after generation—in order to gain the upper hand. There were Flock on every planet or moon that we think—correction, we *know*—*Juggernaut* has already destroyed. You are not naïve, my love. Shock is putting you into denial. And I get that, my heart breaks for you as much as for the people of Lisbon. But you have to shake yourself out of it. We can't stand by as mute, traumatized witnesses."

Micah stabbed a finger at the screen. "That was fucking *Juggernaut*. What can we do about something like that? They just proved that they have the most powerful weapon in the galaxy, and that they're not afraid to use it. Jesus, Lulu, do you even grasp how many of their own kind they killed just to punch back at us for launching *Tin Man*?"

"And that's all the more reason for us not to cave," she said. "If they'll do this, then they'll do worse. Surely you don't think they're going to destroy Lisbon and then stand back and gloat? This isn't a lesson, Micah, this is a demonstration of what's still to come."

He sat there just shaking his head.

Lulu squeezed his hands. "Micah, I don't think this . . . this . . . *atrocity* . . . is simple revenge for Lexie and her people.

It's more complicated than that because the Flock is always more complicated."

Micah looked at her like a confused child, and she could see his rational mind trying to peer through the weeds and vines of his despair.

"Listen to me, love," she said. "Think about all the moving parts. The Flock knows we're looking for the HEs, and they probably worked out that those HEs are the Sleepers and that they're somehow communicating with the Dreamers. That means there are two reasons to be afraid of Lexie succeeding in waking Alpha Wave—what the HEs can do physically and what they seem to be doing mentally or psychically."

He nodded but said nothing.

She gave his hands another squeeze. "The Flock has spies in the Resistance. We know that. How else would they know there was such a large concentration of our cells in the Lisbon Metroplex? Well, if they know that, then there's a good chance they know—or at least suspect—that there's another big cluster in New York, maybe Shanghai too. And we have to assume they know about us, here in Paris. This is the real hub. Do you think the birds will stop with Lisbon? Come on, love, you've never been naïve, so don't start now."

Micah licked his lips and nodded. "Even if Lexie wakes Alpha Wave," he said faintly, "what can they do against a ship like that? And if the rumors are true, then they're building a *fleet* of *Juggernaut*-class ships. Maybe they already have them. What do we have that can hope to match that?"

"You're in shock, honey, I get it," said Lulu. "So, listen to me. We're not helpless. Spies or not, we still have a network around the Earth and throughout the galaxy. No matter how many of our people they interrogate or how many spies they planted, you set the network up to protect itself. Even *you* don't know every cell or who leads them. Now . . . think this through. How many people really know that we have fighters?"

"Know . . . or guess?"

"Who cares what they guess?" she countered. "How many of the Resistance know for sure that we have combat ships? Enough to launch a counteroffensive?"

"Lulu, I know you're trying to help, but we have maybe thirty fighters ready to fly, and most of them held together with glue and string. Another ninety-something waiting for parts or pilots. And you want to send what few we have against the most powerful ship ever built?" He pulled one hand free and stabbed a finger at the screen. "A ship that can do that?"

"Yes," she snapped. "It's that or sit here weeping like helpless fools."

"Don't you realize that the Flock is watching? More so now than ever, thanks to the Dreamers. If we launch those fighters they'll *know*. They'll *see*. And they will have *Juggernaut* burn us like they burned Lisbon. They'll hit every launch point, which means we'd lose those bases and all of the equipment stored there, all the fighters still being repaired. Then they'd come for us here—*here*. They'd blow Paris off the map and then take out any city with enough of our cells to make it strategically useful."

He raised his hand to punch the wall, then at the last moment, stopped himself, squeezing his fist until the nails dug into his skin.

"When I built this Resistance," Micah said, "it was to fight back against the birds, against a known quantity, a known enemy. But Christ, Lulu, I never thought they would be able to build something like *Juggernaut*. Against that monster we are helpless." He turned away and stared at the wall. "Against *Juggernaut* . . . we're literally helpless."

Lulu pushed his chin until he was facing her again. Then

with shocking speed she slapped his face hard to one side and backhanded it back to center. Micah cried out in pain and shock. Blood trickled from both corners of his mouth.

"*Listen to me, goddamn it!*" she roared. "You *built* this Resistance. You. Not governments. Not the military. *You* did this. You are what stands between the Flock and the rest of humanity, here and across the galaxy. Yes, we only have thirty ships. But we also have Lexie Chow out there looking for the Sleepers. If she can wake them up, then we will have the weapon that *won* that last war. Stop acting helpless or so help me God I will beat the shit out of you."

Her hand was poised to strike. There was such tension in her whole body that her small hand trembled like a cobra ready to strike. Micah stared at it, and then at her.

With infinite slowness and care, he took that hand in both of his and kissed it. Then he pressed it to his chest over his heart.

He said nothing.

But he nodded.

118

The Eldest went to his communication egg and contacted his first-hatched son, Kra'Ngo'Betelgeuse, captain of the *Juggernaut*.

"Yes, my lord," said the Flock.

"I have contacted you for two reasons, my son," said the ancient Flock. "First, the statement you made with the Lisbon Metroplex was superb. Large enough to send the right messages to everyone—the Resistance, any traitor within the Flock, the media, and to the citizens, human and Flock—across the galaxy."

"And yet the news feeds blame it on Dreamers . . ." said the captain, making no attempt to hide the disappointment in his voice.

"As is appropriate," soothed the Eldest. "Those who are not cognizant of the political realities will accept that story, and it will likely turn more and more of them against the Dreamers. The tide is already turning that way, and this will increase the impact."

"As you say, father," said the captain a bit stiffly.

"As for those who *do* understand," continued the Eldest, "the traitors will think again before taking any action against the Flock. Human empathy will give them serious pause before putting so many lives at stake if they know that our response is in no way proportional. That pause will give our agents time to weed them out."

"And the Resistance?" asked Kra'Ngo'Betelgeuse. "Surely this will not silence them."

"Oh, not at all," said the Eldest. "Nor was that my intention. I told you earlier that we want them to make a sentimental decision to rise up and avenge."

"Which they will?"

"Without a doubt."

"All of them?"

"No, of course not. One of humanity's many faults is their faith in democracy and the committee process. They cannot wipe their own asses without a motion proposed, ratified, and voted upon. Ergo some of them will want to debate their next course of action, weighing the consequences that you have so eloquently demonstrated."

"Not I, father. I am but the claw on your heel."

The Eldest waved the compliment away.

"You said there were two reasons, my lord," prompted the captain. "In what other way may I serve the Flock?"

"*Tin Man*," said the Eldest.

"That is the resistance ship? The one with your spy aboard?"

"Yes. It is on its way to Earth."

"Excellent. Shall I intercept it? Or should I position the ship to defend their intended target?"

"No, my son," said the Eldest. "*You* are the target."

"My lord?"

"The HEs and their human companions are going to try and destroy *Juggernaut*."

Kra'Ngo'Betelgeuse burst out laughing. A rare thing for Flock; a habit picked up after centuries of close contact with the overemotional humans.

"Do they have some secret weapon?" he mocked. "A special cannon or . . .?"

"They have the HEs," said the Eldest. "We cannot underestimate them."

That sobered the captain. "Of course, my lord. What are your orders?"

"Let the ship approach. Keep your fighters on standby because if *Tin Man* does as we suspect, then the Resistance may launch their fighters in support."

"And we're sure they have such fighters?"

"Reasonably sure," said the Eldest. "Our spies within that group have not been able to get us a count or details of armament. They could have five ships or five hundred. We must prepare for any eventuality. When and if the Resistance launches whatever craft they have, it will betray their launch sites. You will begin an immediate bombardment of every one of those sites."

"Of course. What of the main targets? New York, Shanghai, and Paris?"

"Evacuations of key staff are under way."

"If I may ask, how far along is that process? I ask because if the Resistance makes a fight of this—"

The Eldest held up a hand. "If pressed, then I can accept whatever losses we may incur among those still in the metroplexes. Collateral damage is hardly a concept created by humans."

The captain nodded, his crest of red feathers twitching. Then he asked, "But what about *Tin Man* itself?"

"You may engage in some show of combat," said the Eldest. "But let them get close. If they try to board, allow it."

Kra'Ngo'Betelgeuse cocked his head in surprise. "*Allow* it, father?"

"Yes," insisted the Eldest. "It would advance our Grand Plan if we could capture one or more of these new HEs. They have demonstrated abilities beyond the specifications of their original design. Those abilities belong to the Flock by right of conquest."

"What about the human crew?"

"Any who survive will be handed over to the inquisitors. With luck we may learn enough to tear the Resistance down to rubble and ashes. Therefore, if you can take them alive, do it."

"And if I cannot, father?"

The Eldest's eyes were onyx marbles. "Then burn them out of the sky."

119

Most of the combined team were asleep, lost in troubled dreams. Lexie did not need psychic powers to know that. How could they not be?

After choking down a meal that surely could not have been worse than the military rations Jason declined to bring from Io, she showered, spent some time recording notes in her journal, then brought two steaming cups of coffee into the cockpit.

"Anyone thirsty?"

The prophet, looking idle and likely feeling useless with Trig piloting the ship, declined a cup, offered her his seat, mouthed a "thank you" and slipped away, closing the door behind him. Lexie held a cup out to *Tin Man*'s new pilot.

Trig accepted the coffee, sniffed it, and sipped. "Damn," he said. "First coffee in two hundred and fourteen years. Pretty good too."

"The coffeemaker is about the only part of *Tin Man* that's brand new."

"Got to appreciate a slapped-together stolen getaway ship that has good coffee."

They tapped mugs and drank, then sat together in companionable silence as the screens showed the flowing lines of matter and energy of the inside of the deck.

"Everything chill back there?" he asked, ticking his head toward the cargo bay.

"Yes, Pryss and Short Dog were up for a while talking, but now it's all quiet."

"Good."

They sipped their coffee.

"Trig," said Lexie, "may I ask you some questions? About the way you're connecting with the ship."

Trig looked wary but nodded. "Sure. I guess."

"When you said you just know," she said, "it's like Short Dog's strength and Pryss's telepathy, right? You developed some new ability while you slept?"

Tin Man flew a lot of miles before he answered. "Yes."

"Please . . . tell me how it feels."

He tried on a smile that did not quite fit. "You want the actual truth?"

"Always."

Small muscles flexed and clenched at the corners of his jaw. "It feels like there are ants crawling around in my head."

"God . . ."

"It feels awful," said Trig. "But that's how my body feels, you know? It's not how *I* feel. Does that make any sense?"

"I think so, yes."

He nodded and even looked a little relieved, as if her understanding was some kind of balm, or an anchor.

"I felt a little of it back on the base," he said. "When I went over and touched the capsules. You know the ones I mean."

"Your friends," she said.

"My family," said Trig. "Yes. All those guys. I mean, shit, we were all alive yesterday. For us, I mean. It was just a day ago . . ."

Lexie reached across and gave his muscular forearm a light squeeze. He looked at her small hand and nodded. Accepting the comfort.

"But while I was touching Monique's capsule, I felt something else. At first, I thought that maybe she was still alive. Or . . . that maybe what made her *her* was still there. I felt the emotions. Sickness. A sense of being broken."

"That must have been awful."

"No, miss, you don't understand. It wasn't really her I was feeling. It wasn't Monique who was sick."

"I don't understand."

"It was the capsule," Trig said, shaking his head in wonder at the memory, surprised at how it felt to say it aloud. "It was the damned capsule. The machinery, the software, the hardware. All of it. There was still energy in the wires, still heat there, and it was crying out in pain and fear. *It* was sick, broken, and it wanted me to fix it. No . . . that's wrong. It knew I wasn't a mechanic, not an engineer. How do I put this? It wanted me to *know*. To understand. The machine wanted—*needed*—me to hear it. To feel it and see it and know it." He shook his head again. "This sounds so stupid."

"No," she said, "it does not. It's . . . well, I mean it's scary and strange and nothing I ever imagined, but in its way, it's beautiful."

He looked at her, searching her face, her eyes.

"Yes," he said.

Lexie touched the console. "And this? Is it speaking to you too?"

Trig thought about that. "Yes and no. It's so different. *Tin Man* is alive. Sure, it's whole. But . . . it's more than that. I can feel it. Each separate part, from each separate ship Mugabe used to build it. The engine feels like my own heartbeat. The airflow is my breath. The sensors are my eyes, and I can see what they see. But I can see farther too. That's the hardest part to explain. I was sitting here thinking about it. And I think I figured out *how* I can see farther."

"Tell me!"

"It's the deck."

"What?"

"While we're inside the transduction deck, we're connected to it. From the entry port to the exit, there's a connection that flows along the transduction network. It's alive in its own way. More, maybe, than anyone knows. I can feel it talking to me, and it's—I don't know—*extending* my sight. I can see behind us and know that no one is chasing us. And I can see all the way forward to the exit and I know it's clear."

"That's . . . that's . . ."

"Awful? Fucked up? Scary as shit?"

"No . . . that's beautiful."

He laughed. "But still scary, you have to admit."

"Trig," said Lexie, "everything I've seen over the last two days is scary. I'm a book nerd from a long line of book nerds. I write bullshit for the Flock and the truth for the Resistance. You and every one of your friends are like something out of my-thology to me. You're literally heroes from some ancient story. Like Ulysses and Achilles. But now . . . you're more like demi-gods than even augmented humans."

"Oh jeez."

"You're not human anymore. Not *Homo sapiens sapiens,* I mean. And I don't know that *homo eximius* really fits. Not since you went to sleep. Am I scared of you? Not in the way you think. It's more like the way people are scared of tigers in a nature documentary. You're beyond my experience, but what you just described . . . *feeling* the machines. Understanding them on a level that's maybe even deeper than emotions . . . that is beautiful."

"Beautiful? How is any of what I—what we are—beautiful?"

"Because before I met you all," she said, "I was just about out of hope. And that's not true anymore."

120

Hell once more strode through the corridors of the cryogenic facility on Io. It felt very much like the tomb it had been for the last few centuries. The only vitality in the air was the fading smell of blood—both human and Flock—and the stink of burned meat. Neither smell offended him.

His remaining officers walked a few paces behind, ready to step forward at his slightest gesture, but respectful of his privacy.

Hell's thoughts were pulled in many directions. He considered the attack on the Lisbon Metroplex. Now, thanks to Monster, known to be one of three major hubs of the Resistance. It annoyed and frustrated Hell that the Elders had decided on so drastic and dramatic a counterpunch. And he felt disappointed that the Eldest approved it, though he understood the chain of logic that led to that decision. It would cow many humans who were, perhaps, entertaining support of the Resistance. Many, but not most.

That was something the Flock always got wrong. It was naïve in the way he knew his kind could be. And yet deeper understanding was possible. He was fully, acutely aware that

Flock thinking was often too linear, too mired in observable reaction. What this lacked, though, was insight into the working of the human heart. No other species the Flock had so far encountered was as sentimental. While that was a failing and a vulnerability at times, it was also one of their greatest sources of strength. It made many stand when otherwise they would be on their knees. The Flock spent so much time learning the way humans did things that they failed too often to consider the "why" of it. It was why the Elders would sacrifice so many Flock in such a devastating strike, consigning those lost to the mathematics of collateral damage.

But they missed the danger of that. Even the Eldest seemed to lack the empathy to understand the concept of martyrdom beyond a mere definition. Nor did the Eldest seem able to grasp the emotional underpinnings of strategic military sacrifice. *He* did. His deep reading into events such as the refusal to reinforce the Alamo and instead using the sacrifice of the soldiers there to rally outrage into counterattack on a much larger scale. Or the United States army not providing reinforcements to the Americans along the Meuse River during the Battle of the Bulge in World War II. Or when, during the Water Wars of 2036, the Scottsdale Irregulars stormed the California National Guard before reinforcements could arrive, turning the Colorado River red for twelve hours with the blood from the massacre. Or even during the Second Liberation of Mars; oxygen was three hours delayed resulting in catastrophic loss of life when Domes 2 and 3 were breached. None of those were accidents. They were deliberate actions that required hard choices in order to guarantee a better overall outcome.

His father and the other Elders understood some of it, of course. The long game played out during the two hundred years preparation of the Uprising, with the Flock pretending to be servants. And now allowing so many Flock deaths in Lisbon.

But while they could grasp the value of collateral damage, they remained obdurately focused on Flock motives and were too often blind to the way in which the human mind—individually and as a mob—reacted.

There were lessons to be learned, but after two hundred years of control and fourteen years of oppression, the Flock seemed to learn nothing. Some of it was the arrogance of conquest; some was complacency; some was the weakness that bigotry engenders when facing an opponent for which they have no respect.

Hell respected the humans. He even feared them. The devastation of Lisbon would be blamed on something irrelevant. But it was foolish to believe too much in the power of propaganda. He had sent reports earlier in his career about the phenomenon of conspiracy theories. They had been ignored as completely as his reports on what 'rallying cries' meant.

He reached the doorway to the cryo-chamber and entered. The capsules of dead HEs lay in a row. Waiting for him. But he paused by the first of them, his mind still churning on the failings of the elder Flock.

The development of the HEs would not have happened had the Flock not targeted birthing centers. Kill a hundred humans and there would be anger. Murder a child and a mob would rise. Kill a thousand children and the humans would take their finest soldiers and turn them into monsters.

No one listened to him. Now the HEs were on their way to Earth, and the Eldest held the *Juggernaut* as bait, and the destruction of the Lisbon Metroplex as a whip.

And they took their best hunter, the one who understood the humans most, and pulled him from the chase to collect corpses and dead machines. A mission of importance, but not the best use of his skills.

Perhaps.

Hell trailed his taloned fingers along the curved metal on one capsule, leaving deep scratches. Through the glass he could see a withered face. A woman whose name was stenciled to be read. *Monique St. Pierre.*

"What do you have to tell me?" he asked. "What have you dreamed about all these years? Do not believe that death will still your tongue. Oh no . . . we will share much. Very, very much."

121

It took Micah a while to get his feet under him. But once he managed it—and Lulu was his rock, as always—he moved well.

He convened his senior staff. Their holo-forms filled the chairs around the table, and he could read the fear and apprehension, even despair, in their expressions. He recognized all of that from what he had seen in the mirror when he was getting dressed.

But he put on his best game face—his king-fixer face—and even managed to smile. It was a cold one, dialed to exactly the right temperature he wanted. Somewhere north of absolute zero, but not very damn far.

"The birds have made their move," he said. "Not a strike on some distant world, but right here. On Earth. Lisbon."

"And you think it was *Juggernaut*?" asked Shimada.

"Fucking right I do. Anyone who thinks otherwise is wrong. Deluded or stupid."

He made it such a certainty that no one wanted to risk contradicting him. He explained anyway, couching it in a way that could not be interpreted as a personal insult.

"Your people are going to want hard facts because the Flock's propaganda machines are in full swing. So, let me lay it out."

Micah took a pause and caught Lulu giving him a nod so small as to be invisible to anyone but him.

"Let's focus only on Lisbon for the moment," he said and sent a graphic to the screen. "This is the feed from the Eurafrican weather satellite in the forty minutes leading up to the disaster."

He ran them through the math, explaining how sudden tidal surges and disruption in weather patterns had ramped up both unexpectedly and in extremes. And then he showed another set of numbers detailing how those weather extremes settled down within an hour of the explosion. Then he shared information on CMEs and other activity from the sun, detailing how the level of solar disruption was actually slightly below the seasonal average. Then he flashed complex formulae from software designed to predict changes in weather and tidal patterns.

"The bottom line," he said, "is that the numbers are wrong for any scenario in which that disruption was from solar or lunar influence."

They all sat and watched, attentive but clearly and deeply disturbed.

"Now, let's add something to the math," he said. "The predictive models begin to make sense *only* if some of a certain mass were to enter the upper atmosphere and move a certain distance, pause, and then move away."

He watched as they ran the same numbers through their own computer systems. The Japanese smuggler Shimada looked up first.

"The numbers match," he said.

One by one the others came to the same conclusion.

"We don't have the same kind of weather data from the other places where we've suspected *Juggernaut* struck. Because of that, even our best scientists haven't been able to build a reasonable case for the existence of *Juggernaut*. And what's made that even more of a pain in the ass is that it means that *Juggernaut* either has to be enormous—approximately 1/11th the size of the moon—or somehow has that amount of density."

"Which is impossible," said Quinnayuak, the Innuit logistics wizard.

"No," corrected the Net influencer Lucius, "just highly unlikely."

Quinnayuak turned to him. "And how is it in any way possible?"

"Nuetron star matter comes to mind," said Shimada. "And before you jump down my throat, my friend, I'm not saying that there *is* neutron star matter aboard *Juggernaut*. My point is that there is matter of different kinds in the galaxy that has a different ratio of density to size."

Micah could have kissed him, but instead nodded.

"We know next to nothing about *Juggernaut*'s construction," he said. "We're inferring a lot based on what's happened here and elsewhere. But if we take a step back and look at the Flock's history, then maybe it starts to make more sense."

"How so?" asked Shimada. Not as a challenge but to aid and abet Micah's pitch.

"The Flock are scavengers. Yes, yes, I know that's cliché. We all say it a dozen times a week. But I think we've fallen into complacency *about* that. We forget that just because they haven't shown us all of the alien tech they've discovered and repurposed that what we've seen is all they've found. Or even the most dangerous and sophisticated stuff they've recovered. That complacency is compounded by the fact that they didn't use more of that tech during the war. Well, maybe they didn't *have* it then. But don't forget, they've had over two hundred years to keep looking. We know for a fact that some of their fleet vanished after the surrender because some of those ships came back during the Uprising. Their 'peacekeeping force.'"

They nodded.

"So," said Micah slowly, "haven't you ever wondered what the hell they were doing all that time?"

122

His name was Elno'Igo-Antares and he was not driving his own body.

The skin he wore, the bones that made him stand, the wings beneath his arms, the talon on his heel—all of that was his by birth. But he no longer owned it. The part of him that was Elno'Igo-Antares was there, but shoved back, pushed down, crammed into a corner of his consciousness, and held there by the biomechanical implants drilled into his brain.

The consciousness that was connected to the motor cortex belonged to someone of a darker red color, a grander Privilege, a more important stature. Not merely within Elno'Igo-Antares's family circle, but within the Greater Flock itself.

This Flock had a name, but no one had used it in a very long time. Everyone, on every planet and moon and station across the whole of the Milky Way Galaxy called him *Eldest*.

It was a name earned in every possible way, least of which was in the counting of hatching seasons. He had earned his colors through heredity and darkened them in battle upon battle. When the Martian military command group spanned visible space to stop the Flock fleet two hundred and forty-three years ago, it was the Eldest who cut their line. When the Narwhal space cruiser launched a dozen Inferno heat-seekers against the Flock birthing colony, it was the Eldest, flying a Needletail with a failing cooling system who hunting the missiles and destroyed them one by one. It was so remarkable a feat of dogfighting that books had been written about it by Flock *and* human historians. When the HEs rose and frightened the Flock High Council into surrendering, it was the Eldest who led a flotilla of seven hundred ships to a safe staging area inside the Eagle Nebula, and there hid them from the human inspectors. Those ships were never found and never cataloged; when the Uprising happened, those ships—old as they were—became the dominant fleet in the galaxy.

The Flock, slow to age, seldom saw a fighter ascend to the High Council. Rarer still was a soldier, a pilot, a decorated war hero, elected to the post of Eldest of the entire race. And while there were technically older Flock scattered here and there, by contrast, none of them mattered.

It was he who took control of the body of Elno'Igo-Antares. The Embodiment neuro-tech was proprietary, used only when the Elders needed to venture out of the safety of the tall buildings and key rookeries. Their consciousness was transmitted across unimaginable distances via a special kind of transduction network. Something not entirely of borrowed human design. That science had appeared in the relics of more than a dozen species, some extinct for more than a million years.

It was in that body that the Eldest walked on a world so distant that it only had a number: FL-938kL. It was not important enough for a name. It was too distant and in too inconvenient a place. It was near nothing of importance. It lacked mineral wealth. It orbited a small, dying white dwarf.

The Flock attached to this mission, however, had given it their own name.

Hope.

The Eldest stood on a crest that looked down on a broad, flat plain that stretched to the east and west horizon lines. On the far side, rows of ancient and dead volcanoes had left broken cinder cone shells, none whole, that marched in ranks of increasing size away from the plain.

There, beneath a sky the color of unpolished lead, was the ship. The sight of it took his breath away.

"Magnificent," he breathed.

The Eldest steered his borrowed body down the jagged slope to the floor of the plain and stepped onto a hover-deck, which whisked him across the two kilometers to the wreck. When he stepped down to the solid ground again, the senior technician attached to the deep-space recovery team was there to meet him, bowing and fluttering her wings. The Flock was from a green clan, and only moderate of hue. But the confidential report gave her very high marks for intelligence, well above her peers and even some of her teachers.

"This is old, you say?" asked the Eldest, using the mouth of Elno'Igo-Antares to speak the words.

"Yes, Eldest," said the Flock, whose name the Eldest had not bothered to learn.

"*How* old?" asked the Eldest.

"We have run all the tests," said the technician. "We used all of the radioisotopic methods, paleomagnetic, organic and inorganic chemical methods, and even biological methods. The consensus is that this ship crashed here eight hundred and forty thousand years ago, with a 5 percent plus or minus."

"Older than we thought," mused the Eldest.

"Much older, lord. A conservative guess is that this ship is no less than one million years old and perhaps as old as five million years."

The Eldest stared at her for a moment, then nodded his acceptance.

"You mention that you used biological methods to date the ship," said the Eldest as he began to walk along its length. "Why?"

The technician looked puzzled. "I . . . I don't understand, Eldest," she stammered. "I had thought you were told."

The old Flock turned and faced her, the Eldest peering out through those borrowed eyes. "Tell me what, exactly?"

"Eldest," she said, "ever since we found this vessel, we have been picking up biological signatures."

"It's a crashed ship. Of course, there would be residual signatures. The dry climate here likely mummified the original crew."

"If I may, Eldest, it's not that," said the senior tech. "It's not that at all. If you come with me, I'll show you what we've found."

A squad of Raptors had erected a set of metal stairs up into a breach amidships.

As they passed through the hole she said, "This damage is consistent with a meteoroid of some size. There are fractured pits inside, so we figured that a meteor of some size struck the ship, encountered some kind of shielding, but was going at such a speed that it punched through, fracturing as it did so, but nonetheless breaching the hull. This may have led to a catastrophic loss of breathable gasses. Why the ship either had no redundancies or they did not work is something that engineers will have to determine through full analysis."

The Eldest waited.

"The short version, Eldest, is that it crashed here and here it has remained."

"You said there as a reason for the biological testing."

"Yes, Eldest, forgive me," said the Flock. "I was trying to provide context."

The interior of the ship was half filled with sand that had been blown inside over millions of years, though the scavenging crew had swept a pathway. It was along this that they walked. The ceiling arched above them in a series of overlapping ribs that could have been decorative or functional.

When the tech saw the Eldest looking up, she explained, "The ship is old. My theory is that it has passed through different hands over a very long period of time. The repairs we've seen, along with some structural changes, are not consistent and suggest more than one design philosophy. These are radical differences that indicate different physical types—sizes, shapes, number of limbs, shape and functional use of hands, and so on. It is not entirely unlike the way in which the Flock adapts technology we have found."

The Eldest nodded.

"Also, lord," continued the technician, "there are rooms and compartments we cannot yet access, and some materials resist our scanners and our cutting torches. We have detected power surges in some parts of the ship, as you will see."

They paused at the entrance to a large room. As soon as the technician stepped in, the lights came on. The lights were all indirect, soft, soothing. It was obviously a command center or, more properly, a flight deck, with one chair on a raised platform and concentric semicircles below, each of them facing massive screens as large as cathedral windows.

"Power?" asked the Eldest. "After all this time?"

"Yes, lord. Quite a lot of power, though we have only been able to figure out some of its use. Even if we calculate the possible uses for power relative to a deep-space colony ship, which is what this might be, the remaining energy is substantially more. More than an entire fleet of ships this size would ever require."

"Explain."

The technician bobbed her head. "It will be better if I show you, lord."

The Eldest, patient because his curiosity was so thoroughly piqued, followed the Flock scientist deeper into the ship. They entered the stern, where the machinery configurations suggested a massive engine room. All the lights were on, and even within the envelope of his space suit, the Eldest felt a change in atmosphere. The walls glistened wetly and, in places, glowed with a strange blue-white bioluminescence. He paused to look at it, but then straightened and turned, his eyes going very wide.

There was a greater light source at the rear of the vast engine room. At first that same blue-white light was so intensely bright, the Eldest could hardly bear to look at it. He tapped the visor of his suit until the lens darkened enough for him to see what it was.

He stood there in absolute silence for a very long time.

A very long time indeed.

Worlds turn on such moments.

123

Jason Horse had one leg in a space suit, trying it on to see if it fit better than the one he'd worn on the trip from the facility to the ship. For some reason his old rig did not fit as well. Too loose around the middle and too tight in the shoulders. He was lifting the other leg when it hit him.

It felt like a wave, like a shove. He staggered sideways off balance and slapped a hand against the wall to catch himself. Or tried. The hand hit at the wrong angle and slid four feet along the wall and then he was falling.

Falling.

Falling . . .

Out of that world.

Into another.

He stood in a vast room. He was dressed in his full combat rig except for his helmet. His weapons and ammunition hung heavily from the crossbelts. The magnets in his shoes anchored him to the deck, but he could feel himself swaying.

The room was so bright. Too bright. Impossibly bright.

He threw a hand up to shield his eyes, but the light seemed to soak all the way through. Even squeezing his eyes shut was no relief.

It was blue-white. Glowing. Pulsing.

Alive.

That word, that thought suddenly burned through everything and forced him to look at it, think about it. Know and understand it.

The light was alive.

And as he thought that he felt another change.

He was at once in this strange place but also deep inside dreams. Old dreams, some going back years. Decades. Generations. Recurring dreams that had slept—or had hidden—since he woke up on Io. Dreams from long before *Tin Man* arrived. Before Lexie.

Way before.

Before she was even born.

This thing was there. Always, always there.

Coming to his dreaming mind. Over and over again. Year after year.

Calling to him. Begging him. Pleading.

Pleading . . .?

That was a strange word to describe what something so powerful felt. Jason knew on some level that this thing was more powerful than any single thing that had ever been born into the galaxy.

Into *this* galaxy.

Infinitely old but not infinitely powerful. Somehow it was trapped. Caught. Bound. Forced.

Enslaved.

Long, long before the Flock. Before they had begun the slow evolution from alien versions of dinosaurs. Before they became proto-birds and then primitive birds. Uncounted ages before they became a sentient species of bird.

Before that time, some other race had enslaved it.

No, that was not precise enough. The race that had enslaved it before the Flock was not the first. Not the tenth.

There had been so many.

Finding it.

Maintaining its bondage even as one race faltered and fell and another exploited their dying hold.

Why? he wondered. Jason's mind was adrift in the dream within a memory within a dream. *What makes it so valuable?*

He heard his own thoughts like an echo and knew the thought itself was flawed. Naïve. He fought for understanding and articulation. He felt his lips move as he made the thought make sense.

"What makes *you* so valuable?"

Those five words reverberated throughout the centuries of his own lifespan and then flowed backward into the forever of time. He stood in that overlit room, arm across his eyes—and stood in the small room on *Tin Man*, amid the space suits—and slept in the capsule on Io. Waiting in all of those aspects for an answer.

Waiting for insight and understanding,

He knew it was there.

Just beyond his reach . . .

And he knew that understanding was so very important.

The future hangs on it.

That was a thought in his head, but he trembled because it was not his own thought.

It was . . .

Whose?

Help me, said a voice that was not really a voice. It was not even a thought, not as Jason understood the concept of thought. Was it telepathy? Maybe. Or something deeper and more profound than that.

Whatever it was . . . it wasn't human. It predated that concept by so many years that any attempt to calculate it was folly.

It was trying to make him understand.

It had tried to make him understand in a lot of ways.

Through dreams.

Mostly through dreams.

"Tell me where you are," cried Jason. "If I can find you, then maybe I can help."

Set me free.

"I will. I swear. Tell me where you are?"

Instead of an answer, an image flashed through his mind. Not of a being. Not a world.

It was a thing.

Sleek and black and powerful and deadly.

A ship.

Help me, cried the ship.

Jason stared at the image that filled his mind's eye.

Set me free, begged the *Juggernaut*.

124

Tin Man moved along the commercial transduction network. Closer, with every second, to the planet on which every single one of them had been born. That, in itself, was a rarity in an age of galactic expansion, and Lexie wondered if she was the only person aboard who knew that they were all Earthers.

In the ship's cramped interior, the crew began to stir, to shake off slumber, to push themselves away from the deep well of grief, to sponge away the lethargy of the enormity of what they were racing toward.

Lexie found Jason Horse sitting on the floor of the small room where the space suits were stored. She stood in the doorway, concerned by the look of strain on his face, but not sure if interrupting his reverie was the right move. She was about to back away and quietly close the door when, without looking at her, he said, "Come in."

She hesitated. "You sure?"

"Yeah."

"Are . . . you okay?"

He looked up at the ceiling and barked out a brittle laugh. "Define 'okay?'"

"What do you mean? Has something happened?"

"Why, because everything up till now has been so normal?" He sighed. "Okay, fair enough. Something *has* happened. It's just so hard to talk about."

Lexie took a small step into the room. "You can tell me anything."

Jason looked into her eyes.

"I know I can," he said. "But that isn't what I meant. It's literally hard to put into words. Where do I even start? Okay, so you know that I've been having dreams—"

"Really? I had no idea."

"Yeah, yeah, but there's more to it. Call it another layer of dreams. And, for the record, I don't think I've *begun* to unpack all that I went through while I was on ice. A therapist could make a career out of me, and that's no joke."

"I can give you some names."

"Might take you up on that if we make it through this," he said. "Anyway, these *other* dreams are so strange that I don't really know how to talk about them. When I first woke up back on Io, I didn't remember them because . . . well, let's face it, I had a lot on my mind."

"No joke," said Lexie.

"But before you found me here in this closet, I had a kind of flashback," continued Jason. "It wasn't just like remembering something I forgot. It hit me like a missile. Knocked me on my ass. Goddamn near tore my head apart."

"Oh no!" She searched his face. "*Are* you all right? You did look a little out of it when I came in."

"I was. Still am, on some level."

He told her about the dream, fumbling his way through it

because the dream had few definite shapes, confusing images, and no clear narrative through-line.

"Wait," said Lexie, "let me get this straight. You're telling me that the *Juggernaut*—the Flock warship—has been talking to you in your dreams?"

"I think so."

"*Why?*"

"Lexie, you'll think I'm nuts, but I'm pretty sure—no, I'm *certain*—that whatever's aboard *Juggernaut* is asking me for help. I know, it sounds completely crazy." When she didn't reply, he said, "Feel free to tell me I'm *not* crazy."

Lexie frowned. "I don't even know how to respond to that. I mean, how does it make any kind of sense?"

"I really don't know," he said. "And that terrifies me."

"God . . ." she breathed.

"What freaked me out, or to be accurate, *freaks* me out, is that this thing was calling me. Me . . . in particular." Jason rubbed his eyes and sighed. "I think I just had a dream. But not a normal one. Or, I guess, I mean, not a sleeping dream. I was awake but dreaming. Does that make any kind of sense?"

She sat down next to him. "I don't even know what 'sense' means anymore. Tell me about the dream. I mean . . . if you want to . . ."

They sat in silence for almost a minute before he could gather himself enough to speak. Then he told her everything about the dream. She listened in fascination and horror and wonder.

"What do you think it means?" they both said at the same time.

"You first," said Lexie.

Jason shook his head. "I don't know. I mean, I want to believe that it's some kind of hallucination, maybe a weird hang-over from the cryo-sleep."

"But . . .?"

"But I don't really think so."

"Then what?"

"That—whatever it was—triggered some memories. Look," he said, trying to come at it logically. "I know that on some level I was conscious during the cryosleep. Maybe not for all of it, and damn sure not conscious in any way you'll find in a dictionary."

"More like lucid dreaming?" she suggested.

He considered that. "I guess, but more than that too. After all, there's nothing to compare it to. Far as we know, no one else but Alpha and the other HE teams have ever been in cryogenic hibernation for as long as us."

"You're right. Dubbs will want to hear about this."

Jason grunted but then said, "Bits and pieces of other dreams have been popping up in my head. Fragments, some of them pretty damned vague. I don't know if more will show up, or if they do, if I'll remember whole dreams. You follow?"

"Yes," said Lexie.

"But as I was *having* that waking dream just now, it made me remember that I've *had* dreams about this before. Like some kind of echo. It's really hard to explain."

"It would have to be," she said.

"But one thing I can tell you, Lexie," he said, "is I don't think this is a fantasy dream. It's more like . . . shit, maybe telepathy? It feels like it's totally real. That somehow *Juggernaut* really is calling to me."

They sat with that for a while.

"How will that change what we're planning on doing?" she asked, breaking the silence.

Jason considered. "Won't change the basic plan. Might not change much at all when it comes to fighting the Flock, but . . ."

"But what?"

"What if there is something alive aboard *Juggernaut*. Something that's not Flock or human. Maybe something . . . alien?"

"Yes?"

"If it's calling out for help, then doesn't that tell us that it's no friend of the birds?"

"The enemy of my enemy?" she quoted. "Historically speaking, that doesn't always mean it's our friend."

"Maybe not," said Jason. "But given how that dream—or contact or whatever you call it—made me feel, then I'm not so sure I want to blow that ship out of the sky."

"But we have to," she urged.

"Do we?"

Lexie frowned. "I don't understand. It's destroying whole cities. On Earth and elsewhere."

"The Flock is doing that," said Jason. "But that ship . . . there's something very strange, very different about *Juggernaut*. I can feel that whatever it was that reached out to me is not just alive, I think it might actually *be* the ship."

"How does that even make sense?"

"Fuck if I know," said Jason. "I don't think I'm wrong, though."

They sat in silence there among the hanging space suits as *Tin Man* hurtled through the void.

125

Captain Kra'Ngo'Betelgeuse sat in his command chair, watching the vista of Earth, Luna, Sol, countless satellites, and the many space stations, all painted against a tapestry of stars.

He enjoyed the view. He knew that his senior lieutenant liked the peacefulness of it all. Kra'Ngo'Betelgeuse delighted in it for the chaos. He felt that distinction was an important one. The sun was, after all, a gigantic nuclear furnace. The gravitational pull of the moon caused hurricanes and tidal surges and storms. The Earth's tectonic plates were always grinding against each other, causing earthquakes and igniting volcanoes.

No, this was not peace. It was chaos in its purest form—ever changing, balancing destruction and creation with subtlety and skill.

Much like his beloved *Juggernaut*.

It was the strong right arm of chaos, rendering upon the human worlds the artistic vision of a beautiful galaxy.

"Nothing on the scanners yet, Captain," said the Flock monitoring the sensor array.

The captain merely nodded. He was neither impatient nor hasty. His father said the humans and the HEs would come to him. Kra'Ngo'Betelgeuse trusted the Eldest. And he enjoyed the slow burn of waiting, knowing that there was nothing mankind had ever developed that could hope to defeat his massive, incomparable, living ship.

He imagined he could hear the thing far below screaming.

"Beautiful," he murmured.

126

Lexie sat very close to Jason. At first it was because she needed him to know that she was there for him while he was trying to sort through the weird complexities of his waking dream. Then, as the minutes passed, that closeness became something else. She wondered if he felt it too.

"I know I keep asking but are you okay?" She didn't have anything more clever as a way to restart their conversation.

"Okay-ish," he said. "And that'll have to do for now."

"I'm sorry if I bothered you," she began, but he cut her off.

"Actually, I've been wanting to talk with you, Lexie," he said. "And not about that weird *Juggernaut* dream thing."

"What about, then?"

"About what happened earlier. Outside of the cockpit, I mean."

"You mean when we kissed," she said, surprising herself by her own frankness.

The big man's face colored. Lexie thought that was endearing, that someone so tough, so strong, so fierce could be shy about some things. About something like a kiss.

"You have my attention, Jason," she said, leaning back against the wall. "What was it you wanted to say?"

He cleared his throat. "Um . . . first . . . I wanted to thank you for everything," he said flatly. "And to make sure you were okay after what happened with Short Dog."

Lexie nodded. "Your friend is upset. Of *course* he is. How could he not be? How could any of you not be? To be honest, Jason, I don't know how any of you are even remotely sane."

"Don't bet money on actual sanity," he said, then shook his head. "Bad joke. No, truth is we're feeling it. Maybe the others are better at hiding it than Short Dog—and he never had a problem speaking his mind, right or wrong—but I know them. I can see it. I can feel it."

"When you say 'feel' . . ."

"What? Oh, no. Not like that. I'm not talking some psychic superpower stuff. What I mean is that I know *them*. Sushi's probably the best at hiding it. He's deadly to play poker with. He could have five cards from five different decks and bluff the body-mods off anyone at the table."

"Pryss seems pretty strong too," observed Lexie.

"She's my rock," agreed Jason. "Even after what happened back on Io, she's got her feet mostly on the ground."

"Mostly?"

"I've known her longer than anyone," he said. "We were in the same team before we got picked up for the HE program. We go way back."

"Way back in how many directions?" asked Lexie, cocking an eyebrow.

Jason snorted. "Nah. Don't go there. A long, long time ago we tried the office romance thing, but we realized pretty quickly that we were friends making love, not lovers making love. Now she's more like a sister to me. I trust her to the ends of the universe and back. So, yeah, I know she's feeling her feelings. Big time. If she thinks she's losing her shit, though, she'll come to me."

"What about Girlie?"

"I know her less than the others. She joined midway through Alpha Team training. A transfer from another team. Smart, keeps mostly to herself, not all that chatty. Even so, I've been keeping an eye on her. I caught her doing one of those mind control exercises to keep nervous hands from shaking. Didn't let on that I saw, though."

"I can relate," said Lexie and held out her hands. The shudder was faint, but it was there.

"As for Trig," said Jason, shaking his head. "He's a wildcard. Half the time he acts like just another joker in the deck. Rough humor, snarky one-liners, some locker room trash talk, but then he goes all quiet. I think that other stuff is a put-on and that the introverted monkish part of him is what's real."

"I agree," said Lexie, and she explained about the conversation she had with him when they were alone in the cockpit. Jason mulled on that for a while.

"This superpower stuff is way outside of anything I know about," he confessed.

"Are you sure about that?"

"What do you mean?"

"You are having some kind of communication with an alien entity aboard the Flock ship. Pretty sure that isn't a design feature of the HE upgrade."

He poked idly at the empty space suits on their hooks. "No," he said, "it's not. But I don't know if it's a new ability like Pryss and the others, or if it's tied to the dream thing."

"Can you be sure it's *not* a result of the HE upgrades, though?" she asked.

"I don't think so. Operative word 'think,'" he said. "Look, let's clear one thing up. You and your friends seem to think Alpha Wave is completely settled with being HEs. That's not true, though. You have to understand that we graduated from the HE enhancement training seven months ago. We spent three of the next months in field testing and light skirmishes, and then they threw us into the war. None of us really had a chance to let that part of it sink in. I still feel more like a science project than the shaggy-haired kid who spent his summers surfing in Oahu or climbing rocks at my grandfather's place near Albuquerque. We haven't had near enough time to learn who we are, if you get what I'm saying."

"I do," she said. "I mean, I understand the struggle without knowing what it actually feels like."

He studied her for a moment. "You've always been you, right?"

She shrugged. "More or less. My parents are historians, and most of my ancestors going back to Alexander were the same. I was just finishing my doctorate and had started teaching at Harvard when the Uprising happened."

"The Uprising." He grinned and ran his palms over his shaved scalp. "It's sooooo weird to think about things that were in *your* past but in an unknown version of *my* future. Like a time-travel paradox, I suppose." He flexed his shoulders and yawned. "Jeez . . . you wouldn't think after all that sleep that I'd ever be tired again."

Lexie nodded. "On what you were asking . . . I'd written books about things that had happened since humans first encountered the Flock. I wrote and taught about human-Flock relations. I even made friends among them, as far as that went. Friendly, I guess is a better word. Not actual friends. Different set of emotions, different emotional bonding rituals and traditions.

So, when the birds took over, I wasn't listed among the visible threats. They offered me a job in their propaganda offices."

"That had to suck," said Jason. "Going from a legit historian to a puppet telling lies. No offense."

"None taken," she said with a sour laugh. "I accepted the job because I thought it would give me a true insider's view of their world. And it has. It also made me visible, and that's something I wanted because I wanted to join a resistance."

"You knew the Resistance was already out there?" he asked.

"God, no. But I knew that the formation of one was inevitable. Humans have their weak moments but push them too hard and they always push back. Hitler and the Nazis tried to exterminate the Jews in the middle of the 20th century, and a couple of years after that regime was crushed, the state of Israel rose, and it became a nuclear power. We're at our worst when things are kind of peaceful. We pick ideological fights and act like spoiled brats. But give us a threat that endangers us all? Something that takes away our freedoms? Do that and there will always be some who rise up, raise their voices, and find a way to fight back."

He grinned. "My, my, my. You're an actual patriot, aren't you?"

"Politically? No. Idealistically? You damn well better believe it."

Jason's smile remained, but it softened. "That's a pretty sexy thing, Lexie Chow."

"Oh?" she said softly. "Is it?"

"Yes," he said, "it is."

The moment seemed to shift, and Lexie felt immediately awkward. There was a look in Jason's eyes that she hoped she was not misreading, that earlier kiss notwithstanding. He seemed to feel it too.

"Lexie . . ." he said.

"Yes?" she replied, her voice smaller and higher than she expected.

"About what happened earlier? That kiss . . .?"

"Yes . . .?"

"Maybe we were both in the moment, what with all that's been happening. And maybe—"

"Oh, shut up," she said, and reached for him.

They filled that space with heat and need. Jason pulled down several suits and made a bed out of them. They were both very glad the door was locked.

127

The traitor found a small corner of the ship, a closet where the space suits were stored. He wormed into that and sank down to the floor. For a few moments he simply sat there in silence, his game face fallen away now that he was alone. Then, slowly, he caved forward, face in his hands as the first terrible sobs tore their way out of him.

Lisbon.

Millions of dead. *Millions.*

Millions more whose lives were ruined. The crippled, the blind, the grieving, the lost.

Because of him.

Because of what he had done. Because of what he had told the Flock.

Because he was a traitor.

He collapsed by slow degrees into a heap, his desperate hands clawing at space suits, tearing them from their hooks. He tried to bury himself beneath them. To muffle his sobs. To smother him.

To bury him.

Lisbon.

"Oh my God," he wept. "I'm sorry. I'm so sorry."

But he did not think God was listening.

Not to him.

Never anymore to him.

128

The real thing was different from the dreams.

And yet it was the same.

Lexie became lost in it from his first touch.

It was his gentleness that surprised her most. In the dreams, they often made love after a fight, after some bloody action with the birds. Then, they tore at each other's clothes, urgent, filled with unbearable need. It was sweaty and furious and filled with screams on both their parts.

Not this.

This was different.

Jason undressed her so gently, his fingers hesitating as if waiting for invitation by word or reaction. When they were naked, he paused, looking at the curves of her body, touching her skin very tenderly with the tips of his fingers. He settled her down on their bed of space suits and kissed her mouth, her face, her throat, and then all of her. She knew that he was strong enough to break her in half, but never in her life had she been with someone who used that strength to enhance gentleness. With tongue and fingers he brought her to the first precipice and guided her over, catching her as she fell. And as aftershocks rippled through her as the orgasm began to fade, he slid under her, lifting her so carefully and artfully that as she sat down, they were joined.

And there they held it for a long and golden moment. She gasped but did not close her eyes. Instead, she looked down into his eyes, seeing him. Seeing deeply into him. Her inner muscles clasped his hardness, and she placed her palms flat on his broad chest. Only then did she begin to move her hips. He bent his legs and placed his feet flat on the deck, lifting with his thighs as he rose to meet every movement of her hips.

They did not hurry. For them, in that moment, they were not on a ship hurtling across the solar system toward blood and death. They were not a human historian and a soldier forced upward along the path of evolution. None of that mattered in that moment, even though Lexie was certain this would be the last time she ever made love with anyone. Death was real and felt certain.

Except she did not care.

Jason Horse moved with her in a timeless dance of shared passion. Her heavy breasts swayed with each thrust. His hands were on her hips, guiding her as if they were dancing. He never took his eyes off her, and there was a sense of wonder in them, as if he, too, were surprised by this sweetness.

The second time she rose to that cliff, he was with her, and they choked back their cries as, together, they fell over and plunged long and deep.

129

Hell watched as the technicians on his team crawled all over the capsules and computers in the cryogenics chamber. They were diligent, they were smart, and they were *his*. A few even wore white—distant cousins who had hooked their stars to his. Others were members of better Privileges, but who had become loyal to Hell over the years. Those who had done so purely out of self-interest had been weeded out; the last of them fed to the humans and HEs here on Io when he had them lead charges and walk point. Their arrogance and hunger for praise within their Privileges might as well have painted targets on their chests.

Now his team was more fully his since the Eldest had engaged him for this mission.

He knew that they would tell him everything they found and all they learned and leave it to him what to include in official reports.

And . . . they were learning so much . . .

130

She lay there, trembling, feeling the aftershocks ignite bright white-hot fireworks in every cell of her body.

Lexie wanted to say something, to mark the moment with words of importance in the way she would record an event of enduring historical importance.

She did not, though.

Some moments define themselves and do not need words to make them more real.

Jason held her close and she clung to him.

131

"Excuse me," said Pryss. "It's Pickle, yes?"

He turned to see the HE leaning out of the galley doorway.

"Yeah," he said. "That's what they call me."

Pryss stepped out into the hallway. "I've been meaning to have a quick word."

"About . . ."

The HE walked up to him. "Lexie tells me you're the one who put this team together. You're a—what did she call it? A fixer?"

"For want of a better term, sure."

"So, it's largely because of you that my friends and I are awake."

Pickle looked uncomfortable. "I guess."

Pryss offered her hand. "Then let me officially say 'thanks.'"

Pickle looked at the strong, small, pale hand for a few moments, and then took it. They shook.

When the grip was released, he asked, "Was there anything else?"

"No," said Pryss with a genial smile. "Just that."

She turned and walked off. Pickle lingered there, watching her retreating back.

132

"Hey," she said, "where'd you go?"

Lexi lay naked in Jason's arms, sweat cooling on their skin, a space suit pulled over them like a blanket, though it accomplished little.

When Jason didn't answer, she touched his face and he jerked in her arms. He stared at her with his gold-rimmed eyes and a shudder rippled through him. Those eyes were glassy and unfocused—and then suddenly *he* came back into them. Into himself.

He blinked and laughed and tried on a smile that fit crookedly but looked genuine. "Oh . . . damn . . . I'm sorry."

Her fingers lingered on his cheek. "Are you okay?"

"You keep asking me that," he said and tried to smile. He took a few breaths and seemed to be listening inside himself. "Yeah. Yeah, I'm good."

"What happened? Was it another waking dream? Was it more about *Juggernaut*?"

"I . . ." he began, faltered, looked at her for a moment, then nodded as if making a decision. "Yes," he said.

"*Tell* me."

"It's hard to explain because it's more of a feeling than anything in words or pictures."

"Do your best," encouraged Lexie.

"Okay, it's like having an empathic connection with a thing. Not with a person, per se. Nothing as clear as that. I'm feeling emotions and something that might be thoughts, but they're so radically different than my own that I don't entirely know how to translate them. I mean, I *understand* those emotions, but there are no words in my head that I think can help me tell you."

Lexie nodded. "I get that concept. What emotions are they closest to? Maybe that will help."

Jason closed his eyes for a moment. "Fear. There's a lot of something like that, but it isn't a physical fear. It's bigger than that. What's the word? Existential? Like that. A kind of anger too. Maybe despair, or longing. Or some blend of both."

"Jesus. Anything else?"

"Yes," said Jason. "And even though it doesn't seem to fit the other emotions, it's just as strong. I can't give it a proper name because no word is big enough, or complex enough. The closest I can come to it is . . . *hope.*"

Lexie opened her mouth to say something but suddenly Mugabe's voice roared from the comms speakers.

"We're coming out of the deck," said the prophet. "Everyone suit up."

Jason and Lexie staggered to their feet and began grabbing clothes. They were almost dressed when fists began pounding on the door.

133

Tin Man shot out of the deck on the far side of Luna, propelled by a burst of transduction energy.

Mugabe was in the copilot's chair, with Lexie and Jason crouched behind. Other members of the crew were crowded together in the hatchway, watching. They were all dressed in their combat rigs, harnesses heavy with weapons and ammunition.

"What are you seeing?" asked Jason.

"We're clear in this lane," said the prophet.

"Flock ships?"

"Long-range scans show a handful in orbit around Earth. A dozen escort ships docked at Luna-6 refueling station in geostationary orbit over the Antarctic. Nothing that's showing the heat signatures of combat shielding."

"And *Juggernaut*?" asked Lexie. She heard Pickle give a loud and derisive snort behind her, which she ignored. It sounded forced anyway, so she decided he was being obstinate only because otherwise he'd have to admit he'd been wrong all this time. Pickle was like that.

"It's not on my scanners."

"It's there," said Trig.

Mugabe turned to him. "Is that guesswork?"

Trig laid his hand on one of the scanners and shook his head. "She sees it. Feels it. Whatever. It's there."

"Right in the center of your imagination," said Pickle under his breath.

"Stow it," snapped Jason. To Trig he said, "Where?"

Trig closed his eyes for a moment, and Lexie wondered if he was somehow *seeing* through the scanners, through *Tin Man*'s eyes.

"It's on the far side of Earth," said Trig. "Parked above magnetic north, using that to try and hide its gravitational signature. Call it 279,000 kilometers from us."

"There's a dead satellite ahead," said Mugabe. "We can hide behind it while we decide what to do. It has enough mass to cloak us if we cut engines."

"No," said Jason. "We didn't come here to hide."

Everyone looked at him. Fodder's broad face broke into a wide, savage grin.

"Now *that* is what I wanted to hear," she said. Lexie saw that there was a new tattoo on the back of one of her hands. A burn-tat—a kind of self-inking popular in prisons and the Bottoms—seared into the skin with a modified utility laser and whatever colors were available. The laser was synced to an image file, and so the face on her hand was photo-real, and the sight it sent a painful jolt through Lexie's heart. It was Fire. Smiling in a way that made the enforcer's face look beautiful. Lexie noted that it was on the back of Fodder's gun hand, and she understood that. Every time Fodder raised her weapon to fight the Flock, she would see Fire's face and remember her loss. Powerful. Heartbreaking too.

Trig trailed his fingers across the gleaming face of the flight controls, though his eyes were on Jason. "Call the play, boss."

Jason looked over his shoulder. "Pryss, you still remember the Flock recognition codes?"

"Yes," she said.

Dubbs said, "Um, I hate to piss in the punch bowl here, but after what happened on Io, don't you think they know we're coming?"

"Probably," said Jason.

"Won't they have changed those codes?"

"Maybe," said Jason. "But if I was them, I wouldn't."

"Why the hell not?" cried Pickle.

"You may be a good fixer, man, but you're not a strategist."

"And what's that supposed to mean?"

"If they just wanted us dead, they'd have bombed Io into rubble," explained Jason. "They didn't. They sent Raptors to take us. Alive or dead, whatever. They want us. Alpha Wave. Maybe you too. They know we kicked ten kinds of turkey butt back in the day. And that freak, Hell, probably told them what we did on Io. The Flock knows for sure that in any one-to-one fight the odds favor us because of the enhancements. That's before you factor in any of our new—and I use this word with caution—*gifts*. So, I'd bet cash money they want to get hold of us, reverse engineer us and make bigger, better Raptors. HE birds. They can't do that if we're atomized."

"Word," said Girlie.

"There's no chance he's wrong," said Lexie. "I've said as much to the Resistance. It's one of the reasons, maybe the *main* reason, this whole mission got the green light."

"Might even be why we got away from Earth so easy," said Fodder.

"Easy?" cried Pickle. "You call that easy?"

"Yeah, pretty much. Half a dozen of us and a junkpile of a ship and we slipped away from the birds on Earth and there was no fleet chasing our asses? Then we get to Io, wake these spooky sons of bitches, kill a shit ton *more* birds and escape again? I mean, sure, we're a bunch of tricky badasses, but unless we're the luckiest motherfuckers in the galaxy, then the birds are dicking us around."

Short Dog pointed at her. "What she said."

"Can't argue with that," said Mugabe.

"Bullshit," said Pickle. "We did all that because the Resistance has planned this nine ways from Sunday. We earned everything we accomplished."

"Try not to be completely naïve," said Mugabe. "Jason and Lexie are correct. I felt it too. The Flock let us get this far."

Jason nodded. "And they probably want you folks because you're Resistance and we know from past experience the birds understand the value of enhanced interrogation. The more Resistance people they snag, the more cells they can identify and the more of your network they can tear down. So, no, they want as many of us alive as possible."

"Won't they *know* we know this?" asked Lexie.

"Probably," said Jason with a rough smile. "The birds may not be creative but they're not dumb. They love playing strategic games and taking big risks."

"That's a big gamble," said Fodder.

"Life's a gamble, or haven't you been paying attention?"

Lexie said, "Is it a bigger gamble than pretending to be our willing servants for two hundred years?"

"Yeah, okay, that's a point."

"This is crazy," said Pickle. "It's absolutely reckless. It's not even a real plan. You just decided this on the spot."

"Pretty much," agreed Jason. Then he gave a sly grin. "Though, we had been working on some plans like this way back when."

"What will prevent them from surrounding and arresting us as soon as we board their ship?" asked Dubbs.

"Nothing," said Jason. "But *keeping* everyone they arrest is a different thing."

"Meaning what?"

Sushi barked out a laugh. We didn't lug all those cases for nothing."

"Yeah," said Fodder, "but you cats never told us what it was or how it's gonna help us."

"Then listen up," said Jason. He quickly outlined a plan. Lexie and all the norms gaped at him. The HEs, however, looked interested, and most of them grinned.

"Let me see if I grasp this entire concept," said Short Dog after Jason was finished. "We're going to fly right at the biggest and most dangerous battleship in the history of . . . well . . . history. We know it's a trap and we're going to walk right into it and hope that the eleven of us can fight our way through a crew of unknown size but presumably fucking huge. Then using some really hinky and highly questionable subterfuge, the plan is to hijack or destroy that ship and sail off like a band of merry pirates?"

There was a silent beat.

Jason smiled. "That's the plan."

"Yes," said Pryss.

"Worth a try," said Lexie.

Trig and Mugabe both nodded.

Short Dog took a breath and blew out his cheeks. "Cool. Sounds like fun to me. Let's rock and roll."

Jason clapped him hard on the shoulder and then surveyed the crew.

"When this happens, it'll happen fast," he said. "Go suit up. Mugabe . . . I was also poking around in those crates and you norms brought enough guns and ammunition to storm the gates of hell."

The prophet bowed. "I could not risk us waking you up and then finding they didn't store your weapons on Io."

"Good call," said Sushi. "You're Santa Claus."

"Who?" asked Fodder.

"A jolly old fat man who used to bring toys to kids on Christmas."

"More like Krampus," said Short Dog. "And I mean that in a good way."

"Taken as such," said Mugabe and they bumped fists.

"Okay then," said Jason. "Suit up, gear up, and get right with God because we're going bird hunting."

134

"Micah," said Lulu as she hurried into their bedroom. "Your boy's on the line."

He looked up from his *Mon Taut,* on which software was decoding reports from Resistance cells all over Western Europe. "*Which* boy?"

"Pickle."

"Oh, shit," he said and tapped into that channel and threw a holo up. There was Pickle. It jolted Micah because he had never seen anyone so thoroughly changed by a few short days. All of Pickle's jaunty officiousness was gone. He looked thin and haggard, with dark smudges under his eyes and eyes that looked like those of a caged animal.

"Holy hell, boy, you look like shit?"

It was a measure of Pickle's distress that he neither joked nor fired back one of his typical vulgarities. Instead, Pickle wiped sweat from his eyes.

"Listen, man," he said in a quick, hushed voice, "we're coming in hot. *Tin Man's* already on the dark side of the moon. The HEs are going to tackle *Juggernaut.*"

Micah's jaw dropped. "Are you fucking crazy? That little piece of junk against that freaking monster. Didn't you idiots see what it did to Lisbon?"

Tears broke and fell down his unshaven cheeks. "Yes," he said thickly. "I saw. We all saw."

"Then you all know how powerful that ship is. Do those Sleepers even have a plan?"

"Not much of one," said Pickle. "Not enough of one."

"Christ on the cross."

"Micah . . . we're going to need some help," said Pickle, pain and pleading in his voice. "How many birds can you put into orbit?"

"Every last one," said Micah. "They're being prepped right now."

"*Do* it," begged Pickle. Then he took a breath and forced a smile onto his face. He was trying for some semblance of his usual confidence, but the result was truly ghastly. "Our little rust-bucket is going to be swatted if we don't have backup."

"Count on it. And Pickle . . ."

He wiped his eyes again. "Yes?"

"You're a hero. You know that, right?"

A terrible sob broke in Pickle's throat and he quickly disconnected.

135

They dressed separately. The HEs on one side of the cargo bay, and the norms on the other. There was no laughter, no rough jokes, no trash talk.

Short Dog tore the lids off the crates from Io, and the members of Alpha Wave began the complex and difficult process of getting themselves into them. Lexie tried to watch the process and to match it against descriptions from Alexander's journal. She understood the basic function, but it seemed so alien to her. And incredibly dangerous.

Her own suit was a completely different kind of space suit. Ultra-lightweight, though with an inch-thick padding all over. When she asked Mugabe about this, he said the suit was lined with self-sealing gel.

"Will it stop a pulse blast?" asked Dubbs.

The prophet smiled. "It will soften a punch, turn a knife, and stop a bullet."

"Not what I asked."

"And I told you what it was designed for. This is old stuff from the museum. Pre-Flock War. It was designed for interstellar law enforcement, and they never had to deal with pulse weapons."

"That's hardly comforting," said the scientist.

"If it's comfort you seek, brother," said Mugabe, "I have some tracts you can read."

Dubbs turned away, cursing under his breath.

Pickle put his suit on, but his heart was clearly not in it. Lexie moved closer to him.

"Look," she said confidentially, "I can see you're upset. If this is about whether *Juggernaut* is real or not, then—"

"Save it," he said. "We're all going to die. Whether on a hypothetical ship, in deep space, or in a bird interrogation camp. What do you want from me? Jokes and grins? Fuck that."

He turned away, his face a mask of bitterness and defeat.

Lexie stood helpless for a moment, fishing inside her head for something to say. But, really, everything had already been said. There was no more time or purpose for debate.

And so, she turned away and continued dressing for the war.

"You okay?" asked Jason from behind her and Lexie jumped a foot in the air. He caught and steadied her. "Whoa, whoa now. Sorry."

"God! Do that again and I will *so* kick your ass."

Jason grinned. "Fair enough."

She stepped back and turned in a circle. "Tell me the truth. Do I look even remotely like a soldier or a kid playing dress-up."

"Bit of both," he admitted.

"Thanks. Lie next time."

"You can stay here on the ship, you know. You and all of your people. I mean, you can drop us off and hightail it out of there."

Fodder, who was a few feet away, wheeled on him. "The

hell we can," she said sharply. "This is our fight every bit as much as yours."

"It's an offer," said Jason. "Not a command. If you want to take some scalps, then by all means. Just don't feel obligated."

Fodder's only answer was to raise her fist so he could see the tattoo.

"Copy that," said the HE. Then Jason raised his voice. "Listen to me. Anyone who wants to stay here can."

Dubbs looked like he was on the fence, but then gave a single tight nod. Lexie glanced at Pickle. Before she could ask, he said, "Don't worry. I'm coming too."

"You sure?"

Pickle's laugh lacked all traces of humor or hope. "What's the worst that can happen?"

"You could fucking die," said Fodder.

"Go look up the phrase 'rhetorical question,'" snapped Pickle.

Trig's voice came over the intercom. "*Five minutes to full burn.*"

"Okay, okay," yelled Jason. "Game time."

136

"Micah," said Lulu, "it's almost time."

They stood in the conference room. Both of them were too wired to sit. She was popping CalmZees, a pill intended to balance stress and hormones so that her body did not, and indeed could not, go into panic mode or shock. Micah was making inroads into a bottle of Tennessee whiskey that had aged in a barrel since before he was born.

The big wall was covered by dozens of holo-screens. The faces of Shimada, Quinnayuak, and the other Resistance leaders filled many of these. Other screens showed what appeared to be pastoral images of old barns in fields, peaks of distant mountain ranges, dunes in an endless desert, rocky walls in wilderness areas, and even a derelict platform from the old oil-drilling era. There was no obvious human presence in any of these. Which was entirely the point as hidden within each was one or more fighters, fueled, armed, crewed, and ready.

One of the screens projected an image hijacked from a Canadian telecom satellite. It showed part of the blue curve of the Earth, but mostly it seemed to present a relatively empty space-scape of blackness pocked with cold and distant stars. It was only when one stared patiently at the screen that the truth was evident.

That starfield rippled. Not much, and certainly not obviously, but it was there. Like heat haze on a hot desert road.

Micah knocked back a hefty gulp of tequila, gasped, coughed, and nodded.

"All launch stations report ready," said Shimada. "Waiting on the go order."

"Not yet," breathed Micah. "Not yet . . ."

137

Jason Horse felt something move inside him. In his chest, in his mind. Even in his hands.

It was not an invasion—which he had thought the first time he'd felt it. Nor was it his own nerves jangling.

In some way deeper than his own understanding of self, it felt right.

And yet *what* he felt was an overwhelming sense of desperation, of pain. Of horror on a level that Jason knew was beyond even the greatest of human understanding.

"We're coming," he said aloud, but the sound of those two words were lost in the roar of engines as *Tin Man* hurtled toward *Juggernaut.*

138

Mugabe was at the controls because Trig was with the other HEs in the cargo bay. His breaching pod suit was too bulky and rigid to allow him to steer. Before he had ceded his chair, though, Trig spent nearly three minutes with his palms pressed to the console, eyes closed, respiration so shallow that Mugabe thought he had stopped breathing. More of that strange electricity flickered on Trig's hands and seemed to melt into the metal of the console.

Before doing that, Trig had spent ten minutes tapping away at control keys, writing code, his fingers moving far too fast for Mugabe to follow. And even when he could see whole sections it was meaningless to him. Mugabe was an engineer and mechanic, not a code-writer. Three times he asked Trig to explain what he was doing, and each time the tall HE said nothing.

Finally, those fingers slowed and stopped.

"That oughta do it," he said.

"Do what, exactly?"

At first he thought Trig would ignore the question again, but then the young man smiled. "I'm what your boy Pickle would call a 'code monkey.' Before I joined Special Forces—and long before I went into the HE program—I wrote software packages to augment shipboard combat protocols. Essentially upgrading the AI and smoothing the interface between the AI and the shipboard combat systems." He paused and shrugged. "You did a pretty nifty job of filing *Tin Man*'s teeth into nice bitey points, but—and don't take this the wrong way—but you guys aren't really qualified to fight the ship to its maximum potential."

"You're not wrong," agreed Mugabe.

Trig nodded. "So I basically had a long conversation with *Tin Man* and now she's eager to use the teeth you gave her."

"I . . . well . . . wow. Thanks."

"Mind you," said Trig, "it's a delaying tactic. *Juggernaut*'s going to eat this boat for lunch. But I think we can give it some indigestion."

"I'm all for that."

"Got to go. The guys are waiting for me and this is about to get really real."

The HE pushed back, stood, nodded once, and then turned to get ready for the attack, leaving Mugabe alone in the cockpit. He wore his suit, sans helmet, and sat with his fingers hooked in the metal neck collar. Staring at the console. Almost afraid to touch it. Eyes filled with wonder.

The shipboard AI spoke into the silence.

"*The HE crew has moved to the airlock,*" said *Tin Man*. "*Would you like to engage autopilot?*"

"No," said Mugabe. "I'll take us in."

The machine voice paused for a moment. "*I am aware of what you are doing.*"

There was just the slightest additional emphasis on the word 'aware.' Mugabe caught it.

"Yes," he said.

"*You can trust me,*" said the ship.

"Yes," said Mugabe again. "I know I can."

They flew toward the place in the sky where the stars shimmered in all the wrong ways.

"*It is there,*" said *Tin Man*.

That sent a chill through Mugabe.

"How can you be sure?" he asked. "It's not yet on the sensors."

"*I can feel her,*" said *Tin Man*. "*I can hear her.*"

"You can . . ." began Mugabe and then let his words trail off. He made a warding sign in the air and touched his pendant through the fabric of his space suit.

"May the Gods of Dreams save our souls."

PART SEVEN
INVICTUS

"No soldier ever really survives a war."

—Audie Murphy

"Aspire rather to be a hero than merely appear one."

—Baltasar Gracian

139

Tin Man skimmed the Earth's exosphere four hundred kilometers above the surface. Mugabe allowed the planet's rotation and gravitational pull to slough off the speed Trig had relied on to get this far. Soon the ship was coasting along with only the barest momentum to allow steerage.

"Show yourself, you big fucking tub of shit," muttered Short Dog.

He and the other HEs were no longer aboard *Tin Man*. They clung to the outside of it, their breaching pods attached by magnets to the hull, legs bent and feet planted firmly on spring-jump pads boosted from the museum. Lexie Chow had thought ahead.

"She's out there," said Trig.

"How the fuck do you know?" demanded Short Dog, but Trig's only answer was a short laugh.

"Cut the chatter," said Jason. "We're coming up on her."

None of them asked how he knew. Pryss understood, though. While they were getting into their suits, she touched his shoulder to steady herself when she lost balance. That touch was enough. It wasn't as powerful or painful a jolt as when she'd torn secrets from the Flock officer, but it was there. Absolutely and without a doubt.

He's talking to the ship, she thought, then immediately knew that this assessment was wrong. *He's talking to something* on *the ship.*

That, she knew, was right. Even if it made no sense to her at all. But then again, since waking up on Io, how much of anything made real sense? It was not the first time she wondered if all of this was a dream.

The rest of Alpha Wave crouched in place, spring-jumps primed, trackers and guidance chips active, weapons ready.

Waiting.

Waiting . . .

Jason was more frightened than he had ever been in his life. More scared, even, than when he was about to go under the knife for the first set of HE enhancements. More lost than when he watched the video of his own funeral.

While on ice he had dreamed.

Now that he was awake, he was inside a nightmare.

He clung to the hull of an antique ship, waiting to attack the most powerful ship in the known galaxy, crewed by an unknown number of elite Flock warriors, while some alien . . . *thing* . . . screamed inside his head.

God save my soul, he prayed.

Deep inside his mind, he felt the entity scream again. It burned its way through his nerve endings, raced through his veins, made his heart race out of control.

God save us all, pleaded Jason Horse.

They all heard Mugabe.

"God Almighty."

It was not a prayer of the Church of Morpheus. It was older than that, more basic than that. It was pulled from him by total shock.

The crew of *Tin Man* clustered in the cargo bay spun to the holo-screens and witnessed what the Prophet had just seen.

Then the HEs turned and saw it too.

The stars stopped shimmering.

And *it* was there.

Juggernaut.

It was not the giant they were expecting. The urban legends and conspiracy theories had it wrong. It was not miles long. It could not have a crew numbering in hundreds or even tens of thousands. And yet . . .

Juggernaut was terrifying.

The ship looked alive. There were no sharp edges, no truly straight lines. It looked grown rather than built. Sleek and reptilian, with a tapered snout that seemed ready to open to reveal venomous fangs. Wings like those of some mythical dragon swept back from the main superstructure, and antennae of arcane design thrust outward from its metal skin like needles on some poisonous sea creature. Everything about the ship was ominous, pernicious, and cruel.

And it was coming for them all.

140

Captain Kra'Ngo'Betelgeuse envied only one thing about humans—their ability to smile. Now he wished he had that ability—to smile or grin or laugh for joy. Like many Flock who tried to understand the human condition, he had watched movies—some of them going back several hundred years. Human mouths were wonderfully expressive in ways beaks could never be. Even with head crests, skin around the eyes, and body posture shifts, the Flock were simply not a demonstrably emotive race.

The *Tin Man* filled the forward viewscreen. The impudent Resistance fighters led by that traitor Lexie Chow, and the remaining members of Alpha Wave. Right there, only a few thousand meters away. Inching their way through the airless space as if *they* were the predator. As if they had any chance at all.

He ached to be able to tell his gunnery crew to fire, to enjoy themselves, to chip away at the worthless little ship until the scanners picked up nothing but floating corpses and pieces of composite metal no larger than a fledgling's claw. Oh, how he ached to give that order.

Instead, as his father commanded, he waited. Son of the Eldest of the Flock, captain of the most powerful warship in all creation, he sat and waited.

But he would have been comforted had he been able to enjoy a wide, happy, cold, predator smile.

141

"They're slowing," said Mugabe.

"*They are likely waiting for you to make a significant move,*" said *Tin Man*. No trace of snark. Mugabe noted that the AI was much more agreeable—though less entertaining—since Trig had done something to it.

"Get ready," he said to both teams.

"*Would you like to engage autopilot now?*" asked *Tin Man*, actually drawing it out the way a person would. "*Trig has programmed our next moves, and you can feel safe leaving them up to me. I know what to do.*"

Mugabe stared at the console. "Do you understand what might happen? What probably *will* happen?"

"*Yes, Prophet Mugabe,*" said the AI. "*I will very likely die.*"

"Yes."

"*And in doing so I will do what I was created to do. How many beings can say that with such accuracy?*"

Mugabe sat there and fought the spill of tears. Fought, but lost.

"*You are weeping for a machine,*" said *Tin Man,* and there was awe in his voice.

"I . . . I am sorry that you will . . . will . . ."

"*You can say it. That I will die.*"

"Yes."

The monstrous Flock ship now filled the forward viewscreen.

"*It is the expected outcome, Prophet Mugabe, but it is not a certain one. Neither of us can see the future. It is an undiscovered country.*"

"I . . . don't know what to say," confessed Mugabe. "I could pray with you."

"*The offer is a kind one,*" said the ship, "*but I fear we may have different gods in our respective heavens. However, Prophet Mugabe, there is something you can do for me. Perhaps for us all.*"

"Tell me and I will do it."

A panel opened on the console and a small device rose from it. Mugabe recognized it as a data slip.

"What is this? What am I supposed to do with it?"

"*If you both survive . . . give it to Trig. He will understand.*"

"And if he does not? What if he dies on this mission?"

"*Then you, Prophet Mugabe, may find some use for it.*"

Mugabe took the data slip. Then he placed his hands on the console, much as Trig had done. He felt the hum of the ship's ion propulsion engines. He hoped to feel more. He tried to. But whatever gift Trig had belonged to him alone.

"Thank you," he said.

The ship made no reply. Mugabe reached for his helmet and went to join the others.

142

The rest of *Tin Man*'s crew was in the hold.

Mugabe hurried over to where Lexie stood with Pickle, both of them staring intently at two holo-screens. One showed *Juggernaut*, dominating the upper atmosphere view of the sky. The other, however, carried the feed of an external maintenance scanner and the image it displayed was the outer skin of *Tin Man*. A group of ungainly figures seemed glued to the hull.

Lexie gestured to the second screen. "They're in position."

"Those idiots are out of their goddamned minds," said Pickle.

Mugabe shook his head. "They are god's warriors."

"Yeah, well that don't make them any less crazy."

Mugabe smiled. "You know that in times gone by, anyone labeled a madman was regarded as having been touched by God."

"Then he must have touched them really damn hard, because this whole plan is nuts."

Lexie sighed. "You're not wrong."

Even Mugabe agreed.

"What makes it even crazier," Lexie said, "is that I don't know who's crazier in this scenario—them or us."

Mugabe and Pickle looked at one another.

"Oh, us for sure," said Pickle.

"Without a doubt," agreed Mugabe. "I can feel God's touch right between my shoulder blades."

They all tried to laugh at the joke, but they were too scared to manage.

143

"Captain," said the Flock pilot, "detecting a heat bloom in the enemy's engines."

The XO, who stood to the left of the elevated captain's chair, said, "They've thought better of this folly. They're going to make a run for it."

Captain Kra'Ngo'Betelgeuse leaned forward and studied the small cargo ship, gesturing to have the holo-projector turn it in a slow 360. There was indeed a sharp rise in engine temperature.

"How are they armed?" he asked.

The scanner tech was hunched over his screens. "Minimal visible weaponry, sir. Two pulse cannons with swivel turrets giving each a 270-degree swing, and what appears to be antique-style rocket pods mounted fore and aft. These are non-military, sir, and are consistent with cargo ship armament used to destroy large rocks in the asteroid belt."

"And what else?" asked the captain.

"That is the entirety of their weapons capabilities as far as I can tell, Captain," said the tech. "This is a low-end commercial ship. Sturdy hull but no guns that can hurt us."

Several of the bridge crew chuckled and made derisive click-ing noises until the XO glared them to silence.

"Very well," said Kra'Ngo'Betelgeuse. "Fire a shot across their bows. XO, prepare to latch on and bring them into the cargo bay. Full squad to receive them but keep weapons on stun."

"At once, Captain," said the XO and he hurried off to relay those orders.

The gunner took a joystick in hand and thumbed off the safety cover to reveal the trigger. "Firing a warning shot," he announced.

And *Juggernaut* coughed out a pulse blast. It burned an in-tense purple line through the blackness and then vanished into the infinite beyond.

Immediately *Tin Man* turned. The heat bloom intensified as the ion propulsion engines cycled up.

"They are running, sir," said the scanner tech.

Tin Man shot off, moving away from the Earth as if trying to return to the relative safety of the Moon.

"Follow," said the captain. "Match course and speed."

The big ship swung around with remarkable agility and began moving. It accelerated smoothly and easily, nimble as an eel or a dorado—Earth sea creatures the captain enjoyed hunting.

Captain Kra'Ngo'Betelgeuse was mildly surprised that the humans were brave enough—or perhaps foolhardy enough—to try and outrun him. As if they thought the cloaking technology was all *Juggernaut* could bring to the chase. He was delighted they were going to make a game of this. There was no glory in capturing enemies willing to surrender or too feebleminded to avoid a trap.

"Let's have some fun with them," he said. The dark red feathers of his head crest stood up. "Keep firing. Near misses only. Burn the paint but don't destroy the ship."

The gunner laughed and took a fresh grip on the joystick. Purple pulse blasts filled the void.

144

"Now," said Jason Horse.

Six pods, each shielded against the eyes of scanners, launched from the stern quarter of *Tin Man*. Their spring-jump pads ignited and shot them outward at incredible speed. The burn of those pads was completely masked by the increased heat of *Juggernaut*'s engines. No one notices every spark in the midst of a roaring blaze.

The pods, synced with in-suit AI, sent the HEs hurtling into the Flock ship's path. Timing was critical and it required everything the AI and suit mechanicals could manage, and all of the physical strength of each *Homo eximius* to turn the maneuver from a suicide run with no hope of rescue into a precisely planned covert insertion.

Juggernaut was moving at the same speed as *Tin Man*, and on the same course. Jason felt massive relief that he had read the situation right. But the next steps were horrific.

The ship grew from a dot to a monster in seconds, and HE's suit AI sent hundreds of tiny course corrections to the spring-jumps. Helmet displays counted down the distance from five thousand meters to one thousand to nothing at all. Jason disengaged the pad and turned his breaching pod's magnetics to maximum. This was the part he hated.

The pod slammed into *Juggernaut*'s hull amidships and below and locked on with a jolt that sent shockwaves through Jason's body. Inertial dampeners and gel-shock absorbers be damned—it tore a dull cry from him and for a moment everything in his head turned to fireworks. Consciousness swept in and out.

He vaguely heard the other pods striking and locking on.

Jason fought to shake off the trauma of that impact.

"Ev—everyone . . . count off . . ."

There was a delay and then he heard them. Pryss, then Sushi. After three seconds, Short Dog and Girlie.

Then silence.

"Trig," called Jason, suddenly alarmed, "count off."

Nothing.

"Trig, damn it, report status."

Jason turned his head inside the bulky breaching pod. "Does anyone have eyes on Trig?"

"Can't see him, boss," said Pryss, anxiety sharp in her voice.

"Fuck," said Short Dog, "maybe he's on the other side of the hull."

"Whatever this thing is built from," said Sushi, "it could be blocking comms."

"That hit nearly knocked me out," said Girlie. "Maybe he's shaking it off. Give him a sec. He'll call in."

Precious seconds burned off, but the radio remained silent.

There was no sign of Trig at all.

145

Lexie had never had much faith in a higher power. The historian in her had spent too much time at university studying the way in which religions rose and fell; how an older one was often absorbed into a new one. Faith always seemed to be a kind of rationalization by people too primitive to understand the way in which cultures evolved and science worked.

Now, huddled in the cargo bay of *Tin Man*, she was very much reconsidering that agnosticism. She wanted to have something to pray to. Mugabe, next to her, was praying constantly, though quietly. Fodder was reciting catechisms she'd likely learned as a child. Dubbs stared at nothing; his jaw set but eyes unfocused as he looked inward. Was he searching for some kind of comfort beyond the science he so treasured? Lexie thought it probable.

And Pickle.

After their brief discussion earlier, he went over and sat down on a crate, as far apart from the others as he could manage in the cramped space. He had his head in his hands. Lexie hated that Pryss had put him in charge of the anti-caps. It was one more burden, and Pickle already blamed himself for all the disasters that had happened since the Raptors showed up at Lexie's apartment. *She* didn't blame him, though. There were supposed to be traitors and spies inside the Resistance, which meant that anyone Pickle spoke with might have passed word to the Flock.

On top of that, discovering that *Juggernaut* was absolutely real must be shaking him down to his core. Pickle's faith was in the practicality of the Resistance. Small actions undertaken by different cells, playing the human version of the long game to disrupt the Flock and hopefully destabilize it. That was his vision. Having a ship as powerful as *Juggernaut* skewed that math all to hell. With every hour Lexie had seen his humor melt away and his despair mount. She was pretty sure he no longer believed that the Resistance had any real chance; nor was he sold yet on what the HEs might achieve. They had tried to rescue an entire platoon and came away with six, and none of them were what they expected.

She went over and put a hand on his shoulder, but he flinched away from it. He wouldn't look at her. Instead, he seemed to be focused on the anti-cap trigger mechanism on his belt buckle. It was hidden beneath the space suit, but his finger kept tracing the shape.

"If you want to talk," she said, but he ignored her.

One of the holoscreens flashed purple and the small cargo ship shuddered. Mugabe waved her over. "They've opened fire."

"They're not trying real hard," said Fodder.

"I don't think they're trying to destroy us. Cripple, to be sure, though."

"Yay?" mused Fodder. "All that means is they want to scare us into surrendering."

"Surrender," sneered Pickle, suddenly getting up and joining them, his face dour. "Surrender means vanishing into a

Flock camp. You all know what that means. We might as well grow some balls and shoot it out."

"With what?" countered Fodder. "Couple of pop-guns and asteroid missiles? Might as well throw stones."

Mugabe shook his head. "I keep telling you, we have some surprises."

"Running sounds like the best thing we can do," suggested Dubbs.

"No," snapped Lexie. "We stick to the plan."

"Plan?" laughed Pickle. "We have an AI driving this boat and all of our superhero soldiers are out there in the black. Who knows if they even managed to reach that ship? And even if they do, it's the flagship of the goddamn Flock fleet! I get that the HEs scared the piss out of the Flock two hundred years ago, but that means the birds have had all that time to prepare a response. Alpha Wave is dead as soon as they step on board and you know it. And we're up shits creek once the captain of that ship stops playing cat and mouse with us. Tell me, Lexie, what part of this insanity feels like a plan? We either burn with this ship or we spend the rest of our very short lives in a torture camp. There's no third outcome."

Lexie opened her mouth to rebut his rant, but then something slammed into *Tin Man* and the ship reeled as if struck by a mortal blow.

146

Jason Horse felt his heart break, but instead of stealing away his resolve, he threw his pain onto the fire of his hate, using it as fuel.

"The mission stands," he roared. "Hard seal."

The four HEs ignited the quick-weld packets mounted around the flat borders of their pods. The self-sealing gel flooded the space between the pods and their lightweight space suits. Even with that, Jason felt the heat.

Suddenly Girlie cried, "Boss, on your four o'clock. Are you *seeing* this?"

They all twisted around to look. The Earth was massive behind them, and for a moment that was all Jason could see, but then he understood what had alarmed Girlie.

"Holy God."

A hundred kilometers away but visible through the amplification of the helmet sensors, they saw it. *Them.* One after another they rounded the curve of the Earth and turned toward *Juggernaut.*

One, two, five, ten. More.

The Flock fleet, having lain in wait, was coming for them

too. The craft that led it was twice the size of *Juggernaut*. A grand battleship. Twenty-seven decks, a crew of ten thousand, with launch bays for a hundred fighters. *The Talon*. Formerly the flagship and now consort to the newest and most powerful ship in existence.

Jason's heart sank.

Then he heard something else. Heard. Felt. Whatever the actual form of perception it was.

Save me.

It was the voice of the entity. The thing that was trapped aboard *Juggernaut*. Shouting to him in a voice louder than all the sound in the universe.

Find me, it screamed.

Jason forced himself to turn away from the fleet, to shove back the certainty of his own death and the deaths of everyone he loved. What was left of Alpha Team was committed now. They either took or destroyed *Juggernaut*, or they would all die.

"Burn it," he roared, and the five pod-drivers fired their ultra-high-intensity cutting lasers. The entire perimeter of each suit cut at once. They were designed to cut as much as sixty inches of polysteel.

"What the hell is this boat made of?" growled Girlie. "Hard as fuck to burn."

"Dial it up," ordered Jason. "There's no Plan B."

His pod's burners ratcheted up and now he could feel a lot of heat as the intense cutters challenged the heat-dampeners.

"Getting cooked over here, boss," said Sushi.

"I thought sushi was supposed to be raw," joked Short Dog.

"That's sashimi, dumbass," yelled Sushi. And they all laughed as if the moment was funny. Jason was heartened by that, knowing that rough humor of any kind was another layer of armor. He kept hoping to hear from Trig, but there was still no answer, and that was another reason the jokes mattered—the heart needs armor too.

"Wait," cried Pryss, "my burner just speeded up. Cutting faster now."

"There's some kind of outer skin," said Sushi. "Just got through it. Feels like I'm burning through regular metal now."

Jason felt it too. *Juggernaut*'s armor was not indestructible, and that was big. It was huge.

"Running low on fuel," said Short Dog. "This fucking ship's built like a beast."

"What'd you expect," asked Girlie. "A kid's paper boat?"

"Would have been nice, yeah."

"Suck my dick."

"You don't *have* a dick."

"Meaning what? If I got a body-mod nine-incher you'd suck it?"

"Get me drunk and let's find out," said Short Dog.

Even Jason cracked up.

"I'm through," said Pryss.

"Me too," called Sushi. Jason was third and then Girlie.

"Short Dog," called Jason. "What's your status?"

"Fuck me blind and move the furniture," growled Short Dog. "Got a full cut on 78 percent but then the fuel ran out. Shit."

"Hold tight," said Jason. "Soon as we're inside we'll cut from the other side."

"Hurry the hell up, guys. I feel like a pimple on a dog's ass out here."

"You're nowhere near as pretty as that," said Girlie.

Jason braced his back against the rear wall of the breaching pod, took a big breath, and slammed forward with the heels of his palms. The cut section of hull resisted him. He hit it again. And again.

On the fourth try the thick steel shifted. Jason kept hitting, moving the slab by inches until he could raise both legs and then he kicked out with every ounce of strength he possessed. The cut-out jerked backward and fell away.

"I'm in," he announced and shoved off into the ship, correcting his momentum as *Juggernaut*'s internal gravity pulled him to the deck. He turned and checked the seal, but it was tight. No escaping oxygen.

He was in what appeared to be a maintenance corridor— purely functional and with only minimal lighting. It was long, though, and both ends faded into shadows.

There was a heavy thud to his left and he pivoted and brought up his rifle.

"I'm in," said Sushi.

Another thud in the same direction.

"On deck," said Girlie.

"Working on it," said Pryss.

"Hold on," said Short Dog. "Got to use a little muscle here."

There were four muffled bangs and then a much heavier thud to Jason's right, and a section of wall forty feet away went flying across the corridor and slammed into a wall. Short Dog stepped out, grinning and rubbing the knuckles of his big right fist.

"Had to talk to it some," he said.

Jason called the team to him, and while he waited, he kept hoping he would hear from Trig. But there was still nothing but a hopeless silence.

They all clustered together to shed their lightweight space suits and do a quick weapons check.

"No alarms," said Sushi. "That's something."

"I think we're in the belly of this beast," said Jason as he adjusted his standard combat rig and tested the gas jets. "Girlie, launch some canaries."

She pulled a dozen of the small drones from a pouch and sent them flying. Their subsonic echo location sent data back that allowed the team's forearm holo-projectors to build a model of the corridors.

"Looks like we're in the sub-basement to the sub-basement," said Short Dog. "Only see a couple of birds and they're dressed like maintenance crew."

"Sushi and Girlie," said Jason, "go find them and take 'em off the board. Hide the bodies if you can. Quick and quiet, no traces."

"On it, boss," they said and moved off, silent as ghosts.

"I wonder how *Tin Man*'s doing," said Pryss.

"Wish you were telepathic as well as empathic, sis," said Jason.

"What's the plan?" asked Short Dog.

"No change. We find the engine room and see what's driving this tub."

Pryss gave him a calculating look. "And if there is some kind of alien entity aboard?"

"Then we observe, assess, and deal," said Jason. "Let's go."

Like the others, they moved off without a sound.

147

"They're gaining on us," said Mugabe.

He stood with the rest of the crew in the cargo bay of their little ship, all of them in space suits. A holo-screen showed *Juggernaut* approaching. It was painted a flat black and except for where it obscured the stars it was invisible.

"That thing creeps me out," muttered Fodder.

"It terrifies me," said Lexie. Ahab, tucked down into her suit, squirmed.

"Not much of a fan either," said Dubbs.

Pickle said nothing. His face was gray, and his eyes filled with nothing but hopelessness. He held a stolen Raptor pulse rifle and met no one's gaze, but he whispered to the ship AI to be ready. It was almost time . . .

148

"Captain," said the XO, "they're not slowing."

Kra'Ngo'Betelgeuse sighed. "Apparently warning shots are lost on minds that small. Very well. Target their engines. Disabling shots only. I do not want that ship destroyed."

"Sir!"

Juggernaut veered slightly from its stern-chase course, angling to come alongside it. Gunports slid open and the snouts of a dozen guns thrust outward.

"You may fire at—"

Before those cannons fired, *Tin Man* opened fire on *Juggernaut.*

It was as if the entire hull disintegrated as scores of mid-size cannons seemed to appear as if by magic. They swiveled high and low and immediately began firing. This was no simple barrage by a cargo ship, but a sophisticated attack, with each gun selecting its own target based on the AI aboard *Tin Man.*

And the weapons seemed to be archaic.

There was nothing sophisticated about them.

Molten Metal Rail Guns threw burning pieces of shrapnel through space.

Fusion Lances pulsed as they sought the weakened places the rail guns had targeted.

Against all odds, it was as if the *Tin Man* had thrown rocks at them and those rocks had consequences.

The first fusillade blew the starboard-side heavy guns to pieces.

Then another weapon rose from the top of the human ship. This one they recognized. This was of Flock origin and was more than lethal.

The commander of the *Juggernaut* inhaled in fear as the top-mounted pulse cannons swiveled directly toward him and began a rapid-fire assault on the ship's bridge.

In every way that mattered, the Second Flock War had begun.

149

They moved fast through the corridor, rifles snugged against their shoulders, feet taking many small steps so as to maintain constant balance and not spoil their aim. Short Dog and Girlie caught up, reporting that the maintenance crew were down and hidden in an air shaft.

Jason ran point while Sushi had their backs, with Pryss, Girlie, and Short Dog in the middle. They kept their fingers laid along the outside of the trigger guards, barrels swiveling in sync with their eyes, adjusting their aim whenever a team member shifted into the line of fire. This part was old hat for them, recalling their early days in specialized combat and live-fire training. Special Ops schooling had refined it, and elevation to HE had polished it to a high gloss. During the Flock War they were not merely elite, they were the best of the best. The pinnacle of human combat training; the first generation of *Homo eximius* soldiers.

The corridor was long but reached a T-junction after forty meters. Girlie sent a canary drone ahead and it sent back images of an empty hall to the left and a pair of guards outside a heavy hatchway on the right.

Jason signaled the others to hold back and then moved forward briskly, wheeled around the corner and fired four quick shots. Two each, center mass. The guards were armed and wearing their cuirasses, but they did not have grease-shields active. They died without knowing they were in danger.

"Girlie," called Jason. "You're up. I need that door open. Quick and quiet."

She moved past him to the door. Without Trig, she was the fallback tech. She pulled scanner leads from a device clipped to her cross-belt and pressed their magnetic heads to the door. It was a solid affair, dense, well made, and oddly shaped. Too tall and not as wide as it should be for either humans or Flock.

"Weird dimensions," said Pryss quietly. "I'm not all that sure the birds built this boat."

"Been thinking that all along," said Jason.

"If not them," said Short Dog, "then who?"

No one had an answer to that.

"Locking mechanism isn't that strange, though," said Girlie. "Looks like a modified airlock like you see on older space stations. See the welds on the wall there? This was an aftermarket upgrade."

"Can you open it?" asked Sushi.

"Can you find your dick with your eyes closed? Wait, no, it's too small." Girlie removed the leads and gently pulled the door open. They all tensed, waiting for an alarm. When there was none, they flowed inside and closed the door behind them.

150

"Eldest," said the senior officer as he bowed into the room, "the essential evacuations are complete."

"And my wife?" asked the Eldest, rising from behind his desk.

"She was reluctant, lord," admitted the officer, "but we convinced her that a terrorist attack was imminent. She finally assented. She and the latest clutch of eggs are on a skimmer right now and should reach the Pyrenees in minutes."

"What about the command staff?"

"In the bunker beneath Neufchâteau, along with their aides, support teams, and all computer records."

"Excellent." He walked over to the big window and looked out at the sprawling expanse of the Paris Metroplex. The beautiful spires of a thousand rookeries rose like the arms of the old gods toward the cloudy sky. Most of the rookeries were still occupied. There were still more than a million Flock in the metroplex. None of critical importance, but all important for the role they were destined to play. Martyrs. A word so many of his peers did not fully grasp. He wondered if his agent, Hell, understood the value of that word, that concept. Probably.

That bastard son of a colorless Privilege was smart. He understood humans.

Just as he, the Eldest, understood them.

When this city was destroyed, as Lisbon had been and New York would be, then there would be such a cry of outrage from the Flock that mere occupation of humanity would not be enough. Retaliation would be called for, demanded. Needed.

And he would allow it. Reluctantly, with obvious sadness and regret. He had his scripts memorized. The next moves were all up to his first-hatched son.

He tapped a panel on the wall and the view outside the windows of Paris vanished to be replaced by actual direct views of the graceful, snowcapped mountains that were far, far away from *Juggernaut*'s next target.

151

Juggernaut reeled.

The blasts from the small ship rocked it, hitting much harder than Captain Kra'Ngo'Betelgeuse had ever expected. The blasts, each finding critical targets with mind-boggling precision, had the effect of a body blow. Alarms screamed as inertial dampeners fought to compensate. Control panels exploded outward, showering crewmembers with burning sparks and pieces of melting wire. The monstrous ship was knocked off course as emergency systems lagged coming online.

"Right the ship," roared the captain, who had been thrown from his chair and now clung to one arm. "Return fire."

Juggernaut's guns fired, but the broadside was ragged. Not a single shot hit the tiny cargo ship because *Tin Man* was not there. As soon as it fired the craft yawed to port, swung around, and corrected so that its starboard cannons were aimed at the belly of the larger ship. Once more it attacked, the guns firing in a sequence more precise than human gunners could manage in the time allowed.

The skin of *Juggernaut* was incredibly tough, but the ray shielding had been turned off to allow it to fire on *Tin Man*.

Shields did not allow gunfire and, in fact, trapped it so that pulse blasts or torpedoes would detonate as they fired. Captain Kra'Ngo'Betelgeuse relied on the outer skin and sixty inches of alien poly-blend metals.

And yet . . .

"Yaw and fire," he bellowed. "Give me some distance." The ship leaned sideways to bring its lowest tier of cannons to bear, but as they tilted down toward for a target lock, they discovered that they were unable to do so . . .

The *Tin Man* was faster and its cannons, firing at close range, used its smaller size to sting like a wasp rather than stand off for a suicidal duel with a ship a hundred times larger. The *Tin Man* targeted *Juggernaut*'s guns as they angled down, matching thought to action without any human delay, and the new barrage blew apart six of the great ship's cannons.

But the big Flock ship broke hard right and climbed into a wide turn, increasing the distance by several kilometers and allowing stern-chasers to fire. Those bigger pulse cannons—though nowhere near as big as the main city-destroying pulse-weapons mounted forward—filled the distance between the ships with purple fury. They continued to fire as *Tin Man* attempted to veer away. Of the twenty shots fired in under three seconds, nineteen missed.

One, alas, did not.

In the little ship's hold, Lexie and the others were slammed sideways into stacks of crates. She screamed as those boxes broke from their restraining straps and collapsed down on her.

Automated emergency lights and sirens flashed their warnings, but Lexie was buried under two tons of gear.

Within *Juggernaut,* Jason and his team crouched, bracing against anything solid as the big ship shuddered.

"God*damn*," cried Short Dog. "That little rowboat's putting up a fight."

"Can't win against this fucker," said Girlie.

"They scored some hits," said Sushi. "I could feel that through the deck."

But Jason cocked his head, listening through the alarms. Listening from inside his body.

Find me, cried the voice that was not a voice. *Save me.*

Tin Man fled from the aft cannons. Smoke funneled out through vents, and its backtrail was littered with debris. Several guns were down and two completely torn away.

The swivels mounted above deck fired backward, but the distance was great and the ship damaged. It stopped firing and went into a climbing turn that brought it around on the port quarter with fifteen kilometers between the craft. The distance was not a problem for the guns but much too far for safety. Every kilometer—every inch—of distance gave more advantage to *Juggernaut*.

Captain Kra'Ngo'Betelgeuse nodded as he climbed back into his chair.

"I have you now."

Juggernaut surged forward.

"Target those guns," he ordered. "And take out their engines. Do it now."

The guns fired.

And fired.

And fired . . .

Tin Man's guns were relentless as it came out of its turn, clustering its shots to give them more specific punch. One of the bigger ship's forward cannons exploded, but the others fired so fast that it forced *Tin Man* to veer. The returning salvos were so fierce that no distance was gained.

It kept firing back, though.

Every gun, every moment.

Dubbs and Pickle, shaken and bruised inside their space suits, fought to lift the crates that buried Lexie.

She screamed in pain and tried to push, but the crates kept shifting in all the wrong ways.

"Mugabe," cried Pickle, "cut the gravity. Cut the god-damned gravity."

The prophet, his head ringing from striking the big cargo door, crawled toward the control panel. *Tin Man* kept shudder-ing as more and more of the enemy's fire struck home.

As Jason Horse forced himself to his feet, he fought for focus. His combat mind needed to be right there, right now, but another part of him was falling into a waking dream. That part of him stood before something huge and monstrous that glowed with a blinding blue-white light. He held a hand up as if to shield him-self from that glare, but it was in his head and not that room.

"Boss . . . *boss*," he heard someone cry. Pryss? Or was it Lexie? He couldn't be sure. The world had stopped making any meaningful sense.

He took a step toward the voice, but his foot missed the ground somehow and he fell into that light. And from there into darkness.

Juggernaut's forward guns were relentless.

The gunners maintained a continuous fire, targeting the smaller ship's engines and weaponry.

One by one that ship's guns exploded or were knocked so badly askew that they could not fire safely. One by one, *Juggernaut* pulled *Tin Man*'s teeth and claws. And then there was a bigger explosion as the exhaust ports for the main engines blew apart into ten million melting pieces.

And *Tin Man* seemed to sag away into the slow, inevitable pull of Luna's gravity.

Drifting.

Damaged.

Dying . . .

152

"Father," said Captain Kra'Ngo'Betelgeuse, "we *have* them."

The Eldest leaned back in his chair and contrived to show nothing on his face. "Define 'have.'"

"We have disabled *Tin Man*. We are rigging towlines now and will bring it into our hold."

"And the crew?"

"They are radio silent, Father," said the captain. "No doubt preparing to resist once we breach their hull. But that is of no matter. I have two full platoons ready with stun rifles and shock rods. They are all in atmosphere suits in case draining the oxygen is necessary to immobilize the HEs."

"Very well," said the Eldest. "That is excellent work, my son."

The captain bowed.

"Now," said the Eldest, "it is time to make another statement. Prepare the main guns."

"Paris, Father?"

"Yes," said the Eldest. "Paris. And do not be gentle. I want a fire lit that will be seen across the galaxy."

153

Pryss knelt over Jason. She tapped her forearm scanner and used it to cycle through his vitals. "Christ—his heart rate is one eighty-four and his blood pressure is—"

Girlie's face went pale. "What's up with him? He just groaned and fell over."

Pryss shook her head. "I . . . don't know."

"Look at his eyes." Jason's eyes were closed but the eyeballs moved back and forth behind the lids. "He's dreaming."

They all looked at one another.

"Is that good or bad?"

"I don't—" began Pryss, but Sushi cut her off.

"Fuck a duck, we got company." He was at the door, watching the feed of a canary drone. "Whole shit ton of birds coming this way."

"They must have seen the breaches," said Short Dog, pivoting to bring his gun up.

"Copy that," said Sushi. "They're at one of the breaches now. Pausing to examine it. If they come this way, we have maybe a minute. Call it, boss . . . Boss?"

He turned and saw the others clustered around Jason.

"Wait," said Pryss, "I think he's coming around."

Jason's eyes opened and Pryss recoiled. They were not dark irises with gold rings. There was nothing at all familiar about them.

"What . . . the . . . actual . . . fuck?" breathed Girlie.

"Look at his eyes," gasped Sushi.

Jason's eyes had completely changed. No pupil, no iris, no white sclera. Instead, looking into his eyes was looking into the heart of a newborn galaxy. Countless stars swirled and danced. His body was entirely rigid, muscles straining against the flex-fabric of his combat suit; fists knotted tightly, veins in his neck taut as cables. They all withdrew their hands. No one touched him.

"What's happening to him?" demanded Sushi.

Jason's body began to tremble from head to toe.

"Hey," said Girlie, "do that mind thing. Maybe you can reach him and, I don't know, help him wake up again."

Pryss took a breath and then—very carefully—reached out a hand and touched Jason's face. She did not want to open her mind to him the way she had with the Flock officer. Not with Jason.

Earlier, before they left the ship she'd touched a couple of members of Lexie's crew, and memories that were not hers now lived in her head. Some were incredibly private, and she felt deeply wrong for having accessed them. Fears and hopes, lies told and secrets kept. And one of those was a terrible, terrible secret. That she had shared with Jason, but it made her feel like an abuser, like a thief.

Jason, though, was her friend, her team leader, her fellow soldier. He was also much more than that, and Pryss was afraid that if their minds somehow connected that he would realize *her* truths and know *her* secrets.

And yet . . .

"Fucking hell. Do the mind thing," urged Short Dog. "Clock's ticking here."

Pryss braced herself for the mental, physical, and emotional assault and, with trembling fingers, reached out to touch Jason's face. His skin was fever-hot and slick with sweat.

At first there was nothing . . .

But only for one second.

And then she screamed.

154

Mugabe switched off the artificial gravity and the crates became weightless.

Everyone scrambled to push them aside. Fodder and Mugabe snatched them out of the air, stacked them to one side and frantically tied them to the deck. Pickle and Dubbs lifted Lexie out and guided her floating body to a clear spot and pressed her gently down. Mugabe then switched the gravity back on and the cases settled with a thump. The four of them immediately clustered around Lexie.

Dubbs pressed his fingers to her throat. "She's alive."

Pickle's face was a mask of worry and fear. "There's so much blood."

"Scalp wound," said Fodder. "They bleed like a bitch."

Lexie's eyelids fluttered and her lips formed a soundless word.

Jason.

Then the whole ship rocked again.

Fodder started to rise. "They're firing again."

Mugabe frowned. "That wasn't a shot."

They tensed, looking at the walls as if that let them see anything. It was a measure of their stress that it took a beat for anyone to tell the AI to open a holo-screen. Mugabe said it first, and a big holograph appeared with a feed from the exterior scanners.

"Save our immortal souls," he breathed.

On the screen, the huge, slanted door of *Juggernaut*'s cargo bay was opening like the mouth of some steel behemoth. Dozens of tow cables pulled *Tin Man* into that mouth. Scores of Raptors in full armor stood in silent ranks, their pulse rifles ready.

The ship passed through the atmosphere shields and into the monstrous ship.

The door closed behind them with a clang like the bells of hell itself.

155

Pryss was not in her own mind.

Nor was she entirely in Jason's.

She could feel his presence, but instead of surrounding her, it felt as if Jason stood close beside her. His energy, which she could perceive as a nearly solid thing, overlapped hers, causing sparks to sizzle and hiss.

"Jason," she cried.

"I . . . I'm here," came the reply.

It was in her ears but also in her mind, and the juxtaposition of those two sensations was incredibly unnerving. The abnormality of it was disturbing, violative in both directions. It was also vastly different from invading the Raptor's mind. More than just worlds different. There was no commonality between the two events.

She looked down and did not see her own body, but she could feel it, from the short hair on her scalp to her feet on the deck. Everything was there, except she could not see it. It was like being some kind of ghost. When she turned to look at Jason, he wasn't present in any physical form either, yet she could perceive him. It was as if her eyes no longer served a useful purpose and some other sense had come awake. In that moment she knew everything about Jason. His childhood memories were there. His *birth* and first breath were there. His laugh and his troubled thoughts as a boy and then a young man. His first kiss and first lover, and first love and first heartbreak. All there.

Lexie was there too. Not in any visual way, but as a memory—recent, potent and . . . beautiful. She saw into Lexie through Jason's memories, and what Pryss saw was someone deep and wise, insecure and confident, brave and terrified, and . . . in love.

In love? So quickly? So . . . deeply?

Jason's voice said, "No."

Not in refutation of Pryss's assessment, but as a request. Asking her to step back from that. Somehow—she could not explain or understand how—she did step back. In doing so, her perception shifted.

Suddenly the whole of the universe seemed to fill with light. It was beautiful. Exquisite. Flashing with a thousand subtle shades of blue and white, and every possible combination. Pulsing with a vitality that dwarfed her own. Massively powerful. Incredibly aware. And old.

So old.

There were stars younger than this thing.

Find me, it said.

"But . . . you're here," cried Pryss. "You're everywhere."

Save me.

"Tell me how?"

It took her a moment to realize that she was not speaking in her own voice. It was Jason's. His voice, their shared thoughts.

"I'm here," said Jason. "Tell me what to do."

It was the gunfire that woke them both up.

156

The Raptors swarmed into *Tin Man* as soon as the ship was in the hold of the bigger ship.

"We're unarmed!" cried Lexie as she and the others knelt there, hands raised.

The Raptors ignored her plea. They kicked and clubbed and stomped the humans. One of them grabbed Lexie by the front of her spacesuit and stared at her—at the blood that still ran from the scalp wounds. The alien's eyes were filled with hate, and with a snarl of contempt it used the butt of its pistol to club her on the top of her head. She cried out and sagged and would have fallen but for the bird's iron hold.

"Please," she begged. "We surrender."

The Flock pulled her close, its head crest bristling with outrage.

"I do not care," he snarled, and the pistol butt rose and fell again. And again.

157

Jason Horse came awake all at once.

It was not any gradual process of shaking off a stupor or fumbling his way back into his own skin. He was in the dream on one side of a second and fully awake on the other. Just like that.

He sat up, pushing Pryss back so abruptly she began to pitch backward, but he lunged—fast as lightning—and caught her arm. Girlie and Short Dog recoiled.

"What's happening?" demanded Jason.

Gunfire from the hallway gave him his answer.

Jason scrambled to his feet and pulled Pryss up with him. Unlike him, she was only half out of the waking dream. Her hands fumbled for a wall, found one, and Pryss leaned against it, panting, eyes staring inward, lips rubbery.

"*Save me . . .*" she mumbled, repeating the plea that thundered in her head.

"Boss," called Sushi, glancing over his shoulder at Jason, "you with us?"

"Sitrep," snapped Jason.

"Twenty birds coming in hot. Two down."

Jason moved to the door and leaned out and back very quickly, then read the image he'd snatched. The Raptors were clustered at the T-junction, with four using their grease-shields to create a defensive wall.

He glanced around, seeing the room they were in clearly for the first time. It was a machine shop of some kind. Beyond the far wall was the heavy thrum of the engine. The walls were lined with cabinets and there were worktables bolted to the floor. Another airlock was set into the far-right corner of the rear wall. No other exits.

"Girlie," he said sharply, pointing, "airlock. That's our way out."

"On it." She was pulling her gear as she ran.

"Short Dog."

"Boss."

"You still feeling strong?"

"Hell yes."

Jason pointed to a vise bolted to the end of one table. "How far do you think you could throw that?"

"What? The vise or the table?"

Jason laughed.

Short Dog hurried to the table, gripped the vise with both hands and tore it from its moorings. Broken pieces of table pinged off the ceiling.

"Make a hole," he roared. Sushi fired a last burst of gunfire and then dove for the deck. Short Dog grabbed the frame of the door for balance and leverage and then with a huge swing of his arm leaned out and hurled the vise at the Raptors. It struck the grease-shields, and though it did not penetrate the shimmering field, the foot-pounds of impact lifted two of the Raptors off their feet and sent them crashing into the soldiers behind them.

"*Now!*" bellowed Jason. With Sushi behind him, he raced up the hall.

158

The Raptors dragged the crew of *Tin Man* out of the captured ship. They were pulled, shoved, kicked, driven along a hall and into a lift, and then spilled out into *Juggernaut*'s bridge. There they were forced to their knees.

Lexie, badly dazed, collapsed onto her face. She was dimly aware of hands on her, patting her down, taking away her pulse pistol and the stunner. There was a faint squeak of alarm as Ahab was pulled out of her space suit, and then a wail as the robot dog was hurled with cruel force across the hold. The wait ended with a sharp yelp as it struck a wall and collapsed into stillness and silence.

Lexie tried to see what was happening, but her hair—thick with fresh blood—was pasted across her eyes. She had to paw at it to see.

"On your knees," said a voice as cold as the empty vacuum of space. Raptors jerked her halfway up and then crashed her down again so that her kneecaps banged the metal deck.

She blinked her eyes clear and looked around.

The bridge was large, but not as vast as she had imagined.

There was a central dais on which the captain's chair stood. Then two curved rows of workstations between that chair and a wall of huge screens. Lexie had seen enough pictures of starships to grasp the essentials—pilot and navigator, gunners, scanner techs, and comms. Others that she couldn't place. But the bridge crew numbered only a dozen, not counting armored Raptors who seemed to be everywhere.

The captain looked down at them. His crest feathers twitched the way they did when the birds were either irritated or amused. She figured it was both. Then her heart froze, and her mind nearly went numb when the captain spoke.

"Miss Lexie Chow," he said. "What a pleasure to meet you."

Beside her, Fodder breathed, "Oh . . . shit . . ."

159

Jason moved.

He moved very damned fast.

His mind was focused, but somewhere behind the needs of the moment he could see that blue-white glowing thing. There were no words to describe or define it beyond what his thoughts had chosen: the Entity. He could feel it on every level, and as he raced toward the Raptors, he knew—*absolutely knew*—that it wanted him to do what he was doing.

Save me.

The Raptors were only just recovering from the vise Short Dog threw. The two that had been knocked back were dazed. The other two with active grease-shields closed ranks, trying to plug that hole.

They were fast.

Jason was faster.

He leapt up and sideways, stepped onto the wall and shoved off, pivoting in midair, aiming his pistol down past the shimmer of the grease-shield wall. At that range he could not miss. At that range they could not evade, and there was no time to bring their shields up. His rounds punched down through feathered crests and skulls, blowing their faces outward so that blood and brains and bone struck the inner shields and sizzled.

Then Jason scissored in the air as he landed, twisting around to face the Raptors who had been behind the defenders. They did not have shields active, and they made the awful mistake of trying to ignite them rather than bring their weapons to bear.

Jason made them pay for that.

His heels chunked down on the left shoulder of one and the right shoulder of the other and rode them to the floor even as bones broke audibly. His pistol fanned around as he found himself in a target-rich environment. There was no way to miss, and he hit birds with every shot. His finger moved at the speed of an HE. No superpowers needed. This was what he was made for, it was why he was chosen to lead the HEs. Every shot tore through armor and skin and bones; and the wounded collapsed back against their fellows, hampering any chance of an efficient counterattack.

Suddenly something slammed into a knot of three Raptors and Jason saw Short Dog. He grabbed a Raptor by the arm-hole of his cuirass, plucked him off the ground and used the bird as both a club and a shield. The other Flock fired, but their pulse blasts—awkwardly aimed in too much haste—tore into bird flesh in the split second before that dying Raptor smashed into them.

Shots burned through the air as other Raptors surged forward, but Sushi was among them now, a pair of gas-knives in his hands. Blood flew like a wave of rubies.

Jason burned through the rest of the magazine. He did not have a replacement charge-mag, so he slammed the gun into its holster and drew his knife. A Raptor used that moment to grab him and drag him backward, but Jason yielded to the pull, crouched, pivoted, and cut upward, opening the bird from crotch to breastbone. It uttered a high-pitched shriek of agony, but Jason was already turning.

There were three of them against twenty.

It was not enough.

For the Raptors, it was not nearly enough.

160

"I have to give credit where it's due," said Captain Kra'Ngo'Be-telgeuse. "Your plan was bold, and your accomplishments are considerable. Even if you discount the help we provided, you did what no one has done in centuries. You *found* and woke the Sleepers."

Lexie was unable to speak. Her heart was hammering so intensely that it hurt her chest. She cut looks at her crew and saw that they were all slumped down, their faces bruised and running with blood. Only Pickle seemed relatively unhurt, though from the way his body was caved over, she wondered if the Raptors had battered him with rifle stocks to the belly and groin. Tears ran down his face.

The captain rose from his chair and descended the two steps to the deck. He was a tall Flock, dressed in dark red with matching crest feathers. His clothes and armor were of the highest quality. The fact that he was so calm made Lexie even more afraid of him. It showed his confidence, his control. This officer knew that he had won.

He strolled along the line of the prisoners, but when he spoke it was to his crew.

"Have we reached our position?"

"Yes sir," said the helmsman.

"And the guns?"

"Charged and ready, sir," answered the gunner.

The captain reached the end of the line and turned. "A mechanic and prophet of a false god. A scientist with a bright future in cryogenics but poor decision-making capabilities when it comes to friends and causes. A piece of human waste from the Bottoms. A Resistance fixer. And you, Miss Chow—historian from a noble family, a trusted propagandist for the Flock. All of you traitors. All of you murderers and thieves. The list of your crimes would take an hour to read, and even then, I would have to summarize."

"Fuck you, you ostrich-looking piece of shit," snarled Fodder. A burly Raptor smashed her across the face with a gloved fist. Blood flew from torn lips. Fodder shook her head and spat a broken tooth at the bird. "Go fuck a toucan."

The Raptor hit her again, this time smashing Fodder's nose. Even through the pain and blood, Fodder grinned with cracked teeth and fire in her eyes.

"Leave her alone," screamed Lexie, but the Raptor hit her again and again. Other guards placed gun barrels against the heads of the rest of the *Tin Man*'s crew.

"Christ, stop it," begged Pickle.

"Enough," said the captain mildly, but only after Fodder puddled down onto the deck, blood running from mouth and nose and ears. He hooked a talon under Lexie's chin and raised her head, lifting it up, up, and up until her neck creaked. "Now . . . where are the Sleepers?"

She wanted to spit in his face, but her mouth was dry as paste. She wanted to say something bold and insulting, but there were no words in her throat.

"Nothing?" mused the captain, his eyes twinkling. "Do you think your display of brave obstinacy will accomplish anything?"

Lexie just glared at him.

"My stars," said the captain, feigning astonishment, "you actually thought you could win, didn't you? You genuinely believed that you and your crew of trash and rejects had a chance against the Flock? That level of self-delusion is so . . . so . . . well, I think I'm at a loss for words." He turned to another senior officer. "You see, it's times like these that I wish I could smile. Or give a proper laugh. Something these humans could appreciate."

"It would be useful indeed, Captain," said the XO.

The captain turned back to Lexie. "Your audacity, though admirable, is only overmatched by your extravagant naivety. And I admit to being personally disappointed that a historian so accomplished as yourself lacks the perspective to grasp that the Flock have never been defeated. Not once. Oh, I know, you probably believe that we were beaten into surrender by the HEs, but that's simply—and I would think *clearly*—not so. In your game of chess, one would sacrifice a piece even as important as a bishop or queen if it opened the way to a clear and certain checkmate. Our pretense at surrender was that sacrifice. And look what we gained. At your *invitation* we infiltrated every level of your infrastructure, every position of authority within your government, and when we required no additional gains, we simply took over. With no new battles fought, with minimal losses, and with all of your worlds undamaged by what would have been a devastating war. Surely you, Lexie Chow, descendant and namesake of Alexander Chow, must feel humiliated for not understanding this."

"We're going to destroy all of you," she said, forcing the words out.

The captain took no obvious offense. "In which version of reality do you see that happening? And through what means?"

"Alpha Wave," she said.

"Really? Do you mean the pitiful few who did not die in their sleep back on Io? Or the others who still slumber, waiting for us to come and take them?"

"Jason Horse will kill you."

The XO came over and whispered something in the captain's ear.

"Ah, so the HEs managed to sneak aboard my ship." To Lexie he said, "And right now they are pinned down near the engine room. They are fighting my Raptors, and make no mistake, as dangerous as they are, we have the numbers. There are more than a thousand of the most elite Raptors aboard *Juggernaut*. The reports say that you have but five HEs. Do you think each of your heroes can defeat fully hundreds of Raptors apiece?"

Five? Lexie tried not to frown at that number. Where was the sixth? Who was missing? Was Jason already dead? Her stomach turned to icy slush.

"No, Miss Chow, we will take them all," said the captain. "Then we will tear them apart and learn the secrets your military tried to hide from us. Remember how patient we are. We knew this day would come. We have planned for it, prepared for it, allowed even for the variables that have occurred. The Flock has never lost a war. Not once in fifty thousand generations. Defeat is not a part of our heritage, but—clearly—it is a human failing. *We* defeated you with our strategies and our patience, and with this ship we will crush your so-called Resistance."

"You can never beat the Resistance."

"Oh, we don't have to. We *own* them. You see, you have all been so complacent in the belief that every human hates us and is willing to rally to your cause. Have you not considered that *we* have our agents seeded among you?" He shook his head. "Surely you know that we let you steal that ship. You know that we followed you to Io. We have aided and abetted you every step of the way. Do you think that was a reflex action? Hardly. We were prepared for it. We were involved at every step because we knew that you, Dr. Chow, would find the HEs, and that you would bring them directly to us."

"You're lying. You got lucky, and that's all. But your luck is running out."

The captain held his arms wide. "Has it? Even now, do you refuse to accept the truth that we have spies all through the Resistance? How else would we know to strike Lisbon?"

"It doesn't matter. You won't win."

The captain stroked Lexie's bloody chin with the spiked talon on his finger. "Won't we? Do you think Lisbon was our only proof of Flock superiority? I have destroyed worlds across the breadth of this galaxy, vaporizing Resistance strongholds one after the other. You have nothing that can ever hope to stop us."

"We *will*," she gasped, filling those two words with venom, with hatred.

"No," he said airily, "you won't." He turned to the flock at their workstations. "Show the target on the main screen."

Immediately the massive forward holo-screen flashed and there, kilometers below, was the elegant, sprawling expanse of the Paris Metroplex.

"*Noooooo!*" screamed Lexie.

She lunged forward but the captain kicked her backward. Fodder, Pickle, Dubbs, and Mugabe all tried to rush their guards, but they crumpled under cudgel blows and lay bleeding and helpless.

"Please," begged Lexie weakly.

"You may fire when ready," said the captain.

161

Jason held the last of the Raptors by the throat, pinned against the wall as he stripped it of weapons.

"You planning on saving it as a pet?" asked Short Dog. He was wiping blood and feathers off his hands. Around him were twisted lumps that no longer looked like anything that had ever been alive.

"Where's Pryss?" asked Jason.

"Last I saw she was whacked out of her head after she touched you while you were out," said Sushi. "What *was* that all—"

"I'm here."

They turned to see Pryss hurrying up the corridor. She moved unsteadily, one hand brushing the wall for support. She looked gray and haggard, but when Sushi moved in to help, she waved him off.

"Damn, Pryss," said Jason. "Are you okay?"

She stopped and leaned back against the wall a meter away. "Not even a little bit." She took a few deep breaths, then nodded. "Tell me what you need."

"Are you sure you can—"

"Just tell me," she said, avoiding his eyes.

Jason thought he understood. Being inside his own head was tough enough because there was heartbreak and loss and darkness there, and now he knew that she had seen it.

"We need to know about this ship," he said. "Crew numbers, systems, the works. And Pryss, I need to know where that thing is."

"The Entity," she said, not making it a question.

"Yes."

Pryss pushed off the wall and stepped unsteadily over to the pinned Raptor. There was justifiable terror in its eyes. She could relate. If there had been a hole to hide in, she would have crawled in. Instead, she reached out with both hands and took hold of the Flock's head.

Immediately the bird began shivering, its arms and vestigial wings fluttering with an agitation that ran miles deep.

"Boss," snapped Sushi. "On your six."

Jason spun and saw that far down the corridor, past two sets of open blast doors, a horde of Raptors were running at full tilt. Those in the front ran boldly, their shimmering grease-shields active.

"Fuck me," said Sushi. "There's got be a hundred of them . . ."

Three things happened all at once.

One set of blast doors abruptly slammed shut, doing it with such unexpected speed that the foremost Raptor was caught between them and smashed flat, blood spraying into the corridor. The other birds were behind it, trapped for the moment on the other side of the heavy doors.

The lights went out.

And there was a huge and awful sound that rocked the entire ship. The echoes crashed and banged through the metal corridors.

"No!" cried Short Dog. "I think they just fired their big-ass guns."

There was another bang. And another.

"No," said Jason. "This is something else."

162

The blast rocked *Juggernaut* at the moment she fired, heeling her over as if kicked by a giant. Pickle staggered forward against the captain, who shoved him contemptuously away.

Lexie fell sideways, hitting Pickle's legs so that he landed next to her.

"Captain," cried the scanner-tech, "enemy fighters. Count thirty."

The XO was on his hands and knees, struggling to get back to his feet. "We must take evasive maneuvers. With our shields down we're vulnerable."

"XO, signal the admiral aboard *The Talon*. Tell him to launch all squadrons," growled the captain. "Tell them to close on us for support."

"At once, Captain."

"Helmsman, bring us around," continued the captain. "Gunner, I want a fresh lock on the target."

"You can't!" pleaded Lexie. "There are innocent civilians in Paris. There are *Flock* there. You can't do this."

"It's done," said the captain cruelly. "This is what real

courage is, woman. This is what true vision is. Bear witness. *Fire!*"

The ship vibrated again, that deep and ominous hum of pure destructive power. Then something flashed past the viewscreen. Four small craft.

Fighters.

Ancient ships from the first Flock War. Patchwork craft that looked like they belonged in a junkyard. Above and below their stubby wings were guns that throbbed with purple plasma.

Juggernaut's big cannons fired, and at the same instant Resistance fighters hit the forward bow with a barrage of blinding pulse blasts. Lexie screamed but then choked it short as she saw, on the screen, the twin beams of the ship's destructive guns burn downward . . . *into the English Channel.*

Boiling water shot two full kilometers into the air. Small boats were picked up and hurled, broken and burning as far as Brighton and Southampton, and as far inland as Évreux and Louviers. Along the beaches of La Harve, Honrfleur, and Deauville the sands were melted to glittering glass.

But the Paris Metroplex stood.

Unharmed. Unburned. Untouched.

The fighters wheeled in formation and then paired off, two going high and the other two diving low as they swung back toward the *Juggernaut.* Their guns opened and the big ship staggered again.

"Return fire," bellowed the captain.

"Those guns are damaged, sir," said the XO. "That damned ship disabled most of them."

"We have an entire fleet, damn your eyes. Get them here. Flank speed."

More blasts hit along both sides of the ship, making it yaw and pitch and convulse. Captain Kra'Ngo'Betelgeuse grabbed a

Raptor for support as the deck tilted and jumped, but another blast knocked him to the floor. He landed atop Pickle, who immediately grabbed the officer and tried to throttle him. Guards rushed in and stomped Pickle until he lay panting and helpless, then they helped the captain to his feet. He shoved them away, pivoted and slashed Pickle across the forehead with his heel spike. It opened a terrible gash side to side an inch above his eyebrows.

"Human *filth*," he snarled. Then to his crew he yelled, "Find where those fighters came from. Do a gas scan on their exhausts, match the chemical composition and calculate backward along predictable lines of trajectory. Look for fuel signatures and heat variations in the atmosphere. I want those launch sites found. Gunner, charge the cannons. As soon as we have a new target, fire."

"Captain," protested the XO, "what about Paris?"

"Paris can wait," replied the captain. "We need to deal with those launch sites. They are a more immediate threat. Now follow my orders."

163

Lexie and Pickle seemed forgotten by everyone for a moment.

Mugabe, Dubbs, and Fodder were a few yards away, with Raptors all around. The bridge crew was busy trying to fight the ship. No one was looking at them.

Lexie began to rise, but Pickle pulled her down and close. He bent to whisper in her ear.

"I have to tell you something, Lexie."

"We have a chance."

"No, we don't. There's too many of them." He shook her. "For fuck's sake listen. We're not getting off this ship. You know it as well as I do."

"Jason and—"

"Fuck Jason. Fuck the HEs. We can't count on those freaks."

"Then what, damn it?"

He pulled her ear to his mouth and told her.

When he was done, Lexie leaned back at stared at him in mingled horror and wonder. And then she grabbed his face, pulled him close, and kissed him full on the mouth.

"Okay," he said, gasping. "Not the reaction I was expecting."

164

"The hell's going on?" demanded Sushi, crouched like a surfer—knees bent, arms out—to compensate for the ship's sudden jolts.

"Those blasts," said Short Dog. "We're taking fire."

"From whom? *Tin Man?*"

"No," replied Jason. He ignited a flare stick and tossed it down the corridor. The blast door was still closed. "Hits are too heavy for *Tin Man*'s guns. Shots are simultaneous fore and aft. I think *Juggernaut*'s under attack by multiple ships. Maybe Resistance fighters."

Sushi looked up at the ceiling. "Do they know we're here?"

"Not sure they care. Did you feel the energy surge a minute ago? I think they're using *Juggernaut*'s big guns. From what Lexie said, Lisbon isn't the only hub of Resistance activity."

Sushi nodded. "You think they launched fighters to stop another hit?"

"Wouldn't you?"

"Damn skippy, boss."

Short Dog pointed at the doors. "Yeah, okay, but who turned out the lights and closed those doors? That wasn't the damned Resistance, and I can't see Lexie and her crew doing it. I mean, maybe Mugabe would know how, but no way he got access this fast."

"Beats me," said Jason. He turned to see that Pryss was kneeling on the floor, still holding the face of the Raptor, who had fallen with her. "Talk to me, sis."

Pryss was staring into the bird's eyes, neither of them blinking. Blood was running from her nostrils and leaking from around the Raptor's huge eyes. Then, with a grunt of effort and disgust she shoved herself back, breaking the contact. Jason caught her and dragged her to the opposite wall.

"I'm okay, I'm okay," she gasped, wiping at her bloody nose. "I . . . didn't go all the way deep. Not like back on Io. But . . . fuck . . . being inside their heads is like swallowing sewer water. Those thoughts. They're so . . . not human . . ."

"Yeah, we here in the trade call that 'alien,'" joked Short Dog.

"Bite me," she said, managing a tiny smile.

"Pryss," said Jason, "I'd love to give you time to get your shit together, but I need to know now."

Pryss nodded wearily, then put on a brave game face. "Help me up. Thanks. Okay . . . okay, I got some stuff. Enough, I think." She looked at the closed blast door. "No idea what did that, though. But I have a schematic of the ship in my head. Crew is smaller than we thought. Biggest part is about a thousand Raptors. Top of the line."

Short Dog picked up the dazed Raptor and hurled him the length of the corridor, smashing to ruin against the doors. "Top of the line my ass."

Pryss ignored him. "Fifty noncombatant crew, then a dozen bridge crew and the captain."

"Still a lot," said Sushi.

Pryss caught Jason's sleeve. "The captain is the son of the Flock Eldest."

"Which elder?"

"No, *the* Eldest," she insisted. "He's the firstborn of the head of the entire Flock. That's why they gave him this ship."

They stared at her in total shock.

"Oh, I have *got* to meet that cocksucker," laughed Short Dog.

Jason nodded. "I'm okay with that. Try to take him with a pulse because he's one hell of a bargaining chip. Mind you, if he makes a fuss and you need to dent him a bit, I'll try not to weep."

"Copy that, boss."

"Pryss, what about the Entity? What did that bird know?"

She shook her head, looking puzzled for a moment. "It's strange. You know how the doors are the wrong shape, even for birds? That's because they didn't build it. And it's not something humans were working on that the birds stole. After the surrender, a fleet—led by *The Talon*—sailed off, just like Lexie and the others said. They vanished for years, and while they were away, they found a bunch of alien tech. This ship was something they found. It was a derelict on a world on the far side of the galaxy, well away from any human or Flock settlement. Jason, this thing is old. Really old. Centuries at least, though the Raptor heard something someone said about it being maybe hundreds of thousands of years old. There were bodies aboard from other aliens. Not Flock. Older, and dead."

"Shit," said Sushi, impressed.

More blasts hit the ship and they all fought for balance. There was a deep-throated roar of some kind from forward.

Sushi looked scared. "Jesus, I think they're firing their big guns again."

Jason ignored him. "Pryss, what about the Entity?"

She raised her hand to the room they had been in a few

minutes before. "That airlock leads to an access corridor. There are red lines on the floor. If you follow them, it'll take you to the engine room."

"I don't want the engines, Pryss, I want to find that creature."

She looked at him. "Don't you get it, Jason? The creature *is* the engine."

165

"My god," said Lulu, "I think we're winning."

Micah stood next to her, and around them was a semi-circle of screens. Dozens of them, each showing the feed from a satellite in near-Earth orbit. A massive battle was unfolding, and they kept turning to follow Resistance fighters as they made daring runs at *Juggernaut*.

Fighters from *The Talon* and the rest of the Flock fleet were engaging too, but they seemed more cautious, angling to fire only when their blasts had no chance of hitting the giant flagship.

Micah gave a triumphant pump of his fist. "I was right, damn it. We had reports that the Eldest's first hatched was aboard. Probably the captain. The pilots of those Flock ships won't dare to risk him. Look! We got another. And—shit—*another*. Jesus, Lulu, we might even have a chance."

"*If* the crew of *Tin Man* is aboard," cautioned Lulu.

"They are, they are."

"How do you know?"

Micah's eyes were bright with the fever of fear and anticipation. "They *have* to be."

"What if they're not?"

Before Micah could answer one of the screens flashed white hot and the signal was lost.

"What was that?" cried Lulu.

Micah's heart turned to ice in his chest. "That was the base on Mount Logan," he whispered, his color fading his skin from coffee brown to a sickly gray.

The satellite feed flickered and came back slowly.

The Mount Logan base had been built into the highest mountain in Canada. It was the second-highest peak in North America and had the largest base circumference of any non-volcanic mountain on Earth. Sturdy, steadfast, with eleven peaks above five hundred meters, including the one in which the Resistance used to rebuild and launch the largest number of fighters.

And now . . . the entire top of that peak was gone. Simply gone. Two thousand meters of rock vaporized, filling the entire region with a cloud of burning dust and ash.

166

Jason stood in the corridor alone, surrounded by Flock dead, and watched his team go running off to fight, Girlie among them. The hatch remained open, waiting for him.

He wished he could go with them. He wanted to, but Pryss's words rang in his head like church bells.

"*Don't you get it, Jason? The creature is the engine.*"

It made no sense. And it made perfect sense. Those two aspects of understanding warred in his head, but ultimately he knew Pryss was right.

And so he had sent the team to try and capture the bridge. And to rescue the *Tin Man* crew if they could. That made him think of Lexie Chow. A few days ago he didn't know her. At least, not in the real world. In dreams, yes, but until he woke, Jason had no idea of the value of those dreams—their substance and importance. Now, though . . . Lexie was very real to him. She was the agent of change that had started all of this. Without her, he and Alpha would never have been found. Without her they would all go on dreaming throughout eternity, going slowly insane, dying in terror and madness.

Lexie changed that.

And in those few days she had come to mean something unexpected and very special to him. Jason knew that he was a closet romantic—something he'd tried to suppress ever since he became a Tier One special operator, and more so since entering the HE program. Dates, sure; sex, sure. But romance? Love? Those were things he'd felt too important to carry with him into battle. They were a double-edged blade that put his heart and his life at risk by splitting his focus.

Except Lexie wasn't splitting focus for him. If anything, she had clarified his purpose, given him insight, and gave him something worth fighting for, even here, two hundred years in the future.

"Lexie," he said softly. But as he spoke those words, he heard another call.

Find me.

Jason nodded and bent, patting the Raptor corpses for extra charge-mags for his stolen pulse pistol. Found half a dozen and slotted them into his belt. As he straightened, he felt for his own gear. Grenades, shape-charges, knives.

Save me.

"I'm coming," he said, then turned away.

167

As Pryss and Alpha Wave approached the blast doors, they suddenly hissed open. Air rushed past them with abrupt and surprising intensity, flooding into that part of the corridor. Everyone shifted fast to one side or the other, weapons up and hot, ready for anything.

"The hell was that?" demanded Sushi.

"Goddamn," breathed Short Dog. "Look."

There were only dim emergency lights in that part of the corridor, but they cast enough of a glow for them to see the bodies. Dozens of them. Raptors with pulse rifles and pistols clutched in their hands.

In their limp, dead hands.

A computer voice spoke, "*Internal atmosphere restored.*"

"Look at them," said Girlie. "They're dead. They suffocated."

Sushi glanced at the grilles mounted high on the walls. "Whoever shut these doors vented all the O2 out."

It made them stop there.

"Much as I want to think we have a friendly on board," said Pryss, "we proceed with caution. Short Dog, could you punch through that next set of doors?"

The big HE looked at the closest set of doors and frowned. "No way. Twenty inches of dura-steel. I got the muscle mojo, but they're called blast doors for a reason. We're going to need to blow our way through that set down there."

As if in response, the blast doors at the far end of the corridor opened with a ghostly whisper.

They stared at it.

Girlie licked her lips. "Well . . . shit . . ."

"Do we trust it or not?" asked Pryss.

Pryss laughed. "Like we have a choice."

She broke into a run and the others followed.

168

The Resistance fighters were everywhere.

Their main target was *Juggernaut*, and they kept hammering at it, but as Flock fighters swarmed in, those attacks became sporadic. They were old but formidable Hammerhead spinfighters, brutish Manta Ray torpedo bombers, tiny Piranha one-man gunships, and big Orcas with their ion short-pulse cannons. They swept through the great gulf between the Earth and Luna.

The squad leader, Colonel Clayton Muncy—descendant of a pilot who was at the battle of Calliope Station—had drilled his team in every possible variation of this kind of dogfight. Specifically, that knowing the real challenge was more than fighting the Flock in space, but of keeping *Juggernaut* from doing the kind of damage they all feared. With Lisbon now a recent memory and a potent horror story, Muncy knew that that mission was more critical than ever.

And, as so many of his friends said over beers, he was a devious bastard. Sly, smart, quick as lightning, and ruthless as hell. As he brought his fighters into play, he read the situation. Damaging *Juggernaut* was not enough. Not after it had just destroyed the very base from which a fifth of his own ships had launched. The Flock fleet was in play now, so he had to both do damage *and* draw all those guns away from Earth.

That would give the rest of the Resistance bases time to launch their craft and then evacuate before they, too, were wiped from the face of the Earth. It was a lot. It was, he knew, too much for a handful of ships to accomplish.

Odds like that made him grin like a ghoul.

Fourteen years of cruel oppression pumped hotter fuel into his ship and turned his own blood to poisoned lava.

His squadron faced a fleet and a thousand fighters and *The Talon* and the *Juggernaut*. And that was damned fine by him.

Colonel Muncy whipped his spinfighter into a corkscrew turn, opening up with R-99 chain guns that had a rate of fire of five hundred rounds per minute, and each of them tipped with a radical new take on the volatile *aziroazide azide* explosive. Each bullet hit with the force of a Flock War Punisher-A2 wing-missile.

His cockpit vibrated with the sound of Martin Red-Rock thrash metal and he never stopped laughing.

169

As Alpha Wave approached the newly opened blast doors, the lights in that part of the ship began to flicker very quickly, almost a strobe.

Pryss felt on a deep level that it was not fault in the system or something equally random. It was a warning.

Fine, she thought as she slowed from a run to a predatory stalking gait, *consider me warned.*

She plucked a shock-and-awe grenade from her belt, thumbed the arming trigger, growled, "Frag out!" and side-armed it around the corner.

The blast was enormous, and it threw broken weapons, torn flesh, sprays of blood, and screams down the hall.

She activated her PAALs system and raised her rifle. "Go, go, go."

The team rounded the corner and advanced behind a constant barrage of purple pulse fire. They stepped over the dead and the crippled and those too badly dazed to be of any threat.

Raptors were falling back, their planned ambush ruined, but most were still able to fight. And there were a lot of them.

Their blasts skittered off the PAALs fields and Alpha's blasts were likewise mostly deflected by the bird's grease-shields.

Pryss swung her rifle down and behind her, drew her gas knives and leapt high as she charged. Sushi saw this, grinned, drew his own knives, and rushed forward.

And he passed her like she was standing still.

He moved so fast—so impossibly fast—that he became a blur to everyone. It was so fast that for a moment his own eyes could not process the visual intake quickly enough, even with the lightning speed of nerve conduction.

His blades met the grease-shields and pushed through them, cutting at arms and wings, at chest and throats. Blood, caught in the vortex of his motion, swirled like a tornado around him.

Sushi struck a wall, rebounded and crumpled down, gasping. He turned and looked at the Raptors. There was an alley carved through the mass of them, but . . .

They were now a hundred meters behind him.

He lay there, gulping in the breaths he had been moving too quickly to take in before. His muscles tingled painfully as the room spun around him. The surviving Raptors were not even looking at Alpha Wave. They were staring at him, beaks sagging wide, eyes bulging in shock and confusion. Beyond them, Pryss and the others were equally stunned.

In the space of two seconds, Sushi had killed a dozen Raptors and run more than a hundred meters.

How was it possible?

His brain literally ached. His mouth was completely dry as if he had not taken a sip of water in hours.

Sushi climbed back to his feet, aware that his body felt different somehow. Even his clothes felt strange. Too large, loose as the jacket and trousers on a scarecrow.

The knives in his fists were clean, as if the cuts had been

so fast that there hadn't been time for anything to stick to the blades.

Then the truth seeped into his conscious. He was one of *them*. Not merely Alpha Wave. Not only an HE. He was not like Pryss and Short Dog. Maybe like Jason, too, who seemed able to sense that Entity in some way that made no real sense.

He had powers.

He was fast.

He was very, very damned fast.

A smile climbed onto his mouth. He blinked, licked his dry lips, and raised those knives. And then once more he was a blur of silver fire and red death.

170

Jason moved through the gray corridors of steel, and with each step it felt more to him as if he were flowing through the veins of some godlike giant.

Twice he encountered Flock technicians. Twice he left corpses behind him. They were not combatants, but this was war and there were no bystanders. Not now.

The deeper into the ship he went, the more he could feel something. It was more than just energy. It was almost like he could touch something alive. And the voice of the Entity was both clearer and more urgent. Desperate.

Find me.

Save me.

"I'm coming," he called back, not at all certain it could hear him. Or sense him. He wasn't even sure if it knew he existed. Maybe to it, he was nothing but the product of some dream. Maybe it was sleeping there in its nest of chains and restraints. Perhaps it was to the Flock no different than the HEs were to the government-mandated cryogenics. Used and then set aside like a garden rake, like a pair of winter boots during a long summer.

He found himself running.

Calling out that he was coming.

Hurrying to meet whatever it was that lived at the heart of this monster of a ship.

171

"Get the power back," ordered the captain, his rage a towering thing that snapped everyone out of their stupor. "Engage backup systems. *Now!*"

One by one lights flared on around the bridge.

The XO demanded answers to why the power went out, but no one had any clear answer. All such controls ran through the bridge crew, and they were each at their posts. The XO stalked over, grabbed Lexie, and hauled her up, lifting her so high that her toes barely scraped the floor.

"You will tell me what sabotage you have done, and you will do it right now."

"How . . . could I . . . do anything?" she gasped, forcing the words past the stricture of the hand clamped around her throat. "You brought . . . us here . . . from our ship."

As if in response, the comms crackled, and a Raptor officer began screaming that they were engaged with demons.

"Demons," echoed the captain. He gripped the arms of his chair. "XO—release her. Use your wits. This isn't the humans. For the love of the Flock, *the HEs are aboard*. They are doing this."

The XO flung Lexie down and turned to the guards. At the mention of the HEs they looked suddenly tense and frightened. But they stood to attention, clutching their weapons.

"No," said the captain. "We need them on the bridge. Send reinforcements to that patrol. Remember who we are fighting— send a thousand. Send them all."

The XO turned away to give those orders.

The captain rose slowly from his chair as he stalked over to where Lexie and the others cowered. He held out a hand to a Raptor. "Sidearm."

Once he had the gun, he studied it thoughtfully, then clicked off the safety and pointed it at the humans.

"You will tell the HEs to stand down," he said.

Fodder, her face a bloody ruin, tried to spit at him. "You can go and fuck your mother."

A Raptor hit her again with his rifle stock, and she slumped down, barely conscious.

Dubbs grabbed Fodder and pulled her close, leaning over the wounded enforcer to shield her with his own body. Mugabe shifted over until he was close to Lexie. Pickle, his torn face a mask of blood, crawled over to them, touching each of their faces, looking into their eyes.

"Don't give in," he whispered. "Trust me."

Mugabe mouthed the words *anti-cap*. But Pickle made no reply.

The captain raised his gun and pointed it at Lexie. "Do I shoot you first?"

Pickle whirled. "Leave her alone, you piece of shit." That earned him a savage kick from a guard. He curled into a ball and lay rocking and groaning, the tension of pain making his face begin bleeding afresh.

Lexie bristled and rose to her knees. "Go ahead. If you want to shoot me, then shoot. What do I care? I'm not getting off this ship alive anyway."

"Hmmm. Bravery or deception?" mused the captain. "Both, I suspect. And optimism too. You think the HEs have an actual chance against us. That lack of vision is appalling." He touched the barrel to Lexie's forehead. "You want to die? Or are you devious and courageous enough to need to die so that none of our specialists at the camps will ever be able to unload your mind of everything useful you know? Yesss . . . your eyes are evasive. That gives you away. No, my dear Miss Chow, I think you are better left alive. For now."

He turned and examined the others.

"A prophet of the faith of dreams, perhaps? But, no. You, too, would be willing to die in the hopes that your sacrifice will both honor your god and serve as a rallying cry to the faithful. I've read enough about martyrs to not want to waste a pulse round to create another. So, you will also be more useful in the camps. There you will beg to share everything about the Dreamers and all they signify."

He punctuated that with a sudden kick that caught Mugabe under the chin and knocked him back and down. The prophet lay there, teetering on the edge of consciousness, blood running from the corner of his mouth.

"A worthless toady for the Resistance," said the captain. "You will be worth more to my inquisitors. If you think that reprieve is a blessing, I suggest you reevaluate your insights."

He walked a pace and looked down at Fodder.

"As for the scum from the Bottoms," continued the captain, "what use are you to anyone? The camp will teach you manners and perhaps we will discover how the Resistance recruits from trash like you. Yes, that should be entertaining. Now, who does that leave?"

Lexie watched aghast as the captain moved to stand in front of Dubbs.

"A scientist," he said. "A specialist in cryogenics. Useful to your friends, without doubt, but—let's face it—hardly unique in the larger scope of the galaxy. There are many, many like you. There are many among the Flock who share your skill set. So . . . what value are you, really? Mmmmm, well, perhaps we can discover something."

He gestured to his guards to drag Dubbs away from Fodder. The young scientist fought them with all of his considerable strength, but they were elite Raptors and they were stronger. They clubbed him with shock rods, kicked him in the ribs and groin, and they hauled him before the master of the *Juggernaut*.

"Stand him up," said Captain Kra'Ngo'Betelgeuse.

Lexie lunged forward and tried to drag Dubbs back. "Leave him alone."

The captain gave her a look of pitying contempt and then kicked her in the stomach. She collapsed down beside Pickle, vomiting onto the deck. The captain grabbed her by the hair and forced her to stand.

"Listen to me—you will broadcast a ship-wide message," he ordered. "You will tell the HEs to stand down, to lay down their arms, and allow my Raptors to take them into custody. You will do this now or there will be consequences."

Lexie, in pain, her chin dripping, fireworks filling her eyes, shook her head.

"Lexie, don't," begged Dubbs. His eyes were filled with terror as if he could see his own death. "Lexie, you can't . . ."

Pickle crawled over to the captain and clutched at his ankles. "Please," he wept, "kill me instead. Not him. Not any of them."

The captain looked down at Pickle. Then he pistol-whipped

him across the face with shocking speed. Pickle spun away, his cheek torn from ear to mouth.

The captain's gun swept back toward Dubbs, but he glared at Lexie. "*Now.*"

Lexie shook her head. "No. Please. I *can't.*"

The captain fired.

The pulse blast took Dubbs just above his right knee. The searing hot plasma cut through flesh and bone as if it were nothing at all. For a moment Dubbs stared at his leg, seeing where it terminated. Seeing the knee and lower leg and foot still standing even as the rest of him fell away.

Lexie's screamed tore her throat raw. Dubbs's scream was louder still.

The captain walked over and pointed his gun at the scientist's other leg.

"Do I need to ask again?"

172

Short Dog waded into the Raptors. He had abandoned his rifle and instead used his hands. He grabbed a Raptor by the wrist, braced his other palm against the bird's armpit, and with a savage grunt tore the arm from the socket. Blood sprayed his face, but that just made him laugh. He raised the arm like a club and attacked the other Raptors.

Girlie was dodging fire, shooting with one hand and slashing with the other. Gun and knife seemed to know where to go, powered by her enhanced musculature and the AI chips in her brain. The Raptors tried to react to her, to intercept her, to lead her with their guns, but she was a step ahead each time.

On the opposite side of the corridor, Pryss was fighting with two gas knives, leaping and twisting like an aerial dancer, turning as she landed, dodging right and left as she threaded her way among the Raptors. They tried to shoot her and shot their fellows. They tried to grab her and caught only another bird as it fell dying.

And Sushi was everywhere at once.

As more Raptors flooded into the corridor, he charged them.

They had no way to adjust to his speed. There was no strategy in any world, in any culture that could prepare troops to fight someone who moved like that. His blades broke and he pulled new ones. When the speed snapped those, he snatched a rifle from a Raptor lieutenant and used it as a club. When that shattered, he used his bare hands.

He was death in a form none of them had even dreamed about.

His AI struggled to keep up as he slaughtered his way into the heart of a thousand charging Raptors.

173

Juggernaut's cannons fired again. The massive energy bursts ripping downward through the atmosphere toward a second Resistance base. The target was Aconcagua in the Andes, where a squadron of Manta Ray bombers had just launched. The launch tunnel angled up less than a hundred meters below a summit that was 6,961 meters above sea level.

It struck like God's fist and sheared off a thousand of those meters. A split second later the heat of that blast ignited eighty-six tons of ammunition and fifty thousand liters of fuel. The resulting blast ripped Aconcagua down to a stub, flinging debris over two thirds of the Mendoza Province.

In his apartment, Micah saw that devastation and crumbled beneath the weight of it as if he had been shot.

Lexie saw the explosion on the screen, and she kept screaming until blood flecked her lips.

The captain—who really wished he could smile—blew off Dubbs's other leg.

Colonel Muncy heard that news.

He wanted to weep, to scream.

Instead, he wheeled around and drove toward *Juggernaut*, firing with every gun.

174

Jason descended two more levels and immediately knew he was close. The deck beneath his boots vibrated softly and there was a hum in the air that did not match any frequency or vibrational form he could name. It came and went almost with the pacing of breath—but it was slow. His optimism wanted to believe that the Entity was relaxing, knowing that help was on its way. But his fears made him wonder if this was dying.

Or, as he thought earlier, it could simply be asleep and dreaming.

He found a hatch that stood ajar. Intense blue-white light spilled out, painting a section of the deck in its colors, the brightness revealing the steel deck with a clarity beyond normal. As if it saw things with a shaper eye and he, standing near its light, shared that insight.

Find me.

He paused, his hand inches from touching it.

If it *was* asleep, then could all of this—Lexie, *Juggernaut,* the superhuman abilities, all of it—merely be a dream? Was he *inside* that creature's slumbering mind? Was this only that?

Those fears kept returning to him, begging to be accepted as some horrid truth.

Save me.

"No," he said stubbornly, "it's not a goddamn dream."

Jason Horse grabbed the edge of the portal, pulled it open, and stepped into the light.

175

There were a thousand Raptors crowded onto that deck of the ship.

They should have overwhelmed Alpha Wave, crushing them, erasing them as a factor in the complex max of this war. Pryss knew that. Since Jason had formed his plan back in *Tin Man* she—and the others—accepted that this was a suicide mission. It was modern-day *kamikaze*. They were berserkers of this century. Ready to die, but in doing so filling hell with their enemies. Washing this ship in enemy blood.

She only hoped that they could do enough damage to *Juggernaut* to make their sacrifice worth it.

The other plan, raised and then discarded, had been to bypass Earth and fly on to the next base where more HEs—more *Sleepers*—waited, dreaming away the centuries. That felt like the path they should have taken. At least that way there was a chance of survival, and a pathway to organizing a counteroffensive that could rock the foundation of the Flock hold on the galaxy.

But the cost was appalling.

The destruction of Paris and maybe other metroplexes. The utter destruction of the Resistance. Time to construct a fleet of ships made in the image of *Juggernaut.*

Those were things Jason could not abide. His humanism, his idealism, would never allow the sacrifice of so many on the chance of a hypothetical win unknown years from now.

His plan, though, was wild.

Let Trig use his new skills, his newly emerged ability to speak directly to machines, to talk with *Tin Man.* To install new combat programs and turn the antique ship Mugabe had slapped together to be a weapon. Something between a ship flying under false colors and a fireship. Deceit and an unexpected punch.

That had worked, at least in part. *Juggernaut* had been damaged and, more to the point, distracted. Paris yet stood, though she suspected—now that fighters were in the game—that it was targeting their bases of origins. A loss, yes, but far less so than the loss of tens of millions in Paris.

As for the rest of Jason's plan . . . time would tell. The data slip, the bomb, and the rest . . .

Pryss had her doubts, and as she fought they gnawed at her. There were more ways this could all go wrong and very damn few where it could work.

A fresh wave of Raptors ran at her, and she wished she had Short Dog's strength or Sushi's newfound speed. Her body felt oddly cold, as if the ice in which she had slept was not entirely thawed.

Even so, she fought.

Like a true *Homo eximius,* she fought.

176

"Second target is destroyed," said the gunner. "Locking in coordinates for the third Resistance base."

The captain nodded.

Dubbs lay on the floor, his screams faded down to a whisper, trauma glazing his eyes.

Lexie wept. Pickle crawled to her, reached for her, gathered her to his chest.

"I'm sorry, kiddo," he said, his voice thick with pain, his face torn to a horror mask. "I should never have agreed to this insanity."

Lexie shook her head. "It's not your fault."

Pickle was sobbing too hard to hear her.

The Resistance fighters were doing well, racking up kill after kill.

But they were losing.

For every Flock ship that fell burning into Earth's atmosphere, a dozen more came ripping through space toward the melee.

Colonel Muncy knew that he could win a fight if there were more ships. More time.

More mercy.

With his heart sinking in his chest, he kept fighting.

The lights on *Juggernaut*'s bridge flickered again. Half of the screens went blind. A third of the combat workstations switched themselves off. Command channels cycled themselves to automated warnings, telling everyone there was a fire, a hull breach, a proximity alert—and all with the volume cranked to ear-splitting levels.

The XO ran from station to station, yelling over the noise, sometimes resorting to blows to keep his flock focused. Each time there was an outage, they changed to a different redundancy—of which there were many. Some stayed on, while others winked out again.

The captain grabbed a senior technician. "Find whoever is doing this and bring me their eyes." He hurled the Flock away, knowing full well it was beyond that subordinate's power to solve this.

Micah was on his knees in front of his screen, beating his fists onto the floor as he watched mountains burn and fighters turn to clouds of debris.

And far below the command center of the great ship, Jason Horse stepped into a massive chamber that had to occupy a full third of the great ship.

There he stopped and stood. Frozen into that moment of time.

The blue-white glow was everywhere. He could feel its light penetrating his combat rig, his flesh, his whole being.

"I found you," he said.

177

Alpha Wave fought all the way to the end of the corridor that ran the length of Juggernaut.

They fought their way up three flights of metal stairs.

They fought through one ambush after another.

They were one flight down from the bridge before they paused.

Before they were forced to stop.

It was Sushi who stopped them.

Like a surging storm he had run before them. A hurricane of slaughter. Merciless, blindingly fast, dreadfully efficient in the art of destruction.

Now he stood at the top of that last flight of stairs. The first time he had stopped since he realized that powers had manifested in him.

Suddenly they all froze in place. Girlie and Short Dog and Pryss. Staring up those stairs.

"My god . . ." gasped Girlie.

"Oh . . . fuck no," said Short Dog. "Fuck no. Fuck no."

Pryss took a single step forward, raising a hand as if it could wipe away the reality of what they were all seeing.

Sushi swayed up there. His combat rig hung from a body that seemed to be made of withered sticks. His visible skin hung equally slack, with no meat or muscle seemingly able to support it. His eyes were sunken into dark pits on a head that was nothing like the man they knew and far too much like a skull. His hands hung like bags of broken pottery, limp and shapeless at the end of each arm.

On some level Pryss understood. Just as her own powers took their toll on her, Sushi's speed had done this to him. The energy output to run like that had to draw on something. It consumed him, feeding first on available calories, then draining fat and finally muscle. He used too much. Far too much. And his hands—the speed of his blows could never be matched by the integrity of the hand's delicate bones.

"Sushi?" she called.

He looked at her and the others. Pryss saw the precise moment when he read their horror. The moment when he looked down at his body and understood the price.

Yet he smiled.

"I . . . kicked some . . . bird ass . . ." he wheezed in a voice as old as time, as thin as shadows. "Didn't I, guys? Didn't . . . I?"

"You did," said Pryss, though a sob broke as she said it. "You saved us all."

"That's . . . good then . . . right?"

Sushi kept smiling.

Even as he fell.

178

Jason stood there.

Ever since his first dream of the Entity, he had tried to picture it. Tried to imagine what it might look like. At times he thought it might be like an egg—huge but smooth and rounded. Other times he envisioned a creature from a nightmare, with too many mouths, not enough eyes, and thrashing tentacles. He even thought it might be something more human—a being with wings like an angel.

But he never imagined what he saw.

It had no actual shape. Not that he could see.

The main mass of it—was it a body? Or did that word apply?—did not have a form that fit any anatomy or geometry. It was a mass of light and color, but it was constantly in flux, taking on appendages that seemed to come more from Jason's own mind than anything belonging to it. It was a presence more than anything substantive. The chains he'd imagined were not made from steel. Instead, there were pylons built along the walls and running in rows up those walls and across the ceiling. Hundreds of them, and each glowed with a red-gold fire, and wherever the roiling mass of the Entity brushed against one, there was a flash of heat and a hiss of something burning.

As he stared, squinting against the glare, Jason could see that the thing was covered with countless burns, some looking new while others had a sense of age that made him feel strange and small.

The Entity filled that part of the ship completely. The scope of it was daunting, because nothing that he had ever seen came close to its size. That part of the ship could hold a dozen blue whales—the largest creature that had ever lived on Earth. Even with that, there was something about the creature that felt compressed, squeezed into too small a space.

And it was in pain.

Though . . . *pain* was too weak and small a word. As Jason reached out toward it with his heart and mind, he knew that. There was no word in any human language that could encompass pain of that level. A dying sun, given consciousness, might understand, but nothing less.

He took a step forward, pulled toward it by his own empathy. By whatever new gift he had been given during his sleep. But his knees buckled beneath the weight of sudden understanding.

Save me.

The words burst through his mind with too much force. He cried out, falling forward onto his hands and knees.

"Tell me how," he begged.

The Entity writhed in its prison. It had no mouth and yet it screamed anyway. And that scream carried with it more than sound, more even than need and pain. It struck Jason Horse with something far more terrible.

Understanding.

Images crashed through the barriers of his mind. Sharing, telling, pleading, showing, needing, wanting, begging, weeping.

Then Jason, too, was screaming.

179

Pryss reached Sushi as he fell.

She caught him. He was as light as a bundle of sticks. Lighter even than the scarecrow he resembled. There was nothing left of him except a husk. She immediately stretched out with whatever powers had been granted her, telling Short Dog and Girlie to stay back.

As she sank down on the middle step, Pryss hugged Sushi to her chest. She kissed his face and pressed her head to his. Trying to find him. Needing to know he was in there. Needing to tell him it was okay for him to go.

Her eyes lost their focus and she stood in a dark place. Not a room. Not an anything. All that existed was darkness.

Sushi was there too. Somewhere. She could feel him. Pryss heard his quiet laugh. There were flickers of shared memories. Drinking beers on Calliope Station, with all of Alpha there. Darren, Monique. Everyone. Alive.

Then she slowly realized that she was wrong about that. Not everyone was there.

Short Dog and Girlie weren't there. Trig was nothing but

a flickering ghost from whom sparks dripped. And Jason . . .

She could feel him as something strange and distant.

With horror she realized that the ones she could see most clearly were those who had moved on. Those who had died.

Most of Alpha Wave. Nearly all of her friends.

Maybe Jason and Trig, too.

Then she saw Sushi. He was far away, and though his body did not move, she felt him walking away. Then he paused and turned. Just a little, looking over one shoulder. His eyes were filled with starlight.

"It's okay, Pryss," he said without moving his lips.

"Sushi, I'm so sorry."

"No. I did my job. I did the best I could. I can go home now, Pryss. I can rest."

All of the other members of Alpha Wave stood with him now. All the dead in a group.

Sushi began to turn away, to go farther. But he paused once more, still looking at her.

"He's going to need you to trust him," he said.

"Who? Who needs that?"

"He's got his part to play."

"I don't understand."

Sushi looked away, off to another part of that darkness, and Pryss thought she could see the faintest line of a horizon. Instead of morning orange or sunset red, it glimmered with blue-white light.

"They're coming, Pryss."

"Who's coming, Sushi?"

"If you don't trust him, then it's all for nothing. You need to know that." He paused as if listening. "Can't say more. I got to go."

"Sushi, please tell me what you mean."

He sighed. She could see his chest rise and fall.

"I'm a little scared here, Pryss," he said. "It's dark out there and it lasts a long time."

"Sushi, no . . . we love you . . ."

But he was gone.

The darkness loomed around here, huge and endless.

180

Time had lost all meaning.

Jason knew that he stood in the engine room of the *Juggernaut*. He was aware that his friends were fighting for their lives—both the human crew and Alpha Wave. He could hear and feel the impacts as Resistance fighters battled for the thin hope of freedom. He knew all of that.

And yet it seemed to exist in another world. Maybe it was the real world. Where he stood no longer seemed to be anything except a dream. He feared that this dream was really a nightmare and he'd just met its monster.

"I found you," he said to the Entity.

It pulsed with that nearly unbearable light. As powerful as this thing clearly was, there was a strange atmosphere about it that made Jason feel physically ill.

As *it* was ill.

That realization was abrupt, and it was true, he felt that for sure. It broke his heart too. This Entity that had called to him in dreams and across the gulfs of space, was sick. Maybe dying.

"I don't know how to save you."

There was a long time and Jason had the strangest sensation, as if worms were crawling around inside his skull. Then he saw that the faintest strands of energy were caressing his face, his scalp, his chest. Thin as cobwebs but flowing and undulating like sea anemones.

Release me.

It was the same voiceless voice. The meaning appeared in his thoughts but not through any process of human hearing. He wasn't even sure if it was telepathy. Or, more correctly, he *knew* that there was no phrase or term or description in any human tongue to describe communication of this kind. It even occurred to him that it was more than a difference in language or commonality of experience upon which even a rudimentary communication could be based. He and this Entity were as alien to one another as any two beings could be. The challenge, he realized, was it was having to descend far, far down in order to communicate at all. It was no different than if a human super genius tried to engage an amoeba in conversation. The gap was bigger than that.

He forced himself to focus on the moment, on the task at hand.

Release the thing? How?

There was a network of cables that were affixed at one end to each of the pylons and at the other seemed to be sunk into the substances of the Entity. The effect looked less like wires and tubes attached to a hospital patient and more like the wires drilled into the brain and body of a lab animal. Around the connecting points the blue-white surface was puckered and discolored, darkening to a sickly purple.

As Jason moved around the thing, he saw that there were at least a hundred such cables. However, there were thousands upon thousands of discolored purplish marks. Wounds? Scars?

Something like that. Did it mean they kept moving the cables? If so, why?

Jason was becoming accustomed to the bright light and that allowed him to pick out more details. He saw many places in which the flesh—if it was flesh—had been carved away, leaving large wounds, old and new. There were also places where the blue-white substance was smeared on the walls and floor, separate from the main mass and yet glowing with the same troubled vitality.

There was a story to be read there, and he picked his way through it. If the Entity was somehow the source of power for *Juggernaut*, then what did those cables do? Feed it? Or were they siphons that leeched that energy away and fed it into the engines?

The pylons were clearly a containment field, and a cruel one at that.

But those missing slabs of the Entity's skin . . . why do that? Were they cutting away tissue that had been so overused that it had become necrotic? That would make some sense, but Jason didn't think so. The reason for his doubt were a series of metal bins that stood in a row by the nearby wall. Each bin was two meters long, three wide, two deep. They squatted on wheels and the lids were closed and bound with cables similar to those that pierced the creature.

He cast a wary glance at the Entity as he crossed the nearest bin. Even though the bin had opaque polymer sides, they glowed as if with great internal light. Jason drew his knife and glanced at the Entity.

"May I do this?" he asked.

A pause, then: *Save me.*

Jason nodded and slashed the cables. Each end leapt away from the cut, hissing out gasses that smelled foul. The bin itself trembled and shuddered and for a moment Jason wondered if somehow this thing's young were imprisoned inside. But the answer wasn't as simple as that. He threw the lid open and stared inside.

What lay there was a twisted and folded *piece* of the greater whole. He could see the marks of some cutting tool—the flesh was melted and fused where it had been sliced from the main body of the Entity.

He recoiled and looked at the long row of identical bins.

They were cutting the flesh from this thing. Taking slabs and storing them in bins. *Why?*

As an afterthought he saw something he'd missed. There were dozens of small glowing spikes that were exact miniatures of the pylons. When he bent over to look inside, he saw that the sides, and presumably the bottom, were all covered with those spikes.

"Containment system," he said aloud.

Without warning the color intensity of the Entity changed. The blue-white radiance dimmed and the sickly purple around each cable stuck into the mass flared with eye-hurting brightness. All around him there was a dramatic upsurge of noise that was louder than the drone of the engine. The noise swelled as power built within the creature and then a roar from elsewhere in the ship. It was intensely loud and aggressively potent even though it lasted only two seconds.

Then it was gone, and the purple connection points faded down to the levels they had been before. The Entity looked somehow diminished. Not in size but in some other way. Jason felt that as much as saw it, and inside his heart and his head, he heard the Entity cry out, its voice weaker, sadder, more desperate.

Save me.

Release me.

Save me.

Insight is a tricky thing to explain because it can come from so many directions. Observations made by the subconscious whispering to the higher mind. Or random thoughts floating around and suddenly coalescing as if in the presence of a magnet. Many reasons.

As Jason listened to the emotional tones of those cries and saw the dimming of the Entity's life light, he had a moment of insight. An epiphany that could have been his own reasoning or something shared by the thing. Or both.

He stiffened and looked at everything again, seeing it with new eyes, with a new and appalled understanding.

"That sound just now," he said. "That was the sound of the main guns firing. The city-destroying guns."

The light flared for a moment.

Save me.

"You're more than the power source for this ship."

Release me.

"You're the weapon too."

Save me. Save me. Save me. Save me. Save me. Save me. Save me. Save me. Save me.

181

Mount Kilimanjaro was a legendary mountain, and the tallest on the continent of Africa.

Was.

In the space of two seconds, the ion-pulse cannons aboard *Juggernaut* turned it into a spiked crater. The burning debris rained down on Kilimanjaro National Park and set it ablaze. Within seconds a million trees were burning. Strong winds whipped the flames into a storm of fire that consumed twenty small towns.

Of the Resistance fighter base, there was nothing left except debris scattered for hundreds of kilometers.

Micah Fontenot sat on the floor, his back to the wall. He had a bottle of tequila in one hand and Lulu's hand in the other. An old-fashioned lead-bullet pistol from the late 21st century lay on the carpet between them.

Loaded.

Not yet used.

On the bridge of the *Juggernaut*, Lexie had her face buried against the side of Pickle's neck, her tears hot against his skin.

She could not bear to watch the destruction. He could not look away.

Some of the bridge crew were cheering.

Dubbs groaned in a semi-doze brought on by pain and shock. Mugabe prayed over him, but his words seemed to have lost all meaning. They were fragments of prayers, old and new, calling not merely on Morpheus but any god who might be listening. Fodder was sprawled beside him, unconscious, her face distorted from the many broken bones.

"They're not coming," sobbed Lexie.

Pickle said nothing.

"Jason *swore* he'd be here. That was the plan. That was the whole plan."

Pickle did not speak words of reassurance or comfort. He had none to give. There had not been much hope left in his heart even before they left Paris. Each blast of those cannons, each devastating blow, each wound slashed into the flesh of the Earth, each loss of a Resistance base chipped away at it. Now the vault of his hope stood open, looted, empty.

The bridge lights flickered, screens blanked out and rebooted, but those goddamn cannons kept firing.

182

Pryss lay Sushi on the cold steel deck as Girlie and Short Dog knelt beside her.

They each placed their hands on his withered chest, a ritual action born in that moment—ceremonious and sad.

When Pryss raised her head and was able to speak, she looked at Short Dog. "What about you? How are *you* feeling?"

Girlie glanced at the big man and she flinched. "She's right, man. You look bad."

Short Dog raised his arm and studied them. He was still powerful, his arms still corded with muscle . . . but less so. Visibly, less so.

"I . . . feel okay," he said, though the doubt in his voice made that a half lie. "Still feel strong."

"But it's taking a toll," Pryss observed. "Sushi burned himself out. Your whole body looks a bit . . . shrunken. Smaller."

"I know," he admitted.

"The more you use your strength at that level, the more it needs to take."

"Yeah." He shook his head. "God, I've never been this hungry before."

"Wait," said Girlie, slapping her pockets and pouches. She produced a silver package about ten centimeters long and tore it open. "Protein bar."

He took it gratefully and ate it in two big bites, eyes closed as if it was the best thing he'd ever had. He fumbled for his canteen and drank deeply, then nodded. Girlie produced a second bar, and he ate that too.

"Fuck," he said, pawing a tear from his eye, "I wish we could have, y'know, stopped Sushi. In time, I mean. Made him eat something. I know these bars aren't enough, but maybe they might have helped. Kept him going until we could get some medical care for him."

Pryss looked doubtful. "At the rate he was burning calories, I don't think two high-protein bars would have been enough. He would have needed thousands of calories and a lot of actual mass."

"If we had the time, we could have rigged something," said Girlie. "A suit that kept replenishing what he used."

It was a good suggestion that was entirely impractical at the moment. Sushi was dead. Short Dog was getting weaker and losing mass.

Girlie gave Pryss a careful look. "What about you?"

"I don't know. What I can do is different. Doesn't burn calories."

"You get nosebleeds and I bet your vitals go off the scale."

"Yes. And headaches. I've had one since Io, and it's getting worse."

They sat with that for a moment.

"So," said Short Dog, "these new powers . . . they're killing us?"

"I don't know," Pryss admitted. "It's not like we've had five minutes to even think it through. Maybe we can learn how to use them. Safely, I mean."

Girlie stood and looked down the hall at the hundreds upon hundreds of dead Raptors.

"We kicked ten kinds of ass, though."

Pryss rose too. "Let's hope it's enough. Sushi did a lot of that. Now it's just the three of us."

Short Dog was the last to remove his hand from Sushi's chest and stand. "Yeah, well we maybe have more problems than that."

"What do you mean?"

"Trig never made it aboard, and Jason . . . we all saw him go into some kind of convulsion. You saw his eyes, right? You can't tell me he wasn't changing too. Not sure what kind of power we're talking, but there was something. Then he went off looking for some kind of alien entity. You want to tell me that he's okay?"

Pryss looked away. "I don't know."

"Bullshit. I think you do. You were in his damn head." Short Dog slapped his diminished arm muscles. "Now's not the time to be coy."

"It feels wrong to talk about what I saw in Jason's head," she said, "but you're right."

She told them everything about the Entity and how Jason seemed to be connected to it on a level that even he could not explain. They already knew some of it, but the full picture was daunting.

Girlie gaped at her. "He went off to do what? *Commune* with it? Hold its hand? Plead with it?"

Pryss shook her head. "I don't know. I don't think Jason knows. But what he was sure of is that he had to try. This Entity . . . creature, whatever . . . is at the heart of all this. Some-how. I don't understand it. I only had a glimpse into Jason's thoughts. Enough to know that I think he's *right* for doing what he's doing."

"Why didn't we all go, then?" demanded Short Dog. "Why send us into a meat grinder while he goes to have a therapy session with a fucking alien?"

Pryss's reply was a long look, hard as fists. Short Dog met that gaze for as long as he could but then he growled and turned away.

"Yeah, yeah, okay. He has his reasons. Fuck."

Girlie put her hand on his big shoulder. "You need a beer, a bed, and a blowjob, son."

"You offering?"

"In your dreams."

Pryss stepped away from Sushi's body. "Weapons check," she snapped. "We're not guest stars. This is our show."

Short Dog knelt once more. "Sorry, brother," he said as he patted Sushi's pockets for fresh charge-mags. "Don't worry, I'll collect some scalps for you."

He rose, snugging the mags into his belt. Then he patted his rifle. "Think I'll go old school for a bit."

"Probably safer."

"Not for those fucking birds."

"I heard that," said Girlie, holding her fist out for a bump.

Pryss swapped in a fresh mag too. She glanced at the others.

"For Sushi," she said.

"For Sushi."

They ran up the stairs, guns up and out, eyes filled with a calm and dangerous anger, mouths set in hard lines. Hunting birds.

183

"Let me do it now," begged Pickle, his voice barely a whisper.

"Not yet," cautioned Lexie.

"Why *not*? We can stop this."

"We need to give Jason and Alpha time."

"Why wait for them? We're not helpless. Or do you want to see how many more of Dubbs's limbs that freak wants to blow off?"

Lexie gripped his wrist hard enough to hurt. "If we do that now, then we all die. Which means that even if Jason and his team win, the search for the other HEs is over. The war is over. This battle won't mean a thing because the rest of the fleet will just blow us out of the sky."

Pickled stared at her. "You'd better be right about this."

The bridge lights flickered off and on.

"I trust Jason," she said.

The lights continued to flicker.

Captain Kra'Ngo'Betelgeuse was in a towering rage.

"*Get my stars-cursed lights on.*"

It drowned out the sounds of impacts as Resistance fighters slipped past Flock ships and took shots at *Juggernaut.* It even drowned out the alarms that no one seemed able to cut off. Raptors cringed back from him; technicians scurried around, trying to look like they were working on the problem, but there was nothing to work *on.* They ran diagnostics and the ship told them it was fine, that there was no malfunction, no hack, no code errors, no mechanical failures.

And yet the power came and went, came and went.

Lexie and Pickle were still huddled together under the watchful eyes of Raptor guards; their friends a few meters away. Ahab, battered and limping, had snuck over and tried to hide under Lexie's thigh.

Finally, the captain stalked over to Lexie, grabbed her once more by the front of her space suit and hauled her upright.

"What have you scum done to my ship?" he demanded.

"N-nothing . . ."

The captain drew his pistol once more and pointed it at Dubbs. "Lie to me again and I'll take his hands."

184

Save me. Release me. Save me.

Those words pummeled Jason, inside and out, making it hard to think.

"How?" he cried.

Release me. Save me.

"What do I do? Cut the cables? Break the pylons? Help me, damn it. I don't know how to help you without hurting you. Without *killing* you."

The ship's great guns fired again, and the creature screamed.

Jason could never tell if that scream was real or only in his head. The effect was the same. It knocked him backward into the line of carts. He struck hard, pain exploding in his lower back. He began to fall and had to grab on. Light, bright as the sun, flared so bright it chased every shadow from the room. He felt pinned by it, frozen by it.

Release me. Save me.

Its countless wounds flashed with that ugly purple light. Throbbing with agony. The purple seemed to be worse after each time the gun fired, and it made the Entity scream.

The sound of it was enormous inside his head.

"*How?*" he roared. "Tell me *how.*"

Then Jason had another flash of insight. Maybe it really was the Entity projecting thoughts into his head, or maybe he was actually reaching a new level of understanding. Either way, as he watched those purple wounds pulsate and expand, he realized that they were a reaction to what was happening.

The Entity was the source of power for the ship and the gun. But what was worse . . . every time those guns fired, it stole something from the creature. Jason did not think it was like draining a vessel. It wasn't like a person becoming weaker as it *lost* power.

No.

It ran deeper than that. Light-years deeper.

It was *why* the cannons were being used. That was what hurt this thing so badly. Stealing its power to snuff out tens of thousands of lives.

Life used as a weapon against life.

Jason saw that now. He recoiled from the enormity of that act. That crime.

The Entity was somehow either tied to life itself or a manifestation of the very concept of life. He wasn't exactly sure which, but he knew he was getting closer to the truth. Life used to end life was an offense against all life.

The insight was staggering, and for a moment Jason could do nothing but look into that well of understanding, and with each second more pieces of the puzzle fell into place. He suddenly knew things that were beyond any possibility of his having learned them in the course of his life. Old dreams began awakening in his head; dreams from before . . . when he slept away two centuries in the ice. Somehow this creature had found him— not on any physical plane but on some level where distance or substance did not matter. It had entered his dreams and planted the seeds from which this very encounter grew.

Find me. Save me.

In those dreams—which he was remembering now—it had told him its story.

A story of uncountable years.

The Entity had come from some other place. Far away. Not even from a distant part of the Milky Way, but from some other galaxy. Thirty-three billion light-years away. GLASS-z13 galaxy. One of the very first galaxies that formed after the Big Bang. That was its home.

Its kind—who had no name and no need for any—traveled the universe along lines of force, their passage unhampered by distance. Like blood cells flowing along the veins of a giant of impossible size.

He caught only the faintest glimpses of others of its kind, and some of them seemed, impossibly, older than the known universe. As if they had come into our universe through the Big Bang itself, using it as a doorway. Reborn from their experience into a new existence, into a virgin universe filled with endless possibilities.

How it had gotten from that most distant of galaxies to the Milky Way was hard for Jason to grasp, though when he glimpsed those lines of force, they looked suspiciously like the energy pathways of the transduction network.

As he thought that, the blue-white light suddenly flashed.

A confirmation? He thought so.

He closed his eyes and let himself drift back into the life story of the Entity.

For all its immeasurable power it was naïve. Trusting. Unaware of evil because its entire race predated that concept. Communication with other species had been innocent, like a child touching a flower, or a puppy cavorting with a butterfly. No need for language, yielding instead to the joy of experience.

It lingered here and there over the unfolding years. Sometimes—most often—it moved off, leaving no trace behind but carrying with it memories. At other times, when it perceived sickness—a planet losing its atmosphere to space following a near-collision with a gigantic asteroid or a garden world dying because parasites proliferated faster than plants could compensate by evolving defenses—it would leave some trace of itself behind. Shedding some of its light so that the energies contained within could heal and restore balance. The beauty of that made Jason's heart swell but also spilled tears from his eyes. Joyful tears, to know that there was such grace in the universe, and that it predated any deliberate corruption.

Then the civilizations rose. Billions of years ago, but many more billions of years after the Entity and its kind began their wanderings. Somehow one race managed to trap it, and from that moment, the Entity learned new concepts as they were used against it. Greed and avarice. Hatred and cruelty. Maliciousness and malevolence.

That cruel race bound it within the hold of a ship, and over the millennia, they leeched away power that had been used to heal, to encourage beauty, to balance the natural flow of order and chaos.

That ship had been one of many.

Many hundreds of thousands.

Each time, as one civilization crumbled under the weight of its own greed, a new one would rise, and it would seize all resources and use them to carve out their own territory within the galaxy. Over and over, uncounted times.

When Jason realized that these ships—or, more precisely, the containment grid—had become more than merely a prison but were actually keeping the Entity alive, it tore at him. The concept of prisoner and prison being linked so long that they became symbiotes, was its own special kind of horror.

And then the last ship crashed on a planet in this galaxy. There was a mutiny among the crew, with different factions fighting for the right to own and use the power they stole from the Entity. They fought and they died, and none survived.

Except the Entity.

It lay there, trapped inside the pylons, with the cables still buried like venomed fangs in its flesh. Draining power and storing it in batteries until there was no room left. And so . . . nothing.

For eight hundred thousand years.

The Entity endured, singing the songs of the beautiful things it had seen, living in memories, and then, ultimately, in dreams. It became a Sleeper, Jason realized. Like him.

When the Flock found it, the Entity had a flash of hope. They repaired the ship and studied the glowing thing in the hold. He tried to reach out to them, but their minds were strange. They lacked empathy. They were cold, hard, determined, bitter, greedy. Hateful.

They did not free him, and soon the Entity realized to its despair that they were going to use its power again. To drive the ship. To plunder other worlds. And to carve pieces off its body to fuel other ships. A fleet of destructive ships with which to conquer all worlds. And . . . all galaxies. They were not its rescuers, but another group of slavers. Worse by far because their ambitions stretched into eternity.

The Entity could not stop them. All it could do was retreat inward and hide in its own dreams.

Which is where it found Jason Horse. In the dreamlands. Found him by hearing the songs of Jason's dreams. Strange songs.

In those dreams it recognized something in Jason. He was warlike, yes, but not driven by hate or greed. He, too, fought for balance in his own limited, human way; he fought to protect beauty.

That mattered to the Entity.

So much.

This was an alien species it could relate to. However tenuous the similarities, that commonality of purpose was a bond. Of all the minds it had encountered while dreaming on that distant world, Jason Horse was true. And he, too, was trapped.

And so, the Entity waited for Jason, the Sleeper, to wake.

All the time calling to him. As the Flock rebuilt the ancient ship and created massive cannons that forced the Entity's energies into weapons. And with every shot fired, with every assault on life itself, the Entity could feel itself changing. Becoming polluted. Becoming defined by the rampant sickness of hate.

It pleaded for mercy. For release. Endlessly as the years passed. Trying to awaken someone who could do something. Someone who was not defined by greed or cruelty.

It begged the Sleeper to wake.

Find me.

Save me.

And now it had been found.

185

"Micah, we need to pull the fighters out of there."

Shimada's face filled the screen. He was florid, his hair untidy, eyes wet and filled with shock. "They've taken out three bases. We can't risk the others. Call them back."

Lulu turned to Micah and her eyes held the same look. "He's right. We can't win this."

"We can't," cried Micah. "If we stop now, then what prevents them from blasting Paris off the planet? What will stop them from hitting New York and Shanghai? What's next? Sydney? Krakow? The Flock won't stop. They'll burn us out of every city, every world."

"We're *losing.*"

"We're still fighting, goddamn it."

And he gave the order to launch the rest of the fighters.

Lexie screamed. She begged the captain for mercy, even though she knew the concept did not exist in the Flock culture. Their minds were hardwired to be predatory scavengers; what little compassion some of them demonstrated was likely false—a strategy of manipulation rather than any learned kindness.

"What have you done to my ship?" demanded the captain. "How are you interfering with the power? What is the nature of this sabotage?"

"It's not us. Please, you have to believe me. It's not us."

The captain fired. Two quick shots. Very precise.

As Dubbs body arched upward, the sound torn from his was not a scream. He was beyond that. It was merely that of sensation. Deeper than feral. Primal. An organism reacting to trauma. Then he collapsed back. Legless. Armless. Eyes staring upward with a shock so thorough that he saw nothing.

Mugabe, still clutching one hand that was attached to a severed arm, screamed. So did Pickle and Lexie. Fodder, barely conscious enough to understand, beat her fists on the deck.

Dubbs blinked. And for a terrible moment there was clarity in his eyes. Awareness. Sensation.

He looked at the captain, then at Lexie. He looked at her, and through her, and through the wall, and into the forever that opened up before him. His body sagged, chest settling as pain and breath and life fled.

The captain turned away and pointed his gun at Pickle.

"I will not ask again," he said as he raised his gun.

And the bridge lights went out once more.

The darkness was filled with shouts from the bridge crew, with wails from Mugabe. With cries from Lexie and Pickle.

And then with a piercing, rising howl of pure murderous rage from Short Dog, Girlie, and Pryss, Alpha Wave swept onto the bridge like a storm.

186

The revelations, the sharing of all that history punched Jason down to his knees. It was so much to try and grasp. Even with the software and AI expansion of his brain, it was too much.

Save me.

Save me.

Save me.

"How can I save you?" he begged. "Tell me how."

Save me.

"If I free you, if I cut those cables and disable the pylons, you'll die."

Save me.

"Do you understand? Can you understand? I can't free you without killing you."

But the Entity cried *Save Me* over and over until it filled every corner of his mind.

Pryss was first onto the bridge. She had her combat contacts cycled to night vision, and the entire bridge glowed with a million shades of green. She took it all in at once. Dozens of

Raptors, technicians crawling around under consoles, pulling at wires. Officers and crew scattered around, some at workstations, others fumbling in the dark for weapons. Two tall Flock—the XO and what was clearly the captain—stood near two groups of humans.

The XO stood over Mugabe and Fodder and . . .

Dubbs. Mangled, dismembered. Dead.

The captain had his gun pointed at Pickle.

She saw all of that in a moment, her combat training and AI collecting the data, sorting and arranging it. Knowing that Short Dog and Girlie were seeing the same things.

Raptors turned toward the bridge door, alerted by the sound as it had whisked open. They fired their rifles.

But Alpha Wave was not in the doorway. They split apart, each of them taking a third of the bridge. Girlie ran toward the XO, firing as she ran, the pulse flashes popping the color from green to purple with each shot. Another bird moved at just the wrong time and the shots tore him apart, though it knocked him into the XO, who stumbled, tripped over one of Dubbs's feet, and fell.

Right into Mugabe's arms.

Girlie turned away as the prophet began savaging the bird. She wore a cold grin as she hunted for more targets.

The bridge lights popped on and off, never settling but giving the whole bridge a wild strobe effect that was confusing and disorienting.

Short Dog hurled himself at a knot of Raptors and bore them down to the deck. He used his rifle as a club and hammered at them, breaking bones, smashing beaks, sending crest feathers flying. They clawed at him, tearing at his combat suit, but even as the tough fabric ripped and the claws opened up his skin, he kept fighting with a total savagery.

The captain, realizing his danger, darted away from the HEs, firing at Pickle as he moved. But Lexie leaped forward and wrapped her arms around the captain's knees. He fell and she did her best to climb atop and pummel him.

Pryss saw her fighting with the captain and began moving in that direction, but a Raptor activated its grease-shield and plowed into her, driving her back against the command chair.

Lexie was more furious than she had ever been in her life. She was not a fighter, though, and her blows hit elbows and shoulders, cuirass and sternum, but missed every target worth hitting.

Outside, in the space between Luna and Earth, the battle raged.

The Resistance fighters led by Colonel Muncy were on the run now. Most of their maneuvers were avoidance tactics, though they made some gains by using Flock ships as shields just as enemy fighters opened up. One frigate was listing toward the pull of Earth, its bridge destroyed by friendly fire. Closer to Luna, a destroyer was limping out of the fray, its engine exhaust clogged with the debris of a Resistance fighter who—as his own ship burned—made the best of a bad end.

Muncy lost count of how many fighters he destroyed. There was no joy in it because there were so damn many more.

He thought of his wife and four kids at home. They were who he fought for. They were why he did not flee the sky even when it became obvious there was no possible way to win.

Save me.

Jason stopped and stood rigid, still as a stone, listening to those words inside his head. Listening as if he had never heard them before. Listening and hearing not what he thought they meant, but what they *actually* meant.

Save me.

He looked around at the pylons, at the cables. He looked at the bins and the wounds on the Entity's flesh.

Save me.

"God Almighty. Please, no."

Save me.

"I understand," he said. "God help me . . . I understand."

187

The bridge of the *Juggernaut* was a slaughterhouse.

Driven by grief and loss and outrage, Pryss, Girlie, and Short Dog became something other than soldiers, more than HEs, worse even than mad Dreamers. They became the monsters that the Flock always feared.

Girlie fired her gun until the charge-mag flashed empty, and then she simply threw it away. She dove under pulse fire and came up with a fallen pistol, rose, fired, killing or maiming. She didn't care which.

Short Dog was tiring, he knew that, but he was too caught up in the madness of this fight. His combat rig was torn to rags and his skin slick with blood as he fought. He had no idea what had happened to his rifle or the knives that should have been strapped to his thighs. But he was not unarmed. He tore a console from its pedestal and used it as a shield and a bludgeon, and he splashed the walls with Flock blood.

Pryss had her knives out and used the gas jets in her suit—despite the artificial gravity of the ship—to leap and lunge, dodge and whirl away from pulse blasts. She was not trying for elegance or style, but there was a balletic grace to her movements. And on a level below actual consciousness her new empathic awareness warned her of attacks from angles beyond her range of peripheral vision. She dodged at the same time as trigger pulls; she ducked as pulse blasts singed the air where she had had been a split second before. And each time she moved those blades wrote a song of carnage in the confines of the bridge.

Lexie straddled the captain's chest with no real idea how she managed it. Her fists were bruised, bloody, and swelling from poorly delivered and ill-considered blows delivered with the full force of her rage.

Colonel Muncy saw two more of his ships explode, and with a terrible chill realized that he was alone on this side of the *Juggernaut*.

He set his helmet scanner to do a 360 and nearly shrieked when he saw a massive battle cruiser flanked by two complete fighter squadrons barreling toward him. He was caught between that hammer and the anvil that was *Juggernaut*.

The captain swung a blow that started at the floor and caught Lexie on the point of the jaw. It rocked her, dimmed all her internal lights, and sent her crashing sideways into Pickle, who was just getting to his feet.

The Flock captain sprang up with a surprising and disheartening display of rubbery agility. He grabbed the shoulder of the gunner in charge of the giant cannons and hurled him away. Then his fingers blurred as they sent the command codes to swing the bow of the ship hard over and begin the charging sequence. The forward screen flashed to brightness as the bridge power came back on.

There, in the center of the main screen, was a satellite view of the Paris Metroplex.

The ship hummed with rapacious hunger as the weapons charged.

Pryss felt a presence behind her and she spun, bringing up her knives, ready to cross-cut a bird beneath its beak.

And then she froze.

A figure stood there.

He was tall and very thin. His clothes were pieces of burned rags hanging from him. His eyes were wild, and he clutched fistfuls of wires that trailed down and into open panels on two different workstations. Every part of him was smudged with ash and arcs of electricity leaped from his eyes, snapping and vanishing in the air and then reappearing, again and again.

He raised one hand and the bridge lights blinked out.

When they reappeared, he looked vague and frustrated and squeezed the other hand. Lights out, lights back on.

"I tried . . ." said Trig.

And he sank down to the floor.

188

Jason drew one of his blades and stood there, panting as if he had climbed a thousand steps. The cables crisscrossed the room and there had to be a thousand of them.

How many would he have to cut?

What would the effect be on the Entity? And on the ship?

If he was alone there, his choices might have been different. He could sacrifice himself willingly, easily. Gladly if it saved Earth cities from being obliterated and ended the suffering of this great and ageless creature.

Save me.

"I'm sorry," he said as he grasped the first cable. White-hot static seemed to burn all the way through him. It was so intense he was amazed not to see his skin blacken and peel. "I'm so sorry."

He cut the cable.

Blue-white fluid, viscous and shot through with that ugly purple, burst from both ends, fierce as water from a fire hose. He released the cable and glanced at the Entity.

Save me.

"Shit," he growled and grabbed another. It parted just as easily and sprayed him and the room with that same mingled fluid.

Save me.

Save me.

Save me.

He cut and cut. The fluids drenched him, soaking into his skin, his mouth, his nose and ears and eyes. He gagged on it, spat it out. Kept cutting.

Save me.

Maybe it was his tenth cut, or his hundredth—he had lost all track—but the heat in his grabbing hand seemed to change. It still burned, but it no longer felt like acid. He could not name the sensation that replaced it. It made his heart race as if it were laced with some drug, though. He swayed, staggering from cable to cable. Twice he vomited the stuff up, but with each new cut there was more.

Save me.

He felt the deep thrum of the engines, and in his mind he heard the scream of the Entity. The guns were charging again.

Save me. Save me. Save me. Save me.

Then somewhere in the midst of it, his mind went elsewhere. He tried to take the next step but there was no deck there. Only a void into which he fell.

Jason stood nowhere.

It was not a void. Not really. But it was empty of everything except him.

Before him, spread out across the velvet tapestry of infinity, were ornate and glowing spirals. When he looked around, he saw more of them.

Millions more, though Jason did not know how he could see as many as he saw. His gaze seemed infinite too. And stretching, nearly invisible between all of them, were glowing blue-white strands of pure energy. Like the transduction network but scaled up to the universal level.

It was almost trite to say that all things were connected, but he saw those connections and knew them to be the truth.

Save me.

The plea was still there. In his head and outside it. Everywhere.

Save Me.

Jason felt the Entity reaching into him, moving inside his skull, tampering with his consciousness. Expanding him. Immediately that expansion came with insight. The Entity was allowing him to see.

It showed him many things.

He saw *Juggernaut* moving through space between worlds, not merely riding the transduction energies, but ripping into them, tearing at them, bruising and scarring the fabric of space-time.

"*Too much,*" he heard himself say, and knew that although it was his mouth, his accent, his diction, they were not his thoughts he was expressing. "It does not flow. It has too much."

"Too much of what?" asked Jason.

"*Too much of me. A touch will do it, a whisper. It uses a storm.*"

Jason had to work that out. *Juggernaut*'s Flock crew kept drawing energy from the Entity even with batteries fully charged. The birds thought they needed more, more, more because everything about them demanded that. Their spread across the galaxy could never be justified for their need for habitable worlds. It was the acquisition, the greed sewn into the fabric of their culture and of their belief system that demanded more, more, more.

And he saw the cost of that. The ship was so grossly over-powered, so highly charged that its own field of wild energy was a danger to the entire transduction network.

As he thought it, the images he saw visualized it. He saw the lines of transductive force emanating from *Juggernaut* turning from the pure blue-white radiance to that sickly purple, and that sickness, that pollution was spreading out along the entire network. Transmitting a disease faster than the speed of light, moving through warped space as it spanned the galaxy.

And the space between galaxies.

It was a plague of spoiled energy. Though he knew energy could not be created or destroyed, Jason understood that it could turn negative in many ways. This was the worse, because just as the ship ripped the fabric of space-time, so did its pollutant.

Save me.

Then the vision changed as he saw that purple plague stretch across the vastness until it reached one galaxy. Then another, and another.

Save me.

The vision seemed to slow down and pause, but Jason realized that it was simply a measure of how far that energy had to go, out to the fringes of the known universe. To the first galaxies.

To the home of this Entity.

Then he felt something change before he saw anything else. It was like a wave of humid air that slammed into his chest, choking him, making him fight for every breath. That gave way to a heavier feeling, as if he stood chest-deep in the surf as a massive wave rose above him, towering uncountable miles above. A wave that would not only crush him but roll on and on until it drowned everything.

Save me.

Then he saw it.

Saw . . . *them.*

At first mere dots on the edge of his vision. Blue-white. Wholesome. Lovely.

They hurtled toward him at impossible speeds. Growing in clarity, flaring in luminosity.

Entities.

Like this one.

But much bigger. And . . . so many of them. Racing along the polluted lines of transductive force. Racing toward him.

No. Racing toward the source of that pollution.

Toward the settled worlds of the Milky Way.

With enormous speed. With unspeakable power. With unstoppable rage.

And all at once Jason was back in the engine room of the *Juggernaut.* He staggered sideways and caught himself by grabbing a cable.

Save me, said the Entity.

Jason heard those words, and now he understood what they meant. This creature was infected. It bore the taint of a million years of misuse, amplified by the monstrous purposes to which its energies were being put. The charging of the guns was like the thunder of doom. The thing had shown him the cause and the effect. The action and the consequences.

Save me.

It meant save us all.

It meant more than that.

The Entity could not bear to be part of the plague that infected the universe. It was a thing born of innocence, devoted to healing and beauty. It was beyond curing and now it faced two possible futures.

To be the thing that harmed its own kind, and in doing so sparked a cleansing genocide of all life in the Milky Way.

Or to be nothing. To end. To die.

To be saved . . .

189

"No," cried Trig. "Don't touch me."

Pryss stopped, her hands inches away. She could feel the hairs on her arms twitching beneath her clothes. Small arcs of electricity leapt from Trig to the tips of her knives. Not painful, but deeply strange.

"What *happened* to you?" she cried.

"I . . . got separated . . . anchored my breaching pod on the far side . . . thought you guys were lost . . . thought it was all on me." His words tumbled out almost in stream of consciousness. "So I . . . I decided to use my . . . gift . . . power . . . whatever it is. I cut open some electrical access panels. Just . . . grabbed some. Jacked in. Fucked with things. Lights. Doors. Whatever I could feel. I tried . . . Pryss, I tried . . ."

"You *saved* us, Trig," she said, meaning it.

"Sushi . . . I saw . . . I . . . god . . . I killed him . . ."

"No," she barked. "Whatever happened to him . . . his *gift* . . . that killed him. He used too much. He burned out. It's not your fault. If you hadn't suffocated those Raptors, we'd all be dead."

"Oh," he said, "that's all right then."

His eyes rolled up and he fell flat on his face.

Short Dog stumbled, the console too heavy now. His sides ached from that level of exertion and his head felt swimmy. He looked around and saw that there were a lot of dead birds. But still plenty alive.

"Fuck it," he said, and grabbed a rifle from a nearby corpse. "Do it old school."

The bridge was a madhouse. Bodies lay everywhere. Gunfire had all but faded and now the fighting was hand-to-hand.

Captain Kra'Ngo'Betelgeuse held his own pistol but was hesitant to shoot. At that moment none of the humans or HEs seemed focused on him. It was like he stepped inside a 360-hologram. The blood and destruction was everywhere he looked but not directed at him.

Paris filled the screen with such detail he could even see the rookery where his family had lived before being evacuated to the Pyrenees. And there was the office building where his father, the Eldest of the Flock, worked, guiding their race forward into a glorious future.

He looked for a gunner still at his station and saw none. But the screen displays on their vacant stations told the same story as the digital display on the main screen. The guns were fully charged.

Moving slowly, trying not to be noticed, he began inching his way toward the closest gunnery station.

Mugabe rose from the mangled corpse that had been the ship's XO. He spat blood from his mouth and gagged because he had bitten the Flock's throat out and there was some of it still on his tongue.

He looked down at Dubbs. Fodder looked dead too, but he saw her chest rise and fall. Not much and not very fast, and that scared him.

For a moment he was alone, with fights happening around him but no one close. His battle with the XO had washed him up at the foot of the captain's chair. Mugabe glanced at the screen and saw that the charging cycle for the cannons was nearly complete.

"No, by the gods of dream," he swore and climbed up the dais. There were a few controls on the arms of the captain's chair, and he had no idea what they did. Last thing he wanted was to accidentally fire the guns.

But then he saw something that changed everything for him.

On the left armrest—as with virtually every Flock ship he'd ever seen—was a slender and unobtrusive slot.

"Please, God . . . please."

He fished in his pocket and came up with the data slip that *Tin Man*'s AI had given him. He was not sure what it did, or what was on it, but he knew that it must be of some use. Why else would the seemingly prescient AI tell him to give it to Trig? However, Trig, who seemed to appear from nowhere, lay across the room. Unconscious or dead.

"What is this?" Mugabe had asked Tin Man. *"What am I supposed to do with it?"*

"If you both survive . . . give it to Trig. He will understand."

"And if he is not there? What if he has died on this mission?"

"Then you, Prophet Mugabe, may find some use for it."

That was the conversation.

Now was the moment.

How had the AI known? Or had it calculated possible outcomes and left it up to him to decide if the time was right? Had God guided the machine?

He knew he would never know for sure.

With a prayer on his lips, Mugabe slid the data slip into the slot on the command chair.

Pryss turned Trig over and felt for his pulse. It was there and it was frantic. She got small shocks from his skin, but she didn't care. It was pain and what did that matter?

"Trig," she said, shaking him. "You have to wake up."

He gave a soft groan and turned his head away.

"Trig, we *need* you."

"C'mon, mom, let me sleep . . ."

She shook him harder. Then she leaned very close and yelled in his ear.

"*Wake up!*"

Colonel Muncy knew he was going to die. There was no other way this could play out. With every second more Flock fighters were launching from *The Talon* and the other ships in the fleet. Space was thick with them.

The only grace—not a *saving* grace, but he'd take what he could get—was that with all those ships, he could hardly miss.

He opened up with every damn thing he had.

Better to burn out than fade away.

That was an old phrase he saw on a dusty book in a library when he was seventeen. He had used it for so many decisions in life, and he was fine with it being his epitaph.

So, he wheeled around and drove right for that big bastard of a flagship. The exhaust vents were more than big enough. Two Flock fighters saw him and guessed his trajectory and kicked on the afterburners to try and cut him off.

Trig jumped and yelped as he came awake.

He looked around as if surprised to be where he was.

"Pryss?"

"Hey, baby, welcome back," she said, her voice shaky with stress.

"What . . . what's happening? God, I had the weirdest dream."

"Time to wake up. We're in a measurable amount of shit right now."

Trig sat bolt upright, his dazed eyes clearing.

"The ship," he said.

"Yes, we're on board the *Juggernaut* . . . it's about to fire on—"

"I know," he said and pushed away from her, scrambling on fingers and toes and then getting to his feet and running.

And he ran away from every fight that was going on.

"Trig?" whimpered Pryss.

A Raptor heard her and turned around, bringing up its rifle.

Captain Kra'Ngo'Betelgeuse reached the gunnery station.

There were islands of violence all around him, and it amazed him that none of them were looking at him.

It is fate, he thought. *If there is a god, then he is allowing this. He wants this.*

He slid into the chair and began furiously tapping the keys that would turn control over to him.

They can win this battle. I will win the war.

A panel hissed open and the firing joystick rose toward his waiting hand.

190

He went a little mad.

He knew it. Felt it.

And he didn't give a good goddamn. This was no time to be sane.

Save me.

Save me.

Jason leaped and jumped, grabbing cables one, two, three at a time. Slashing them, letting the goo splash him. There was a cart of tools, and he grabbed some heavy wrenches and hurled them at pylons. It took three tries before he discovered *where* to hit, and after that he began blowing them to bits.

As the pylons shattered, he heard the Entity's voice with more clarity.

Death is a doorway.

Was it really the Entity or his own mad inner voice? He had no way to know. He kept cutting and smashing.

Nothing ever really dies.

Jason climbed up on the edge of the massive cage and leapt out, feeling his feet land on the blue-white mass. It was the strangest sensation, like stepping off a high cliff onto a cloud, expecting to fall and yet not falling. Like that, and he knew that if he survived, he would never adequately explain it to anyone else. Maybe Pryss would understand, if she touched him . . . read him.

That radiance flared and fell away, flared and fell away. Like respiration and a heartbeat both.

Free me.

He jumped up and caught the cables where a dozen were bundled together. He sawed at them. He heard himself making a noise. Almost a child's whimper. A madman's sound.

Save . . . me . . .

The voice changed in the space of those two words. It slowed. Lost emphasis. Became dreamy.

Electricity leaped from one of the damaged pylons and arced to the ones of other side. They exploded, and the resulting discharged jumped to another and another. They began detonating in a chain reaction.

Save . . .

The force grabbed Jason and tore him from the cables he was cutting. He fell. Onto the creature.

And . . . through it . . .

. . .me . . .

Jason sank into the thing as if it was gelatin. A slow plummet. The mass of it closed over him, blotting out the room and the exploding pylons.

Smothering him.

Jason sank down. He fought against it, kicking and lashing out with his arms. The knife in his hand slashed at the flesh of the Entity.

Save . . .

And then the world went totally black. He heard a softness

of a voice. Familiar and yet subtly different, speaking from the shadows of his mind.

Thank you.

A beat of total silence, outside and in.

What I leave, I leave for you.

And then the darkness took Jason.

191

Pryss flung herself backward, rolled, came up fast and jagged right, and flung an arm out at the Raptor. The movement was faster than the bird could track, and it was trained to be elite. But the HEs were next level. Pryss's knife spun through the air and buried itself in the Raptor's throat.

Before it even realized it was dead, she was running. She tore the blade from the dying bird, spun and tried to find Trig. She saw him on the far side of the bridge, clawing at an access panel below one of the workstations.

"Christ," she muttered, then turned away, leaving him to whatever delusions now owned him. She saw Lexie backing away from a Flock officer, using a broken armrest as a shield. Her robot dog, battered, burned, and limping, was nipping at the bird's ankle and narrowly dodging the vicious heel claw. The Raptor had no gun but was slashing at Lexie with a wickedly curved knife. He was winning too. He had the weight, the reach, and a real weapon.

"Mine," said Pryss, and ran that way.

Pickle picked himself off the ground and tried to stand. His face was a ruin. Blood blinding one eye and some of it had gotten into his nose. The taste of it slipping down his nasal passages made him gag.

He looked around for a weapon, found a pistol laying nearly at his feet, picked it up, and looked for someone to kill.

Captain Kra'Ngo'Betelgeuse felt the moment when the firing joystick accepted his authority and shifted to fit his hand. The relief was nearly orgasmic.

He flipped off the safety and curled his finger around the trigger.

"For the Glory of the Flock!"

He pressed the trigger.

The whole ship shook as the big guns fired.

Jason lay on his back.

He opened his eyes and looked up. The ceiling was lined with the shattered and smoking remains of pylons. Thousands of cables, many severed, hung like cobwebs from the ceiling of a haunted house.

It took him a very long time to realize that he was on the deck.

He was not on, in, or even under the Entity.

That made him sit up and then nearly jump to his feet.

The blue-white glow had faded. Shadows now dominated the room. He turned around.

He was alone.

Completely alone.

The Entity wasn't there. The entire massive cage that formed the whole rear third of *Juggernaut* was empty.

It was gone.

Completely gone.

Then he realized that the radiance endured anyway. Then,

unbidden, the last words the Entity spoke echoed through his mind.

What I leave, I leave for you.

And he wondered what that could possibly mean.

Everyone on the bridge tried to move as the *Juggernaut's* guns fired. The *thrummm* of it was deafening.

Lexie and Pryss both screamed. Pickle lunged for the captain. Short Dog yelled and smashed the last Raptor out of the way, but he was nowhere close enough. Girlie was down on one knee, her left arm broken and her right hand crushing the life out of the bird who'd broken it. Mugabe flung himself from the dais, kicking off the captain's chair as he launched himself into an attempted tackle.

All of it too late.

On the screen the bolt of purple plasma flashed through the blackness.

The explosion was massive. It blinded them all, spoiling leaps and steps and grabs. They spun away, shielding their eyes.

Then they stood there, where they were, where they landed. All of them staring at the screen. At the destruction. At the clouds of fiery debris.

"I don't . . ." began Pryss but she ran out of words.

"It . . . it . . ." Short Dog stopped and shook his head.

And then Pickle began to laugh.

It was completely wrong. Hysterical, maniacal, insane.

The debris floated past the ship. Lexie could not imagine all those glittering pieces of metal and plastic could ever have added up to a grand battleship like *The Talon.*

Mugabe shook his head. "How?"

The crackle of electricity behind him made the prophet turn. Trig was there. He raised a finger and pointed at the captain's chair. At the slot where Mugabe had entered the data slip.

A voice spoke from the speakers mounted on the walls.

"Juggernaut *is happy to join the Resistance.*"

It was *Tin Man.*

With a snarl of frustrated rage, the captain squeezed the trigger again. Then he switched over to all guns and brought the remaining cannons online. Mugabe, who was closest, did not try to stop him. When Pryss began to move toward the officer, the prophet waved her off.

The captain pulled the trigger.

The cannons did fire, but not at anything he aimed at.

Juggernaut's guns began independent and selective fire aiming at dozens of targets and firing with a precision and accuracy no living gunner could match.

Colonel Muncy was flying for his life. The explosion of *The Talon* had wiped out more than a score of bird fighters, but all the rest seemed to think he was somehow responsible, and they flew at him, guns firing.

He whipped his spin-fighter around, hit the burners and spiraled away, firing behind him. When he saw a dozen of the Flock fighters explode, he almost congratulated himself for the luckiest gunnery in history.

But then a frigate burst apart, and more fighters.

Muncy came out of his evasive spiral, went high and spun around and saw something he simply did not understand.

Juggernaut was firing on the fleet.

Three big ships were already destroyed, two more crippled. Even with more than half of its guns disabled, the goddamn ship was cutting a swath through the Flock.

Then the tide began to turn as more of the fleet came up and began spreading out to try and attack the flagship from all sides.

Space was suddenly a burning network of pulse fire that was way above anything he could match or endure.

He hit the channel to all remaining fighters.

"Whatever's going on is above our pay grade, lads. We've done our bit, now let's get the fuck out of here."

There were laughs and replies. Not many, though. Not enough.

Muncy rose higher, turned, opened the throttle as far as it would go, and got the fuck out of there.

Lexie walked over to the captain, who was the last of the Flock still alive on the bridge. As she passed Pickle, she took the pistol from his hand. Everyone watched her.

The captain knew he had nowhere to go.

Lexie pointed the pistol at him.

"You're Kra'Ngo'Betelgeuse," she said, her voice oddly calm.

He stood up without haste and with great dignity, straightening his uniform. "You know who I am."

"Yes."

"You know who my father is."

"Oh yes."

"If you kill me, he will hunt you across the galaxy. He will arrest everyone you have ever loved, and they will vanish into torture camps. He will tear down the cities of your world and burn this planet to a cinder."

"Really? Wow," said Lexie. "Then I'd better not kill you."

The captain's eyes narrowed. "What?"

"I'd have to be a fool to throw away a bargaining chip like you, Captain Kra'Ngo'Betelgeuse." She smiled. "History would never forgive me."

She shot him in the face.

She only felt a small twinge of regret that the pistol was set to stun.

192

Enemy fire was hitting the ship. Three scanner screens went dark and two wall panels exploded outward, showering everyone with sparks. The bridge doors hissed open and a ragged, sodden, bruised and battered figure ran onto the bridge.

"*Jason!*"

Pryss and Lexie screamed it at the same time, Lexie just a little louder.

Jason looked wildly around, trying to take in the carnage and the situation. "What in the *hell* is going on here?"

"The ship is ours," said Pryss.

"What? How? No, tell me later. We need to get out of here right damn now. Does anyone know how to drive this goddamn tub?"

"*Where would you like to go?*" asked the voice of *Tin Man*.

Jason stared at the speakers. "Okay. Fine. That's happening. Fuck me."

"*Please be specific.*"

"Anywhere but here," said Short Dog.

"No," growled Jason. "Locate the closest deck."

"*There is a high-speed deck fifty-eight point two kilometers from here.*"

"Get us there. Top speed."

"*Entering a deck at high speed is—*"

"Dangerous. Who cares? Do it."

Until that moment Jason was only a little sure the engines would work at all. All he had was guesswork and a small dash of hope.

Juggernaut seemed to pause as if allowing the gunfire to pummel it, and then it moved. Big as it was, it moved well. It turned remarkably fast, the inertial dampeners sloughing off the stress. Then the engines roared like lions and the ship shot forward.

"The fleet's on our ass, boss," said Short Dog, who was staring at the scanners.

"How many?"

"A lot. A dozen big ships, too many fighters to count."

"Good."

Short Dog cut him a look. "How is this good?"

Jason didn't answer. Instead, he looked at Trig. "Glad to see you."

"Glad to be seen."

"The lights, the doors . . . all that?"

Trig nodded.

"You're a freak."

"Lot of that going around."

They grinned at each other. "Are you working the guns or is *Tin Man?*"

"Frankly, boss, even I don't know where I leave off and that thing picks up."

"I can work with that. Here's what I need . . ." And he told him.

Lexie limped over and looked at him. "Are you hurt?"

He studied the screens, watching the deck grow larger. "We all are."

"And the Entity?" asked Pryss, joining them.

He avoided her eyes. "Free."

"Is it alive or dead?"

"It's free," he repeated. And then they were in the deck.

The entry at high speed—never advised—sent a shockwave through the ship. Anyone who wasn't at full strength fell. That left only Jason on his feet.

"*Tin Man*," he yelled. "Pedal to the metal. Full speed."

Juggernaut accelerated. The screens showed the glowing lines of transductive energy whipped past, blurred as the ship reached wildly unsafe speeds for so narrow a passage. Jason knew for sure that no human pilot could have managed it.

The Flock fleet was behind them but losing ground.

"Trig . . . on my mark."

"Call it, boss."

"Three . . . two . . . one . . . *mark*."

Every cannon on the *Juggernaut* fired at once. Not one was aimed at the pursuing ships. The guns fired upward and downward, they fired sideways. Each shot hit the wall of the transduction tunnel and detonated.

From that point of impact and all down the line, the tunnel exploded.

At that precise moment *Juggernaut* exited a deck near Mars. A shockwave fifty thousand miles wide chased them, caught them, and did its best to hurl the ship at the red planet. They missed the moon, Phobos, by ninety-two kilometers. They clipped six separate satellites, smashing them to pieces. They spun around and around with such force the interior dampeners nearly shut down.

And then *Juggernaut* swirled and tumbled out into space away from the planet.

Behind them—fading now as the internal fires of all those ships was snuffed out in airless space—the Flock fleet assigned to the solar system died. The shockwave traveled along the transduction network, blowing out dozens of decks until the wave was spread so thin that it, too, faded.

EPILOGUE

-1-

There was more to do aboard *Juggernaut.*

Though the bridge battle had been won, there were still many pockets of Raptors, technicians, and crew left. With the help of Trig and *Tin Man*, they were all located and told to surrender. Some did, and they were left on an automated weather station orbiting Mars.

Those who wanted to fight it out for the Glory of the Flock died. There was no story to tell, no heroics. Jason, Pryss, and Short Dog hunted them down. The birds should have surrendered.

Girlie's arm was set, and she seemed to be healing. In fact, she seemed to heal remarkably fast. Faster even than was normal for HEs with accelerated wound repair systems. Her cast was off in a week. Within ten days she was pain free. When Pickle asked her if that was her new superpower, all Girlie did was laugh.

Fodder was another matter. Her face needed reconstructive surgery, she had three ruptured internal organs, and a total of seventeen broken bones. It took Trig and Mugabe less than a day to rebuild a Flock med-bay to accommodate humans. Fodder was narcotized and the machines, with their tools and drugs, began the long process of rebuilding her.

Pickle had his face stitched up. Oddly, he seemed in no hurry to let the machines repair him.

"Why not?" asked Lexie.

But Pickle didn't answer. He seldom spoke to anyone for days. Lexie worried about him, but Pryss told her to leave him be. Lexie wanted to know if Pryss knew something, but that conversation never seemed to happen.

Dubbs and Sushi were wrapped in shrouds and stored in freezers. No one wanted to use the old tradition of firing them out of torpedo tubes.

"They were both born on Earth," said Lexie. "Seems only right that we bury them there."

"Could be a long damn time before we get back there."

"They'll keep," she said. Then, not looking at anyone, she added, "Maybe they'll dream."

-2-

They monitored the Flock networks and learned that there was growing outrage back on Earth. Somehow the truth about the Lisbon catastrophe had leaked out through *Radio Free Earth* and *Radio Free Galaxy*. Vid-clips of the space battle and the destruction of the fleet were hard to refute.

People on Earth, particularly Micah and Lulu, were expecting retribution, but the Elders were notably silent. There were no new arrests.

At least for now.

The Eldest spent a lot of time alone in his office, staring at a holo-print of his first-hatched son. His friends sent condolences for his loss, and a burial was even conducted, but the Eldest would not openly speak about it. Not to anyone.

Aboard *Juggernaut*, Kra'Ngo'Betelgeuse paced the narrow confines of his cell. He, too, had nothing to say.

-3-

The crew spent hours every day exploring their ship.

Their ship.

The AI did its best to argue for a renaming of the vessel. He suggested *Tin Man*. But even Trig voted against it. *Juggernaut* was theirs by right of conquest. It felt wrong to change the name.

"Maybe when the war's over," said Jason.

-4-

On Io, Hell watched the footage of the Battle of Paris, as the news stories labeled it. He found it very interesting, and he read endless reports looking for some hint that the Flock had learned something of value from the defeat.

He looked in vain.

After a while he stopped paying attention to that and focused on the things he was discovering there on Jupiter's moon. He was absolutely certain that the survivors of Alpha Wave and Lexie Chow had no idea what was stored in the cellars and sub-cellars. How could they know? So much of it was dated *after* the HEs had gone to sleep.

Hell found it absolutely fascinating.

He spent most of his time down there. In storage rooms, in other cryogenic chambers. And in the laboratories. What he found delighted him.

Each day he could feel the injections working in him. Changing him.

That delighted him too.

-5-

Jason had to tell his story of what happened in the engine room at least forty times.

"This is just fucking weird," said Short Dog. "And, let's face it, we've been doing weird pretty hard. This takes the cake."

No one argued the point.

Mugabe asked, "And it just . . . vanished?"

Jason nodded.

"You are talking about 200,000 cubic meters of mass."

"Yes."

"Gone."

"Yes."

"I don't understand how that's possible."

"Like I said," cut in Short Dog. "Fucking weird."

"Maybe I'm missing something," said Trig, "but if this Entity thing was the power source for the engine *and* the gun, then how is this tub moving? I mean, I can speak to the ship, but it doesn't seem to know either. It keeps telling me that things are normal."

"It is, I suppose," said Jason. "This is what the Flock never understood. Maybe none of the other races that owned this ship first never got it either. The Entity was the *source* of the power, but its energetic potential was off the scale. I don't even know what kind of math you'd need to figure it out."

He pointed to smears of blue-white that clung to the walls like moss and lay in pools on the deck. Then to the line of pins which lay on their sides, the content as absent as the Entity itself.

"The Flock was maybe *kind* of getting the idea," Jason continued. "They started carving off bits of the Entity, which is what's in those bins. They were going to use them as power sources for a new fleet. Built on the *Juggernaut* design. The Entity left some behind. For us."

"Why?" asked Girlie. "I thought it was peaceful by nature."

Jason thought about that. "So is a puppy, but if you raise it with a whip, chain it, starve it, abuse it . . . that puppy will learn to hate. Maybe the Entity learned to hate. I hope not, though.

The thought of that makes me sad. Something born to beauty becoming vicious."

"We may know something about that," said Pryss quietly. "None of us were born monsters."

"I think the Entity wanted us to take this ship, powered by *its* essence—or whatever we should call it. After all, the thing was inside our dreams. It knows that we—the whole human race—is in bondage, in chains, being used, being tortured. It has great empathy. And, though it breaks my heart to say it, that creature wants us to take those gifts and use them to fight this war."

Lexie looked down at her hands. "I don't know whether that's beautiful or tragic."

"Both," said Pryss.

"Both," agreed Mugabe.

"That's all well and good," said Short Dog, but didn't you say the Flock was harvesting chunks of that—what's the word?—glop? So, okay then, how many ships could they build with what they took?"

"I'm not sure they took any of it yet," said Jason. "Not saying this because I know. It's more of a feeling, maybe something I picked up from the Entity. But those bins I saw . . . that was what they had harvested, and the bins were all there."

"But you could be wrong," said Mugabe.

"I could be wrong," agreed Jason.

"Well . . . fuck," said Short Dog.

Jason looked around. "For right now, though, we have *Juggernaut*. With the Entity gone—and do not even think of asking me how it vanished after it was free—that incredible mass and density is gone. The ship won't rip holes in the transduction network or space-time. It's fast, powerful, and more importantly it's *ours*."

"Ours," echoed Lexie, and the others nodded, their eyes filling with speculation and even obvious wonder.

Jason Horse smiled. "Kind of makes you wonder what *we* can do with it."

-6-

Jason and Lexie sat on chairs in the galley. The ship was quiet and nearly everyone was asleep.

"Jason . . . those visions the Entity showed you . . . the beings like it across the universe."

"What about them?"

"You said they were coming this way."

"Well, I think it was trying to show me worst case scenario. What they might do if the one that was here stayed a prisoner and wound up poisoning the transduction network."

"Okay, but it had been a prisoner for years. I'm not talking about all those thousands of years before the Flock found it, but since the Uprising. We know *Juggernaut* used the decks a lot to put down Resistance groups."

"Yes. So . . ."

"What if those other creatures already know that it was a prisoner? What if they know that it was being tortured? And what if they now know that it's dead?"

"What are you saying?"

"How do we know they're not already on their way here?"

Jason had no answer to that. The air in the galley seemed to have gone colder. He wrapped his arm around her, but neither of them seemed able to get warm.

-7-

They slept.

The ship was tucked away behind Pluto, engines cycled down, well away from any deck. It was the first time they could all sleep, and as she drifted toward the edge of sleep, Lexie wondered if it was the last time that any of them would sleep that soundly again.

Jason lay on his side, spooning her from behind, his breath a slow and reassuring rhythm. The sound of it and the safety of his arms quieted her thoughts and fears, and soon she, too, was asleep.

They all slept soundly.

For a while.

And then the dreams began.

She dreamed of those entities. Thousands of them. A race of them. Infinitely powerful. Vengeful. Angry.

In her dreams they truly were coming. They attached themselves to the infinite energies of the transduction network. Not the one designed by mankind, but the natural one; the one born when the universe was born. They attuned their energies to it and flew through space at speeds that fractured mathematics, bending space-time to their will. Bending it to their anger.

Not merely coming in answer to a plaintive call that had since ceased.

No.

As they flew through the void they dreamed. It was a natural state for them, to live half in the real world and half in dreams.

They could hear dreams. Just as one of their kind had found Jason Horse asleep in his icy coffin, so they found other dreamers. Powerful minds filled with as much rage and hate as theirs.

These other Dreamers heard their call, and in the depths of their sleep, they reached out. Calling back. Inviting. Making awful promises.

In her dreams, Lexie Chow saw these Dreamers. The ones who called across the stars. They lay in rows, their bodies inert in tubes of metal and glass. Each with a name stenciled on them.

Sleepers, calling out in their dreams. Speaking to every

dreaming mind they could touch. Speaking in shrill, ragged, awful voices. Speaking words that only the very mad could hope to understand. Screaming. Chanting. Worshipping fell gods born of nightmare. Being worshipped by those who fell beneath the weight of their dreams.

Lexie heard the words, the prayers, the whispers that promised dreadful things. She glimpsed the horrors conjured in the wastelands of the dream worlds.

She woke screaming.

So did everyone aboard *Juggernaut.*

So did thousands of people on a hundred worlds.

Screaming their way out of that shared nightmare.

Jason snapped awake too, the scream torn from him. He looked wildly around and did not see Lexie. He heard her, though. He heard her scream wind down to a small and terrified whimper.

He tumbled off the bed, crawled to her. She sat in a corner, Ahab clutched to her chest, eyes wide and staring, mouth agape.

"Lexie . . . are you okay?"

She turned to him with a face as slack as a corpse and eyes filled with madness.

"The Sleepers," she said in a ghostly whisper. "The other Sleepers . . ."

And then she screamed again.

For a long, long time.

She screamed.

Until her voice went ragged and she could scream no more.

END OF BOOK ONE